F.46 778C

TRANS Z - (MJFR)

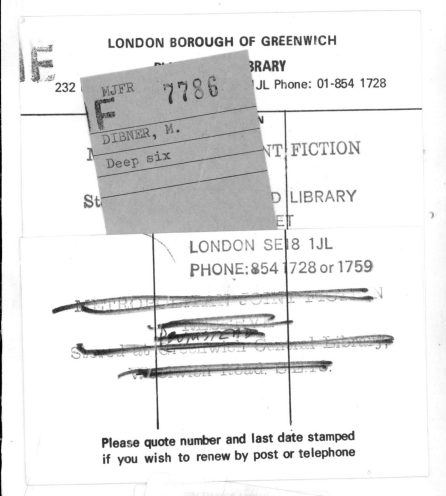

**Please quote number and last date stamped
if you wish to renew by post or telephone**

THE DEEP SIX

The Deep Six is about life on board an American cruiser in war-time. It is a somewhat alarming account, mainly because the crew are a rather alarming collection of people. The captain is a reluctant and inexperienced sailor; the executive officer is contemplating suicide; one of the junior officers roams the ship in search of homosexual adventures; and the ship's doctor spends all his time drinking in his cabin.

The ship, the Atlantis, makes contact with a much superior Japanese naval force. How will this strange collection of men react to the violence of sea warfare?

THE DEEP SIX

MARTIN DIBNER

CEDRIC CHIVERS
PORTWAY
BATH

First published 1954
by
Cassell & Co. Ltd
This edition published
by
Cedric Chivers Ltd
by arrangement with the copyright holder
at the request of
The London & Home Counties Branch
of
The Library Association
1974

ISBN 0 85594 977 5

705

Printed in Great Britain by
Redwood Press Ltd, Trowbridge, Wiltshire
Bound by Cedric Chivers Ltd, Bath

For the men and the boys

'There are three kinds of people;
those that are alive,
those that are dead,
and those who are at sea.'

ANACHARSIS

I

IT was an accident. It happened during a routine test-firing drill, the way any accident can happen at sea.

A junior grade lieutenant named Alec Austen was in charge of the forty-millimetre gun mount aft. Lieutenant Commander Dooley, the gunnery officer, was observing the drill. Two test rounds for each barrel had been loaded into the trays and the gun crew was standing by. The target—a burst from one of the cruiser's old three-inch guns—floated past. Austen gave the order to commence firing and the pointer squeezed the firing key.

The guns were set to fire singly and the first round from each barrel went off nicely. The second round on the port gun jammed or misfired and there was a jarring explosion. The breech bulged and jagged pieces of hot metal flew in all directions. There was a lot of smoke and some of the men screamed and coughed and some of them fell to the deck.

A loader named Loomis was hit by a chunk of the breech block and was instantly killed. Two other men, Parry and Hackmeister, were severely wounded and the rest of the crew suffered cuts and burns of one sort or another.

Oddly enough Lieutenant Commander Dooley broke his leg. He had stationed himself behind the gun mount holding a stop watch and was well out of range of the explosion. He tried to vault over the splinter shield of the director tub. The heel of his shoe caught the lip of the shield and he fell eight feet to the deck level of the twenty-millimetre clipping room.

The gun captain, an enlisted man named Frenchy Shapiro, jumped on the mount and unloaded the remaining live round from the starboard gun. It was a very brave and foolish thing to do. He cleared the breech and heaved the hot live shell over the side.

Austen took charge of the casualties. He administered morphine to the two wounded men to ease their pain. The attendants arrived with stretchers and carried them below to sick bay along with dead Loomis. Later, when Austen wrote his report of the casualty, he said some very fine things about the gun captain. His report carefully avoided any reference to the gunnery officer's peculiar accident. He had known for some time about Dooley's fear of guns, but he had not believed Dooley would actually try to run away and he was sorry he had seen it happen.

Captain Meredith, the commanding officer, gave orders to cease all exercises. The tiny task group, which had been patrolling the western approaches to the Aleutians, now set its course for Adak to transfer the wounded and pick up a gun replacement.

The official report of the casualty was carefully drafted from Austen's preliminary report and typed by the captain's yeoman. It now rested with the ship's classified mail until it would enter the official channels of Navy red tape.

Meanwhile Loomis was dead and Parry and Hackmeister were in very poor shape. Loomis was buried at sea the next morning. He had been the youngest man in Austen's division, a bright-eyed funny kid with a big smile, who played a concertina, who never drank whisky, whose mother's milk was not yet dry on his clean pink face.

They buried him in the icy waters somewhere north east of Attu. His grave was the latitude and longitude in the ship's log. The honours were brief. It was a damp chilly morning and the ship had no chaplain and the captain had small taste for such melancholy affairs.

The ship's engines were stopped. The ship's surgeon, Commander Blanchard, held a closed Bible and said a few words. Frenchy Shapiro held on to Loomis until the boy's shrouded body slid into the water. The men shivered and ducked the spray. The wind blew and the broken body slid from the fantail on a smooth pine board and Blanchard's words and Loomis were soon lost in the bubbling wake.

It was an accident and the war was full of all kinds of accidents. It could have happened to anyone. It was just too bad it had to happen to a nice kid like Loomis.

IT was almost dawn when the *Atlantis* dropped anchor inside the mouth of Kuluk Bay. The sea was calmer here. The hook grabbed the bottom and clouds of rust and scale poured from the ship's chain lockers and settled to her scabby grey decks.

The Word was passed for in-port routine. The men scattered from their stations. Some of them lingered about the weather decks though it was not yet sunrise. The ache of the early morning watch still lay in their bones. They stood at the rails and stared about them wonderingly. The nearness of solid land seemed strange after weeks of nothing but the cold rolling sea.

Alec Austen dismissed his gun crew and headed for the ward-room. As he passed the galley deckhouse a sailor named Slobodjian plucked at his trouser leg. Slobodjian was crouched against the bulkhead, peeling onions. It was an incredible pile of onions. Huge tears poured down Slobodjian's smooth brown cheeks. He swiped at them with his skinny arm.

'When you gonna paint my picture, Lieutenant ?'

'Any time you say, Slobodj.'

Slobodjian regarded him with soft brimming eyes. 'You're all the time saying that. But you never do.'

'I never know you'll be here when I get back with the paints.'

Slobodjian averted his eyes. He knew what Austen meant. The last time the ship had anchored in Kuluk Bay, he had gone ashore without permission and borrowed an army major's jeep and toured the island. When they caught him and returned him to the ship, he was thrown in the brig. He protested mildly. He had done no wrong. The major's name was Khargheusian. It was plainly printed on the warm parka that Slobodjian had found on the seat of the jeep. All Armenians are cousins. Everyone knows that. How can you punish a man for seeking his cousin ?

Apparently they could. Slobodjian was given a summary court martial. He chose Austen, his division officer, to defend him. Austen convinced the court that Slobodjian's escapade was harmless and not entirely devoid of a certain humour. The prisoner was released with a warning and an indeterminate sentence to the onion pile. He accepted it as he did everything else in the Navy—with an air of faint contempt and an edge of inborn resistance to authority.

Now he wiped his eyes and nose with a languid expert sweep. 'You can start painting right now, Lieutenant.' He smiled his foolish secret smile. 'I'm going to be around here for a long time.'

'You're damned lucky,' Austen told him. 'Jumping ship in wartime is desertion. They shoot deserters, buster.'

'For that I would thank my cousin the major.' He regarded the pile of onions thoughtfully. 'I do not think he was a real Armenian. Armenians are understanding and very affectionate and sentimental.'

'The major was sentimental about his jeep.'

'I really don't believe he was an Armenian at all. He would have understood how I felt.'

'Saroyan would have understood.'

'Saroyan?'

'Don't you know Saroyan?'

Slobodjian shrugged and the tears fell heavily among the pale sweet onions. 'Saroyan, Khargheusian, Slobodjian—we're all cousins.' He looked obliquely at Austen. His smile was again secret and foolish.

Shoes scraped the near-by ladders. The engine-room gang came out of the ship like maggots from a rotting carcass. Mouldy smiles cracked their pale unshaven faces. The promise of sunshine and fresh air charged their hard etiolated bodies like an aphrodisiac. It warmed the marrow of their lonesome bones.

The sun edged the rim of the grey and brown hills. The men clustered together in an olio of faded denim, grease, and tattoos. The steel deck rang with their harsh jokes and cursing.

'Zombies,' Slobodjian observed coldly, reaching for another onion.

One of the men led a hot dog on a string. It bounced in a

4

rubbery fashion along the deck. He clucked at it seriously, jerking the string and making it behave in a lively manner.

'C'mon, Fido,' he urged. 'That's a good feller.'

The others watched and shouted and jeered although they had seen the performance many times before. The sun broke through the thin fog. Chipping hammers rang out and winches creaked. The big cargo nets were rigged and swung out. A supply barge headed for the *Atlantis*, low in the water. On the signal bridge a torrent of flags and pennants hung to dry flapped wildly, bright as circus streamers.

The fog lifted and the sun warmed the men and the sight of the surrounding hills pleased them. It feels good, they thought, to be anchored in the bay again.

The squawk box blared. '*Lieutenant Austen report to the captain on the bridge. Lieutenant Austen report to the captain on the bridge.*'

'You're a very important man, Lieutenant,' Slobodjian said softly.

Austen frowned and climbed the ladder to the bridge deck. The loaded barge was approaching the ship's side. Mail, meat, and ammo, he thought. It's better in here than out there. Another time out there would be one too many, he thought, remembering dead Loomis. He took a deep breath and knocked on the captain's cabin door.

The captain was sitting on his bunk examining a large water-colour portrait of himself. He was a beefy handsome man. The paper seemed overcrowded with his fleshy image. He squinted his eyes and held the portrait at arm's length.

'It's nice, Alec. I like it.' He rubbed his ample stomach and belched with the full authority of his four stripes. Austen was tempted to salute.

'Thank you, Captain.'

'Wish you had painted me wearing wrinkled khakis, though.' He looked at Austen hopefully. 'Instead of those dress whites. Not very salty, you know.'

Austen studied the portrait deliberately for several long moments. He was annoyed. He had undertaken the task with misgivings from the very beginning. He knew it would create a special relationship between him and the captain that would cause resentment among some of the wardroom officers. But the captain repeatedly brought up the matter during Austen's bridge watches, being careful however to insist that it was not an order and thereby making it more difficult for Austen to ignore.

And now he wants khakis. Somehow he was unable to imagine the captain in wrinkled khakis. The captain's khakis were never wrinkled. He was scrubbed-looking and immaculate and faintly aromatic. Like a damned prize bull, Austen thought bitterly.

'Unless you feel this is the real me,' the captain said.

'I could try another one, sir.'

'Won't hear of it. I really like it, Alec. It has an authentic quality of the sea. It really looks like me, too. Damned if it doesn't.' He chuckled and his cheeks rippled softly. 'A very good likeness.'

'I thought so,' Austen said.

'Fine, my boy. Now here's what I'd like you to do. Go ashore and get a frame for it.'

Austen stared at him.

The captain chuckled. 'It's all arranged. I've sent a signal to the beach. There's plenty of wood moulding left over from the officers' club the Seabees built. They're expecting you. Pick out any of it you want, Alec. Something suitable for this kind of a picture. Use your own judgment.' He held up the portrait and cocked his head to one side. 'This is really one hell of a beautiful piece of art, the more I look at it. You're a talented young man.'

'I don't know about getting ashore, Captain. I'm in the duty section and there are no leave parties.'

'Hell. You arrange for your own relief. You'll be back on board in time to stand your next watch. Check out with my yeoman. He's got all the dope on the framing and who to see and so forth.'

'Yes, sir.'

'Don't get the idea it's a pleasure trip.' The captain rummaged through a stack of dispatches with a wet, curled thumb. 'That forty-millimetre replacement barrel of yours should be standing by.

Check with the ordnance officer in ComNorPac—here it is.' He
pulled a paper from the file. 'We requested the replacement three
days ago. Find it and get it the hell on board.'

'Aye, sir.'

'I'm sending that boy's effects in with you.' He looked at Austen
guiltily. 'Did you write a letter to his parents?'

'Yes, sir.'

'Too bad it had to happen. And in a damned routine drill.
Let's see now, what was his name?'

'Loomis, sir. Edward Loomis, seaman first class.'

'And the other two.' The captain wiped his forehead nervously.
'It looks like one of them may be blind permanently.'

'That's Hackmeister, sir. Louis Hackmeister, gunner's mate
second.'

'That's the one. Commander Blanchard says he doesn't have
much of a chance.' He drew a deep breath. 'Well, Blanchard is
going in with you, to get this Hacksomething and the other one
to the naval dispensary. They're both being transferred.'

'It's going to leave the division shorthanded, Captain.'

'Hell, Alec, two less to worry about. We're taking aboard a
new draft from the States anyway.'

'Hope they're better than the last draft, sir.'

'I know, I know. They're sending us the scum.'

'Hackmeister and Parry are tough men to replace. They were
a pointer-trainer team on that gun.'

'You can train a new team, damn it. The papers are made out
and they're officially transferred.'

'It's still a rough deal for them, Captain.'

'What's so rough about a shore billet?'

'Well, the hot dope is we're heading for the States for an overhaul. Those two will be left behind.'

'If you're foolish enough to believe the crew's scuttlebutt, I feel
sorry for you. This ship's heading right back for patrol just as
soon as the gun's aboard. And Admiral Marcy.'

'An admiral?'

'And his staff. Now don't pump me, Alec,' he added sharply.
'And tell your crew to forget about the States.'

Marcy, Austen thought. He was impressed. Anyone who knew about Pearl Harbour on December seventh knew about Admiral Marcy. 'It sounds very important,' he said.

'Get going,' the captain said. 'Check out with the exec., please. I forgot to tell him. Matter of form, of course.'

'Aye, sir.'

The captain opened the door. 'How's Dooley's leg?'

'It'll be in plaster for some time, sir.'

'I've been told you're running the gunnery department very efficiently.'

'If you listen to the crew's scuttlebutt you're liable to hear anything.' His grin faded. 'Is Commander Dooley being transferred, Captain?'

'Blanchard recommended it but Dooley himself begged to stay with the ship. Showed real guts.'

Austen didn't say anything. The captain was admiring the portrait again.

'In wrinkled khakis and a salty cap this would be a masterpiece. Now get that framing, will you?' He waved impatiently.

'Yes, sir.' Austen saluted and went down the ladder. Wrinkled khakis, he thought angrily. And a little ammonia rubbed into the cap device to give it that salty look. And it's going to hang in the admiral's cabin. Sure as hell the admiral will want a portrait. In wrinkled khakis and dress whites.

And there are dress blues and the new greys. A hell of a war, he thought. With Paintbrush and Pencil in the North Pacific, or The Boy Artist with Popgun and Water Colours in the Aleutians.

He grinned. I'll paint anyway. To hell with them, as long as I'm painting. That's better, he thought. And he felt better.

3

THE executive officer sat in the wardroom staring at a cup of cold coffee. He was a thin man with a face like an old shingle.

Austen saluted him. 'Permission to go ashore, Commander?'

The executive officer did not look up. 'Not granted.'

'But I already have permission to leave the ship, sir.'

'No one has permission to leave the ship.'

You'll eat it, Austen thought. 'The captain is sending me ashore on a special mission. I thought he must have advised you, sir.'

'No one has advised me of any such thing.' He looked up. 'Is this ship's business, Mr. Austen?'

'It's the captain's business, sir.'

The executive officer turned his red-rimmed eyes morosely back to the coffee cup. 'Permission granted,' he said sourly.

'Thank you, Commander.'

'In the Navy, Mr. Austen, we do not give thanks for routine acknowledgments. I might add that we also conduct our business through prescribed channels. Chain of command. How did you reach the commanding officer without clearing through me, please?'

'The squawk box said for me to report to the bridge, sir.'

The executive officer waved his hand impatiently. It was a thin blue-veined hand, delicately blotched. 'I know, I know. I heard the squawk box. Most irregular, Mr. Austen.' He took a small black notebook from his pocket and pencilled an entry.

'If you'll check with the captain——'

'Never mind, Mr. Austen. You have your permission. Your division will still be held responsible for stowage of ammunition and supplies. Have you arranged for working parties? The barges are alongside, you know.'

'I'm going aft to handle that detail now, sir.'

'Very well. We're not in port for long and we do not intend to wait around for stragglers.'

'Aye, sir.' Austen saluted. The executive officer did not appear to notice him. He was staring into the coffee cup again.

Austen went below to the Fourth Division compartment. It was a living space cluttered with men and tiers of metal bunks and a disordered assortment of fighting equipment. There was a strong odour of men's bodies. Locker doors slammed. Blowers dinned. Pipes of different dimensions and colours snaked along the overhead, looking like the bright intestines of giant animals. Some of the men were on their knees chipping paint. The insane chatter of their hammers was almost deafening. Beneath its din jazz music blared from the squawk box.

Frenchy Shapiro leaned against a bulkhead. He was studying the division's muster list. He gnawed serenely at a huge sandwich. Austen threaded his way through the overcrowded passage to Frenchy's side. Frenchy watched him thoughtfully.

'What's to-day Boss? Monday the what?'

'How the hell should I know?' Austen still smarted from his interview with the executive officer. He eyed Frenchy's sandwich. 'What're you eating? More of that Brownsville salami?'

'I wish to God it was.' Frenchy parted the thick slices of bread. 'Horsecock and cheese.' He looked at Austen with faint challenge in his lidded blue eyes. 'Wanna bite?'

'I'm hungry but not that hungry.'

'If it's the kosher salami you're holdin' out for, it's all gone. I ate the last hunk three days ago.'

'This is a crisis, Frenchy.'

'There's more on the way, Boss. Maybe in to-day's mail there's a couple salamis.' He carefully extracted a curled streamer of viscose from his teeth. 'Whoever's selling this crap to the Navy for salami, they should oney drop dead.'

He grinned and pointed the sandwich at the sailors who were chipping the deck paint. 'Looka them bastids work, Boss,' he said proudly. 'Ever since the Word gets around we're heading for the States.' He misinterpreted Austen's troubled expression. 'C'mon, eat a sandwich. It can't kill ya.' He reached inside the denim shirt and produced another huge sandwich. 'Here.' He rammed it into Austen's hands. ' Eat.'

'Thanks, Frenchy.' He chewed slowly. It was harder sometimes to speak to Frenchy Shapiro than to the executive officer. 'It's too noisy in here. Let's go someplace where we can talk.'

'Sure, Boss.'

They went into the enlisted men's head. The water raced

through the troughlike urinal and splashed noisily to the
deck.

'My private office,' Frenchy said. 'Won't you have a seat?'

'Look, Frenchy. This scuttlebutt about us going to the States
. . .'

'The hot dope is we're taking some big-shot admiral back with
us.'

'We're not taking any admiral to the States.'

'We ain't?'

'No, Frenchy. He just came here from the States. It's Admiral
Marcy. Red Eye Marcy, the one there was such a stink about at
Pearl Harbour. He's coming on board and we're not going to the
States.'

Frenchy stopped chewing. 'Who says?'

'The skipper. He says.'

'Look, Boss. Itshay me evernay.'

'Straight dope, Frenchy. And they need a working party right
now to handle stores. After noon chow another working party—
all hands, to stow ammunition.'

Frenchy was not listening. 'This is the straight dope, Boss, from
the skipper himself?'

Austen nodded. Frenchy's crooked face sagged. The sandwich
crumbled in his big fingers.

'I can't pass no such word to the boys.'

'You'll have to.'

'But this time it was for real! I coulda swore——' The food
had soured in his mouth. 'What about the busted gun?' he said
angrily. 'We can't go out there with one of the goddamn guns
busted, can we?' His voice rose shrilly. He flung the remnants
of the sandwich into the urinal. 'What about Parry and Louey
Hackmeister? They're both sick guys. We can't go out there
with guys sick as them two. Hackmeister's gonna stay blind, ain't
he? I don't want no blind men on the guns. Those two guys
have gotta go back to the States to be treated. And how's about
Dooley, the gun boss? With his busted leg? What about him?'

'Take it easy. Parry and Hackmeister are being transferred to
the dispensary on Adak.'

'They ain't gonna put gold braid like Dooley in no dispensary. He rates Bethesda and if I know him he'll get it.'

'You're wrong, Frenchy. Dooley's staying on board, busted leg and all. I'm going ashore to pick up the new gun barrel. Ensign King'll handle the division while I'm on the beach.'

'Okay, Boss.' He wiped his eyes with an angry sweep of his sleeve and saluted a little and wiped his nose. 'We been out here too long and we ain't gonna be able to stand it much longer without cracking up. Honest to Christ, Boss, we gotta have something else to look at beside each other and the goddamn bulkheads and the goddamn sea.'

'Maybe having an admiral'll make things different.'

'You could get Nimitz and King and Halsey, Boss—*gurnisht helfen.*'

'What?'

'It ain't gonna help.' He shrugged. 'I'll take care of the working parties and Ensign King.' He followed Austen along the passageway, grumbling. 'Loomis didn't do too bad. He oney got himself killed.'

'That's a hell of a thing to say.'

'This is a hell of a ship, Boss.'

4

AUSTEN remembered the first time he had met Frenchy Shapiro. Austen had just reported aboard the *Atlantis*. She lay alongside a Navy dock in Panama. It was a warm night. The sky was choked with stars. It was Austen's first night watch as officer of the deck.

Shapiro was a rawboned man in his early thirties. He was hollow-cheeked and pale-eyed. His red nose was hopelessly battered. An off-centre chin gave his lined, wise face a slight smirk that could have passed for disrespect. A tight curl of dirty blond hair lay under his squared white hat. He saluted Austen casually.

'Tide's dropping, sir. I slacked off on all lines.'

' Very well.' He searched Shapiro's expressionless face. 'The officer I relieved said nothing about the lines.'

'Your first watch, ain't it?'

'Does it show?'

'I seen worse.' He eyed Austen carefully. 'You're the new Fourth Division officer, right?'

'That's right. I relieved Lieutenant Hogan.'

Shapiro dug into his shirt pocket. 'Mind if I grab a smoke?'

'Not at all.'

'How about you?'

'Thanks.' They lit up.

'I'm Shapiro, bosun's mate first.'

'Glad to know you.'

'Likewise.'

They shook hands solemnly.

'Mind if I say something?'

'Shoot, Shapiro.'

'You didn't get to know Lieutenant Hogan, did you?'

'No. He shoved off before I got a chance to ask him anything.'

'I ain't surprised.'

'Did you know him well?'

'I'm in the Fourth Division.'

'Fine. We'll be seeing a lot of each other.'

Shapiro looked at Austen a long time. 'I hope you mean that.'

'Why shouldn't I?'

'Hogan never came around to see us.'

'That's too bad.' He thought for a moment. 'Do you talk like this with the other officers?'

'Hell, no.' He shrugged. 'Do you mind?'

'No,' Austen said slowly, 'I don't.'

Shapiro grinned. It was a crooked arrangement of teeth, chin, and lip. 'I figured you had a kind face.'

'Thanks.'

'Lieutenant Hogan did not have a kind face. He had a face like the exec. Have you had the pleasure?'

'I've met the exec.'

13

'Hogan was one of his boys. They were like this.'

'Why didn't he visit the division compartment?'

'Why should he? He slept in officer country on clean sheets. He ate off china in the wardroom with t- blecloths and napkin rings. Tell me, Lieutenant Austen, you seen our compartment?'

'I've seen it.' He was surprised to see tears in Shapiro's eyes.

'Hogan came in once—eighteen months ago. When he reported aboard. He never came again. He got in good with the exec. and he let the division's leading p.o. handle everything.'

'What's wrong with the division?'

'What ain't? It's shot to hell. There's no morale. The guys steal. They hate each other's guts. And it's filthy dirty.' He wiped his eyes. 'I can put up with all kinds of muck. But I can't live like a pig.'

'You think it was Hogan's fault?'

'He never gave a good goddamn about the men. If he had, things wouldn't be so bad. Just a week ago we had a knifing. God knows what'll happen next.'

'I'll have a talk with the men to-morrow.'

'Jesus. They'll die from the shock.'

'Who's the leading p.o.?'

'Ski. Kracowski. Bosun's mate first.'

'I thought you were the bosun's mate first.'

'I got more time in than Ski. I just never got along with Hogan. I told him things to his face. So he made Ski leading p.o.' He shrugged. 'Not that I give a good goddamn. I just like a clean compartment to live in. Not a pigsty.' He wiped his eyes fiercely. 'Don't get the idea I'm looking for any favours, because I ain't.'

'You're not going to get any.'

'All I ask is an even break.'

'You'll get an even break. So will every man in the division.'

Shapiro lit a cigarette. 'Maybe you're gonna slap me on report for insolence or something. I don't care. I been aboard this rust-bucket too long to care. But being you're the new Fourth Division officer I figure you're entitled to know what cooks.'

'Nobody's getting slapped on report.'

14

'A smart officer'll soon find out if he treats the enlisted man like a human being, they'll go to bat for him in a pinch.'

'Fair enough.'

'On a ship there's no telling when a pinch'll come along.'

'I'll remember that.'

They smoked quietly. The lights of El Centro cast a ghostly loom through the web of frangipani and palms. The night air was hot and sweet with the perfume of jasmine. Two sailors returning to the ship sang noisily as they wove along the wooden dock below.

'Lucky bastards,' Shapiro said. His voice softened. 'They may as well enjoy it while they're here.'

'Why do you say that?'

'The hot dope is we're heading out of here any day now.'

'Where to?'

'Frisco. Then the Aleutians. That's the scuttlebuttt.'

Austen grinned. 'I've heard of sailor's scuttlebutt.'

'Hungry, Lieutenant?'

'I could eat something.'

Shapiro went below. He returned in a few minutes with a pot of coffee and some sandwiches. They ate quietly.

'This is a terrific sandwich,' Austen said.

'It's salami. My old lady sends it from Brooklyn.' He chewed thoughtfully for a few moments. 'Ever been in Brooklyn, Lieutenant?'

'Many times.'

'You worked there?'

'I'd go on sketching trips.' He remembered something. 'Once I went to Coney Island with a girl. We ate hot dogs at a place called Nathan's.'

Shapiro looked dreamy. 'Brooklyn,' he said. 'Everything's got to be special.'

'What do you mean?'

'Like Nathan's hot dogs. Like the people. People don't die in Brooklyn. They drop dead. It's got to be special.' He gulped some coffee. 'You married, Lieutenant?'

'Not yet, Shapiro.'

'The guys call me Frenchy.'

15

'Frenchy?'

'I know. It's also special. I had a teacher at P.S. 128. She insisted the name was spelled C-h-a-p-e-r-e-a-u. Should I argue with the teacher? So ever since then the guys call me Frenchy.' He grinned reminiscently. 'She was lovely. *Zoftik*. It broke my heart when she ran off and married the gym teacher.'

'You were only a kid, Frenchy. What difference could it make?'

'Listen. You don't know Brooklyn. In the 8B nobody's a virgin.' He finished his coffee and lit a cigarette. 'Hell, I wasn't hardly seventeen when I was goin' steady with Babe.' He looked dejectedly at his cigarette. 'Babe,' he muttered. 'Also special.'

'You're married, then?'

'What else?' He stared gloomily across the docks.

'What's wrong with it?'

'Aah, what the hell.'

'I'm sorry. It's none of my business.'

'A guy can take oney so much.'

'Did you see her when the ship was in the States?'

'Nah.'

'Why not?'

'I quit going home.'

'Any children?'

'A little girl.' He scratched his head. 'What the hell. I'll give it to you straight.'

'Spill it. It's a dull watch.'

'Eleven years this April, we're married. I was only a kid, but I had plenty of push. I had a bagel run. First with a bike. Then I got a little truck. On the side it says, "Frenchy's Fresh Bagels Daily." I'm working like a dog but the money comes in. Soon I'm handling *zemmel* and *chalahs*. They want lox, I bring lox. Bumble Bee salmon for Mrs. Chaim Yonkel, I'm delivering Bumble Bee salmon. I take on sidelines—cream cheese, smoked fish, herring. I'm bringing in seventy-eighty bucks a week and I'm my own boss. All in the first year and a half.

'Is Babe happy? Like hell. She's ashamed. It ain't a dignified business. Here I'm working sixteen-eighteen hours a day and for her it ain't dignified. All day she spends in the beauty shop or eating chink on Fulton Street or in Loew's Metropolitan with her tongue hanging out at Clark Gable. All night long she tells me I should get in another business, like her mah-jongg friends' husbands.

'A fine business. I know these guys. Street-corner bums, every one of them. Yehoodlums. Strong-arming laundries, stink-bombing the movies, mixed up in dirty rackets. Me, I'm keeping my nose clean and making an honest dollar.' He stopped. 'What the hell. It's my *tsuris*. You don't have to listen.'

'What about your little girl?'

'Yeah. The kid.' His voice softened. He brushed a sleeve roughly across his eyes. 'You ever hear of cerebral palsy, Lieutenant?'

'I don't know much about it, Frenchy.'

'My kid, my little Edith, is born with cerebral palsy. A beautiful baby like that—blue eyes, blonde hair—a regular doll face. It's a terrible thing.'

'It must be.'

'At first we didn't know. Then little by little it begins to show. She don't say mama or anything. She don't walk. She don't make sounds. She don't even see when you make goo-goo eyes at her.'

'Couldn't doctors help her?'

'We had her to the biggest specialists. A waste of money. We never gave up hope for a long time. I used to go to her crib. I'd say Kitchy Koo or Looka the Birdie, Edith. I'd see her eyes are watching me. I start to think she's getting better. I yell for Babe to come in and look and just about then the kid's head flops sideways and her tongue hangs out and she's slobbering all over herself.

'And Babe would bawl and tear out her hair. My fault, she said. My crazy family. And eat? My God she ate. She used to sit around fressing and bawling all day long. It got so she could hardly bend over to pick up a charlotte russe if God forbid she dropped it.

'What the hell. I took it as long as I could. So I shipped out. Just like that. Eight years ago. Like it was yesterday.'

Austen carefully extinguished his cigarette. Water slushed softly between the pilings and the ship's side. The quartermaster came over and saluted stiffly.

'Permission to wake reliefs, sir?'

'Very well.' He looked at his watch. The time had passed swiftly. 'Do you hear from home, Frenchy?'

'Babe writes. I'll say that for her. She mails the salamis for my old lady. The old lady can't write but she's smart as a fox. She's living with Babe and the kid.'

'It should be some comfort for Babe to have her.'

'For dames like my wife there's no such thing as comfort. Like she says in her last letter, she wants to move to Flatbush. All of a sudden Brownsville isn't good enough for her.'

'It'll be a change.'

'She wants an elevator apartment with a tapestry-brick front entrance.' He shrugged. 'Go argue with city hall. She gets an allotment. It's her money.' He blew his nose. 'Sometimes I get to thinking maybe I'll go home. Just once. But the idea of seeing the kid kills me.'

The quartermaster returned. 'Reliefs are up, sir. The log is ready to be written. My relief is standing by.'

'Very well. You're relieved.' He turned to Frenchy, who was staring moodily across the water. 'You should, you know. It would be a wonderful thing to do.'

'What would?'

'Go home and see Edith.'

Frenchy flipped his cigarette across the rail. 'Look,' he said, 'I'm running.'

5

AUSTEN went to the quarter-deck and saluted the colours, preparatory to leaving the ship. The officer of the deck was an ensign named Mike Edge. He was thickly built, with close-set cunning eyes. He was a 'mustang'—an ex-enlisted man—and the responsibility of gold braid sat on him like a suit of ill-fitting armour. He looked at Austen suspiciously.

'Nobody's supposed to leave the ship.'

'Captain's orders, Mike.'

Edge watched him uncertainly as Austen went down the ladder and took a seat alongside Dr. Blanchard in the motor whaleboat. He glared at Austen as the boat shoved off.

There was a light chop across the bay. Parry and Hackmeister were propped on canvas cushions in the bow seat. A sick-bay attendant sat between them, sheltered by the blue-grey canopy. They spoke to each other in low whispers.

Hackmeister's eyes were heavily bandaged. He sat with his big hands folded in his lap. Parry was younger and neater. His patched, eager face grinned at Austen out of the shadows. Austen did not look at the blanket over Parry's legs. He remembered clearly how the legs had looked after the gun exploded. He watched Hackmeister, whose head was bent so that his chin touched his deep chest.

A good sailor, Austen thought unhappily. Through now. He tried to think of someone in the division who could be trained for Hackmeister's job on the gun. All he could think of were Hackmeister's dead eyes.

The attendant was laughing and Parry's face brightened. Austen knew they were pleased because the ship was not going to the States after all and they would miss nothing but the resumption of another harsh patrol to the west.

'Ain't these guys lucky, Mr. Austen?' the attendant said. 'Getting a nice safe shore billet while us poor bastards are going out to sea again.'

'Very lucky,' Austen said. He did not really think they were very lucky.

Parry grinned back at him and winked.

You're a nice kid, Alec thought, and very jolly for a guy who's going to end up with one and a half legs if you're *really* lucky. And what are you going to tell the girls back home when all you've got is one and a half legs? Will you still be jolly? Will you tell them you're fine? Are you going to write letters from the dispensary on Adak and tell them you can't wait to get home and wrap your one and a half legs around their lily-white thighs?

Just stop being so damned jolly about it, he thought. Get mad and hate my guts a little and I'll feel a lot better.

He could not see Hackmeister's eyes, but he could see his mouth. 'Sure we're lucky,' he was saying. 'Want to swap even, Lieutenant?' Black specks of gunpowder and steel splinters that were still imbedded in his cheeks made a startling pattern. Pointillist, Alec thought, trying to ignore the bitter edge of Hackmeister's sudden words.

'Wanna, Lieutenant?' Hackmeister's voice rose to a sudden shout. 'Wanna swap even? I'll go to sea for you and you gimme your eyes. How about it? What d'you say?'

He half rose from the seat, his big hands groping. The attendant held him firmly against the cushions. Parry's grin faded and his hands on the white blanket nervously rubbed the bloody bandages on his legs underneath.

'I'm sorry,' Alec said, his insides freezing. He wondered exactly what he was sorry about.

The attendant patted Hackmeister's knee and chuckled thinly. 'It's gonna be okay,' he said. 'They got a hut full of hot-looking Navy nurses up there.'

Hackmeister shoved the attendant's hands aside. 'A big break for a blind man,' he said.

It was an hour's run across the open bay. They sat quietly for a time. The engine pounded and the cold north wind knifed through the canvas lashings. In the confined space under the canopy the air was choked with the smell of fuel. Austen's head ached from the fumes. He leaned his head back to catch the cold thrust of air. The coxswain towered above him. His swathed legs were thrust apart on the stern thwart. His eyes intently followed the course he steered.

Looking sternward, Austen made out the grey shape of the *Atlantis*. Her four stacks poked skyward. Her tripod foremast, topped by the box-shaped forward gun control station, made a jagged silhouette against the grey morning sky. He took a small sketch block and fountain pen from his coat pocket and sketched in the ship's details. The lines he drew were tendrilly thin. The pen moved swiftly.

20

Dr. Blanchard watched him with an amused smile. He was a compact man with a grey-streaked somewhat unruly moustache. Though he spent very little time in sick bay, his department was the most efficient organization on board. He spent most of his shipboard time behind the locked door of his cabin.

He watched Alec's sketch take shape. The ship's lines were roughed in. The shore line beyond magically appeared with a few deft sweeps of the pen. Austen dipped a small brush into the spray that raced past the ship's side, and wet the paper. He worked intently from a small flat box of colour and rendering quick unstudied washes.

Yellow greyed to neutral for the bland sky. A slash of black tinted with ultramarine defined the ship's sides. Austen rinsed the brush and dampened a portion of the paper again and streaked murky greens and feathery blues to delineate the rough sea. The hills were swept in with umber grading to the paper's whiteness for snow-capped peaks. He used the pen once more to sharpen the details of the ship's structure. Then he held the block to catch the flat force of the wind. A puddle of colour feathered into the still-wet blue-green sea.

'Aren't you spoiling it?' Blanchard wanted to know.

'Makes it interesting this way. Fresh-looking. It's only a spot reference. Sometime I'll use it as a study for a larger painting.'

'The captain showed me the portrait you made of him. He says you're a talented young man.'

'I'd feel a hell of a lot better if the captain'd forget I made that portrait.' The sketch was not drying quickly enough and he blew on it.

Blanchard smiled. 'The wardroom boys complaining?'

'Not directly. But the Word gets around.'

'I wouldn't worry too much about it.'

'How's Dooley's leg, sir?'

'A simple fracture. No problems except he's talked the skipper into keeping him aboard. Only complication is he may get in the way.'

The coxswain leaned down. 'You got any idea which is the hospital landing, Mr. Austen?'

Austen peered over the canopy. The harbour was crowded with many types of small craft. He pointed to a launch with a red cross painted on its deck.

'That's probably it.'

The coxswain swung the tiller and clanged the bell. Soon the whaleboat scraped alongside the landing. A Navy ambulance was waiting.

'Real service,' said jolly Parry. Hackmeister said nothing.

'I'll meet you at the Navy landing, Austen,' Blanchard said. 'I'm going after some medical stores.'

'Yes, sir.' He watched while they transferred the two men. Then the doctor climbed into the ambulance and it drove off.

Austen headed for the base carpenter shop. The roads were deeply mired. Vehicles of all types skidded past him, spattering mud, honking, racing wildly. There was an incredible air of urgency and confusion. No one smiled. Austen was sharply aware of the solid land beneath his feet and minded none of it. He was sorry now he had not said good-bye to Parry and Hackmeister.

There was no difficulty about the picture moulding. He thumbed a jeep ride to the base ordnance office and presented the copy of the dispatch the captain had given him. He sat for a long time. Finally the ordnance officer came out. He was a short chunky commander. He looked at Austen with an exasperated expression.

'We don't know anything about your gun barrel, Lieutenant.'

'My instructions were to report to your office and pick up the papers and then pick up the gun barrel at the supply depot, sir.'

For a panic-stricken moment he felt like a man about to drown in a sea of red tape. 'It's all there in the dispatch,' he added wearily.

'I can read, Lieutenant,' the commander growled. He rubbed his head irritably and stared out of the window. 'It says your gun barrel left Mare Island depot by Army Air Transport. That clears us.'

'The skipper said to report to you, sir. I'd hate to go back to the ship without that gun barrel. We really need it.' He said it

22

quietly and reasonably and the ordnance officer looked at him with respect. His irritation ebbed.

'Who's your skipper?'

'Captain Meredith, sir.'

'Snooky Meredith?'

'He signs the ship's log "Warrington E." '

'Hell, that's Snooky all right.' He snapped at a dozing yeoman. 'Fetch me the ships-present file, son. On the double.'

The yeoman returned with a thick sheaf of papers. The ordnance officer flipped through it. 'Hell yes. The *Atlantis*.' He whistled and grinned. 'Well, well.'

Austen relaxed. The strain went out of him and he almost laughed. The captain's name was Snooky. The ordnance officer beamed at Austen. 'Snooky with a ship of his own. Imagine.' He laughed so heartily that several of the yeomen at their desks sat up startled and stared at him. 'Why the hell didn't you tell me it was Snooky Meredith?'

'I didn't know, sir.'

'Hell, Snooky himself should have come in.' He laughed again. He picked up the phone, still laughing. 'Get me Klondike,' he said. He winked at Austen. 'That's the code for Army supply depot. I'm gonna get Snooky his goddamn gun barrel. He needs it.' He rubbed his jaw. 'If it's on this goddamned island I'll get it. I can't see why the hell they picked Army Air—— Hello? Hello, Klondike. This is Mainstay. Right. Is Sergeant Madjicka there? I know he's busy. So am I. I still want Al Madjicka and no lip. That's right. . . . Hello. That you, Al? . . . Listen, Al, I'm sending over a certain lieutenant from that beat-up cruiser that patrols on the outside. He's chasing down another of your snafus—this time it's a gun barrel from–uh–Parity. They need it real bad, Al, and it's laying around probably in one of those big warehouses where you keep all that liquor. . . . I know. I know. Forget it. So am I. I want you to get this lieutenant his gun barrel. You can't miss it. It's about the size of a coffin. We've had them come in before, but not by Army Air. . . . No, we're fresh out. This is in *your* lap. . . . What's that? Sure he has, in black and white. Look, he's on his way over.

Treat him right. His skipper's an old buddy of mine from the Brooklyn Navy Yard. Furnish him transportation and anything else he needs, Al. . . . Right, Al. Thanks.'

He hung up and wiped his face and scribbled a note and stamped it. 'You go out this door, Lieutenant, and wake up my jeep driver and tell him to take you to where Madjicka is. He'll know. The driver will return here, but Madjicka will furnish further transportation for you and for the gun barrel. See Madjicka and no one else. Steer clear of all that Army brass or you'll miss your ship. Hell, you'll miss the whole damned war. Al's the only guy who knows where anything is over there.'

'Thanks for going to all this trouble, Commander.'

'Forget it. Just tell Snooky to get his ass over here to the officers' club to-night. Tell him that's an order. Hell, tell him it's a command. From his old pal, Al Dickman.'

'I'll do that, Commander.'

'It's not often a commander can issue such an order to a captain, you know.'

'It does seem odd, sir.'

'Well, I happen to be an old warrant gunner and I knew Snooky when he got his first ship. It was tied up in Brooklyn.' He laughed so suddenly and heartily that Austen was embarrassed. 'Well, anyway, Snooky and I are old drinking pals. You tell him about to-night. Don't forget.'

'I won't, sir.' He saluted.

Austen went outside and woke up the jeep driver. They took off in a spray of dark, stinging mud. He could still hear the echo of Commander Dickman's booming laughter. It had the quality of one who had been saving his laughs for a very long time.

Sergeant Madjicka was everything Commander Dickman had said. He greeted Austen briefly and thumbed through a thick file of dog-eared dispatches, yanked one, and held it alongside Austen's copy. It was identical with one exception. The word 'CANCELLED' was stamped lividly across the face of the message.

Very decorative, Alec thought numbly, that shade of purple against that shade of green.

'Why?' he asked the sergeant.

24

Madjicka shrugged his thick shoulders. 'All I know is, there's your gun barrel, Lieutenant.' He drew a series of delicate doodles in the corner of the green dispatch while Alec thought it over.

'I'm going to have to report something to the skipper, Sergeant. Perhaps it's a mistake.'

'Now! Now you said it!' Madjicka's face had suddenly come alive. 'A mistake. Hah!' He relaxed and slumped over the desk again.

A character, Austen thought gloomily. Slobodjian. Edge. The exec. All I ever run into are characters. He was hungry and tired and spattered with Adak mud, and he had not yet found his replacement gun barrel.

Madjicka had a faraway look in his round Czech eyes. 'You know something, Lieutenant? I like you. Besides your skipper being a schoolgirl chum of Commander Al Dickman's, I like you for what you are. You have a kind and gentle face and infinite patience and I am a very busy man here and I envy such qualities.' He leaned closer and looked at Austen affectionately. 'You are taking it like a man. You are not bending my ear or reaming my ass or chewing me out or beating your gums. I respect your restraint. In my position I meet all kinds. You are as refreshing a change from the other type of customers as I have ever had the good fortune to encounter. I'm going to show my appreciation. I want to do something to help. After all, you poor guys are riding that rough sea in all kinds of weather and my heart bleeds for you.'

Alec smiled faintly. The shaft, he was thinking, the well-greased shaft in the hands of a past master. 'Thank you for those kind words,' he murmured. He wondered if Blanchard would wait.

'Not at all, Lieutenant,' Madjicka hastened to assure him. 'The pleasure is all mine.' He lowered his voice. 'Lemme show you something. On account of you got nice grey eyes and you're giving me no hard time like some of the boys in Navy blue.' He spun the file so that it faced Austen across the counter. 'See your dispatch number here?'

'Yes.'

'Follow me. When the time came to stamp "CANCELLED" on

your gun barrel shipment, I made a memo like I always do, to show what the reason for cancellation is. Usually it means it's been replaced by some item on the plane with a higher priority number. Look here. See that entry? AV 48734 replacement priority AAA 743, origin, Parity, etcetera, etcetera. The rest don't mean a damn thing. What you want to know out of sheer curiosity is whose priority put your gun barrel off the plane. Well, I'm not gonna tell you, Lieutenant. Know why? Because I'm ashamed. Because he's a general here. Big brass. He needed this priority real bad and your gun had to wait. You know what replaced your gun, Lieutenant? Here—read it yourself.' He savagely thrust the memorandum under Austen's face. 'One Guernsey cow, Lieutenant. See? The general is from Wisconsin and he's homesick for a little fresh milk. He loves fresh milk. It helps him to sleep. So instead of your Bofors forty-millimetre gun barrel as requested, we got a cow on the island.'

He was perspiring, and Alec was fascinated by the tiny beads that formed as he watched them on the damp red forehead. A small froth of almost imperceptible bubbles lay at the corners of his lips as he talked, his voice rising, the words flooding bitterly, his round, moist eyes staring directly into Austen's.

'Hell, Lieutenant, you don't need your gun as badly as the general needs his milk, do you? You can't drink a gun and you can't expect the general to try, can you? Tell that to your skipper, the one who's such a good friend of Al Dickman's. Tell him they made a mistake. Instead of a gun that shoots bullets they sent one that shoots milk, four barrels at a time. Maybe the general won't mind if you borrowed his cow and took it on patrol with you, instead of the gun.'

Austen turned to go.

'Hey, Lieutenant,' Madjicka cried. 'Where the hell you going? What's the rush, Lieutenant? Don't go now, pal, just when it starts to get funny. No kidding, it's the funniest goddamn thing——'

He shouted at the empty doorway and moved about cursing, pulling at the dispatches like loose hair, tearing them from the file and flinging them to the floor. They fluttered in graceful see-sawing arcs of pink and yellow and green and white and blue.

26

A young major put his pink, spectacled face through a doorway. 'What's the ruckus out here?' he called sharply.

Madjicka turned on him, his face violent with fury and pity and tears. 'Mind your own goddamned business!' he screamed, and bent down to recover the multi-coloured dispatches. The major hastily retreated and closed the door to his cubicle and locked it.

Blanchard was waiting at the Navy landing. An icy wind sliced across the water, driving the whaleboat's fenders hard against the pilings.

'You look cold, Austen, and very muddy.'

'I fell a few times. I walked across half this damned island.'

'You'll appreciate the ship all the more. Where's your gun barrel?'

'Mare Island gun depot, probably.' They walked along the dock to the motor whaleboat. He told Blanchard about the general's cow. Blanchard seemed pleased. He took a pint bottle of whisky from his pocket and offered it to Austen.

'You need it,' he said.

'I need something.' Austen took a long pull. It was very good whisky. He handed the bottle to the doctor. The doctor took a longer pull. Austen looked at the crew in the whaleboat anxiously. They waved at him, happy grins on their cold blue faces. He caught Blanchard's shrewd eye.

'That was a thoughtful gesture, Commander.'

Blanchard shrugged and threw away the empty bottle. 'Won't hurt 'em,' he growled. 'Now let's get back. I'm starved.'

Austen got into the boat. He almost stumbled over Slobodjian, who was huddled on the deck boards, dreamy-eyed and cold.

'What the hell are you doing here, Slobodjian?'

Slobodjian regarded him sheepishly. He started to get up.

'Sit down,' Austen said perplexed. 'How in the hell——?'

'When you went in this morning I went in with you.'

'The hell you did.'

'I sat behind Parry and Hackmeister. My shipmates. I had to wish them farewell.'

'Why not wish them farewell on the ship?'

27

'It's not the same thing.' He looked at Austen innocently. 'I thought you knew I was with you this morning.'

'You lie in your teeth, Slobodj.'

'What can I say, then?'

'Nothing to me. The exec'll want the details, though. You're a fool, jumping ship again.'

'I can't help myself. I have a very affectionate nature.' He smiled slowly. 'I met a cousin of mine, here with the Seabees. Living in a shelter like an animal. Poor fellow.'

'Another cousin?'

Slobodjian nodded gravely. 'Zadourian. He owns an avocado grove in Homestead, Florida. And with all his money he gets sent here. This life is not for the rich, Lieutenant.'

'Okay, Slobodj. How the hell did you get by Mike Edge? He runs a taut quarter-deck.'

'Ensign Edge is a dull-witted beast. Even you will admit that, Mr. Austen.'

'Never mind the cracks. If he finds out, God help you. Move over. Commander Blanchard sits there.'

'You are a much wiser officer than Ensign Edge.'

'That remains to be seen.'

Slobodjian moved forward, watching Austen's bemused face through red-rimmed eyes. He squatted like an Arab beggar and wrapped one of the blankets about his shoulders. Commander Blanchard climbed aboard. The engineer started the engine. The bowhook crawled forward, fumbling and cursing and laughing at the stubborn frozen lines, working them with his stiff drunk fingers.

Blanchard stared at Slobodjian, who stared back with an air of mild loathing.

'What've we taken aboard, Alec? Refugees?'

'He's one of the boys from my division, sir. Returning to the ship.'

'How did he get ashore?'

'A pilgrimage, Commander. A holy mission,' Slobodjian said.

'Knock it off, Slobodjian,' Austen said sharply.

'To me, gentlemen,' Slobodjian continued in a soft sing-song, 'getting on dry land is like going to church. I'm a very religious sailor.'

Blanchard settled down as the boat got under way. 'I think the boy is expressing a very touching sentiment, Alec.' He smiled benignly at Slobodjian.

'Hell, Commander, he's a prisoner-at-large and he jumped ship again.'

'I like what he said. Ask him if he'll have a drink.'

'What about it, Slobodj?'

'A drink of what, Mr. Austen?'

'A drink of what, Commander? He's particular.'

'Scotch.'

Slobodjian shook his head. 'I touch nothing but sacramental wine.'

'Alec?' Blanchard produced a fresh pint from his coat pocket and broke the seal.

'Thank you, sir.' He drank and passed the bottle back to Blanchard, who tilted it and swallowed several times without lowering the bottle. He wiped his lips and passed it to the engineer. It made the round of the crew quickly and Blanchard capped the half-empty bottle and returned it to his pocket.

The boat rocked against the rough sea. Austen sat stiff with cold. The whisky inside him was a warm, glowing island. He noticed the pile of medical stores that Blanchard had procured on the beach. It consisted entirely of sealed liquor cartons. Blanchard grinned at him.

'It's an old Navy axiom, Alec. The sole purpose of any shore-based establishment is to service the forces afloat. Every time we hit the beach I get very professional. It never fails. Medical items only, of course.'

'I'm glad to see it comes in the right kind of bottles.'

Madjicka was right, he thought. The general gets his milk. The doctor gets his whisky. And my goddamned gun barrel sits in a warehouse on Mare Island.

They rode in silence for a while. Austen took out the water-colour sketch of the ship and compared it with the *Atlantis*, which lay ahead of them near the mouth of the bay.

'For the skipper, Alec?'

'Hell, no.'

29

'Not mad at him, are you?'

Austen slowly put the sketch aside. Slobodjian slept and the boat crew was out of hearing.

'I suppose he's all right.'

'That's all you have to say?'

'No, it's not. I think he's weak. I have little faith in him.'

'You don't mean faith. You mean confidence. Save your faith for God.'

Austen looked at him. He was smirking slightly. It annoyed Austen. 'You asked me what I thought of him. I told you.'

'It's very easy to confuse the ship's captain with God after a man's at sea a while.'

'No fear of that.'

'The crew is devoted to him, you know.'

'They can have him.'

'You're bitter about the portrait.'

'He's right out of Gilbert and Sullivan.'

'I've had the same feeling. He doesn't really like the sea, does he?'

'He couldn't face up to the simple duty of burying Loomis. Maybe that's why I'm bitter.'

They were approaching the *Atlantis's* ladder. The boat bell clanged and they drew alongside.

'Looks like we missed chow,' Blanchard said.

They climbed the bobbing ladder. Slobodjian followed them. Austen looked around carefully. Johnson, the O.D., who had relieved Edge, was watching the motor whaleboat tie up at the boom. Austen slapped Slobodjian's behind.

'Beat it. You're in the clear.'

Slobodjian glided away and vanished down the crew's ladder. Blanchard stood by while they unloaded the medical stores. A detail arrived from sick bay. Blanchard nodded at the stores.

'You know where they go, men.' He turned to Austen and winked. Austen thought of his gun barrel. 'Chow, Alec? Something'll be left.'

'Johnson's standing my watch, sir. I had better check with him first.'

'Very well. See you below.' Blanchard turned to go, then paused. 'That boy of yours is a real character.'

'Slobodjian?'

'The holy little bastard lifted the pint of scotch out of my pocket as we came up the ladder.' He smiled. 'Don't bother him. He's given me a few moments of pleasure.' He waved casually and left the quarter-deck. The O.D. came over to Austen.

'Welcome aboard, swabbie. I was getting worried about you.'

'Sorry, Johnny. I wasted a lot of time tracking down the gun barrel. It's hung up somewhere.'

'Hell, Alec, you don't need guns on this ship. You've got the Navy's two best fighter pilots to defend you.'

'Guns look so pretty.'

'Did you run into Dave on the beach? He's picking up a repair part for my OS2U over at Andrews Lagoon.'

'Didn't see him. It's a big island. Very muddy.' He was startled by the sudden crack of pistol fire. 'Who in hell's that?'

'The skipper.'

Ping, Ping, Ping!

'What's the damned fool shooting at?'

'Not afraid, are you? A great big gunnery officer like you?'

'Afraid, hell. I just like to know what's going on.'

Johnson shrugged. 'I'm a flyer,' he said. 'How would I know?'

'You're officer of the deck, aren't you?'

'Under protest. This is your watch I'm standing, remember?'

'Okay, okay. Let me run this damned framing up to him and I'll relieve you. I haven't had chow.'

'Take your time, swabbie. I'll stand your watch.'

'Where is he, Johnny?'

'On the bridge, starboard side.'

Ping, Ping!

'I'll make my report to him and be right back.'

'No hurry, Alec. Better wear a helmet.'

Captain Meredith was taking careful aim when Austen arrived on the bridge. This close the *ping* became a *wham*.

Wham, Wham! The slugs disappeared into the nearby hills.

The empty, smoking shells sprayed overhead and rolled tinnily to the deck. The captain slipped the clip from the .45 and tossed it to his Chamorro cabin boy, who caught it neatly and handed the captain a fresh clip. The captain rammed it home, aimed carefully again, and fired.

Wham, Wham!

'Did you get the picture moulding, Alec?'

'Yes, Captain.' He *would* ask for the moulding first, Austen thought bitterly.

'Good. And the gun-barrel assembly?'

'No, Captain.'

'Why not?' He was aiming again.

'Shipment was cancelled, sir.'

Wham, Wham!

'Cancelled? By whom?'

'By a higher priority, Captain. The ordnance officer sent me to Army Air, who handled the shipment, and Army Air had a dispatch cancelling the gun-barrel dispatch. I saw it, sir.'

'What did you see? Don't be so vague.'

'The dispatch cancelling the gun-barrel shipment. The higher priority.' I'm hungry, he thought. I'm also muddy and tired.

'Whose priority?'

'Some Army general's, sir.'

Wham, Wham!

'I think I hit something, Ben,' the captain said to the Chamorro boy. The boy grinned. 'Which general, Alec?' He frowned.

'I don't know, sir. He wanted fresh milk. He's from Wisconsin. He had a cow shipped up—a live Guernsey cow. The sergeant said he was homesick and the milk helped him to sleep nights. Said the general was homesick. Not the sergeant.'

The captain's finger had been squeezing the trigger. Now it relaxed and the captain's face reddened and he turned and stared at Austen, lowering the pistol and scowling.

'You're wandering, Alec. All I asked was which general. Can you tell me without a fantastic tale about sergeants and cows?'

'I don't know his name, Captain.'

The captain turned and fired off-hand. *Wham, Wham!* 'Didn't you tell them at ordnance we needed the gun barrel before we could put out to sea? Did you tell them that?'

'Yes, Captain.'

'Did the ordnance officer know about this cow?'

'No, sir. The Army sergeant told me about it.'

Wham, click. He tossed the pistol to the cabin boy, who caught it gingerly. 'A cow. A damned Army cow. What a hell of a navy.'

'I'm sure Commander Dickman knew nothing about it. He really tried to help.'

'Who?'

'Commander Dickman, the ordnance officer. He said he knew you.'

'Al Dickman is ordnance officer here and you told him I'm your skipper?'

'Yes, Captain.'

'And he didn't get us that gun barrel?'

'He tried. He was very co-operative after I told him you were the skipper. He did all he could.'

'But he didn't get us the damned gun barrel, did he?'

'No, sir.'

'Al Dickman.' The captain looked moodily at Austen for a moment. Then he stared at the grey mist of hills where he had been shooting. 'See those cliffs, Alec?'

'Yes, Captain.'

'Full of Japs. Hiding out in caves.' He looked sternly at Austen. 'I've been studying up on these islands and I know. Those shore-based Navy intelligence idiots laughed when I told them. They say what I've been seeing is nothing but wild mountain goats and ptarmigan. Hell. I know mountain goats. Used to hunt 'em on Mona Island off Puerto Rico. What I've been seeing is neither wild goat nor anything else but the damned Japs. It's the Navy's own funeral. If they want to live with a pack of fanatic Japs on their doorstep, let 'em.'

He sucked in his ample belly and strode to his cabin. Austen followed. The cabin boy had a silver pot of steaming coffee standing by. Its aroma made Austen weak and dizzy.

'If that's all, Captain, I'll go below——'

'Hell, no, it's not all. Ben, a cup of coffee for Lieutenant Austen.'

'Thank you, Captain.'

The boy poured the coffee. Alec remained standing and sipped it. It was dark and bitter. The captain had stripped to the waist and was vigorously rubbing his pale body with a thick towel.

'Coffee *espresso*,' he said. 'From Italy. I can't stand the wardroom stuff. Too weak for me.' Huge blotches of red showed where he rubbed the towel along his middle. 'Maybe you want cream and sugar. Take care of him, Ben.'

Ben took care of him. 'It's fine coffee now,' Austen said.

'Don't be so damned polite all the time, Alec.' He sat down at his desk. 'Don't you ever get mad?'

'I try not to, Captain.'

'Try it sometime; might do you some good. If anybody treated me like I've treated you the last ten minutes, I'd get mad as hell.'

'I keep reminding myself this is the Navy, sir.'

The captain snorted. 'The Navy.' He drummed his fingers on the desk top. His class ring glinted dully. He took a short sip of the black coffee. 'You're okay, Alec. You never lose your temper. Nothing reaches you. Take me. I'm like Vesuvius. I blow my top at the slightest thing. Like shooting that ·45. Hell. I know there aren't any Japs in those hills. It's out of range and I can hardly see the damned shore line. But——' He turned to the cabin boy. 'Shove off for a while, Ben. This is personal.' The boy went out. The captain drank more of his coffee. 'I get so damned bored with everything. Being captain's a pain in the ass, Alec. I don't like the responsibility of eight hundred lives. And I'm a friendly bastard. I'd like to be pals with the men. But I can't. I have to act like a tin god. So I take it out by slamming a few clips into the ·45 and dreaming there are Japs in the hills.'

He stood up. The dishes rattled. His pathetic expression had vanished. His eyes gleamed brightly. 'Hell, if I thought for a moment there were really Japs out there, do you suppose I'd fool around with a lousy ·45? Like hell. I'd load those damned forties of yours and lay 'em in at point blank range. Armour-piercing and proximity stuff. Tons of it. Then I'd catapult Johnson and Clough and have 'em drop a few loads of hundred-pounders on the little bastards. Then I'd go to work with my main batteries.' He sat down abruptly. 'A Guernsey cow,' he said. He looked at Austen's calm kind face. 'Get the hell out of here,' he said. 'Finish your damned coffee and get your sympathetic pitying face the hell out of here. I can't stand it.'

Austen put the coffee cup down and went to the door.

'I want a complete written report on why you couldn't get that gun barrel on board and no nonsense about sergeants and cows. I mean it,' the captain said sternly. 'An official report.' He leaned heavily on the small desk. 'Oh, the hell with it, Alec. Here. Sit down again. Was Al Dickman glad to hear I had a ship?'

'Yes, sir. He said to tell you to come ashore to the officers' club to-night. He said to tell you it was a command, not an order.'

The captain chuckled. 'That's Al, all right. A damned 'mustang.' Never went to the Academy or anything. A commander now, you said?'

'Yes, sir. A three-striper.'

'Good for Al. Hell, yes. I'll see him.' He waved Austen away. His good spirits were restored. He was going to see his old drinking buddy, Al Dickman. He was already planning exactly what he would wear to the officers' club that night.

Austen went below to the wardroom. The tables were cleared, and covered with their green cloths. There was nobody in the pantry. He poured some coffee from the percolator and drank it quickly, and went to the quarter-deck to take over the watch from Johnson.

6

NO blood ran bluer than the Navy blood in Warrington E. Meredith. No one could claim the wearing of the Navy blue more rightfully than he. A great-grandfather had exhibited unquestionable courage and coolness under fire aboard one of Oliver Hazard Perry's frigates on Lake Erie the tenth of September, 1813, and an untarnished succession of Navy officers made it a matter of family pride and tradition down the years.

Along came Warrington E., and the unwavering line of gold-encrusted admirals and commodores whose portraits graced the east wall of the conservatory overlooking the Cliff Walk in Newport, seemed destined to founder and sink.

Young Meredith, Annapolis '19, had mildly intimated that he did not like the sea and never had. His stunned mother and near-prostrate grandmother regarded him severely across the hero-filled room and demanded to know why. Grandpapa had gone down with the *Maine*. Papa had failed to return from a secret naval mission no more than a year ago. It was unthinkable that Warrington would choose any other fate for himself.

Unfortunately Warrington preferred to go on living. He was an amiable soft-faced youth who had favoured practical-joking to the Navy sciences at Annapolis. He was weakly handsome and looked much stronger and tougher than he really was. His fresh-water blue eyes were surprisingly intelligent, which might explain his reluctance towards the sea.

He had a weakness for tailor-made uniforms and the gaiety of Navy social life around Newport. In fact, everything about the Navy that did not go to sea was quite all right with him, and these were the sentiments he transmitted to his mother and grandmother at the time of graduation.

He never had a chance. Though he reminded them of his shortcomings in naval sciences and mathematics and his enduring respect for dry land, he was doomed. The unwavering line of heroes glared down at him, and his mother and grandmother glared up at him and Warrington E. reluctantly went to sea.

His first command was an ancient destroyer recently converted from coal. He promptly ran her into a respectable portion of the Brooklyn Navy Yard. In the investigation that followed the glorious record of his forebears was recalled, but unhappily so was Lieutenant Meredith, to a shore billet in Newport.

Restored to his bailiwick he blossomed. He married well and

36

his wife, who was lovely and ambitious and proud to be a Meredith in a society where the Merediths sailed with God, loved him well. She entertained cleverly as Lieutenant Meredith's wife and finally as Commander Meredith's lady she was lavishly entertained in return.

Their chafing-dish suppers by candlelight became a local tradition and his salty tales of the sea, heavily laced with old Newbury rum, soon earned him a reputation he secretly knew he did not deserve.

By the end of 1940 he almost welcomed the prospect of war. Good men and ships were scarce and the Navy, remembering the Brooklyn Navy Yard as well as the *Maine*, kept a thoughtful eye on him. He attended the Naval College and brushed up on tactics and studied hard and fared well. His loving wife sewed the fourth gold stripe on the sleeves of his blues and Snooky was sent to sea. He relieved the commanding officer of the *Atlantis* in Dutch Harbour, shortly after the Japanese had bombed it and dug their garrisons into the cold slopes of Attu and Kiska. The *Atlantis* began the rigorous patrol of the island chain.

He had a way with his men and soon won their hearts. He knew their first names. He sampled a ration of the crew's chow daily and raised hell when it fell below prescribed standards. He was friendly and jocular and sympathetic, and he was all of these without violating the dignity of his rank.

The endless patrols became a bitter routine. The days lengthened into weeks and then months without relief. The men grew sullen and morose. New drafts of inexperienced men made matters worse. The captain persisted in his campaign to keep his ship a happy ship although by this time he had had enough of the sea. But he rightly knew that a maximum degree of loyalty upward could mean the difference between saving and losing the ship, and he did not want to lose it. The fates of Papa and Grandpapa were still fresh in his mind. So was the image of his snug harbour in Newport. He had been away from the chafing dish and the flowing bowl long enough and he hoped to return in a condition to enjoy both to the fullest extent.

The captain's gig pulled alongside the landing dock of the Adak officers' club. Captain Meredith stepped out and sniffed the icy night air like a coon dog, his eyes bright with the promise of good hunting.

He had removed the stay from his blue cap. It gave a rakish sea-dog air to his red happy face. The gold insignia was green with tarnish and he wore a fine non-regulation poplin parka coat with a shaggy fur collar.

The coxswain was a soft-spoken boy from the Georgia Bible belt. 'Any orders, Captain?' He was shivering with cold.

'Just stand by for me.' He stared up the long series of steps. 'Why don't you tie up here, Galagher, and the three of you get up there with those jeep drivers.' He winked in the dark. 'Might get yourselves a snort of whisky up there.'

'Be mighty welcome, Captain,' the bowhook said. 'I'm cold as hell.'

Galagher glared at him. 'We'll be all right, sir. We'll be ready for you whenever you want.' ·

The officers' club was perched on a hill of snow and mud over-looking the harbour. The captain started up the long flight of wooden steps. He could hear music and the shrill laughter of women. Leave it to Al, he thought happily. Good old Al.

The crew trailed behind him, Galagher slightly in the lead.

'Looks awful good,' the bowhook whispered.

The engineer was a stocky sullen man. 'All I want is a look at some of them Navy nurses.'

'Not me. I just wanna feel.'

'Fat chance you got.'

'I just wanna feel is all. Anything.'

'Quiet,' Galagher hissed. 'The captain might hear you.'

'So what?' the engineer snarled.

They continued in silence. At the top of the hill the captain called them together. Through the brightly lighted windows they could see the officers dancing with Navy nurses. A hot com-bination of sailor musicians was playing 'Sweet Sue.' It looked warm and cosy inside.

'Just a word, men,' the captain said. 'Remember you're the seagoing Navy. Every one of these shore-based boys would give a year's pay to swap with you. You're the *élite*. Your conduct represents the reputation of the entire ship and all your shipmates. Don't let 'em down. Remember that, won't you?'

'Yes, sir, Captain,' Galagher said fervently. The other two did not say anything. The captain turned briskly and went into the clubhouse. Galagher's eyes never left his portly figure.

'There goes a real skipper,' he said with the dewy-eyed reverence of an altar boy.

'Let's find us a drink,' the engineer said.

'Christ. That's more like it,' said the bowhook.

Four hours and fourteen drinks later the captain emerged from the warm festive main lounge of the clubhouse. He glowed. The world was all right. He looked around for Al Dickman and the two nurses he had promised to bring out with him. They were nowhere around. He waited for a few minutes. Christ, life was sweet again! And the knockers on that redhead he had danced with! Dickman had called them the most formidable forward twin mounts in the North Pacific Fleet.

The club was closing and the departing officers and their dates jostled him. He looked about anxiously for Dickman and the girls. The others brushed past him, shouting and joking, buttoning their greatcoats against the cruel wind. The jeep drivers and command-car chauffeurs were racing the motors grimly, rubbing themselves to keep warm. They watched silently as the drunk laughing nurses piled into the cars. The good smell of ripe whisky hung over the night air like a mist of heavy perfume.

The captain's boots slithered on the wet platform. His feet slipped and he landed in the snow.

'Whoosh!' he said thickly. He scrambled up and leaned against a column. The hell with Dickman, he thought. He straightened up carefully and bawled at the sky.

'*Atlantis*—AHOY!' He fell down. He sat in the snow, shaking it from his red happy face.

A hand reached under his arms. It was the faithful Galagher.

'Where the hell you been?'

'At the gig, Captain. I heard you shout, sir——'

'Help me up and knock off the chatter.' The spill had bruised him. He could feel the dull pain through layers of drunkenness. He had eaten too much king-crab salad. His stomach felt like a suspended lead ball inside him.

'*Atlantis*, ahoy, damn it!' he shouted.

'Right here, Captain,' Galagher whispered anxiously. 'Up you go, sir.' He strained. The captain did not budge. A web of anger had stifled his high spirits. The little redhead, he thought. Betrayed him. She and damned Dickman. Gone now. Redheads, he thought. Probably curled up on the back seat of a jeep warding off the lower-echelon attacks of a three-striper dentist.

He stared up at Galagher. 'Name and station, sailor,' he barked.

'It's me, Captain, the coxswain——'

'Sound off, damn it!' he bawled at the cold stars.

Galagher froze to attention. 'Galagher, Francis X., coxswain, V-6, USNR, sir.'

'Very well,' the captain mumbled.

'If you'll raise up a bit, I think we can make it, sir.'

He helped the captain to his feet and guided him painstakingly down the slippery flight of wooden steps. At the edge of the landing the captain's feet shot from under him. He took the panting weakened Galagher with him.

'Sorry, Captain,' Galagher cried, scrambling to his feet. 'Clumsy of me, sir.' The captain's fingers clawed Galagher's face.

'Whoosh!' the captain exclaimed. 'Damned clumsy!'

'Hey, you guys!' Galagher yelled in the direction of the gig. 'Bear a hand here, on the double!' He dabbed at his bleeding cheek.

The bowhook and engineer, who had been unable to find a drink, had retired in disgust to the gig. They shuffled over sleepily.

'C'mon, c'mon,' Galagher urged, glassy-eyed with fatigue.

The bowhook reached under the captain's arms. The engineer balked.

'Me touch gold braid?' he said, recoiling. He backed away and watched them. They carried the captain to the gig. He sprawled under the canopy, his head thrown back and the pale pink folds of his neck exposed. The boat got under way and headed into the dark icy harbour. The wind blew hard and waves slapped the bow harshly.

Galagher braced himself on the stern thwart and steered for the ship. He hoped the O.D. was someone trustworthy who would understand the captain's dilemma. Mr. Austen, perhaps, or one of the pilots. Not Ensign Edge. God forbid! The Word would be all over the ship by morning chow. He closed his eyes and gripped the tiller tightly. His free hand sought the battery of bright medallions at his throat. He mumbled a fervent Hail Mary for the captain.

The engineer's tousled head appeared from below. He sniffed the cold air. 'What a load the old man's got on!'

'And why not? He's the skipper, ain't he? He's got a right, ain't he?'

'He's singing dirty songs. Hear him?'

'I don't hear a thing. You better get back to your engine where you belong.'

The engineer spat. 'What you looking for? A Navy Cross, wise guy?' He wiped his nose across his sleeve where the mucus had frozen in a shiny hard streak. Galagher ignored him. His pained honest eyes searched the darkness for the *Atlantis*.

In a while the captain stopped singing. He peered through heavy aching eyelids at the surrounding darkness. He knew he was going to be ill. He whimpered a little, remembering all the other times he had been ill like this. In officers' clubs, in passage-ways, in wardrooms and brothels, in men's rooms (and one time in a ladies' room, he recalled), in foyers and gutters and gardens. And now in the cockpit of the captain's gig. A fine figure of a captain, he thought. In his own gig. He searched weakly for a handkerchief.

The engineer had crept forward to harangue the bowhook. He paused and listened and shook his head sadly.

'I think he's still singing,' he said.

Galagher made a skilful approach to the swaying ladder.

'Captain's gig!' he shouted, and was relieved to see Lieutenant Austen's face at the head of the gangway. He threw over the tiller and the bowhook grabbed the line and held the gig close

41

aboard. He kicked over some fenders and the starboard gunwales brushed the sides of the ladder gently.

Inside the gig the captain belched softly and tried to arrange his clothing. He wiped his soiled hands on the fine sennit work that framed the ports of the small cabin. He felt somewhat better now. Everything was going to turn out all right, he thought. It always did, he remembered. He closed his eyes sleepily.

Galagher peered in and was almost overcome by the foul stink in the tiny cabin. He shook the captain's arm lightly and the captain nodded. Galagher helped him to the handrail. The fresh air revived the captain. After a few tries he managed to reach the platform of the accommodation ladder. With Galagher's support he made it carefully and without mishap to the quarter-deck.

He returned Austen's salute with considerable effort. The men on watch had come to attention and stared at their skipper with a variety of expressions, none of which escaped the captain. Galagher still supported him. He brushed the man's hands away. He swayed slightly and tried to focus his gaze on Austen. Dimly he felt a sense of rage and shame.

It had to be Austen, he thought drunkenly. Of all the officers on the watch list Austen had to be the one to receive him in this condition. The talented, the handsome, the quietly disapproving Austen. His young friend. His crutch.

He stopped swaying. With a convulsive effort his shoulders straightened. His chin rose from the damp folds of his soiled collar. Galagher moved away gratefully to attend to the security of his boat and crew for the night. The quarter-deck was silent. Below, the gangway creaked and the gig's fenders crunched softly against the ladder.

The captain raised his hand. 'Just a moment, Coxswain.'

Galagher stopped. He had hoped the captain was not going to express his gratitude for all he had done. It would be embarrassing before the others. And Galagher was a modest sailor. He wiped his aching eyes and touched the dried blood along his cheek. Tears of gratitude started easily as they did in his altar-boy days. He faced his skipper with lighted eyes, tormenting his body into the fixed rigidity of attention.

The captain pointed a grey-gloved finger at him. 'Place the man under arrest, Lieutenant Austen.'

Galagher sagged as though the captain had struck him.

'Throw him in the brig. Three days' bread and water.'

'Aye, Captain.' Austen's face was expressionless. The quartermaster scribbled wildly. 'What are the charges, Captain?'

'You can damned well see,' the captain said coldly, 'he threw up all over my dress blues.'

He turned and left the quarter-deck, weaving slightly. No one said anything. Galagher walked slowly to the side where the gig lay.

'Tie up to the boom and secure,' he called to the engineer. He came back to the O.D. shack. His aching body shook with silent sobs. 'Let's go,' he said savagely to Austen. 'You heard what the captain said.'

Austen was wakened by someone shaking him. It was Ben, the captain's cabin boy.

'What's wrong, Ben?'

'Captain Meredith want to see you, sir.'

'Now?' Austen looked at his watch. It was 5.20 A.M. He had slept an hour since being relieved at the quarter-deck. He sat up. 'What the hell's wrong, Ben?'

'He don't say, but maybe he plenty worried, sir.' He grinned. 'Walking up and down that cabin all night, I guess. Say for you to come and not to dress. To come now.'

'Hell, it's a cold wet climb up there. You sure he's sober?'

'Yes, sir. Maybe too damn much sober.'

Austen buttoned a raincoat over his pyjamas and followed the boy to the captain's emergency cabin on the bridge.

The captain had bathed and changed his clothes. He wore a suit of exotic silk pyjamas over which he had wrapped a Chinese robe. His back was to Austen when he entered. An elaborate dragon was woven in scarlet silk on the back of the robe. Austen noted his water-colour portrait leaning against a bulkhead, framed and ready for hanging. It looks very nice, he thought. Even if it is the captain. Dress whites, he thought. The big sorry slob.

'Sorry to get you up, Mr. Austen.'

'At your service, Captain.'

'I will try to be brief and to the point.'

'Yes, sir.' The formality worried him. Now what the hell have I done? he wondered.

The captain lit a cigarette and puffed vigorously. 'When I returned aboard this evening I gave you a certain task to perform, if you recall.'

'Yes, sir.'

'I suggested that you throw that coxswain, Galagher, in the brig.' He paused. 'On three days' bread and water.'

'Those were your exact orders, Captain.'

The captain winced. 'Orders! You know very well——Damn it, Alec, you know damned well the condition I was in. Plastered to the gills.'

'I'm sorry, Captain. I had no idea.'

'Hell, Alec, that poor kid Galagher almost broke his back lugging me here from the club! He deserves a Distinguished Service Medal. And I slap him in the brig.' He stared at Austen anxiously. 'It was my own fault, you know. Galagher didn't throw up on my blues at all. Did it myself.'

'I really don't know what to say, Captain.'

'You don't have to say a damned thing. I'm ashamed of myself. I don't know what the hell gets into me to do a thing like that.' He continued to stare at Austen's expressionless face. 'For Christ sake, say something nice, will you? Get me out of this jam. All those men heard me. I can't afford such ridicule, Alec. How the hell can I get the boy out of the brig and not lose face?'

'He's not in the brig, Captain.'

'What do you mean, he's not?'

'He's probably in his sack fast asleep.'

'How come?'

'The kid was broken up by what happened. And exhausted. I took him aside and told him to forget about the order. I also straightened it out with the man on watch. You're really in the clear, sir.'

The captain beamed at him. 'Fine, Alec. Splendid. You used your head, boy.'

'Thank you, sir.'

'Well, well,' the captain said. He looked thoughtful.

'He really wanted to go to the brig. He's very devoted to you, Captain, and I had a hard time talking him out of going to the brig.'

'You did, eh?' The captain sat down heavily.

'Yes, sir.'

'He wanted you to carry out my orders, but you said no.'

'Well, Captain——'

'Disobeyed my orders, Alec, didn't you? My direct spoken orders.'

'Yes, Captain.'

The captain was muttering to himself. He tittered and then laughed and then the laughter possessed him so that he was unable to control it. His vast body shook and Austen, watching it, could only think of one thing—oatmeal. Two hundred and sixteen pounds of solid oatmeal.

'Go away,' the captain blurted between the sickening laughter and tears. 'Get out of here.'

'Do you want a written report of the incident?'

The captain leaped up, a swollen tower of gaudy silken rage. 'I want nothing,' he screamed, 'except a little respect from my officers and men. A little dignity. I want every one of you to stop laughing and sneering behind my back. And you especially, Lieutenant. Your contempt for me is too damned obvious. I should break you for it. You and your damned insolence.' He looked about wildly and his eye caught the framed portrait. He gripped it and stared at it and then at Austen. 'This insulting joke of yours—this caricature of a pompous self-satisfied idiot——'

For a moment Austen thought the captain would hurl the portrait at him, but his violent rage ebbed. His arms dropped. His jowls shook and the tears poured down his red-flecked face. 'Go on,' he said in a collapsed voice, 'get out of here and leave me alone.'

'I'm sorry you said that about the portrait, Captain.'

'Alec.' The voice was calm.

'Yes, Captain.'

'You really mean you like the portrait?'

'Yes, sir.'

'The frame is very handsome.'

'Thank you, Captain.'

'I'm sorry for what I said.'

'That's all right, sir.'

He almost stumbled over the cabin boy in the dark pilot-house. He had been crouched near the door, listening.

'For Christ sake, Ben. You scared the hell out of me.'

They stared at each other in the darkness for a moment. Both of them grinned. Alec climbed down the cold ladder to his cramped room. He was shivering and his body was drenched in cold sweat. He crawled into his bunk and after a while he slept.

7

NEXT morning pilot Dave Clough flew out the replacement OS2U. It was hoisted aboard and secured to its catapult. Flag signals wigwagged from the bridge. By sunrise the small task force, consisting of the *Atlantis* and three destroyers, was headed out of Kuluk Bay. Admiral Marcy and his staff were already on board. Preparations were made for several days of intensive exercises.

The Fourth Division muster report was late. Austen searched the ship for his division petty officer, Frenchy Shapiro. He found him astride one of the bitts on the fantail, morosely watching the ship's wake.

'What about the muster report, Frenchy? It's late.'

'Would you leave me alone, please, Mr. Austen?'

'Like hell I will. Let's have the muster report.'

'Please, I beg you.'

Austen walked around the bitt and looked at him. 'What's up?'

'I just wanna be alone, that's all.'

'No bad news in the mail, is it?'

Frenchy shook his head. Two chiefs who were having a smoke on the other side of the fantail looked over curiously.

'I'd like to know what's wrong.'

'Everything. I'm ashamed.'

'Ashamed of what?'

'Myself. The Navy. After eight years, this should happen——' He stood up suddenly, half crouching. 'Look at these dungarees.'

Austen looked at them. They were so new the packing wrinkles were still in them. 'They look fine. It's about time we got some new ship's stores on board.'

'Take a good look,' Frenchy pleaded.

Austen examined the dungarees closely. A little wide in the hips, he noticed. 'Frenchy, you're getting middle-age spread.'

'Uh-un. Look. No fly.'

'That's odd.'

'Not for Waves it ain't.'

'Ah. Wave's dungarees. Now I see.'

'Eight years, Boss. And this has to happen to me.'

'Swap 'em in. They must have others.'

'Sure they do. Two thousand pairs. All for Waves.'

'The fortunes of war, Frenchy.'

'The shame of it, Boss.'

'I'm overcome. Forget the muster report. Ensign King'll handle it.'

'Thanks, Boss. I'll be okay in a little while. This is a blow.' He wiped his eyes. He looked very sad. 'All these years I'm dreaming that some day maybe I'll get into some Wave's pants. I never dreamed it would be like this.'

A sailor named Salvio came running out of the Number Three Hatchway. His delicate olive face was pinched with fear. He ignored Austen. 'You better come down the compartment, Frenchy,' he whispered.

'Beat it, Sal. I'm having troubles enough.'

'No kidding. You better.' He looked furtively at Austen. It's Ski, Frenchy. He's raising hell down there.'

'I can't be bothered, Salvio. Scram.' Frenchy waved him away.

'I swear to God on my mother you better come, Frenchy.'

47

'This is a day I won't forget.' Frenchy slid off the bitt and hitched his new dungarees. 'The first guy makes a crack about these dungarees, God help him.'

Salvio teetered nervously on his toes. 'Hurry, will ya?'

'Want me to go along?' Austen asked.

'Hell, no, Boss. I can handle that guy.' Frenchy and Salvio went below. Austen lit a cigarette. He had had practically no sleep that night and he felt drowsy. Salvio returned in a few minutes. He was alone.

'You better get down there quick, Mr. Austen. Them two guys are gonna kill each other.'

'Ski and Shapiro?'

'Who else?'

Salvio darted away and Austen followed him. When he reached the Fourth Division compartment he had to push his way through a thick ring of tense silent men. Shapiro and Kracowski stood inside the ring facing each other. Four men held their arms. Austen pushed his way through the ring.

'Let them go,' he said quietly.

'They'll start swinging, sir.'

'Let them go.' He tried to keep his voice steady. The men's arms dropped and he stood between them, facing Kracowski.

'What's the trouble, Ski?'

'Find out for yourself, wise guy.'

There was a muffled snicker. Most of the men remained silent. There was a purplish swelling under Kracowski's right eye. Austen saw that his knife sheath was unbuttoned and the knife was gone from it.

'Where's your knife?'

Kracowski regarded him with an expression of contempt. Austen turned to Shapiro. He was breathing heavily. He grinned crookedly at Austen. A long thread of blood stained his open shirt. Wire-thin, it coursed evenly from the nipple of his right breast to the navel. The blood had puddled there, and even as Austen watched the rise and fall of stomach muscles sent the tiny pool trickling.

'Everything's under control, Boss.'

'Where's his knife?'

Nobody moved. Austen looked around at the circle of faces. Kids from home. Familiar faces with blue eyes and brown eyes and grey eyes. Curious, tense. Street-corner faces. In the next compartment he could hear a working party scraping old paint from the deck. On the deck above a loading crew in the after main battery was going through a routine drill with dummy ammunition. He heard the breech slam home and the gun captain's hoarse shouting.

'I want that knife. Now.'

There was an uneasy silence. Somebody kicked the knife from behind Kracowski's leg. It slid into the ring.

'Pick it up, Salvio.'

'Me, sir?'

'You.' Salvio picked up the knife gingerly and squirmed out of range. Somebody said an unkind word and the men laughed at Salvio.

'Let 'em slug it out, Mr. Austen,' somebody called out. Others nodded. Eyes brightened. Everyone watched Austen's taut face.

'How'd this fight start, Ski?'

'You oughtta know.' He spat on the deck.

'Why me?'

'You started it.'

'How do you figure that?'

'Hell. By busting up the division is how. I been the leading p.o. a long time, see? No chicken-livered junior grader is gonna come along and foul things up just like that.'

'That's all you have to say?'

Kracowski sneered. 'Ain't it enough?'

Austen turned to Shapiro. 'What's the story?'

'No story. Everything's under control.'

A sailor named Willis spoke up. 'Ski started it, sir. He come through here an hour ago and started heaving everybody's gear around. He smeared a bucket of gun grease on Shapiro's bunk. Some of us tried to stop him but he pulled his knife. He cut up some of the men's mattresses and stuff like that. Then Shapiro showed up and he tried to cut him.'

49

'He swung on me,' Kracowski said. 'Looka my eye.'

'He had his knife out when Shapiro hit him is why,' Willis said.

'Let 'em fight it out,' a voice pleaded. An excited murmur agreed with him.

'They've been at it ever since you made Shapiro leading p.o.,' Willis said.

'Listen,' Austen said, 'are you guys crazy? You're supposed to be a gun crew—a team—— What the hell are you trying to do?'

'You shouldn't have broke me,' Kracowski said.

'Listen, Ski. Shapiro outrates you, for one thing. But I let you hold the leading p.o. spot as long as I could. This compartment used to be filthy. You did nothing to change that. You can't handle the men, you're surly and unreasonable and you play favourites. Since Shapiro took over the place is clean. I get working parties when I need them. There's some spirit and morale and discipline and that is what I must have and that is what is being delivered. Not by you but in spite of you. And above all, the men like it. At least a dozen have volunteered to tell me so. That's good enough for me. I like cleanliness and discipline. You don't. If you don't like the way the division is running I'll okay a transfer to another division. Would you like that?'

'Go to hell.'

Austen stepped so close to him that Kracowski stumbled backward, a flash of fear in his eyes. 'Get this, Ski. You can get a summary for this. And for your other cracks. And for your fancy knife work. You don't have a leg to stand on. But you're not going to get a summary, Ski, because I'm not putting you on report. A summary means Mare Island prison and the States and I'll be damned if I'll get you a free ride out of here to the States. You're going to stick around with the rest of us and suffer.'

'You're awful cocky, ain't you, with your one and a half stripes to back you up,' Kracowski said. 'A real brave son of a bitch, ain't you?'

'Slap him down, sir!' someone said angrily.

'It won't work, Ski,' Austen said softly.

'Chicken, ain't ya? Real chicken.'

'Go on, Mr. Austen. Don't take that stuff.'

'It won't work.'

'Nobody's gonna know, Mr. Austen. Lay it on.'

Austen shook his head. His tight fists relaxed. 'I'd know.'

'Let 'em fight, sir. Shapiro'll kick the guts out of him.'

'Nobody's fighting,' Austen said.

'I'll fight him,' Ski said. 'I'll fight anybody.'

Austen closed his eyes. A wave of nausea gripped him and his head ached. He wiped his mouth. When he opened his eyes Kracowski's scowling face confronted him. He wanted to smash his fist against it.

'Salvio.'

'Yes, sir.'

'Take a look above in the after main battery. Let me know if the loading crew's cleared out yet. I don't hear them.'

Salvio slipped away. The men spoke in excited whispers. Austen raised his hand wearily. 'Keep the chatter down, men. The Word better not get around.'

He looked at Shapiro's wound. It had done no more than break the outer skin surface. The blood was already drying.

'Feel up to it, Frenchy?'

'Me? Sure.' His face was pale and his body muscles twitched. 'Sorry you had to take that crap from Ski,' he whispered.

'So am I. But I had to.'

'I know, Boss.' He frowned. 'Ski should know better.'

'I'll let you have the honour of teaching him.'

'I guess it better get settled once and for all.'

'I suppose so. I suppose that's the way things have to get done.'

Salvio returned, his eyes bright with excitement. 'The gun room's empty, Mr. Austen. Those guys secured from drill.'

'All right, men. Drift up there easy. Shapiro and Ski stay here with me for a minute. Willis and Salvio, cover the two hatches and keep any outsiders away. When all the men here are in the gun room, dog down the hatches. Nobody gets in after the fight starts and nobody leaves until it's over.' He looked around. 'Okay. On your way and for Christ sake don't look like you're going to Madison Square Garden.'

The room emptied except for the three of them. Kracowski

stood apart, his face yellowish and still scowling. His blunt fingers worked the seams of his dungarees. Shapiro was wiping his sweaty hands on his shirt. Two red spots showed high on his cheekbones.

Austen, oddly enough, was thinking of his Quaker father and a time of his childhood when his father had punished him for playing at war with a wooden sword. And he thought of Goya's etchings of war atrocities—spread violated thighs and bloodied breasts, scowling moustachioed faces under quaint military caps. Etched in acid and blood, he thought, gruesome and lascivious and at once great art and timeless.

'Come over here, Ski.' Kracowski shuffled over. Austen gripped each man's arm. 'I want the two of you to listen for a minute. I couldn't say this to the whole division, but I can to the two of you. This fight is a violation of my duty as an officer. You know that. But more than that, it's against my principles. I hate fighting. I've hated it since I was a kid. I've been raised to hate it.'

'If you hate it so much, what the hell you doing out here?' Kracowski asked.

Austen ignored the remark. 'When the fight's over, it's finished for good. It's dead. It doesn't really matter who wins. What does matter is that the division isn't affected by it. Whether you like it or not, we're in this together. We're a team. We shoot the guns. It can mean the life or death of every man on board.

'When one of you is knocked out or quits, it's over. The winner is leading p.o. You don't have to shake hands or kiss and make up or anything else. No strings. But from then on I insist on loyalty to the men and the ship. I insist on a job well done. Is that clear?'

The two men nodded.

'Let's get going,' Kracowski growled.

Frenchy wiped his broken nose.

'One more word,' Austen said evenly. 'You've sounded off in front of the men, Ski, in a way that makes me look chicken. Maybe I am chicken and maybe some of the men won't let me forget it. You're cagey enough to know if I laid a hand on you, you could raise the biggest stink the Navy ever heard. Well hear this: I'm ready to beat the living hell out of you any time and any place you say once we're off this ship. And I want you to let me know any time you think I can't do it.' He released their arms. 'Now get going.'

They went topside through the after hatchway to the gun room. The men were waiting, formed in a rough ring. Shapiro and Kracowski stripped to the waist.

'They going to need any seconds, Mr. Austen?'

Austen shook his head. 'It's a finish fight. There'll be no rounds.' He called the two men to the centre of the ring. The babble of voices faded. 'It's agreed the winner is leading p.o. of the division. No word of this scrap must get around the ship, men. The fight's over when one or the other is knocked out or quits.'

He stepped back. Kracowski shoved him and swung heavily at Shapiro's face. A protesting cry rose from the circle, but it was too late. The two fighters were swinging short crunching blows. Neither yielded an inch. The first surprise punch that Kracowski had delivered had caught Frenchy's left ear as he turned. It looked raw red.

Kracowski was a few years younger and heavier than Shapiro. He knew how to use his arms and legs. Frenchy was having a difficult time. He seemed dazed by the unexpected barrage of blows that Kracowski had unleashed. He swerved and ducked and swung wildly. The men urged him to cover up, but he seemed not to hear, and absorbed an incredible amount of blows. Yet he gave no quarter. Kracowski's punishing fists, smeared with Frenchy's blood, hammered like pistons. The minutes dragged. It was brutal to watch. Some of the men turned away.

Shapiro's lips were badly cut and his nose appeared to be a shapeless pulp. He breathed noisily. In spite of the awful beating he took, his small crooked grin remained.

Kracowski was virtually unmarked except for several angry-looking red welts in his mid-section. He was puffing slightly, tiring from the steady, pumping action of his hard fists. He fought with his head down and his feet planted well apart. His thick-muscled arms flailed a constant crunching staccato.

Shapiro finally went down. He remained a moment, bent over,

supporting himself on his hands and knees. Kracowski crowded close over him, his fists ready, a triumphant glint in his small eyes. Frenchy's blood dripped with his sweat on the steel deck.

'Stop it, Mr. Austen,' someone pleaded. Austen shook his head.

Frenchy started to get up and Kracowski sent him down. The second time Frenchy charged into the swinging fists and stood. The two of them slugged it out close together and exchanged a withering series of body blows until Kracowski gave ground.

They were both breathing painfully. Frenchy worked to keep Kracowski out where he could box him until his senses cleared. Twice in mad rhino-like rushes Kracowski broke through. Each time Frenchy timed an upswing in a short brutal arc that stopped him dead in his tracks. They were solid, crunching blows. The second one lifted Kracowski to his heels and he staggered backward into the arms of a sailor who shoved him into the ring again.

The crowd was with Frenchy now. Kracowski crouched cautiously and waited for Frenchy to close. He was feeling the effect of the steady body blows that he had taken and looked furtively to Austen, hoping for a breathing spell. He had gambled on the first surprise. Now the taste of an easy victory was souring. He danced nervously.

'C'mon, you yellow chicken bastard,' he gasped. 'C'mon over and get your face bashed in.' The roll of fat about his middle quivered. Frenchy grinned through his blood-smeared mouth, taking deep breaths, not speaking, watching cunningly how Kracowski strained to hold up his tiring arms. Frenchy moved closer, his body bent, his arms raised and the hard ridge of his knuckles extended. Then he closed in.

He feinted and jabbed in vicious stabs. He worried Kracowski into blind wild rushes. Each time Kracowski's head lowered Frenchy drove an uppercut through his failing guard and smashed it home. Slowly the thick body sagged. Blood oozed from the bruise under Kracowski's eye. The red welts at his midriff showed in deeper-coloured blotches. His arms dropped. Frenchy glanced at Austen, who shook his head, and Frenchy stopped grinning. He drove a cruel knuckled blow and Kracowski's head snapped up. His eyes glazed and he seemed to fold all at once. His bloody fists

54

hung uselessly from the ends of limp arms. He remained upright, shaking the blood from his dazed eyes.

'*Kill him, Frenchy!*'

Frenchy dropped his fists and reached out to catch Kracowski before he fell. Kracowski swung once, weakly. He tried to fight back as Frenchy put his arms around him and carried him aside. Someone poured a bucket of water over their heads. The men pushed close and pounded Frenchy's back and tried to embrace him.

'For Christ sake, give us some air, will you?' he pleaded.

The hatches were undogged and men poured out into the cold bracing air of the main deck. They dispersed quickly. Austen soon found himself alone.

He lit a cigarette and went out to the fantail and sat on one of the bitts. It's funny, he thought. Nobody said anything about Frenchy's dungarees. He studied his fingers. They were shaking.

He tried to laugh. It was no use. His insides were knotted and his head ached. He gripped the woven steel life line and remained there in the icy wind, despising violence with all his heart and somehow ashamed of himself for it. He remembered his threat to Kracowski—any other time and place. What war does, he thought. He wondered if he would go through with it when the time came. He was thankful he was alone.

Later he went below. The men had cleaned up the compartment. It was spotless. They were showering and washing, preparing for noon chow. Some of them grinned at Austen and spoke to him. The others shouted and cursed happily at each other.

He found Frenchy and Ski. They were drinking beer from cans in the centre of a chattering, admiring circle of men. Frenchy's nose looked no worse than it had before the fight. He looked up and saw Austen. He winked at him.

'Cheese it, fellers, the cops.'

Kracowski jabbed him. 'Don't talk disrespectful to the division officer.'

'He's my pal. Right, Boss?'

'Right, Frenchy. I'm everybody's pal.'

'You're okay. Have a slug of beer.'

Austen drank some of Frenchy's beer. It was warm and bitter.

He had not seen a can of beer since they had left Dutch Harbour months ago.

'How'd you like that scrap, Mr. Austen?'

'Fine.' He handed the can back to Frenchy.

'You're a damned good referee.'

'Thanks.'

'I never quit, did I, Mr. Austen?' Ski said.

'No, Ski.'

'I never went chicken, did I?'

'It was a swell fight, Ski. It really was.'

'I never meant all that lip I handed you. No kidding.'

'That's okay, Ski. Everything's fine. It was a swell fight.'

8

THE admiral had a big black cigar for breakfast and sent for Captain Meredith. The captain found him sprawled on a leather couch in his cabin on the flag bridge. He was reading dispatches and scratching his flat, hairy belly. The admiral was a gimlet-eyed stump of a man with a bald, freckled head. His cotton khakis were faded and wrinkled. The captain waited politely at attention, occasionally pulling his starched collar away from his raw neck.

An aide stood near the admiral and read the dispatches over the admiral's shoulder. He was a slight, darkly handsome commander with a freshly scarred chin. A Purple Heart ribbon was pinned to his blouse. He smoked a cigarette. The captain could not resist staring at the bluish-red scars on the aide's slim hands.

He had noticed these scars when the admiral's staff had come aboard and wanted to ask about them. Yet it was difficult to speak easily to these younger line officers who had caught the first full blow of the enemy's attack in the Pacific while Captain Meredith had been comfortably established in Newport. He secretly yearned to have his own set of scars in some not-too-vital portion of his soft white body. He studied his buffed fingernails and waited in mild irritation to be noticed.

The admiral tossed the dispatches on his desk. 'Sign 'em, Sammy.'

The aide grinned. 'Another forgery, Admiral?'

The admiral cackled. 'Right you are. Sammy.'

Meredith felt a slight annoyance. The admiral removed his absurd-looking horn-rimmed glasses. He coughed dryly and tapped the edge of the glasses against his teeth for a moment.

'You've met Sam Griswold, haven't you, Snooky?'

'Yes, Admiral.'

'Well, I've a favour to ask of you. For Sammy here.'

'By all means, sir.'

'He's been needling the hell out of me. He's been on my staff for six months and he keeps needling me for sea duty and frankly, he's no damned good on paper work. I've checked over your roster and it looks to me like your navigator is due for new construction or something. How about a switch? I've a relief for Sam who can fly out from Dutch Harbour and he's a good paper man. Sam here's a qualified navigator, aren't you, Sam?'

'Yes, Admiral.'

'Very modest young man, Snooky. If you'll consider the switch I can have the orders written up while I'm on board and when I leave you in a few days Sam can remain with you.'

'Be delighted to have him, sir.' He smiled blandly at Griswold. 'If it's action you're looking for, I can hardly recommend the *Atlantis*. It's monotonous as hell.'

'I'd like very much to be under your command, Captain.'

'Well.' Meredith looked pleased. 'You're in. Welcome aboard.'

'Maybe it's not going to remain monotonous, Snooky.' The admiral stood up and reached for a cut of plug tobacco. He pulled his black tie away from his scrawny neck and bit off a chew. 'The dispatches are pretty hot. Best dope indicates a heavy force operating somewhere to the west. Consists of two cruisers and six or eight destroyers, plus a force of transports and cargo vessels and their escorts. They're apparently making a hot and heavy effort to land reinforcements. It stacks up to a lot of fire power. Might very well be Hashida himself with that kind of weight.

'No question but they'll try to push men and supplies into Attu and Kiska with all they've got and we're going to have to stop them with all we've got.' He paused and looked sharply at the captain. 'With all *you've* got, Snooky, because chances are I won't be with you.'

'Yes, sir. I mean I wish you were.'

'You'll have to be on the ball, Snooky. If it's Hashida, you'll have your hands full. And I'm afraid we can't help you with any more ships, though Christ knows we could use at least one heavy.'

Commander Griswold started to leave. 'Stick around, Sam. You're in on it, too.' He shifted the tobacco wad and spat into his personal bright brass cuspidor and squinted sidewise at the captain. 'What are you getting for flank speed?' he said suddenly.

'Flank, sir? Thirty-five knots, I'd say.'

'Like hell, Snooky. You're lucky if she'll turn up thirty-two with a tail wind. Hell, when she was launched and running her turbines in croton oil she barely squeezed out thirty-five and that was twenty years ago.'

'Well, Admiral——' the captain hesitated.

'When did she make her last speed runs?'

'Not since that quick overhaul at Valley Joe. That was before I relieved McClaffey, sir. He's been transferred to carriers.'

'You should know the performance of the ship under your command, Captain, shouldn't you?'

'Well, Admiral, let's say thirty, flank.' He turned red.

'In the pig's eye. When the Cramp yard laid her down in 1920 she was rated for three thousand miles at thirty knots. You'd be lucky to get five hundred to-day with glue and baling wire to hold her sides together.'

'The *Marblehead* did all right, sir.'

The admiral grinned. 'Damned right she did. I'm not trying to belittle your ship, Snooky. I just want to be sure she can deliver when the time comes. The ship and you, both.'

'We'll deliver, sir. The ship and the men. And me.'

The admiral regarded him thoughtfully for a moment. He

spat accurately into the brass bowl. 'You sound like a damned sea scout, Snooky. Damned if you don't.' He scratched his belly. 'And damned if I don't believe you.'

'She's a good ship, Admiral, old as she is.'

'Her last major overhaul was when?'

'Two years ago. Maybe a little less. She's had these endless patrols and emergency troop-carrying and God knows what else. It's in the old logs. Panama to Lima to Valparaiso. Out to Borra Borra. Back to Panama. A regular taxi service and no letup. Now this damned patrol to the west. It's been constant steaming, day in day out, for months. There's been no opportunity, really, for a decent overhaul.'

'Original Parsons turbines in her?'

'Yes, sir. They've taken quite a beating since the overhaul. I don't see how the snipes manage to keep them going. Then she's had the prescribed modifications for her class. Top hamper cut down, some new fire-control equipment. We've replaced the one-point-ones with three twin Bofors Forties. We're shy a barrel aft from that casualty last week. There are eight Oerlikon twenties and the old three-inch fifties without modifications. Big guns are the same—ten of those, and the torpedo tubes aft, and the two planes. The planes at least are the new OS2Us.'

'I liked the old SOCs better,' the admiral said. He sighed. 'You've got everything but the kitchen sink, Snooky. How's the crew?'

'Four-oh, Admiral.'

'That's not the way I heard it. You've had a few knifings since you've been up here, isn't that so?'

'Yes, sir.' He coughed dryly. 'Have you seen the men's records?'

'Now how the hell would I see enlisted men's records, Snooky?'

'I'd be happy to show them to you.'

'What's wrong with their records?'

'Out of the last draft of thirty-eight men, thirty-one came from various Navy courts and were assigned to hazardous duty as a means of punishment. Before that the draft was sixteen men— all sent to this ship as a means of punishment. I've been getting the Navy's scum.   Malingerers, petty thieves, homosexuals, and plain, downright troublemakers.   I have the service records to prove it, Admiral.   It's a damned disgrace and I'm helpless to do a thing about it.'

'Snooky, I'm astonished.'

'And the good men who deserve a little Stateside duty have no chance of leaving.   They've been on this damned patrol too long. Their requests for changes of duty are ignored.   No wonder they're stale.   No wonder we have an occasional knifing.'

'Simmer down, lad.   This is the first I've heard of it.   A dispatch goes to BuPers in an hour.   It *is* a disgrace.   What are you doing about it?'

'I figure for every rotten egg I've a good man.   They're maintaining a certain balance.   We're doing all right, considering.'

'Considering what?   A few knifings?'

'That can happen in any crew of men, sir.   Mainly, they're devoted to the ship, every man jack of them.'

'Hell they are.   I respect your loyalty and enthusiasm, but the crew is definitely not at peak performance.   I watched them drag their asses to GQ this morning and I watched them fake the motions of routine drills, and I say to you they are below the required level of performance.'

'They'd go to bat for me, sir.'

'What about your exec?   Would he?'

'I believe he would.'

'He looks awful sour to me.'

'He's had a tough break, sir.   Passed over again.'

'No reason to take it out on the crew.   I've been told he's worse than Hitler.'

'He's quite efficient.   A little exacting, perhaps.'

'Christ, Snooky, you're blind with devotion.   That guy belongs on the beach, not at sea where it's touch and go.'

'I've already discussed his relief with the ship's doctor, sir.'

The admiral scratched his chin.   'Well, keep your fingers crossed.   I've seen sadder lash-ups, but I can't remember where. I'm recommending a major overhaul after this one patrol.   They'll dig up some of the other four-pipers to relieve you.'

'Thank you, Admiral.'

'I sure hate to miss a chance of running into Hashida. Raises miniature orchids and writes poems. Imagine that.' He stood up and stretched, baring a few inches of hairy, flat belly. 'Okay, Snooky.'

The captain saluted and turned to go. Griswold watched him with an odd pitying smile and the admiral noticed it. The door closed.

'What do you make of it, Sam?'

Griswold shrugged. 'Has he ever had it tough?'

The admiral snorted. 'Sure. In every officers' club and whore-house from Newport to Annapolis.' He shook his head. 'I don't know, Sam. I run into the same thing all over the fleet. What the hell do you think it was like at Pearl?'

Griswold slowly extinguished the glowing end of the cigarette in the dead palm of his left hand. 'I'd give him a break,' he said. 'I kind of feel there's something under all that sorry fat.'

'Keep an eye on him, Sam. You asked for it and it may be your own funeral.'

'Not another one, Admiral, please,' Sam said, softly grinning.

Lieutenant Clough lay in his upper bunk as he did every first day at sea, wishing he were dead. Seasickness to Dave Clough was somehow inextricably entangled with a ship's weighing anchor. It would persist in varying degrees of intensity until the anchor, like some mysterious talisman, once more rested on the bottom of the sea.

He shared his narrow quarters with Alec Austen. The compart-ment was in the bow of the ship abaft the warrant officers' head. The room smelled of damp clothes and urine. There were two desks covered with Navy manuals, ship's orders, scattered cigarettes, and Clough's flying equipment. Two blue-grey helmets bumped against the peeling bulkhead. The room was at the ship's water line and the pounding sea did little to ease Clough's malaise.

A handsome sword in a shining black and gold scabbard swung from the bulkhead. It glittered like a cold, hard gem in a rubbish heap. It was Clough's graduation gift from his mother and he had rashly promised to carry it wherever he went.

Austen occupied the lower bunk. It was hopelessly littered with books, art supplies, and his foul-weather gear. There was no other place to stow it. He lay on his back quietly. The aftertaste of warm, flat beer still soured his mouth.

Water sloshed in the warrant officer's head. Clough hiccupped. It was a high-pitched, dismal sort of bark. Austen felt sorry for him.

'How do you feel, Dave?'

'Just fine,' he croaked weakly. 'You got some mail.'

'Mail? Me?'

'Smells very lovely. Not like me. It's in that rat's nest on my desk.'

Austen examined the letter without opening it. Stella, he thought. No one else would write him a letter. He looked at the back-slanted handwriting on the envelope for a long time. He sat down and unbuttoned a newly laundered khaki shirt. The faintly scented envelope excited him. He put the letter aside.

Clough watched his lean hard-muscled movements. Why not me? he thought bitterly. Austen was pinning the metal collar devices in place. I've a dozen shirts, Clough thought. With embroidered silk devices. And I get dozens of letters from the cutest gals in Alameda, Jax, and Boca Chica. Why does this have to happen to me?

'They get Johnny's plane aboard okay?' he asked.

'It took a little time. There was a hell of a sea running.'

'I thought so. I could feel it.' He sat up. 'The morning take-off sounded okay.'

'He dipped once, leaving the catapult. Mighty close.'

'Hell. Johnny's the best.'

'Sure, but maybe the admiral made him a little nervous. He watched like a hawk. He watches everything like a hawk.'

'What's he like?'

'A runty little guy. Struts like a gamecock.'

Clough swung his legs down. 'I got to get out of this sack, Alec. I've had about all I can stand.'

'It's still rough topside.'

'I can't let Johnny fly all my missions. He'll go stale.'

'Wait until you feel right, kid.'

62

'I'm okay.' He licked his dry lips. 'The exec. was around, snooping.'

'Again?'

'Raised hell about the mess in here. Reamed me for still being in the sack.'

'Hell. He knows you're seasick. He should by now.'

'He said if I'm seasick I belong in sick bay. If I'm not in sick bay I should be up and about my duties.'

'He's off his rocker. Sick bay's loaded with seasick guys. It's just an act. He's cheesed off because he's been passed over again.'

'Why does he pick on us?'

'You're the trade-school boy. You tell me why.'

'The trade school has nothing to do with it.'

'It helps.'

'He'll be back to inspect our quarters. We better get it squared away. Help me out of this sack, will you?'

Austen helped him down. Clough stood shakily on the narrow deck between the bunks and the bulkhead. 'I feel great,' he said. He rapped his flat chest. 'I'm getting dressed. My green gabardines. I'm going out on the catapult deck. I'm mustering my airdales and showing them what a great guy they got for a division officer.'

'You'll be wanting your sword, of course?'

'You're a lowborn swabbie, Austen. Jealous of us flying men.' He reached for his clothes bag and pulled out the sharply pressed greens and started to dress. 'Feel terrific,' he said. 'Lick my weight in wildcats.'

'Good boy. Triumph of mind over matter. Can I help you?'

'I'm a big boy now. Shove off.'

'Fine. We'll square away the room and foil the exec. I've got to inspect the guns. Suppose we meet here after chow?'

Clough paled. The green trousers hung in mid-air. 'You shouldn't have said that.'

'Said what?'

Clough winced and held the bedpost for support. The trousers settled around his ankles. 'Chow . . .'

He sat down. His thin face was pinched with pain. He moaned and stretched out on Austen's bunk.

63

'Look, Dave,' Austen said anxiously, 'let me help you to your own sack.'

'No, thanks. I'll be up in a minute.'

'Please, Dave. You'll be more comfortable.'

'Don't touch me.'

'Do you feel like throwing up?'

'Is that an invitation?'

'No, damn it. These are fresh sheets.'

'I'm dying and he worries about the sheets.'

'Come on, kid. I'll help you to the head.'

'Don't come near me.' He lifted his head and stared glassily at Austen. 'My sword, please,' he said. 'It's my dying wish.'

'Die. Go to hell.'

'Tell my mother I died with the sword in my hands.'

'What a dirty trick, Dave. A cheap, sentimental, dirty trick.'

'Your own fault, pal. You said that horrid word.' His eyes widened. 'You had better leave now. I'd rather you didn't see me like this.'

'Do you really want your sword?'

'Please.'

Austen tore it from the bulkhead and tossed it on the bunk. 'You know what you can do with it,' he said angrily, and strode out.

When he returned later Clough slept noisily in the upper bunk. A room steward was changing the bed linen.

'I be done here in a minute, Mr. Austen.'

'Take your time and do a good job. The exec's inspecting the room later.'

'It'll be real sharp, sir.'

'Thanks. How'd Clough ever get up there? He was pretty weak.'

'I set him there, sir, after I made up his bunk.' He smiled. 'No fear of him ever overloading that plane of his. He don't weigh nothing.'

'He hasn't had a square meal since we left Dutch Harbour.' He looked at the man curiously. He was a rangy Negro with big hands that began several inches beyond the end of his white coat sleeves. 'Just reported aboard, have you?'

'Be a month come Monday, sir. I been helping in the officers' galley mostly. Now they put me on to wardroom and room steward.'

'Like it?'

'I like the guns, sir. You going to be firing them guns soon?'

'There's a test-firing drill for the admiral to-morrow. Why?'

'I know them guns like I know my own name, sir.'

'Which guns?'

'Them twenty and forty millimetres. I been trained six weeks on them guns at the AA school outside of Frisco.'

'What's your name?'

'Fowler, sir. Homer Fowler. Six weeks, and then they give me a special mention in my records.'

'For what?'

'For how good I can shoot them guns, sir.' He patted the pillow into place and laid two towels at the foot of the bunk. 'Weren't nobody could shoot them guns good as me, sir,' he said gravely.

'What was your station on the forties?'

'Pointer, sir. I learned local control and manual. They didn't had no director control like is on this ship. Then I was two weeks on the Oerlikon twenties.' His face lighted as he smiled, remembering the guns. 'There's a real gun for a man loves guns.'

'We're shorthanded on our forties, Fowler, after that accident last week. I really need a good man.'

'I'd sure like to be that man, sir.'

'Tell you what, Fowler. Next time you hear the bosun's mate call away AA gunnery drills, you report to me on the forties aft.'

'Yes, sir. I'd be mighty proud to, sir.'

'I'm working up a revised station bill now. I'll check your records. If it shows you can really handle those AA guns, I'll make a place for you in one of the gun crews.'

'Thank you, sir.'

'You know we lost two men this time in.'

'Beside the boy got killed makes three.'

'So there's plenty of room for an experienced hand. We'll see how it goes.'

'You give me the chance, sir. It'll go.' He saluted and picked up his stack of linens and went out.

Austen lay down and opened Stella Greyne's letter. Above him Clough snored peacefully. Beyond the ship's steel skin the sea raced by. Water gurgled noisily in the warrant officers' head.

He read the letter slowly, as though he were listening, as though Stella herself were in the room talking to him.

9

HE had met Stella Greyne before the war at a poster exhibition of the Art Directors Club in New York. He had not noticed her in the chattering crowd, but she had noticed him.

She tapped him with a rolled-up programme. 'Tell me something, will you, please?'

'Be glad to,' he said, startled. He had been raptly admiring the Cassandre entry.

'Where would all these poster artists be without *Gebrauchs grafik*?'

'Lost, I'm sure. I own a complete file myself.'

'Oh. Another artist. You don't look like one.'

'Don't you like artists?'

'I like art. The artist is the necessary evil, I suppose.'

A perspiring waiter sidled by with a tray of drinks balanced over his head. Alec deftly removed two as he passed.

'It must be wonderful to be tall.'

'Has its drawbacks. I never know where to put my knees under a drawing table.' He sniffed the drink. 'Sidecars.'

She sipped her drink. 'Not too bad. Domestic brandy.' She drank all of it and looked for the waiter.

'Let's get out of here,' he said. 'I'll find you some Otard.'

'I can't leave yet.'

'Why not?'

She looked over the sea of bobbing faces. 'I'm here with Godfrey Clemson.'

He drained his glass. Godfrey Clemson. Just like that. He felt somewhat foolish.

'Now, over there,' she was saying as though nothing had happened, 'is a poster I could live with.' She pointed to one that advertised SOOTH, a sun-tan lotion. 'It's simple. The picture tells a story. The sun looks hot. I can almost feel it. And the lotion looks cooling. I feel compelled to run into the nearest drugstore and buy half a dozen jars.' She held his arm. 'Excuse me. I'm a bit woozy from that sidecar.'

'I'm woozy from that fast spiel for SOOTH.'

'Why?'

'That's my poster.'

'It's won a prize.' She stared at him.

'Just an honourable mention,' he said.

She seemed genuinely excited.

'Look at your competition—Bernhard, Carlu, Hurlburt, Bayer, Cassandre—isn't it a lovely Cassandre?'

'Oh yes.'

'So your honourable mention isn't to be sneezed at.'

'I wish you'd come with me,' he said uncomfortably. 'I'd like to get out of here.'

'All right.' She waved at a tentlike man in a midnight-blue suit. He waved back and paddled toward them, greeting friends, shaking hands, posturing, and throwing kisses. He stopped once to listen to a story and his large glistening head shook and he laughed shrilly.

'Must be a very funny story,' Austen said.

'I'm sure he's heard it before. He's like that.' She handed him her empty glass. 'You'd better tell me your name.'

He told her. Clemson arrived exuding steam. His powdered, pink face was caked with sweat. His lidless eyes raked Austen swiftly.

'Can't we go now?' Stella asked. 'It's so stuffy and hot.'

'Not yet, dear. So many of the clients are still here.' He mopped his face with a king-sized handkerchief. 'Run along to 21. I'll meet you there. Fivish. Bob's holding a table for two.' He was still measuring Austen carefully. 'Do I know this young man, Stella?'

Stella, Austen thought. *Cara bella Stella mia,* kid.

She introduced him. When he heard Austen's name Clemson's small eyes gleamed. 'Of course. The SOOTH lotion entry. You

67

know, I voted for your poster, young man, second to the Carlu entry in your division. Other judges couldn't agree. Said they never heard of you. Off the record'—he leaned over and Austen smelled a musky cologne and an underarm deodorant—'power politics, even in art. Shameful, you know.'

'It is,' Austen said.

'No discredit to you, however. Lovely poster.' He turned to Stella. 'Doesn't look a bit like an artist, does he, dear?'

'What should I do?' Austen said in cold anger. 'Walk around in a smock and beret?'

'He's so right, Godfrey.'

'SOOTH's a Kirk & Callahan account, isn't it?' Clemson asked.

'That's right.'

'Staff artist, there, are you?'

'I'm the art director.'

'Really? Big responsibility for a youngster, isn't it?'

'It would be for a youngster. I've got my working papers.'

'Ha ha. Hear that, Stella? Said he's got his working papers. Been there long?'

'Almost a year.'

'Surprised I haven't run into you before. Belong to the Art Directors Club, do you?'

'No.'

'Ad Club, then?'

'I'm afraid not.'

'You should, you know.'

'Why?'

'Well.' Clemson frowned. 'Make the right contacts. Get to know what's going on in the world of art.'

'I know what's going on.'

'You must, to turn out that kind of poster. How about the SOOTH campaign that ran in the *New Yorker* last summer? Your work?'

'Yes, sir.' He smiled. 'Also did the finished art. Couldn't find an artist in town who'd do it for the money we had to spend.'

'Those fresh, bright beach scenes? We wondered whose they were. You didn't sign them.'

'No.'

'Should. Get yourself some free publicity. How did the campaign pull?'

'Pull?'

'Sales. Did it sell the item?'

'I really don't know. The sales department worries about that end of it, I guess.'

Clemson laughed thinly. He had small pointed teeth. 'There's the true artist for you, Stella.' He held Austen's lapel between highly polished finger tips. 'Take a tip from someone who knows advertising art from the ground up. You know, I'm responsible for making a big business out of it, don't you, Austen?'

'Everyone knows that, Mr. Clemson.'

'Of course. Want to be a big money man in the field?'

'Oh yes. I want to make a lot of money. Fast.'

'Of course you do. Everyone does. And a top-money art director knows the selling power of his layouts. His art is without value unless it makes a buck for his client. Makes sense, doesn't it?'

'I guess so.'

'Of course it does. Makes vice-presidents out of bull pen artists. Don't want to spend your life in the bull pen, do you?'

'No, sir. I want to make a lot of money. Fast.'

'You can, Austen.' He looked at him shrewdly. 'How'd you get to Kirk & Cal?'

'From Ayres in Philadelphia. That's my home town.'

'Well, you've heard of Clemson Associates. Of course you have. Blind or a fool if you haven't. Like to talk to you. I can always use a talented and clever man in my organization.'

'Fine. When?'

'Call my secretary for an appointment. Don't go through channels for heaven's sake. Tell her I said for you to call.'

'Should I bring along my portfolio of samples?'

'Of course,' Clemson snapped coldly. 'Think I'd buy a pig in a poke?' His eyes glinted and he bared his teeth. 'Fivish, Stella. Got to run. There's LeFevre from BBD&O. Ta.' He barged off streaming water.

'Let's go,' Austen said to Stella in a tight voice.

She took his arm and they went out into the warm sun.

'He likes you,' she said in a pleased voice. 'I'm sure you'll get a job.'

'I have a perfectly fine job.'

'Not like Clemson Associates. They pay their artists a king's ransom.'

'How do you know?'

'Godfrey tells me everything.' She looked up at him. 'You'd take a job, wouldn't you, if he offers you one?'

'I don't know.'

'It'd mean a lot more money, wouldn't it?'

'I wonder if it's worth it.'

'You're not serious, are you?'

'Of course not. What's your name?'

'How silly. Greyne. Stella Greyne. Please take the job if Godfrey offers it to you.'

'Why?'

'It's kind of nice having you around.'

'I'm glad it's Greyne.'

'Are you?'

'I'm glad it's not Clemson.'

'There *is* a Mrs. Clemson. Godfrey and I are just very good friends.'

'I'm sure you are.'

'He's one of the finest persons I've ever met. And very famous as an art critic.'

'You don't have to tell me about Godfrey Clemson,' he said. The name was beginning to irritate him. They did not speak until they stood in front of the iron gates at 21.

'Here you are,' he said.

'Aren't you coming in?'

'I don't think so.'

'It's very cool inside and Emil mixes a fine sidecar.'

'I'm sure he does. But your friend Clemson made it clear I was not invited.'

'Nonsense. Come in with me.'

'I'd be intruding.'

70

'Please?'

'Sorry. Let's make it another time.'

'I like you. I like you right now and I want to have a drink with you.'

'I'd like you to have a drink with me, Stella.'

'Then the hell with Godfrey. Let's go someplace else.'

He took her arm. 'That's more like it,' he said.

They found a cool dark French place and drank sidecars with Otard. Stella chattered with child brightness about everyone in New York. Austen listened amiably enough. He had few friends and her voice had a pleasing lilt and he was getting a little drunk.

The cocktail crowd began to arrive. Stella looked at her watch once, quickly. Austen stood up.

'Time to go,' he said.

'I'm sorry. Please don't.'

'Fivish,' he said, watching her. She coloured slightly.

'Be nice,' she said. 'Come back to 21 and have dinner with us.'

'And let him see me stinko? I'd never get the job.'

They went out and walked back towards 21.

'Call me some evening,' she said.

'I paint evenings.'

'So do I. At the Art Students League, four nights a week.'

'I've my own little studio. How do you like the League?'

'I've just started it. It was Godfrey's idea. I'm in Vytlacil's life class. Mondays through Thursdays.'

'He's very good.'

'That's what Godfrey says. Why don't you come?'

'Maybe I will. How are the models?'

'Naked. I'm still a little embarrassed.'

'I'll come down Monday.'

'I'll look for you.'

'Good-bye, Stella.'

'Good-bye, Alec Austen.' She watched his tall striding figure until he was out of sight.

The studio was a big draughty room crowded with artists, easels, and paintings. The class worked in oils from the undraped model.

During the model's rest period Austen joined Stella at her easel. She stood with a brush and a cigarette in her hand and wiped a streak of colour across her damp forehead.

He studied the painting cautiously.

'Don't just stand there,' she said. 'Say something.'

'It's quite interesting.'

'Is that all you can say about it?'

'Do you really want a criticism?'

'Of course I do, silly.'

He proceeded to take the painting apart. She did not look at him.

'Is that all?' she said when he had finished.

'That's about it. Oil's a tough medium for a beginner, in spite of what the salesman tells you in the art supply store. It has a way of getting muddier and muddier.'

She was looking at the canvas fixedly. 'Go on,' she said.

She's sore as hell, he thought, but he did not feel sorry for her. 'If you insist on painting in oils, try a limited palette. Maybe just one colour—a monochrome—to start.'

'But I see all those colours. That's why they're there. I paint what I see.'

'All right. You and Rivera. But the knowledge of flesh form and bone structure is important even if you intend to ignore it in the actual painting.' Tears were welling in her eyes. 'How many brushes do you use?'

'This one.' She held up the muddy-looking brush.

'You've got a boxful of very expensive ones. Use them.'

'It's easier just to hold this one and keep wiping it off.'

'Then you'll have to be content with a muddy painting.' She was quietly crying. 'Look,' he said angrily, 'I'm no critic.'

'Then why don't you just shut up?' She wiped her eyes with the sleeve of her smock. 'Oh, go on. Beat it. The model's posing.'

He went back to his painting. He stayed there until the session was over. He cleaned his brushes and palette and put the paintbox and canvas into his locker. He went downstairs.

She was waiting for him outside. They walked to Central Park

72

South. She took him to Rumpelmayers and ordered their ice cream and paid the bill. Later they walked along the park's edge where the ducks slept.

'Sorry I cried,' she said.

'I'm sorry I was so rude.'

She was looking down, trying to match her steps with his. 'No one's ever talked to me like that. I suppose I deserved it.'

'Nonsense.' He was vaguely troubled, wondering how he had ever gotten into this. 'Oils are very difficult to use.'

'Why not just tell me I stink?'

'I don't mean that at all.'

'Yes, you do. You're not like these other artists who keep telling me how wonderfully I'm getting on, hoping it'll mean a roll in the hay. I'm not blind, you know.'

'I don't know what you mean.'

'Just say I stink and I don't know a damned thing about art or oils or anything. I won't mind. It won't make any difference about going to bed with me. You can do that any time. You knew that, didn't you?'

'No. I guess I didn't know it.'

'Well you can. You know it now.'

They walked past the top-hatted cabbies, and a sleepy old gentleman atop one of the hansoms nodded at them. Stella shook her head.

'You know it now,' she repeated harshly.

'I was thinking about something else,' he said gently.

'Thanks,' she said. '*My God.*'

'I was trying to figure out why you paint. You get no pleasure out of it.'

'Darling, dumb Alec.'

'Why do you?'

'Godfrey. He insists I have talent. He says I'm a natural primitive.'

'He'd be the one to know.'

'What do you mean by that?' she said sharply.

'He's the town's foremost art critic, isn't he?'

'Honestly, Alec.'

73

'Isn't that so?'

'You're too good to be true.'

He stopped to light his pipe. She watched the warm undulating flare of the match in his steady fingers. They walked into the shadowy park under the soft yellow lights and looked at the caged animals.

'Godfrey's been very kind to me,' Stella said.

'Look how the lions sleep. Curled up like kittens.'

'He's taught me a lot.'

'The temptation to stroke their fur is very strong.'

'You're not listening to me.'

'I've just started at Clemson Associates. Do I have to hear about Godfrey Clemson twenty-four hours a day?'

'Sorry. How do you like the job?'

'The salary's fine. You were right.'

'You'll do very well, I'm sure.'

'How do you know?'

'I can tell,' she said. 'I know.' She took his arm and bent him over and kissed him. 'That's for the new job,' she said.

'The employee benefits amaze me,' Alec said.

He took her home. She lived in an apartment building on Park Avenue. She sat on the edge of a marble scroll table in the small rococo foyer and searched through her handbag for the door key.

Her head was bent and he kissed her hair and she trembled. He remembered what she had told him and he put his arm around her.

'What are you thinking about?' she asked.

'You know what I'm thinking about.'

'Darling.' She brushed her lips along the knuckles of his fingers. 'You'd better go,' she whispered.

His fingers tightened. 'I'm going in with you.'

'We can't. Not to-night.'

'You said "any time".'

'Yes, darling. I meant it. What about your studio?'

'It's in the Village.'

'Wait here. I'll get the car.'

She went out. He lit a cigarette and waited.

It's dead, he thought. Quit while it's still clean, before it's foul-smelling and dirtied. Women, he thought. Some day I'll find an uncomplicated woman. She will love me. I will love her. Life will be sweet. Hell, he thought. Life will never be sweet. There is no such animal as an uncomplicated woman.

The car drew up to the curb and she leaned over and called to him. He got in. She drove down town, being very careful about the way she drove. His studio was a walk-up on West Tenth Street.

'It's a very handsome car,' he said, getting out.

'It's Godfrey's.'

They went into his building. His studio was on the top floor. It had a fine north exposure. Stella stood inside the entry while Austen turned on some lights. The walls were hung with many unframed canvases.

'Sit down,' Austen said. 'I'll make some drinks.'

'Lord,' Stella said, rooted.

'What's the matter?'

'Are all these paintings yours?'

He frowned. 'Of course.'

'Lord.' She walked into the room slowly. Her bag slipped from her fingers. She moved from painting to painting. Austen sat down and lit a cigarette. He looked flushed and angry.

She seemed completely to have forgotten him. He went into the kitchen and shook loose a tray of ice cubes and mixed two highballs. He carried them into the big room.

Stella was sitting now. He gave her one of the drinks. She watched his face. He realized that she had never looked at him before. Not like that. Her eyes were wet.

'Where did you find those Negro kids to paint?'

'Just knocking around.'

'Just knocking around.'

'Sure. I was in Harlem one Sunday. I saw them and made a few quick sketches. Then I worked them into the canvas.'

'What about the clowns?'

'At the circus. Madison Square Garden.'

'I have never seen such clowns.' She sipped her drink. Her eyes never left him. 'The whores?'

He shrugged. 'Around. I get around by myself a good bit.' He grinned suddenly. 'It's a hell of a town.'

'Alec,' she said.

'Here.'

'Please, darling. I'm very serious. Has anyone seen these canvases?'

'Mrs. Titus.'

'Who's she?'

'My landlady. She also cleans. She's very strict about lady callers.'

'Alec, don't be a bastard, please. Have you exhibited any of these? Any gallery people seen them?'

'No.'

'Why not?'

'I'm not ready to show. None of these are really finished.'

She shook her head unbelievingly. 'Alec,' she said softly. 'Darling. I know what you mean. I understand your contempt for Godfrey.' She put her drink aside. 'Sit by me, Alec.'

He sat next to her.

'I want you to listen very carefully, darling. When I walked in here I didn't believe these paintings. I couldn't believe them. No one will. They're incredible. They made me cry. Did you know I was crying?'

'No,' he lied.

'You're doing a very dangerous thing with your paintings.'

'Why?'

'You're painting souls. Those kids, the clowns, those two ridiculous whores . . . Alec . . .'

She turned and embraced him.

'Do they really make you sad, Stella?'

'Oh yes.'

'Maybe they're finished, then.'

They sat quietly, holding each other.

'I'd never have dreamed it,' she said. She held him away and searched his face.

'You're very good for me, Stella,' he said.

She drew him close. 'There are two things to do, darling,' she said softly, 'and the other one is to paint me.'

He kissed her. Her lips were soft and moist. He would remember that when he started the painting, he thought.

They sat together spent and happy in the dark studio. The paintings gleamed in the faint reflection of the street lights. Their cigarettes glowed in the darkness. Around them the breathing city slept, but sleep was not for these two.

She makes a man of me and a child of me, he thought.

I love him, she thought, and I know now I have never loved before.

They talked softly.

'Strange paintings, darling. Disturbing. Very disturbing.'

'That is good,' he said gravely.

'What will you do with them?'

'Nothing.'

'Would you like Godfrey to see them?'

'No.'

'He'd sell them for you. His clients buy anything he recommends.'

'I was afraid of that.'

She turned on a small light. It illuminated the painting of the two prostitutes. Their pale powdered faces leered at her, carmine-lipped and friendly.

Stella trembled. 'Maybe they should never be sold,' she said.

Alec kissed her. 'It's only important that they be painted,' he said.

'I'm so proud of you, darling.' She snuggled close to him. 'Paint,' she said. 'The hell with everybody. Paint.'

'Good,' he said. 'Wonderful.'

'It's what you're for, darling. Do it.' She sat up. 'You once told Godfrey you needed a lot of money. It's for this, isn't it?'

He nodded.

'Then what?'

'Then good-bye job. Good-bye Clemson.' He stopped.

'Good-bye Stella?'

'I didn't say that.'

'Where will you go?'

77

'To the country someplace. Maine, perhaps. And paint.'

'Just paint?'

'Till the money runs out.'

'Then back on your knees to Clemson Associates.'

'It's worth it. I'd have a roomful of paintings.'

'They'd take you back, of course. I know they would.'

'How do you know?'

'Godfrey thinks you're the best they've ever had. He showed me the water colours you did for the Airlux campaign.'

'They were just layout sketches.' He frowned. 'Do you see a lot of Clemson?'

'We're just good friends.' She sat up. 'I'm beginning to feel sad. It's those damned whores staring at me.'

'Want me to drive home with you?'

'I'm a big girl. Will I see you again?'

'Of course. What about Saturday night?'

'Not the week-ends, Alec. How about Thursday?'

'There's a Basque place near here. They make a terrific *paella valenciana*. And they sell Mexican beer.'

'Will you take me?'

'It's a date. Thursday night. We'll go to Coney Island afterwards.'

'What did you say they serve at the Basque place?'

'*Paella valenciana*.'

She wrote it down. It amused him. He said so.

'I always write down exotic and unusual things,' she said.

'Why?'

'To memorize them. Then I impress Godfrey with my cleverness.'

'You're an odd one,' he said softly.

'He's so damned superior, you see.'

'So you write things down.'

'Yes,' she said in a small voice.

He laughed and kissed her tenderly. He stood in the doorway until her car vanished into Fifth Avenue. The night had turned cold and to the east the sky showed the first faint daubs of dawn.

He went upstairs and set a coffee-pot on the stove. He fitted a fresh canvas into his studio easel and with sure strokes began his painting of Stella.

A light onshore breeze sent scraps of paper kiting along the Coney Island boardwalk. Their shoes made pleasing hollow echoes. The place was deserted. Most of the amusements and vendors' stalls were boarded up.

'It was a fine *paella*, Alec.'

'You were very brave. You did not wince when I told you about the octopus in it.'

'I had already eaten it, you fool.'

'You were very brave. Did you like the Carta Blanca?'

'I am in love with the Carta Blanca. I have never tasted such a beer. I am in love with Basques. Also Mexicans.'

'Are you in love with me?'

'Oh, truly.'

They walked to the Sea Gate end and stopped at the railing facing the sea and watched the dull gleam of the wild surf.

'This would paint nicely,' he said.

'It's too wild.'

'Like Ryder.'

'It's too damned gloomy, Alec.'

'I know. It would never sell.'

'Paint bright things, happy things. It's what people want.'

'I do, sometimes. Right now the war bothers me.'

'You don't think we'll get into it, do you?'

'Don't see how we can stay out of it.'

'What about you?'

'I've a draft number like anyone else.'

'You'd paint anyway, wouldn't you? If you went to war?'

'I'll always paint.'

'You're so sure of yourself.'

'It's all I've ever wanted to do since I was a kid.'

'What made you so sure then?'

'Somebody gave me a paintbox for Christmas.' He grinned. 'I'm lucky, I guess. Some guys chase rainbows all their lives trying to settle on a career.'

'You *are* lucky.'

'And nothing can change me. I can be interrupted—any guy can—by a woman or a job or a war or my belly yelling for food. It's all temporary. Nothing else can touch me.'

'Love, Alec. Love could.'

'Not even love, baby.'

'No one should be that strong.'

'Maybe not. But that's the way it is. A guy like me knows what he has to do and obstacles are temporary and I climb over them or walk around them or live with them until they die.' He crumpled an empty cigarette package and tossed it to the beach below them. 'Write it down,' he said. 'It's exotic and unusual. A very pretty speech.'

'Don't be nasty now.'

'Clemson's arty clique would love it. You can be the life of the party.'

'I like to hear you talk. Don't spoil it.'

'I've talked too damned much. Come on. I'll buy you a hot dog.'

He took her to Nathan's. It was a garishly lighted outdoor stand off Surf Avenue. The countermen rattled the long tongs on the smoking grills, hawking their wares.

Stella and Austen stood in the littered alley and ate hot dogs and fresh ears of corn that steamed in the cold autumn air. They drank foaming root beer from huge glass mugs.

Stella marvelled. 'People can live in New York all their lives and never know about a place like this.'

'Eat your hot dog,' Austen said, 'and stop worrying about people.'

Stella was thoughtful on the train to Manhattan. The West End express rumbled and clacked past the dark fields and tenements of Bensonhurst and Borough Park. It dipped, grinding and screeching around the bend into the tunnel at Ninth Avenue station.

A girl in a man's tattered sweater entered their car. She carried a pile of newspapers under her skinny arm. Her ten-year-old face was freckled and cold.

'*Daily News* and *Mirror!* Morning paper, sir?'

Stella reached out and took one of the papers and handed the child a crumpled bill. She reached for change in a cloth sack that hung round her throat.

'Beat it,' Stella said.

'Your change, lady.'

'Keep it, darling.'

The child just made it through the closing doors. She stood at the edge of the platform and stared through the window at Stella until the train moved out of the station.

'I used to be a kid like that,' Stella said, putting aside the paper. She blew her nose. 'You and your damned boardwalks. I'm getting pneumonia.' She snuggled close to him. 'Nobody handed me paintboxes for Christmas. I had five sisters and three brothers. If you didn't grab, kick, and steal, you didn't eat.' She picked up the paper and stared at the cover pictures. 'What the hell,' she said. 'A million years ago.'

'Where was this?'

'A small town. A burg. It had a rich girl's college. I used to turn green with envy seeing them. The clothes they wore. I wanted a real raccoon coat instead of four hand-me-down sweaters and my sister's flannel drawers. And I wanted a field-hockey stick. Christ.' She laughed and wiped her eyes. 'A lousy field-hockey stick. I stole one when they weren't looking. Imagine. Stealing a field-hockey stick.'

'What did your father do for a living?'

'Not a hell of a lot. He had a sad little farm for a while. I guess he was the lousiest farmer in Montgomery County. He was no damned good at anything except drinking. We were always in trouble, always owing money for something. Everybody hated our guts and being Polish didn't help.'

She stared out of the window. Tunnel lights flashed by.

'Go on,' he said softly.

'You sure you don't mind? It was seeing that damned kid peddling her papers. The little snotnose.' She took a deep breath. 'My old man was always running off and leaving us. I remember once we sat around Reading Terminal. My mother and the nine kids. The old man was supposed to be looking for a job. He'd been gone three days and we were put off the farm. My mother

81

borrowed three bucks and took us into Philly, and we sat in the Reading Terminal eating day-old cakes while my old man looked for work and my mother looked for my old man. We kids thought it was a picnic being in Philly eating cakes. Some picnic.'

'How old were you?'

'About fourteen. I swore I'd get out. I quit school and lied about my age and got a job in a five and dime. I worked the Poconos summers as a waitress. Then I came to New York.

'I heard from the family once. They wanted money to buy another farm. I sent almost all I had saved—about two hundred dollars. I was a waitress, making fair tips, and a few dollars evenings, modelling for a photographer. I never heard from them again. The hell with them.'

The train rocketed through the tunnel. Austen leaned over and kissed her cheek. It was cold and dry. 'I'm glad you gave the kid the buck.'

'Know what I'd like to do some day? I'd like to go to Reading Terminal with pounds and pounds of the richest fattest salted cashew nuts and pass them out to all the dirty-faced kids I see. Let 'em stuff themselves for once in their lives.' She leaned her head on his shoulder. 'I don't know,' she said. 'I don't know if I ever want to look at it again.'

They changed trains at Times Square and took the local to Fifth Avenue. When they came out it was drizzling and the tyres on the nightbird taxis made soft music. They passed a late supper party breaking up in front of the Pierre. The men in tails strutted like old roosters and the women were as shrill and plumed as peacocks.

'There's a painting,' Alec said grimly.

'The model fee is in the upper brackets, darling.' But Stella turned and watched wistfully as the chauffeured town cars drove off. 'Know what?' she said. 'I'd like a nightcap.'

They found a bar in the East Sixties. She drank double scotches. She drank them too quickly. They left the bar. Austen helped her because she could not walk very well. He propped her on the stone fence of an old mansion with formidable Norman turrets. She looked at him owlishly, trying to smile.

'You drank them too quickly,' he said.

'Was what I wannad a do.' Her head lolled. She gripped his coat tightly.

'Why?'

'Many reasons why. Reading Terminal. Snotnose kid. Y're inna draft.' She shook him gently. 'And I'm sick of y'r swee' noble face, see?'

'Come on, Stella. I'll help you home.'

'Whose home?'

'Yours.'

'Don' have a home. Don' have a goddamn thing.' She stopped suddenly. 'I'll go home alone.'

'You'll never make it.'

'Take somebody else home. Lea' me alone.'

'I don't know anyone else, Stella.'

'Millions o' lonely gals, Alec. New York's full of 'em. Typists, shopgals, all kinds, from Dayton, Philly, Tulsa——'

'I'm taking *you* home, Stella.'

'Poor lonesome babes in neat empty apartments, lonely as hell, standin' naked in front of the full-length mirror staring at their unkissed bodies. They'd give anything——'

He covered her mouth. A fat woman with skewers in her hair dragged a sullen-looking poodle past them. She stared at Stella.

'Beat it, you old bag,' Stella snarled through Austen's fingers.

'Take it easy,' Austen said. He lifted her from the stone fence. He put his arm around her and they started walking.

'Where we going?' she asked.

'Home.'

'That dirty word again.' She pushed his arm away. 'I can walk,' she said. She did very well. 'Just one thing.'

'What's that?'

'You asked for it,' she said softly. She did not look at him again.

Stella lay on a Lawson sofa in her apartment. Her eyes were closed. Alec sat across the room in a fireside chair and smoked a cigarette.

'You shouldn't drink if that's what it does to you,' he said.

'What it does to me.   As if you could know.'

'Why do you do it?'

'Isn't that what they always ask whores?'

'I wouldn't know.'   Angry marks splotched his cheeks.

'Go home, Alec.   Get out before you're sorry.'

'Maybe I'm already sorry.'

'Please, Alec.'   She spoke so quietly he barely heard her.   'Go away and don't come back.'

'I'm running.'

She gestured weakly.   'Then sit here close to me.   Hold me if you want to.'   He came over and sat alongside her.   'Darling,' she said.

Darling, he thought.   Broadway for hello and good-bye.

He held her, kissing her hair.   'It's no use,' she said tensely. 'I'm cold and frightened and it's no use.   I'm thirsty.   Please go now.'

'I like it here.'

'I'm thirsty, Alec.'

'I'll get you a drink.'

He went to the bright, tiled bathroom and turned the tap and rinsed the chalky tumbler.   Nylons were draped over the shower-curtain bar.   A shaving mug ornately inscribed with a gilt 'Father' sat on the glass shelf.

He let the water run until it frosted the glass.   It ran a long time.   When he brought the glass of water to Stella she held it away so it would not drip on her dress.   She looked at him curiously.

'Who were you talking to in there?'

'To myself.   People who don't talk to themselves aren't normal.' He watched her and their eyes met briefly.   He nodded towards the bathroom.   'Whose is it, Stella?'

'Whose is what?'

'The "Father" in the bathroom.'

She looked away.   'I hoped you wouldn't see it.'

'It's Clemson's, isn't it?'   He pictured the bloated form in a silk undershirt, braces hanging, jabbing a Kent pure-bristled badger brush into the smooth round mug, jutting his pale morning jowls snowy with lather toward the mirror in that bright tiled bath. 'Isn't it?'

'Everything's Clemson's. The rugs, the furniture, the walls. Me. The mug, too. Now will you go home?'

'Why didn't you tell me?' he said mildly, surprised at his mildness.

'I thought you knew. Everybody knows about Godfrey and me.' She stood up quickly. 'Excuse me,' she said. She went into the bathroom. He heard the lock turn in the door. He heard a crash of china.

He walked to the tall windows and looked outside. He could hear them but he could not see the cars in Park Avenue ten stories below as they raced the brief spells between a green and red light.

A gay Chagall hung on the wall between the windows. He admired it until he remembered it belonged to Clemson.

Cuckold, he thought. Not me. Clemson. Because here I am where he pays the rent. Then why do I feel cuckolded, he thought angrily. He hated the way he felt inside until he looked at the Chagall. Then he smiled because the cow danced and the groom was upside down and the eyes of the peasant bride were blue with invitation.

Stella came to him later, looking pale and her dark eyes red with weeping. They sat quietly on the sofa. It was late and he felt dreamy and lost. Once she started to explain something.

'I smashed it,' she said.

He gently stopped her with his finger tips. A near-by train clattered to its early morning rendezvous and somewhere a milkman's basket clinked Good morning.

She fell asleep in his arms. He went to the closet in the bedroom and pawed among the dresses and suits until he found an afghan. He covered her and kissed her closed lids. She seemed small and lovely under the gay afghan. He went to the windows and looked at the Chagall once more and decided it did not matter who owned it. It was a fine little painting and it gave him a warm sense of delight.

He left before dawn. He knew it was the last time and he would not see her again.

Godfrey Clemson's secretary stuck her lovely head into Austen's small office. 'The boss would like to see you, Alec.'

He followed her trim shape down the long corridor whose walls were covered with the slick art that had made Clemson Associates a nationally known art agency. Austen still carried the stick of NuPastel with which he had been working. His eyes watched the movement of the girl's flanks ahead of him.

Soon there'll be no more of it, he thought sadly. The whole vast city of well-dressed, fresh-eyed, come-to-the-city-from-the-country-gals with their soft confident thighs and showy bosoms. The secretary held the door open and Austen went into Clemson's office.

'Sit down, Austen, sit down.' Clemson wore a pink shirt through which the perspiration seeped like bloodstains. His nails were freshly veneered and glinted in the light of the egg-crate fluorescents over his desk. Austen noticed the framed picture of a rather pleasant-looking woman who sat stiffly between two long-haired girls. He had wondered what Mrs. Clemson was like. Now he knew and he felt sorry for her.

'Sorry to hear you're leaving us,' Clemson said. He wiped his face with a square yard of monogrammed Egyptian cotton.

'This is my last day.'

'Drafted, were you?'

'No. I decided not to wait.'

'Sure envy you youngsters. My generation missed both wars. Too young for the first, too old for this one.'

'Yeah. We get all the breaks.'

'Sure do.' He eyed Austen sharply and his laugh had a hollow sound. 'Going to miss you, Austen. You were just getting into the swing of this organization.' He studied Austen obliquely, avoiding his eyes. 'If you wanted to stay on,' he continued carefully, 'it could be arranged.'

'I don't see how.'

'Oh, a little pressure here and there in the right places. Could tie you into the visual-aids programme. Government stuff, you know.'

'I don't think so, thank you.'

'I'm one of the civilian advisers. Chairman of the Art Aspect Committee, you know. You'd be out of the trenches, Austen, and the job's nothing to be ashamed of.'

'I'm in the Navy and I may as well go through with it.'

'Of course, of course.' He mopped his face again. 'I'd do the same thing if I were in your shoes.'

'Of course you would.'

'Well, we hate to lose you, as I said. Now when you pick up your pay envelope this afternoon you'll see we've added a little something.' He giggled. 'For those Paris cuties.'

'Thank you.' And where does he think I'm going? Austen thought angrily. On the Grand Tour?

Clemson was standing. 'Here's a little reminder from my associates and myself.' He handed Austen a small velvet box. Alec opened it.

'That's very generous of you,' he said, surprised.

'Stainless steel.' Clemson beamed. 'Self-winding, automatic, waterproof, shockproof, dustproof construction with luminous dials and sweep second hand.'

'Thank you very much.'

'Nothing too good for the boys. There's even a blank space for your name and service number.'

So they can identify the body, Austen thought. 'It's a very handsome watch,' he said.

Clemson extended his hand. 'Best of luck, Austen. The very best.'

Austen held the limp moist hand for a moment and then went out. In the corridor Clemson's secretary caught up with him.

'Mr. Clemson says he forgot to tell you something, Alec.' She smiled at him. 'I hope it's that you're staying,' she said.

'I hardly think so.'

Clemson had his black Homburg on his head and pale yellow gloves lay on the desk blotter near him. He was nervously working the filter of his cigarette holder.

'Close the door, please.' Austen closed the door. 'It occurred to me as you went out that I will not see you again. That is, not for some time.' He smiled a little and his pale jowls shimmied.

Austen waited.

'Those water colours for Airlux. I've been checking over the presentation. I'd like you to sign them.'

'Why?'

'First of all, they're very good water colours. Wet and splashy

87

and plenty of zing. Secondly, your signature puts a higher value on them.'

'You mean price, don't you?'

'All right. Price.' He reddened slightly. 'Just sign them.'

'I'm afraid I can't do that.'

'Why not?'

'Those water colours were meant for layout use only and not as finished art.'

'It can hardly make that much difference to you, Austen.'

'It does. I'd rather not sign my name to any paintings I'm not completely happy about.'

'How do you know I'm using them as finished art?'

'Stella told me.'

'Just to keep the record straight, Austen, I'm running this office, not Miss Greyne.' He stood up angrily. 'Damn it, I highly disapprove of this business going on behind my back.'

'What business?'

'You and Miss Greyne.'

'We're just good friends.'

Clemson slid slowly into his seat and fumbled with the cigarette holder again. 'I suppose,' he said cautiously, 'I'm a jealous man. I know that Miss Greyne——Damn it—Stella— is infatuated with you. Temporary, no doubt. A crush, nothing more. But I don't like it. I'm a possessive man, Austen, and I have a strong instinct to protect what belongs to me.'

'Stella doesn't belong to you.'

'I created Stella Greyne, Austen. The Stella you know never existed before I took an interest in her.'

'Are you serious?'

'Even her name. She had a preposterous name a mile long that was impossible to pronounce. I changed all that. I made Stella Greyne—from nothing.'

He was breathing heavily and as he lit a cigarette Austen noted the dark band of sweat under the Homburg. He felt the soft velvet box in his own taut fingers and, looking down, was surprised to see he still held the bright blue stick of NuPastel.

'I have lived by a code, Austen, surprising as that may seem to 'you. Nothing else matters. To me there is only one secret—life. There is only one future—death. And there is only one ecstasy— art. And in my own terms art and love are the same thing.' His eyes glittered. 'Stella is art I have created. I have destroyed art on occasion, when it no longer pleased me. I would destroy Stella if I thought it necessary.'

'You mean you would kill her?'

'Don't be stupid. There are more interesting ways.'

Austen looked down. The stick of NuPastel had crumbled and its bright blue fragments were imbedded in the green velvet.

'Why tell me this?' he said.

'Why?' Clemson's fingers gripped the edge of the desk. 'Because you and Stella are in love and the image of a hero in uniform is more competition than I care to face. I've indulged that girl enough. I know you've been meeting each other and heaven knows doing what else to each other. I'm putting an end to it. Right now.'

'Because Stella is art and not a breathing, living human being?'

'Because she's what I've made her.'

'I feel sorry for you.'

'For me?' Clemson looked surprised. 'Why?'

'You're all screwed up about art, for one thing.'

'I've made a fair living at it.'

'And you're a bit of a phony and it's about time somebody told you.'

Clemson shrugged and began to pull on his yellow gloves. 'Is there anything else you have to say?'

'Yes.'

'Go right ahead,' Clemson said coldly.

'Here's your goddamned watch.' Austen tossed the velvet case on the desk. It sent bright blue particles of pastel skimming on the smooth surface.

'You don't have to be so nasty about it,' Clemson said. He looked pale and frightened.

'Sure I do. Do you think I'd ever be able to look at that watch without seeing your fat, dedicated face? It would be one hell of a way to fight a war.'

'I assure you the gift wasn't my idea,' Clemson said stiffly.

'I don't give a damn whose idea it was.'

Clemson's phone rang suddenly. It was an alien sound.

'Okay,' Austen said. 'I'm going. In case it's Stella, give her my love.'

He went back to his office and packed his art things. He picked up his pay envelope and left the place quietly.

It's as good a way as any, he thought, to quit the kind of painting I never believed in.

10

HE said good-bye to Mrs. Titus and returned to Philadelphia. His father's house stood in its narrow garden blotted from view by a new apartment house he did not remember. As always the house reminded Austen of some fixed stone monster, its leaded windows imbedded like deep-set slitted eyes. Beyond the formidable row of clipped hedge the dusty stream of traffic outbound from downtown Philadelphia raced to the suburbs.

It was cool and dark in the house. The panelled library still smelled faintly of furniture polish and old books. He walked from room to room remembering his childhood.

He joined his mother in the big kitchen. He peered under the lids of the steaming iron pots. His mother watched him from the table where she sat tearing lettuce leaves for salad. Austen kissed her and she looked at him, admiring and proud and yet unsmiling.

She is thinking there has never been a uniform inside these walls, Alec knew. He sat at the table and chewed a piece of lettuce.

'I see the *sauerbraten*,' he said, 'but where are the dumplings?'

'There will be dumplings.'

'There had better be.'

He helped her with the salad. Later they walked to the front sitting-room. His arm was easily round her waist. They sat and he told her about his painting and about New York. She searched his face as he talked, searching for the boy she had somehow lost, not knowing when or how or why she had lost him.

'Your father should be coming home soon,' she said.

'Still the early riser, the hard worker?'

'Still your father, Alec, bless him. Every day except the Sabbath he's up and about his work.'

He remembered his father and the Sabbath. The shades would be drawn on the windows of his downtown store. It was a day of meditation and rest. He studied his mother's smooth delicately boned face. Patience, they had named her. They knew, even then.

Leave it to the Quakers, he thought. His eyes sought the massive dark-framed reproduction of Hicks's 'Peaceable Kingdom'. The animals stared solemnly back at him. He shuddered slightly.

'I hear him coming up the walk now,' his mother said suddenly. 'Meet him, dear, and I'll bring in the tea things.'

He met his father on the porch steps and kissed him. Later the three of them sat quietly drinking tea and talking very little. His father was a grave, somewhat inarticulate man with brown, close-cropped hair and thoughtful eyes. He asked Alec what the single gold stripe on his blue sleeve signified. Alec told him. His father nodded.

'Knew an ensign once, a schoolmate from Friends.' He smiled apologetically. 'In the First World War. Came to no good, I understand. They made him an admiral.'

'Not a harsh fate in these times, Father,' Alec said.

'His name was Cadwalader. Perhaps you'll meet him somewhere.'

'Hardly. I'll be on the look-out, though.'

'The Cadwaladers still attend Sunday meeting in full force,' his mother said.

Alec watched the blob of cars race from the timed traffic light. 'I would like very much to go to Sunday meeting,' he said.

'We are going to-morrow morning,' his father said in a surprised voice.

Alec could not see the shadow of pleasure in his mother's smile, for she had bent over to gather up the tea things. His father coughed dryly and inquired if his good wife were awaiting midnight before serving the evening meal.

How good it can feel to come home, Alec thought as they went into the dining-room, and he remembered Stella.

He slept in his own room in the big four-poster his mother had brought back from Lancaster after Alec's grandfather had died. His mind filled with childhood memories as he lay under the soft folds of the eiderdown in the square high-ceilinged chamber.

When finally he slept he dreamed of the wide field that had adjoined this old house where the new apartment building now stood. He remembered in the odd way of dreams the games of terrible importance he had played in that field, remembering especially one game of war.

He had fought valiantly that Sunday morning with his wooden sword and gun. The pile of laths and two-by-fours that was the enemy castle was about to fall and in the sweet moment of victory he did not hear his father's approach. The wooden sword was snapped in two. The wooden gun went sailing in the air and fell among the timothy and weeds.'

The warriors, both friend and foe, stood by as Alec, led by an ear, was directed homeward.

'Thou shalt not play at war again,' had been his father's stern counsel.

Now he awoke this Sunday morning and as he dressed he reasoned that though he went to war again it was not to play. Breakfast was a leisurely and solemn affair and the three of them walked to the meeting house. They went into the old red brick building, through white panelled doors, and took their seats on the shiny wood bench.

Alec was relieved to see a sprinkling of uniforms among the worshippers. People looked at him and nodded. Others frowned at the uniform. He could not escape the feeling that he was a stranger among them. His mother and father sat calmly staring straight ahead. The room became quiet.

To each his own, Alec thought. Someone had stood up and was speaking in a righteous voice about the lesson he had learned from the golden rule. The dreary voice droned on. You pompous ass, Alec thought. If the spirit really moves you, why not trot across the street to St. Michael's and get it off your chest?

They're in the business. Or else sit down and let these good Quakers meditate in peace.

His mother nudged him. 'Stop muttering, Son,' she whispered.

His father stared at him coldly. Alec was surprised to see tears on his cheeks. The speaker had finally finished. The room was still for a moment. Alec's father stood up. When he spoke, the words were a hammering inside Alec's breast.

'We have learned from the ancient Hebrews,' his father said in his hesitating voice, 'to love our home. To honour it. Their home was a sanctuary from persecution and oppression. It meant freedom for religious meditation. They loved and honoured their home as they loved and honoured God. They knew it was their most treasured possession, to be defended at any cost from their enemies. They loved peace, but loved their home more and fought bitter wars to defend it.'

He paused and all heads were turned to watch him.

'I love my home. I'm grateful to have a son who is going to war to defend it.'

He sat down and wiped his eyes. The hum of whispers rose and fell like the swift sound of insect wings. The minutes dragged for Alec until they walked out into the hushed sunshine of Sunday morning Philadelphia. He held his father's arm tightly as they went down the steps and turned toward home.

That was telling them, he reflected happily. You sweet strange man in your quiet blue suit and your deep-running thoughts. I love you, and were I half the man you are I would tell you I love you.

His father walked silently between them. The city was quiet and clean, and the sun shone warmly through the old maples and sycamores. Alec felt the strong peace of everything about him, of the old house and shade trees, of his mother and father especially.

It's going to be all right to-morrow, he reasoned, when he would leave them for Chicago and officer training. He might never see them again, but the presence of this strength would be a comfort at all times. He was glad he had come home.

They were almost there before his father spoke.

'Just see that thee do nothing to bring shame upon thyself, Son,' he said.

BATTALION B swung out of the grassless dusty drill field and marched hotly toward Michigan Avenue. The officer candidates moved stiffly, unsmiling, the hearts out of them.

The battalion had been punished and detained at the drill field after the other battalions had been dismissed. The drill had been a fiasco. Not only did the battalion march poorly, it was incredibly disorganized in its counter-marching and column-by-twos and in all the other refinements of military drill. It seemed equally divided on the geography of left and right. The disgust of its leaders was evident and articulate and profane.

The 'temporary' ensigns and junior grade lieutenants, erstwhile civilians now dubbed 'sixty-day wonders', marched back to Tower Court wearily. They were heartily sick of the two months of rude schoolboy discipline. They swore softly as they marched. They glared shamelessly at the inevitable bystanders on whom they blindly assessed the blame for their predicament.

The battalion halted at the fringe of the boulevard. Two of the officers limped forward to halt the flow of traffic. It was Saturday afternoon, July, and hot. Chicagoans were rushing to be anywhere else but in Chicago. Drivers sped by heedless of the sweating apparitions in dark-belted topcoats who tried to halt them. The two officers dodged and waved and cursed and had no luck. The rest of the battalion fretted and fumed, their sweat a common river among them.

Alec Austen stood in the fifth line of men, weary beyond caring. Sweat lay like another garment beneath his wrinkled khakis and underclothes and the weight of the dank gabardine raincoat. His leg muscles ached. He nursed a painful face bruise where his neighbour had column-lefted on a column-right command. He thought only of the warm showers and fresh linen that waited in the grim, ivied building across the boulevard.

And then he saw Stella, miraculously, incredibly Stella Greyne.

She stood at the grassy edge of the pavement, shining, slim-ankled, dewy-bosomed, haloed in violets.

He shut his eyes. A mirage, he thought, shimmering from the hot stone floor of the city. When he opened his eyes she was still there, searching the faces in the ranks of men, then breathless and gasping with delight at the wonder of discovering him alive in this graveyard of uniforms and faces.

'Alec,' she called. 'Darling.'

Darling, he remembered. Hello and good-bye.

'Alec!' She whistled shrilly. The men grinned.

'Hi, Stella.' The hot sun and the world's eyes on him and his throat choked with dust.

She teetered at the curb. 'How are you?'

'How do I look?'

'Your nose is bleeding. What have they been doing to you?'

'Terrible things, Stella.'

'There's blood all over you.'

'It's this guy's fault.' He jerked his head at his neighbour. The man grinned at Stella and winked.

'Hit him, darling. He has a cruel mouth.'

'My room-mate. Nice guy. A lawyer. He just don't know right from left.'

'I thought I'd never find you, Alec.'

'I'm right here.'

'I've been around for hours. They said you were drilling. I almost died watching the others march back.'

'We're lousy marchers.'

'What do they expect from artists and lawyers?'

He grinned. It was good to hear her voice. He exchanged places with the man at the end of the line nearest Stella.

'Is it all right to talk to you like this, darling?'

'Court-martial offence.'

'Oh, Alec.' She backed away quickly.

'Ten days in the brig if we're caught. They'll keelhaul me.'

'What's that?'

'Look it up in the dictionary. I had to.'

The two men had finally parted the flow of traffic. They blew their whistles and shouted orders. Auto horns honked like angry geese. The battalion started to cross the boulevard. Stella trotted at Alec's side like a coach dog.

'Beat it, Stella.'

'I'm afraid I'll lose you. You all look alike.'

'The admiral's got his eye on you. Beat it.'

'A real admiral?'

'A lieutenant. But he thinks he's Farragut.'

'The hell with him. We'll go to the brig together.'

'Very cosy. You'd really better go.' They had passed the old Water Tower and halted in front of the barracks building. One of the battalion's officers glowered at Stella.

'Isn't he the little Napoleon?'

Alec ignored her and stared straight ahead.

'I'm at the Drake,' she whispered. 'Call me as soon as you can. I'll be sitting and waiting.'

She watched him march into the building and was relieved to observe that he was only a little out of step.

It was almost dark when he came out. He was freshly shaved and bathed and wore a small patch across the bridge of his nose. His dress blues felt loose and smelled faintly of cleaning fluid.

Stella stepped out of the shadows and took his arm. 'In case you had any crazy ideas,' she said, 'I thought I'd surprise you.'

He kissed her. 'I'm glad you surprised me.'

'Have we a lot of time together?'

'Until 1600 to-morrow.'

'That's four o'clock, isn't it?'

'Exactly.'

'I've been studying up.' She looked at him as they walked. 'You weren't coming to the Drake, were you?'

He didn't say anything.

'You were going to sneak off without me, weren't you?'

'Yes,' he said. 'I was going to do that.'

'You and your damned integrity,' she said.

They sat at the Beachcomber bar and dipped shrimp in the two sauces and drank Navy grog. It was dim in the corner where they sat.

'How's Pygmalion?'

'Who? Oh.' She traced an invisible design with a swizzle stick. 'Mad as hell, I guess. I took his convertible, you know. Left a note but didn't say where I was headed.'

'He'll send the cops, if I know him.'

'You don't, darling. Godfrey would send the finance company.' She took a sip of her drink. 'He's afraid of any publicity like that.'

'Clemson afraid of publicity? Ha.'

'Only because it might hurt the business. I don't care one way or the other.'

'Why'd you do it, Stella?'

'Wanted to see you. Missed you.'

'That's very sweet.' He leaned over and kissed her.

'And I'm sick of his tantrums. Ever since you left.' She smiled. 'I thought I'd die when I heard about the wrist watch.'

'He told you?'

'Without omitting a detail.'

'I'm surprised at him.'

'Just to expose you as a low, ungrateful wretch.'

'I was pretty nasty, I guess.'

'Of course you were. It was wonderful. It actually endeared you to me. A facet of your character I never dreamed existed.'

'There are times when the integrity you mentioned is strained.'

'I'm so glad. It's the part of you that's like me. Guttersnipey.'

They left the bar and walked along the boulevard. The hot daytime city had blurred to night-time loveliness, cool and serene. Stella stopped to admire a window display of silk foulard ties.

'He's a monster,' she said suddenly. 'But a cunning mind. Oh, what a cunning mind he has. Ever notice his face, Alec? Wreathed in jowls and chins and pink as a baby's?'

'I've noticed it.'

'Pure and smiling—until you see the eyes.' Stella trembled. 'They're bald. No lids, no eyebrows. And that glassy stare comes from contact lenses. He's really blind as a bat and won't wear glasses, and uses these damned contact lenses.'

'The hell with him.'

'Of course. I never knew about those damned lenses until one night I reached out of bed for some pills on the night table and I knocked over the glass of water he kept the damned things in. Scared the life out of me. And he raised the roof because they broke. As though it was my fault he has to wear contact lenses.'

'Do we have to talk about Clemson?'

'I hate him. I swear to God.'

'Why don't you leave him, Stella?'

'I did, didn't I? I'm here, aren't I?'

'You'll go back.'

She looked at the window of ties. Her face was pale and her eyes had lost their anguish and seemed spiritless.

'You'd better buy me another drink,' she said.

'No. We're going to eat.'

'You don't trust me to drink, do you? Here I drive two thousand miles to see you and you don't trust me.'

'We're going to Jacques.' If you behave we'll split a bottle of good wine with dinner. Open your big fat mouth and back you go to Godfrey.'

They turned into a side street. She held his arm tightly. 'I'm a little bitch,' she said. 'Busting up your last liberty with my dirty wash.'

'We'll explore the possibilities of that metaphor during the hors d'œuvres,' he said.

They walked towards the lake. Traffic hummed along Outer Drive in a swift procession of blinking lights.

'Such a dinner, darling,' Stella said.

'The champagne made me sleeply.'

'*Sleepy*, dear.'

'What I said.' He clutched a package tightly. 'Fall asleep standing up. Be sure I don't drop this.'

'Come up to the hotel. The room's air-conditioned.'

He stopped and shook a finger. 'None of that.'

'Why not?'

'You know.'

'Nonsense. You can stretch out and take a nap.'

'Don't trust you.'

'I know. What's in that package?'

'Bomb.'

'Well don't look now, Ensign, but your bomb's leaking.'

'Ice water. Surrounding a bottle of wine.'

'You bought more wine?'

'Best champagne. Pressed on me by the management in a moment of patriotic fervour.' They came to the beach. 'Here you go. Over the fence.'

Stella removed her shoes and followed Alec across the soft sand. They found a smooth peeled log imbedded in the sand and sat against it facing the water.

'Look,' Stella said. 'People in swimming.'

'Better than hot slums.' He unwrapped the champagne. The bottle was icy in his fingers. 'Get to work,' he said. 'Two glasses and a corkscrew. In my pocket.'

'Smart boy.'

'Navy is always prepared.'

She produced the items. 'You are a wise man. You have many talents,' she said softly.

He dug the corkscrew in. 'A mere youth. About to give his life for his country.' He tugged. 'The damned cork won't budge.'

'Here. Let me.' She took a scarf from her handbag and wrapped it around the neck of the bottle. She worked the corkscrew for a few seconds. There was a satisfying pop and the pale wine ran over. Alec had the glasses ready. Stella poured.

'*Vive le vin !*'

'*Vive frère Jacques !*'

'You're so thoughtful, Stella. *Vive la guerre !*'

She stopped him. 'I won't drink to it.'

'Why not?'

'I won't drink to any damned war.'

He kissed her cheek. 'You're jealous.'

'Not of any damned war I'm not jealous.'

'Because it's feminine. You see how wise the French are? They know. They make war feminine. Man's true love. Of course you're jealous.'

'They're right about love and art and champagne. I suppose they're right about war.'

They drank thoughtfully. The wine held for a long time. The beach was deserted when they finished the bottle. There was no moon and the lake was still and dark and there were no lights. His head rested on her lap. Her cool fingers played with his lips.

'Alec?'

'Present, baby.'

'I must tell you one more thing about him.'

'Really must?'

'Yes. Then I promise never to talk about him again.'

'It's a deal.'

'He said he hoped you'd die. He hoped you'd be shot down or drowned or blown to bits.'

'Maybe he doesn't like me.'

'He said when that happened he would get rid of me. He'd kick me out for good.'

'A sweet, gentle man.'

'He really carried on. That's when I decided to take the car and drive here.'

'Isn't gas still rationed?'

'There's nothing that bastard can't get if he wants it.'

'It seems so.'

'He said other things that were very nasty. He said he hired you just so he could keep an eye on you. He said you'll never be a successful artist. You're a crazy dreamer.'

'A crazy dreamer? I think I like that. It makes up for all the nasty things.'

'I can't forget the way he said he hoped you'd die. Like a curse.'

'The hell with it. Is it out of your system now?'

'I guess so. I don't know.'

'Get him straight, Stella—without the hocus-pocus of his fancy talk. He's just a glib, slightly absurd salesman. The merchandise he peddles happens to be art. It could be ladies' dresses or used cars. He's fast-talked you into trying to be something you're not. He's doing you no good.'

'I know it, darling. I know it.'

'Then for Christ sake, do something about it.'

'I will.' She bent over him. 'Alec, darling, you do love me, don't you?'

He closed his eyes. She put her arms around his shoulders, cradling him.

'Say you do, darling. I'll leave him. I'll quit him all at once before he can change my mind for me.'

He sat up, the sleep out of him.

'I'm going away, Stella. There's no telling.'

'I'll wait for you, Alec, I swear it.'

Tears glistened in the oval frame of her face. He held her cheeks between his big hands and kissed her.

'You know what you're saying, Stella?'

'I do, Alec, believe me.'

'Do you know? Do you really know?'

'For days I've known, driving like mad through the towns and cities, darling. And the poles flew past singing *Alec I love Alec I love Alec I love Alec* like a broken record.'

'Stella.'

'I was insane with the time it took. I wanted to be with you so badly. Nothing ever hurt me as much as the waiting. Nothing, Alec.'

The breath went out of her and she collapsed against his hard body. He touched the strands of hair near his face, gently kissing them while she cried.

He remembered the years of uncertainty and doubt when he had begun to paint seriously, when all that had sustained him had been the will to paint and a few words of Thoreau—'*If a plant cannot live according to its nature, it dies; and so a man*'—so that now on a night beach in big Chicago the inside of him went weak with the fresh knowledge that there was more for him than the whole absorbing and fanatic purpose of painting. There was love now and he realized, sickening, that as he admitted love he was surrendering a fragment of the oneness he had kept inviolate.

He thought of that and reasoned: To love Stella is also according to nature and I do love Stella.

The only sound now was the whine of late traffic and the muted

sounds of the gently breaking surf. She embraced him. His lips
and hands caressed her wonderful body.

'Trust me now, darling Alec. I love you so very much.'

'I love thee, Stella.'

They embraced on the empty beach in the warm night. Later
they swam naked in the cool fringe of the lake. They splashed
and danced like children in the cool, friendly water, their bodies
wise and ageless, their minds blind to the shrouded, sleeping city.

They spent Sunday together until it was time for Austen to
return. They walked along the street like lovers. When it was
time to leave her, he said:

'Go to my studio and see old Mrs. Titus. She has my paintings
stored away. Do you remember our first night? When you left
that morning I started a painting and worked on it until I had to
come here. It's still unfinished. It wasn't dry when I gave it to
Mrs. Titus and she's kept it apart from the others. I told her
about you. She knows you're coming for the painting some day.
Go to her, Stella, and take the painting. Keep it. It's yours.'

'What kind of painting is it, Alec?'

'It's called "The Wish". It's the portrait of you, Stella.'

'Of me, Alec? I'm afraid.'

'No,' he said. 'Take it.' His laugh was at once robust and
chilling. 'It's a wonderful painting of you.' He kissed her.

'I'm afraid,' she whispered. 'You know me too well.'

'Good-bye, Stella.'

'I'll write,' she said.

She watched him go.

12

HER letter had been mailed in New York that summer. It
had gone from there to Norfolk and from Norfolk to
Panama to Vallejo to Dutch Harbour. It had finally caught up to
the *Atlantis* and Austen in Adak many months later.

Now at sea he slowly read the letter.

Darling Alec,

Godfrey was furious when I returned from Chicago. He had locked the apartment and I had a hell of a time. Had to wake the super in the middle of the night to let me in. Godfrey had told him not to. I was so worn out and just about hysterical. Thank heaven for sleeping pills. Popped two of them into my mouth and slept for a day and a half.

Dreamed I was still with you in Chicago. It was delicious, darling. No one will ever take it away from us. But when I awoke there was Godfrey big as life glaring at me over his pink shirt and white collar and black tie. Wanted to know all about the car and why I had broken into his apartment. He's really a beast and I detest scenes. If you had been with me I'd have quit him on the instant, darling. But I'm weak-willed (not weak-minded, please). I let him rave and rant and agreed to anything he said. Finally we didn't kiss but we made up. I did it just to get rid of him, believe me.

So here I am back in the old plush trap, darling. I tried awful hard to remember about us and the country and your painting. But I simply had to give in. He had the nerve to accuse me of being unfaithful! My God—imagine him accusing me! About the only thing he didn't call me was a whore and I suppose he's a little squeamish about using the word.

I guess I just have no moral fibre. I guess all I have is immoral fibre. What a bitch you must think I am. And I really am. If I had any guts I'd enter a convent. It's where I really belong, darling, away from soft living and temptation. I think I shall enter a convent. Just as soon as I get up from this comfortable bed and have a nice warm breakfast inside me.

I've made up my mind I'm not going to worry about you. You're so damned strong-willed and so fierce about what you believe in. Nothing can hurt you. Certainly not Stella Greyne.

Be very brave darling and win a lot of medals but do be careful so you can come back and go to the country and do your wonderful paintings.

Such a sad letter. Not at all what they have been recommending for the boys overseas. Try to forgive me for everything.

I love you, Alec.

Stella.

P.S.—I think to-morrow I will go over to your old studio and get my painting from Mrs. Titus.

He read the letter several times. He lay back on the freshly made bunk and the letter slipped from his fingers to the deck. He closed his eyes and tried to remember what the painting was like. When the image was clearly in his mind he smiled. He knew Stella would be surprised because in one aspect of the painting she was a nun.

In one aspect, he thought bitterly. In another she was a prostitute armoured in sequins. The hell with Stella, he thought. It's the painting that counts, not the subject matter. The painting will outlast us all. The ship and the war and Stella and me.

Clough's snoring stirred him. He retrieved Stella's letter and stuffed it into a shirt pocket. Poor Dave, he thought. Sick of the sea. What are the dreams of the chronic seasick? he wondered. A saturation of self-pity? Or continuous gliding flight in a shining silver plane effortless in blue skies, the dreamer the golden smiling pilot?

Ah, Stella, he mourned.

13

THE old ship plowed testily through the wild sea. Austen stood on the open bridge, waiting out the last minutes of the morning watch.

Ensign King came out and saluted. He was a sober-faced young man with mild intelligent eyes. 'Ready to relieve you, sir.'

Austen kept his binoculars trained on the lead destroyer. Her hazy silhouette was barely visible in the mist ahead.

'Okay, boy.' He lowered the glasses. 'Course is zero-nine-zero, true, zero-nine-two per gyro and standard compass. Speed fifteen knots, one seven eight r.p.m., boilers two and four on the main line. Zigzagging to Plan Seven. Operating as task Group Forty-nine Point Four in company with DDs *Brant* on port bow, *Clovis* dead ahead, *Washbourne* on starboard bow. All vessels on station. Keep an eye on the *Clovis*. She zigged instead of zagging about fifteen minutes ago. Let's see, now. Captain Meredith is up here in the emergency cabin, admiral's on the flag bridge. Starboard plane is on recon with Lieutenant Johnson, pilot, and Howards, radio-gunner. Scheduled to recover aircraft at 1300.' He looked thoughtful. 'I guess that's it, kid.' He unslung the binoculars and passed them to King.

King saluted. 'I relieve you.'

'Did you check the division compartment this morning?'

'Everything's four-oh, Alec. Shapiro's right on the ball.'

'He's doing a good job.'

'The exec. said he wants to see you after chow. Probably about Slobodjian.'

'Slobodjian? What's he done now?'

'He's on report. The exec's got him up for captain's mast.'

'He's been mess-cooking. He hasn't had a chance to foul up.'

'See Shapiro. He's got the right dope.'

'Who put Slobodj on report?'

'Mike Edge.' He stared out to sea. 'What the hell. Get your chow first. You're relieved.'

Austen went into the chartroom and wrote his log as he had written it many times during the arduous months of patrol. *Steaming as before.* He signed it and notified the captain he had been relieved and went below.

The men sat around the deck in a corner of the Fourth Division compartment and played stud for matches. A match cost a dollar. Frenchy Shapiro had a respectable pile of matches in front of him.

'When we going back, Frenchy?'

'You kidding? We just get out here and already he wants to go back.'

'Listen to him.'

'What's so good back there? Everything's rationed. All the dames go for is gold braid. The liquor's lousy and you can't buy a steak without a fistful of tickets. At least out here you lead a clean life. You don't have to worry about no hangovers, no women trouble. And you're doing something noble and worthwhile for your country.'

'Ya shoulda been a chaplain, Frenchy.'

'Some chaplain. I got drunk at my own *bar mitzva*.' He shuffled the cards. 'Whose deal?'

'Not me. I'm broke.'

'I'm gonna sack out, Frenchy.'

'How about you, Salvio?'

'I'm quittin' too.'

'Chicken out on me, you guys?'

'I got the midwatch, no crap. I better get in some sack time.'

Frenchy scissored up from the deck. 'Then let's get the joint cleaned up. It's looking like a pigpen again.'

The others shuffled to their chores.

'Whyncha drop dead, Frenchy?' someone muttered.

'Out here? Not on your life, sailor. You drop dead out here and they give you the deep six. I ain't ending up on the bottom of this frigging cold sea. Not me.' He smiled and began cleaning his nails with a pocket knife. 'After all, my old lady's got a nice plot in a cemetery out in Jackson Heights, a hundred per cent. paid up.'

'So what?'

'So if I was buried at sea she'd never forgive me. She'd never be able to touch another piece of *gefüllte* fish without thinking some of it was me. So I ain't dropping dead, sailor. Not out here.'

Austen came through the compartment. Frenchy greeted him with a casual wave of the pocket knife.

'What's this with Slobodjian, Frenchy?'

'Mr. Edge slapped him on report.'

'For what?'

'For the time he sneaked off with Parry and Hackmeister.'

'How'd Edge know about it?'

'He seen him get into the boat.'

'Why didn't he stop him then?'

'He thought Slobodj was part of the crew. Later he found out otherwise and blew his top.'

'He could have checked with me first. I'd have squared it for the kid. Now he's up for captain's mast.'

'That guy Edge is striking for admiral. Poor Slobodj don't know what he's doing half the time. He's nutty as a fruit cake, Boss.'

'He's harmless.   I better see the exec.   You know about the test-firing drill to-day?'

'Yes, sir.'

'Well, Dooley's getting out of sick bay to watch it.'

'How many rounds per barrel we firing?'

'Two.'

'You sure Uncle Sam can spare the expense?'

'It's just to test the guns, Frenchy.   Two rounds are enough.'

'Okay, Boss, we'll be ready.'

The loudspeaker blared.   *Lieutenant Austen, please report to the executive officer's cabin.*

Austen grimaced and Frenchy shrugged and watched him go.

The door to the executive officer's cabin was partly open. Austen went in.   The executive officer was rolling up an eye chart and his strained bloodshot eyes focused on Austen, who stood awkwardly on the threshold.

'It's customary to knock before entering, Mr. Austen.'

'I'm sorry, Commander.'

'Are you going to stand there like a clumsy fool or are you coming in?'

'I'm coming in, sir.'

'Please shut the door.'

He sat at his desk and slipped the rolled chart from sight.   His fingers clawed for his eyeglass case, then thrust it away.   He began writing in a small black book.   Austen stood silently while the commander wrote with painful exactness and ignored him.

What the hell, Austen thought.   Officers like King and Clough and the new navigator and even Dutch Fledermayer, the grey-haired dour chief warrant gunner, more than made up for regulars like the exec and Mike Edge and Dooley.   Although Dooley really wasn't a regular.   He just tried to pass for one.

The executive officer had stopped writing and tapped the desk with his little black book.

'The morning you went ashore on captain's business, Mr. Austen, a seaman '—he consulted the book—'Slobodjian, seaman second, went ashore with you.   Any explanation?'

'I don't know what to say, sir.'

'The man's in your division, is he not?'

'Yes, sir.'

'You were in charge of that boat trip, were you not?'

'Yes, but I didn't know Slobodjian was in the boat, sir.'

'That's hardly possible.'

'It's the truth just the same.'

'Sir.'

'Sir.'

'You believe he stowed away, then?'

'He was hidden behind the two injured men. They were covered with blankets. Sir.'

'You knew he was aboard on the return trip, didn't you?'

'Yes, sir.'

'Why didn't you report him then?'

'For what, Commander?'

'For deserting the ship. For returning to the ship intoxicated. Why not, Mr. Austen?'

'I didn't think he was intoxicated. In fact I know he refused to take a drink in the boat.'

'Who offered him a drink?'

'I did, sir.'

'Hardly recommended conduct for a division officer.'

'Well, sir, I know I should have placed the man on report when I found him in the boat on the return trip. But he's in enough trouble. He's already mess-cooking for punishment. I honestly believe he should be sent home.'

'Why?'

'He serves no function in the division except as a source of humour. He's really a simple-minded fellow, harmless, and just not cut out for combat duty.'

'I'm pleased to see,' the executive officer said dryly, 'that along with your other talents you are also a psychiatrist. Unfortunately the Navy has already allocated those duties to the medical officer. Unless you have made some special arrangement with the captain to handle that department as well as gunnery. Have you, Mr. Austen?'

'No, sir.'

'Your man Slobodjian is now declared a prisoner-at-large until next captain's mast.' He stood up. 'I intend to present the captain with a full report of your conduct, Mr. Austen. Your attitude with relation to enlisted men has already been criticized by others and I intend to include such information in my report to the captain.'

'I haven't done anything I'm ashamed of, sir.'

'The Navy was not designed as a social club, Mr. Austen. It has other more serious functions. Since someone has seen fit to include you in the Navy, it is my duty to make you cognizant of its fine traditions and usages. You will do things the Navy way, according to the rules and regulations governing the Navy.'

'Yes, sir. But you sent for me to talk about Slobodjian and I still say he is not fit for combat duty.'

'I shall be forced to add insolence to the list of grievances against you, Mr. Austen. That is all. You may go.'

Austen saluted and went out.

There's a face, he thought grimly. For Rouault. Tyranny, he thought, and cruelty, etched like scars in the bloodless face. Rouault could paint it. Stab, cheek. Slash, mouth. Line. Line. The paint thick and angry. The bastard, he thought. The cold *impasto* bastard.

Dooley was waiting for him in the wardroom. His injured foot was in a cast propped on another chair.

The gunnery officer was a slight, troubled man with a sorry secret. As a boy, someone had set off a Fourth of July firecracker directly behind him. He never recovered from the bang. The rest of his life was a stubborn struggle to deny this fear. He looked for courage in uniforms beginning as a Boy Scout. When the Naval Academy would not have him, he laboured through the ranks of a college NROTC until he made it. By the time he took over as gunnery officer of the *Atlantis* it was almost impossible to distinguish John Dooley from an Annapolis-trained officer. Except for those damned guns. He still flinched and closed his eyes and remembered the firecracker.

Austen poured some coffee for himself and sat down. Dooley had a list of gunnery instructions in his hand.

'Here's the way we're going to run the drill to-day, Austen,' he began briskly. 'We'll start at the forward forties, two rounds per barrel. Work our way aft, firing the forties in sequence. The target as usual will be a burst from the three-inch fifties. After the forties, the twenties.'

'How many rounds?'

'Two for the forties. Five for the twenties.'

'Rough on the twenty-millimetre crews.'

'Why is it?'

'Unloading the clips from the magazines. Right now they're fully loaded. To shoot a lousy five rounds they have to pull out fifty-five rounds by hand.'

'The training is good for the men.'

'It's all they've been doing since we left Panama.'

'Never hurts them to drill.'

'They get stale.'

'Not if their officers are on the ball.'

'Okay.'

'I'm going around with you to each forty. Want to personally observe the men, see how they co-ordinate and respond to orders.'

'Seems like a lot of work for two lousy rounds per barrel.'

'Yours not to reason why, yours but to do or die.'

'Okay. Okay.'

'Any objections, Austen?'

'Hell, no. I just thought I was air-defence officer and I'd like to run the drills my way. The men seem to like it.'

'Never mind the men. I'm still gun boss, wound or no wound.'

Now it's a wound, Austen thought. Next, the Purple Heart. 'What I meant,' he said evenly, 'is that it's going to be a little rough on you, hopping around those slippery decks with that bum gam.'

'I'll manage,' Dooley said tersely.

'Yes, sir.'

'You don't have to "sir" me, damn it. You know I'm one of the boys. Just knock off the "sir"—except around the enlisted men, of course.' He frowned at Austen's unyielding eyes. 'Well, that's the firing schedule. Wanted to indoctrinate you, Alec, so there'd be no hitches.'

'I am now thoroughly indoctrinated.'

'The skipper and Admiral Marcy will be watching. Let's give them a real show.'

'We'll try.'

Dooley struggled up and hobbled out of the wardroom. Austen drank his coffee and was irritated to see that his fingers trembled. He tried not to think about Stella's letter and the executive officer's dry sarcasm and Dooley's shrill authority.

Some day with a few slugs of whisky warming his belly, with a lot of time and a hankering to laugh, he would read Stella's letter again. It was full of laughs. Godfrey Clemson with his glass eyes in a tumbler of water. Like a set of false teeth. And trying to make a cultured lady out of his dime-store whore. What a laugh.

Then why aren't you laughing, Austen?

So far away in time and place, he thought. He sat with his head in his hands for a long time. No one came into the wardroom and he knew it was a good thing. Later when the squawk box called away anti-aircraft gunnery drills he got up and carefully wiped his face and went topside.

His gun crews were ready. He joined Dooley and together they stood by as the forward forty prepared for the signal to commence firing. A sudden clap of gunfire shook the starboard bulkheads. The first target burst from the three-inch fifties appeared high on the beam.

Austen watched Dooley's head duck down. The gun captain winked at Austen and Austen turned away, sickened. The gun mount swung to starboard, its twin barrels quivering in remote control. The burst spread, thinning to pale dirty yellow. Dooley watched the signal bridge. The hoist fluttered skyward.

'Commence firing!' he yelled, and ducked again.

The gun mount lurched with the explosion of firing. Two dark patches, then two more, ballooned above the fading target smoke, high and wide.

Directly over Dooley and Austen the captain stood frowning on the open bridge. He leaned over. 'Compliments of Admiral Marcy. He says the firing stinks.'

'Sorry, Captain,' Dooley said tersely. He visualized his next fitness report streaked with red crosses.

'Secure the mount,' Austen said to the gun captain. 'Turn in a report on ammunition expended.'

'Sure, Mr. Austen. You got a adding machine I could borrow?'

Dooley pretended he had not heard. He limped aft. Austen followed him.

'You're going to have to do a damned sight better than this, Austen,' Dooley said. 'These men need stricter training.'

'You can't expect much better on a limit of two rounds, Dooley. They just about get the target lined up and they're through firing.'

'You heard the captain.'

'Yeah. I heard him.'

'Well, let's see how Number Two does.'

The second forty-millimetre gun crew performed no better than the first. The captain forwarded a sizzling comment from the admiral. Dooley looked ill and rubbed his cast disconsolately.

'How about this third gun crew, Austen?'

'Only one barrel, you know.'

'Of course I know. Can they shoot?'

'I think so.'

Frenchy Shapiro was in the gun captain's station, chewing jauntily. 'What were those guys shooting at, Boss—the stars?'

'This is your battle station, Austen,' Dooley said stiffly, 'suppose you take over.'

'Yes, sir.'

Dooley stepped back carefully until he had a good view of the mount from a distance of fifteen yards. Austen climbed up alongside Shapiro.

'Keep a sharp eye on the signal bridge, Frenchy. The instant they two-block Baker, open up. Don't wait for any signal from me.'

'Who's this big jig on the director?'

'A new guy. Fowler. Don't worry about him. Just do as I say.'

'Okay, Boss.'

'He'll be tracking the minute the burst is up there. Just give him the word when to open fire.'

'Wish we had the other barrel.'

'Use what you've got.'

He joined Dooley on the twenty-millimetre gun deck. The ship was in a turn. Its wake foamed white abaft the fantail. Dooley nudged Austen.

'Aren't you going to give the order?'

'They know what to do.'

'There should always be a mount officer in charge, Austen.'

'Okay. I'm sorry.'

The burst from the three-inch gun appeared high on the starboard quarter. It rapidly drifted aft. The ship's turn brought it dead astern. The flag hoist fluttered at the dip, awaiting a final signal from the captain.

'Stand by,' Frenchy shouted. The gun crew tensed. Two rounds in a metal clip dropped into the loading tray. The signal flag was two-blocked, flapping wildly. The gun mount swung smoothly following the fading burst.

Frenchy's voice was drowned in the instantaneous burst of the single barrel.

Poom! Poom!

The small grey-black bursts thrust themselves dead-centre in the drifting patch of yellow smoke. The gun swung back to its centre lock position.

'Stand easy,' Frenchy said. There was an edge of pride in his raw voice.

'Nice shooting, men,' Austen called out.

The talker in the director tub alongside Fowler raised his hand. 'It's the bridge, Mr. Austen. The captain says the admiral says that's more like it.'

Austen nodded and turned to Dooley. But Dooley was pointing at Fowler. 'What the hell's he doing up there?' he whispered in a horrified voice.

Austen pointed sternward where the target burst was still visible. 'That's what he's doing,' he said.

They repaired to the wardroom for coffee. Dooley looked worried. 'That was a mistake,' he said.

'What was?'

'Letting that steward's mate fire the gun.'

'I thought he did fine.'

'Well, he did. But it's bad stuff. Anyway, the skipper and exec. don't know so we can skip it.'

'Skip what? I don't understand what the hell you mean.'

'Nothing to understand, damn it. Just replace him and we'll forget all about it.'

'Why? Fowler's a damned good man. We need a good man there.'

'Oh, please, Austen. For Christ sake.'

'I've checked his records. He's been to gunnery school. His firing on twenties and forties is the best they've ever seen. It says so in his records. We're damned lucky'—he paused and a frown darkened his lean intent face—'you mean because he's coloured?'

'It's not what I mean. It's a well-known rule.'

'I don't believe it. I never heard of anything more disgusting.'

Dooley stood up, balanced on his good leg. His thin lips had whitened. 'I don't like being called a liar. Not by an officer junior to me, Austen. I've been in this man's navy long enough not to have to take that kind of insubordination. You can take my word—no, damn it. This is an order, as of now. Fowler stays off those guns. He can pass ammunition, nothing more. And that goes for any other niggers on the ship. Get me?'

'You can't be serious, Dooley. A nice guy like you.'

'Damn it, you heard me. It's an order.'

'What about Anuncio?'

'Who's he?'

'Coxswain in my division. He's a Filipino. Colour's approximately raw sienna, with maybe a touch of Venetian red on the cheekbones. Definitely a coloured man. What about him?'

'Never mind the lousy jokes, Austen. It ain't funny.'

'I know it. Sit down for a minute.'

Dooley glared at him, then slowly sank into the chair, wincing.

'We're short three men since we lost Parry and Hackmeister and the kid who was killed,' Austen said. 'Fowler's a natural for handling that mount. I'll go along with you on the taboo if you're willing to forget you saw him up there during this drill. But when the real thing comes along—enemy action—I'd like to have him in there.'

Dooley shook his head. 'No deal.'

'Why not? I swear there's no one on this ship gives me the sense of security he does when I see him fingering that director firing key. How about a break?'

'It would be against my principles to do an underhanded thing like that.'

'What's more underhanded than denying a man a chance because his skin is darker than ours?'

'It's not the same thing.'

Austen stared at him. 'I wonder what made you like that,' he said quietly.

'It's just against my principles, like I said.'

'You don't have principles, Dooley. You're too damned scared to. You're yellow. You don't know a principle from a prejudice.'

'That's insolence, Austen, I'm warning you——'

Austen stood up and jammed his cap on the back of his head. 'Fowler's staying on that gun.'

'Disobey my orders, Austen, and you'll be sorry,' Dooley shrilled. But Austen was gone.

Dooley sat picking at his face and wondering why things like this always happened to him. The sea slammed along the bulkheads. Dishes rattled and the wardroom chairs strained against their lashings.

Dooley winced at the sound of them, shivering, too frightened to move.

Austen went to the bridge. Ensign King was sampling the O.D. ration of the crew's mess.

'I'd like to see the captain,' he said.

King barely raised his head. 'In his cabin, Alec.' He wiped his chin and nodded at the tray of steaming food. 'They eat a lot better than we do.'

'They always did.' He knocked on the captain's door.

'Come in, come in.'

Austen went in and closed the door. The captain was pinning his silver eagles to the collar of his khaki shirt.

'Alec, who the hell's the laundry officer?'

'Ensign Heinz, Captain.'

'These damned shirts are buried in starch. Like a block of cement. I've got a raw red wound around my neck from these damned starchy collars.'

More wounds, Austen thought. Heroes. Dooley and Meredith. Purple Hearts won at the battles of Flinch and Starch.

'I'll mention it to him, sir.'

'I should make him wash and iron these shirts himself,' the captain growled. 'What's on your mind? Admiral's waiting for me.'

'It can wait if you're in a hurry, sir.'

'Is it important?'

'I think it's very important.'

The captain stopped what he was doing to the shirt and sat down. He waved at the chair for Austen to sit in.

'Always got time for my men. Shoot, Alec.'

'Thank you, Captain,' Austen said, surprised. 'It's about one of the gun crews. I used a steward's mate named Fowler on the after forty to-day. We're shorthanded, as you know, and this man was trained in the States. His record on the Oerlikons and Bofors equipment is outstanding.'

'Which gun did he shoot?'

'The last forty, sir.'

'On the crippled mount. I remember. A bull's-eye, wasn't it?'

'Yes, sir. And a burst of smoke is a very poor target to hit.'

'Admiral Marcy mentioned the promptness. No time wasted. He liked that very much.'

'Well, sir. After the drill I was told that I should not use a steward's mate to fire the guns.'

'By whom?'

'The gunnery officer, sir.'

'What do you want me to do?'

'I'd like permission to keep Fowler permanently assigned to that director.'

'Not too easy to arrange now, Alec.'

'Why not, sir? It's certainly for the good of the ship.'

'In what way?' The captain was fumbling with his collar devices.

'Defensively, mostly. And it would do a lot of good morally.'

'Negroes aren't usually permitted in Navy gun crews.'

'I found that out. I never knew it before. Is it or isn't it a ship's rule?'

The captain smiled ruefully. 'It is and it isn't.'

'That's nice and definite.'

'It's usually at the discretion of the commanding officer.'

'Then this will give you a chance to set a great precedent.'

'No, Alec. Defensively you're right. We certainly need a good man on those forties, especially against plane attack. The Japs have a lot of those float-type Zeros out here and they can mean trouble. But it's the worst thing that can happen on board.'

'Why?'

'The men are sullen enough now, Alec. I don't want to start any real trouble.'

'It's a damned shame, sir.'

'I'm still your commanding officer,' the captain said mildly. 'Any obscenities in this conversation will originate with me.'

'I'm sorry, Captain.'

'Good. Now listen. Keep the man in your gun crew for the time being. I'll have a talk with the exec. and Dooley.'

'Thank you, Captain.'

'Of course you realize you're putting yourself in a couple of black books aboard ship.'

'It doesn't matter. Whose?'

'Well, you've by-passed the exec. and Dooley by coming directly to me. Very serious breach of etiquette. And some of the officers and men will find out about your steward's mate. They won't be very happy.'

'I believe I'll survive it, sir.'

'Of course you will. I admire your integrity, Alec. I just deplore your methods.' He waved impatiently. 'The admiral's waiting for me, so run along.'

The captain picked up a bundle of dispatches and held the door for Austen. 'He'd better be good, this steward's mate of yours.'

The admiral waved Captain Meredith to a seat. 'The end of the line for me, Snooky.'

'Sure sorry to lose you, sir.'

'I'll transfer to the tanker when you refuel to-night. Hope you get a decent sea.'

'We're used to it rough, sir.'

'I just don't want to be dunked out of that breeches buoy is all.'

The captain cleared his throat. 'How'd we shape up, Admiral?'

'What can I tell you, Snooky? You were absolutely right about those new drafts of men. Scum. I've heard nothing from BuPers about it, but they probably haven't recovered from the dispatch I sent in. I don't think you'll get that "hazardous duty" routine again.'

'Thank you, sir.'

'The overhaul's been approved, following this last patrol. You're long overdue. They're about done revamping some of the old battle wagons and they'll relieve you shortly. Maybe the *New Mex* and the *Idaho*, but it's not definite.'

'Was I very wrong about ship morale, sir?'

The admiral grinned. 'Snooky, you should have been a football coach, not a sea captain. I'll see what we can do about reliefs for the officers. We're stretched pretty thin over a couple of oceans, but new boys are coming through in good shape.'

'Sounds fine, sir.'

'Now I've set up a few missions for you'—he patted a sealed envelope stamped SECRET—'should help relieve the monotony of the patrol. You'll just have to stick it out. And if you run into Hashida, give him hell.'

'We'll try, Admiral.'

'Sure you will, Snooky. I'm hoping this boy of mine, Sam Griswold, will eventually fill your exec's shoes. That man shouldn't be at sea.'

'Yes, sir.'

'That's about it, Snooky. I've got to get packed. Stick it out till those battle wagons show up. Then you can spill it to the crew they're heading for the States.'

'They'll like that, sir. It's been a long stretch.'

'Hell, look at those poor bastards on Adak.'

'It's not like being at sea, Admiral.'

'And what's wrong with the sea?' the admiral snorted. He stood up, squinting his sharp eyes at the captain. 'What's on your mind, Snooky? Something's worrying you.'

'Well, sir.' The captain pulled at his starched collar. 'It's really a small matter.' He told the admiral about Fowler.

'No problem of mine, Snooky,' the admiral said curtly. 'Work it out for yourself.'

'I have, sir. I'd respect an opinion from you, though, the crew being in the touchy run-down state it is.'

'Off the record, then. If the nigger's competent, then by all means that's where he belongs—on that gun. But you know the Navy as well as I do, Snooky. Maybe better, knowing who your old man was. There are certain customs and usages and come hell or high water they cannot be tampered with. Can't you just ignore the whole thing?'

'Not if Dooley, the gun boss, makes an issue of it. I'm afraid I'd have to decide in his favour in spite of my personal sentiments.'

'Sometimes those niggers make damned good gunners.' He glanced at the closed door. 'Let me tell you a story. You know this boy, Sam Griswold. He's Ike Griswold's boy, and you remember Ike? Licked Army in '15—a little before your time, I suppose. Well, Sam's Ike's boy and I've sort of adopted him since Ike was lost at Pearl. Sam was a two-striper then, running one of those damned converted trawlers in the Solomons. Whole damned crew were fishermen. I forget the name of his tub. They were all named after birds like *Plover* and *Magpie* and *Pintail*—I forget which one he handled. They were Diesel jobs with a couple of pip-squeak AA guns and a prayer. The Japs found 'em one morning.

'They sent over a few bombers from a carrier to sink him. The fighter escorts came in low, strafing. But Sam didn't want to sink. He strafed right back. Most of the crew jumped or were shot up and killed. There was Sam and this one steward's mate left. His name was also Sam, I remember. Funny thing. They actually shot down one of the bombers and crippled a fighter. The two of them stood on that open deck, the nigger and Sam, and fought every goddamn thing the carrier sent over until dark.

They were still afloat. Him and the nigger. Sam says the nigger did the real shooting.'

'What happened to his hands?'

'Sam says he doesn't know. May have been ricochets off the water. They were burnt so much they hardly bled and there were holes you could stick a pencil through.' He slapped the captain roughly. 'Damn it, I've got to pack, Snooky. You trying to shanghai me?'

'I guess I know what to do about Fowler, sir. Thank you.'

'It's your ship, Snooky,' the admiral said, and he cackled. 'You're the Law.'

In the passageway outside the captain almost collided with Sam Griswold, who saluted and stood aside, grinning. The captain hesitated for a moment, controlling his eyes so they did not stare at Griswold's hands. Then he smiled and passed him and went up the ladder.

His own fingers looked clean and pink on the white sennit work of the ladder. Much too clean, he thought. 'I'm a fine captain,' he muttered softly. He remembered the gold-framed portraits on the mulberry wall in Newport and he cursed silently. He dug his polished nail tips into his palms and watched the blood rush back into the tiny crevices.

Some salty sea dog, he thought sadly.

14

THAT night the small task group met the loaded tanker in its scheduled rendezvous. The wind had died and the fuelling operation was handled efficiently and without mishap. The admiral and his staff with the exception of Commander Griswold were transferred. Mail and supplies were taken aboard and the tanker headed for Adak before dawn. The task group set its course to the north-west.

The captain opened his secret orders and read them. He spoke to the crew after the evening meal and told them the nature of the task group's mission.

The men sat around the p.a. speakers throughout the ship and listened. They cheered him when he finished. With the departure of the admiral they had expected to fall once more into the depressing routine of patrol. The promise of almost immediate action gave them new life and something to talk about. The ship stripped for action.

After dark the group ceased zigzagging and made a high-speed run to the island of Attu. The Japanese garrison had dug itself deep into the snow and lay sleeping, unprepared for the surprise attack. The ships had formed in single column and at the pre-arranged hour of 0300 commenced firing.

The blinding red and yellow flashes lit the cold Bering night accompanied by the Wagnerian thunder of the guns. The naval shells raked the enemy airstrip and revetments and set fire to several buildings. No fire was returned during the eighteen minutes of port and starboard runs.

The ships departed as silently and swiftly as they had come. They cruised on various courses at various speeds until dusk. Rendezvous was made with a tanker and escort and as the ships of the task group refuelled the men leaned over the rails and shouted and cursed happily and talked to the tanker crew about their exploit.

The following night the group again sped west south-west. Its target was Paramushiro in the Japanese islands.

The men went to battle stations early. They stood their tense watch through the long hours of a sub-zero night. The sky was clear. The sea shone like a frosty meadow bathed in moonlight. Again the captain addressed the men over the p.a. system. He told them what a splendid job they had done at Attu. This would be greater, he said. This was the first surface attack on the Japanese islands. The whole world would hear about it, he told them. They were a fine fighting team and he was damned proud of every man jack of them.

And they believed him and cheered him and were eager to die for him.

Radar contact was established with the island at 0255 the next morning. All guns were brought to bear, and steel followed steel into the snowy sides of the hills. The cold blue night awoke with the red violence of fire. Enemy searchlights stabbed the sky, believing the attack to have come by air. Faint streaks of fire burst high above the ships as the perplexed enemy retaliated.

Small fires flared out of the dark shore, blossoming like paper flowers. The men of the *Atlantis* forgot their frozen bodies and fought the deadly waiting out of their bones. Once an explosion burst on the darkened beach and showered the sky with a gaudy display.

The ships turned and left as the enemy wildly searched the sky for them. The men secured from their battle stations and went below to an enormous feed of steaks and pie and hot coffee that had been provided by the tanker.

On the bridge, Captain Meredith wiped the smoke from his ruddy face and blessed the wisdom of Red Eye Marcy. He could hear some of the men who were standing the morning watch in the gun nest below the bridge. They were singing. The captain had heard no singing in many months. It sounded very good, he thought. He hummed the tune with them.

15

THE long day began.

The catapult officer issued last-minute orders to the deck crew. It was a dirty grey morning. There had been some debate on the bridge before the word was passed to launch the morning observation flight. A mechanic throttled down the roaring motor and waited for pilot Johnson. The *Atlantis* had turned out of the scouting line and headed into the wind. Its signal for launching aircraft was the Fox flag—white with a red diamond centre. It fluttered at the dip, its halyards slapping in the wind.

Johnson came on deck. He was dressed in heavy flying clothes. He was a happy, straw-haired boy with a toothy smile. He jabbed at the catapult officer, who was dancing and swinging his arms against the cold. Johnson climbed on a wing and swapped with the man who had been warming up the engine. He pulled the thick glasses over his eyes and checked the controls. He gunned the engine once, full throttle, and let it idle. He signalled with his thumb to the catapult officer and pressed back, bracing his body for the jolting take-off.

The catapult officer watched the signal bridge, his hand aloft, his body leaning into the wind. The legs of his khaki trousers flapped crazily.

On the signal bridge the crew two-blocked Fox. The catapult officer flung his arm down and the engine roared deafeningly. The men on the weather decks held their breaths. The plane seemed to strain at the after end of the catapult.

Then it whipped forward with a crescendo of noise. It cleared the ship's side and fought its way into the air. For a moment it dipped towards the ugly grey swells, then was airborne, arching gracefully, mounting steadily until it blended with the endless mist.

The men relaxed and turned to their duties. The ship's company secured from routine general quarters. The *Atlantis* changed course to rejoin the scouting line until the plane rendezvous later that morning.

Austen was below in the warrant officers' wardroom playing a game called Automobiles with his friend, Dutch Fledermayer. The game was an invention born of shipside boredom. The rules were simple. Each player took his turn naming automobiles until one or the other was out of names. He was allowed five minutes. If the opponent could then furnish a name, he was the winner. There were no stakes. There was only the pride of memory and a curious nostalgic delight.

It was Fledermayer's turn. He studied the list of automobiles they had already mentioned.

'Pope-Toledo,' he said.

'Moon.'

'Chalmers.'

'Uh-uh. I gave that one ten minutes ago.'

Fledermayer studied the list. 'So you did. I thought maybe you said Chandler. Let's see. How's about Pope-Toledo? No. I just gave it. Stearns-Knight.'

'Okay.' Austen grinned. 'Chandler.'

'You dog. Simplex.'

'Haynes.'

'Apperson.'

'Winton.'

'Westcott.'

'Star.'

'C'mon now, that's a phony. Just because I give you the benefit of the doubt on Moon.'

'No kidding, Dutch. Durant built it. It flopped.'

'Okay, crook. Duesenberg.'

'It's not an American car. You made up the rules. It's got to be an American car.' He looked triumphant. 'It's out. Dig again.'

'The hell it's out. Duesies were made here. It just sounds foreign.'

A messenger from the bridge stuck his head through the doorway. 'I been looking all over the ship for you, Mr. Austen.'

'I'm right here.'

'The captain would like to see you on the bridge.'

'Be right up.' He reluctantly folded his list of automobiles. 'No finagling with the list now, Dutchie. Don't pull any fast ones while I'm gone.'

'Who? Me?'

'And I'm going to check with the skipper on that Duesenberg. He'll know.'

Fledermayer cocked his big grey head. 'How come you and the skipper are such buddies?'

Austen explained about Fowler. The big gunner frowned and scratched his thick, grizzled head. 'I never seen a nigger in a gun crew. Not in twenty-eight years, kid.'

'Then it's about time, isn't it?'

'I don't know. I just never seen it. You better take it easy.'

'I'll do what I think I have to do.'

'Your ass, sailor.' He scowled at the list of automobiles. 'Hurry back. I got some lulus lined up here.'

The captain wasted no time with Austen.

'Damn it, Alec, why do you get me into such snarls?'

'I don't know, sir. What snarl is this?'

'I've had a talk with the exec and Dooley.' He rubbed his chin. 'They're both dead set against upsetting precedent.'

'You're the commanding officer——'

'Damn it, Alec, don't be impudent. I know who I am. Right now the crew's morale is fine—thanks to those two shore bombardments. But it won't last. They're heroes, they figure, and they want to go home and tell the folks about it and I really don't blame them. As long as we're on this damned patrol it's my duty to keep their spirits up. I've seen this man Fowler's records. He's probably a wonderful gunner. Under ordinary circumstances I'd say sure, put him in a gun crew. But right now all hell would break loose in this ship. Any other time I'd risk it, but not now.'

'Then Fowler goes back to the galley.'

'Fowler will report to the gun you assigned him to whenever the general alarm is sounded. He's going to be there for all drills and exercises anyway, isn't he? As an ammunition passer?'

'Yes, sir.'

'You're the mount officer—use him where you see fit. But remember that his official status is ammunition passer—not in the gun crew itself. Except for general quarters.'

Austen started to say something. 'Now that's all, Alec,' the captain said. 'I've stuck my neck out far enough.'

Austen saluted and left the bridge. He resumed his game with Fledermayer, but his heart was not in it. The gunner watched him and after a few minutes he put aside his list.

'Look, kid,' he said, 'I been in this outfit too long to try to fight it. You short-timers ain't going to be around long enough to make the slightest dent in it. So why don't you just let it lay?'

Austen did not say anything. He looked at Fledermayer's bronzed cheeks in which the sea salt had etched its seams for twenty-eight years. Twenty-eight years of eating it, Austen thought. Not liking it, but eating it just the same. And knowing that the one time he would rebel from eating it would not pass. It would in fact be marked in red upon his record for the life of his career. It would never be forgotten by the Navy or by himself or by the years. So for twenty-eight years he's eating it knowing in two years everything will be all right because he will not have to eat it any more.

'Finish the game, Dutch,' he said. 'I've got a million.' He thought he had. There was Mitchell and Roamer, Wills St. Clair, Maxwell, Stutz, and Locomobile. I'll dump the Dutchman, he thought. I'll dump him hard.

Duesenberg, he thought. I forgot to ask.

Commander Blanchard was in the passageway of officer country fumbling with the door to his cabin. His eyes brightened when Austen appeared through the hatch from the deck below. He smiled.

'Ah. The seagoing Da Vinci.' He looked along the passageway. 'A drink, Alec?'

'Very kind of you, Commander,' Austen said.

'You look like you can use one.' They went in. Blanchard locked the door. His cabin was completely disordered. The ship's roll gave the room an air of constant motion as loose objects slid about.

'No executive officer inspections, sir?'

'He wouldn't dare. And knock off the "sir".'

He produced a bottle from the drawer under his bunk. Austen noted that it was kept within arm's reach from the pillow. The doctor passed the bottle. Alec took a drink. It tasted fine. He had almost forgotten how fine it could be. He passed the bottle back to the doctor. He counted eight until the doctor lowered the bottle from his lips. He lit a cigarette.

'What's weighing you down, Alec?'

'Plenty.' He told Blanchard about Fowler.

Blanchard shrugged. 'One war at a time,' he said. 'And the skipper's right about the crew's morale.'

'Maybe.' He looked thoughtful. 'Ever see a painting by a guy named Edward Hicks? A Quaker, around the early 1800s.'

'I don't know any painters.'

'It's called "Peaceable Kingdom". My father's favourite. That's the only reason I know about it. Full of animals. Fascinated me when I was a kid. A lion, a leopard, a bear, monkeys, people— all together. One big happy family. Like the ship.'

'You've got the wrong ship.'

'Oh no. Wait until I finish. It's even got William Penn in the background signing a peace treaty with the Indians. The kitchen sink, plastered with peace. But as I grew up I began to get a funny feeling about the painting. It was peaceful all right. But I had the feeling the whole bunch of them were ready to fall on each other, tear their throats, maim and kill. I remember the tiger —a pure Rousseau tiger. There's a stupid-looking two-year-old kid with his arms around the tiger's neck. The tiger's paw is raised. Gives me a chill down my spine, right now, talking about it.'

'Do you suppose Hicks meant the suggested violence?'

'No. He was a Quaker. But the violence was undeniably there.'

'And it reminds you of this ship.' Blanchard was examining the label on the bottle. He rubbed it affectionately. 'Man's best friend.' He extended the bottle to Austen, who shook his head. Blanchard shrugged. 'Well, you have your painting. I have this.' He tipped it. Austen counted to ten. Blanchard wiped his mouth. 'Don't look so shocked. I get as much from this as you do from your painting. And I never get drunk.'

'I'm not drunk.'

'Me,' Blanchard said with a brutal grin, 'I can drink a straight line with a ruler.' He reached for the bottle and tilted it. Austen closed his eyes rather than count.

Someone knocked on the door. Blanchard slid the bottle leisurely into the drawer.

'Yes?'

'Commander Blanchard?'

Blanchard got up and unlocked the door. A sailor stood there. He was a young boy, light-haired and fair-skinned, and his soft lips hung apart. He stood cringing slightly. His fingers worked nervously around the brim of the hat he held in his hands.

'Come in. I'm the doctor.'

The boy coughed dryly. The cough may have pained him. He winced and stepped carefully into the room. His eyes shifted from Blanchard to Austen and back to Blanchard.

'It's this finger, sir.' The words tumbled from his lips. 'Swelled up something awful last night. Hurts terribly, sir . . .'

Blanchard examined the finger. 'I haven't seen this before, have I?'

'No, sir. The chief in sick bay, he seen it. He seen it last night again when it begun to swell up.'

Blanchard pressed the finger gently. 'That hurt?'

'Yes, sir, a little.' He coughed delicately. 'Like it's in the joint.'

'How about that?'

The boy withdrew his finger. 'Very much. Like maybe it was broken, I think. Like I told the chief last night.'

'Hmmm.'

'Hurt real bad then. Would you say it's infected, sir? It must be. Infected or broken or something in the joint, the way it hurts.'

'Mm, hmm.'

'Pains shooting all through me, sir, honest to God.'

Blanchard regarded the pale face and terrified eyes calmly. 'We'll take care of it.'

'The chief was awful mad last night when I woke him up. Tried to tell me nothing was the matter with me. He made wisecracks about it, sir. And me in real pain.'

'What kind of wisecracks?'

'All kinds.'

'Be specific.'

'Like telling me, if you'll excuse it, sir, not to go sticking my finger where I hadn't ought to.'

'I'll talk to the chief,' Blanchard said gravely. 'You run along to sick bay now.'

'I've got the watch coming up, sir. In the radio shack.'

'Stand your watch, then report to sick bay. What's your name?'

'Gray, sir. Harry Hudson Gray, radioman third. You can see where the finger's swole, can't you?'

'Yes. Now stand your watch. I'll see you later.'

'Thank you, sir. And you can look at my side later, too. Hurts something fierce, under the ribs, sort of.'

Blanchard touched his shoulder. 'Get going,' he said. The boy went out, shutting the door quietly. Blanchard turned the lock. He took out the bottle. 'The ship's crawling with cases like that. You and your "Peaceable Kingdom".'

'Is his finger bad?'

'The nail could stand some cleaning. Nothing else wrong with it.'

'He looks like a kid of sixteen.'

'Probably is. They lie about their age to get out here. Then they get homesick and cook up all sorts of ailments to get shipped back.'

'Did you notice his eyes? Blank as hell. He worries me.' He stood up. 'I better go.'

'Relax, you artist. Here's the cure. One for the road?'

'Better not, thank you. Hell, it's still morning.'

'It's always here, Alec, when it gets a little deep out there.'

'You hit me at the right moment. Thanks again. I needed it.' He went to the door.

'We all need it,' Blanchard said, unlocking it.

Austen saw Mike Edge in the passageway. He was talking to the radioman Gray, who stood at frightened attention.

'You don't belong in officer country, sailor,' Edge was saying.

'I just come from the doctor, Mr. Edge.'

'Nuts. You don't belong here.'

Austen came over. 'He's all right, Edge.'

Edge blustered. 'He can't go trooping through here without official permission or nothing.'

'He was in seeing Blanchard.'

'He ain't supposed to see him here. That's what sick bay's for.'

'No sense in arguing about it.' He turned to Gray. 'On your way, Gray.'

Edge gripped Gray's arm with a big hairy hand. An expression of unexpected pleasure filled his small eyes.

'Let him go, Mike. He's got the watch.'

'That right, kid?'

'Yes, sir, Mr. Edge.'

Edge's fingers loosened reluctantly. He patted Gray's cheek. 'Here,' he said. 'Lemme see that finger of yours.' Gray held out his hand. Edge frowned. 'Looks okay to me,' he said. He squeezed the boy's hand.

'You'd better go, Gray,' Austen said quietly.

'Hell. He's faking.'

'Just let him go.'

Gray followed the conversation with empty-eyed innocence. Suddenly he spoke up. His voice was pitched brightly high, like a sped-up recording.

'You better, Mr. Edge. They need me something awful in the radio shack. Things are terrible. Radar's out of commission and we're on radio silence and nobody knows where the plane is and we can't let the plane know, not without breaking radio silence. So I better get up there——'

Edge slapped him to silence. Austen stood rooted in horror. Edge rubbed his calloused palm and stared at the boy's cheek. His fingers had marked it with angry streaks. Gray stood unmoved.

'You can see why I must get up there,' he continued as though nothing had happened. 'Even though my finger hurts. And my side.'

'Tell him to knock it off, Austen,' Edge said shrilly, cracking his knuckles.

'And the chief telling me dirty things. My stomach is what really pains,' Gray said calmly. His eyes were empty of meaning. 'I didn't tell the doctor. It's none of his business why my stomach hurts. I can't hardly sleep nights. Twisting pains like a knife turning in me, like somebody's standing over me in the dark twisting this knife——'

'Knock it off!' Edge screamed. He raised his arm. Austen caught it and held it.

Edge jerked it away. 'Naah,' he rasped. 'I ain't gonna touch him. He's nuts.' He shoved Gray suddenly and the boy staggered. 'Beat it, you little pogue, or I'll brain you.'

Gray leaned against the bulkhead. His arms were limp along his sides. Tears started in his eyes.

'Why did you call me that? What've I ever done to you?'

Edge rubbed his knuckles and said nothing. Austen took the boy's arm.

'Come on, Gray.'

'What the hell,' Edge said.

Austen walked the boy to the ladder. 'The nights are terrible, sir,' Gray said quietly, his voice shaking a little. 'Fellows crying in their sleep. Rats creeping all over us. Terrible things you officers never hear about.'

'We hear about it.'

'I can't stand it. No one believes me when I tell them.'

'I believe you, Gray.' He released the boy's arm. Through the open hatchway above them Austen could see the weather deck shiny with spray. The wind howled dismally and the unfastened canvas flapped. 'Think you can make it from here?'

'Oh yes, sir. I'll be fine, Mr. Austen.' He wiped his eyes. 'I'll tell Martha I saw you.'

'Martha?'

'Mother's been giving her the rhubarb and soda and she's going to be well.'

Gently he pried Austen's fingers from his sleeve. The raw stain of a fresh tattoo showed under it—a heart and arrow and a mottled wavering 'MOTHER' framed in flourishes on the thin girlish arm. He started up the ladder.

'Wait,' Austen said, 'I'll go with you.'

Gray smiled. His eyes were guileless and clear, his cheek pale except where Edge had struck him.

'I'll tell her I saw you,' he said and he was gone.

Down the passageway Edge laughed obscenely. Austen had started to follow Gray. Now he stood fast, sickened, and recalled a strange time.

He remembered the framed photograph on Godfrey Clemson's desk. He remembered his revulsion then at something both unholy and unclean. The echo of Edge's laughter still rang in his ears.

Dutch would know, he thought. He found the old gunner in his cabin reading. The glasses he wore looked odd against his sea-tanned skin. Fledermayer took them off and blinked at Austen.

'I know. You got a car I never heard of.'

'Something else, Dutchie. Got a minute?'

'Sure, kid.'

'You shipped out with Mike Edge once, didn't you?'

'On the old *Blackhawk*. I ain't bragging about it.'

'What kind of sailor was he?'

'Edge? A sailor. That's all. Why?' He put aside the book and lit a cigarette.

'I just want to know a little more about him.'

Fledermayer frowned. 'He's wearing gold braid now, by the grace of Tojo and a little toadying. But he's still a goddamn deck hand. What the hell, I don't have to tell you, kid. You got eyes.'

'What's a pogue, Dutch?'

A slow grin creased the wise old face. 'Hell, don't you know?'

'They never told us in training school.'

'A pogue's a pushover. You know. A sweet kid who'll do anything for a candy bar. Hell, a candy bar's called poguey-bait. There you have it.' He frowned. 'What's Edge been up to?'

'I didn't like the way he handled one of the sailors. I wondered about it. I thought you might know something.'

'Well it happens I do. It ain't in his record, of course, or he'd never've been commissioned, even temporary. But ask any Asiatic about Mike Edge. They'll tell you.'

'I'm asking you.'

'Look, kid, what another sailor does is his own damned business.'

'What'd he do, Dutch?'

'Draw that hatch curtain.'

Austen got up and drew the heavy green curtain.

'The old *Blackhawk* was quite a ship. Very Asiatic.'

'So I've heard.'

'Edge was a carpenter's mate, striking for chief. A bunch of us got drunk together. It was in Shanghai. I never took my liberties with him before. But this time we happened to be together. So we ended up in a joint. The gals were real good-looking pieces. Half-breeds, White Russians, Chinee gals. We all grabbed one except Edge. He wanted a little boy, he said. I never knew he was like that.'

'Now you know.'

'Well, they couldn't take care of him. Nobody thought any-thing about it. We were all pretty loaded anyway. Then we goes back to the ship. Everybody sacks out except Edge. He's looking pretty nasty and he shoves off. I asked him where he's going. "To get my piece," he says. I told him he can't get off the ship again. "I don't have to get off the ship," he says with a dirty grin.

'So I forgot about it until the next morning. They fished a sailor out of the drink. A nice kid. I remember him.'

'What happened to him?'

'Drunk and drowned, they said. But the kid had been assaulted. Somebody saw it happen but clammed up. Edge did it. All the guys knew. The word gets around.' He shrugged. 'They never found out.'

'It's a very pretty story.'

'It's the truth, kid.'

'Thanks, Dutch. It makes sense.'

'I always knew he was no good. But I never knew he was a butcher boy.'

Austen went to the wardroom. The late breakfast dishes were cleared and the green baize cloths covered the tables. Mike Edge sat tinkering with a small model steam engine he had built.

Lieutenant Commander Dooley sat in an easy chair. His injured leg was thrust before him. His face was bent over a coffee cup from which he sipped in small sucking breaths. He pretended not to see Austen. Austen poured a cup of coffee for himself and sat down.

'That kid's nuts, Austen,' Edge said.

'Then keep your hands off him.'

'Hell. I hardly touched him.'

'The kid needs help. He's sick.'

'Sick, hell. He's a pogue.' He laughed coarsely. 'I know a pogue when I see one.'

'Okay, Edge.' He sipped his coffee. It was bitter and cold. He leaned through the pantry opening. 'Watch boy! How about some fresh coffee?'

'Be right out, sir.'

Fowler came out of the pantry with a pot of steaming coffee on a tray. He filled a fresh cup for Austen.

'Everything okay on the guns, sir?' he said softly.

'Sure.' Here it comes, Austen thought.

'Going to be a regular drill to-day, sir?'

'Yes, Fowler.'

'What's with me, sir?'

'What do you mean?'

'He give me the Word not to show up at the gun no more.'

'Who did?'

Fowler nodded at Dooley. Blotches of grey showed on his dark intent face. His eyes looked murky.

'He's gun boss, Fowler.'

'You know how I'm on them guns, sir.'

'I talked to the captain. He said it's okay for GQ, but that's all. Otherwise you pass ammunition.'

'No more shooting at them targets?'

'I'm afraid not.'

'It don't seem right.'

'It isn't right, but that's the way it is.'

Fowler turned away. Some of the coffee spilled. 'Wha fo' dey make me put in all dat time on dem guns?'

Austen was startled. Fowler had never spoken in dialect before.

'Wha' fo?' he repeated harshly.

Edge looked at him across the room. 'Get back in the pantry, you,' he snarled.

Fowler stared back at him. His eyes were oddly glazed. 'You gonna tell me wha' fo'?'

'Who the hell you think you're talking to?' Edge gripped the screwdriver and half rose.

Fowler continued to stare sullenly, not yielding. Dooley had looked up, startled at the conversation. He coughed and wiped his slack mouth.

'He's talking to me, Mike,' Austen said.

'No nigger steward's mate's gonna talk to me that way.'

The bosun's pipe shrilled over the squawk box. '*Now hear this:*

134

Relieve the watch. Condition Three, Watch Two. All hands not on watch stay clear of the weather decks.'

Austen followed Fowler into the pantry. He could hear the bosun's voice echoing through the crew's quarters abaft the wardroom.

'Don't fool with Edge, Fowler. He's looking for trouble.'

'He called me nigger.'

'I know. I'm sorry he did. Try to forget it.'

'He done it before.'

'He'll probably do it again. He's like that.'

'I don't like for nobody to call me nigger like he do.'

'You're in a spot here, Fowler, can't you see? Try to avoid him.'

'I don't have to take that stuff.'

'Sure you do. So do I.'

'It ain't the same for both of us.'

'It's worse for me.'

'How do you mean?'

'Do you think I like watching them push you around? Do you think it's easy not being able to do something about it?'

Fowler's big hands reached for a towel. He wiped the coffee where it spilled on the small tray.

'What about it? Will you try?'

'Yes, sir. I'll try.'

'Good.' Austen noticed a thick batter in a deep bowl on the shelf. He sniffed it. 'That's delicious. What is it?'

Fowler's tense face relaxed. 'Sweet-tater pie. For Lieutenant Johnson, sir.'

'Why for him, Fowler? I'm jealous.'

'Being he's a Georgia boy I promised him a tater pie.'

Austen dipped a finger and tasted it. 'I'm sorry I'm not from Georgia,' he said. He peered into the wardroom. 'Edge is banging again. Guess it's safe.'

'Mr. Austen, sir?'

'Yes?'

'I'd like to thank you.'

'Forget it. Just be careful, will you?'

Fowler nodded. Austen went into the wardroom again. He sat down near Edge and stirred his coffee.

'Lay off him, Mike. Things are tough enough.'

Edge jabbed at the engine. 'He's been asking for it.'

'Slobodjian didn't ask for it. You got him clapped in the brig.'

'Teach the little jerk not to jump ship again.'

'Couldn't you've checked with me? I'd have done the same with a kid from your division.'

'I don't handle my division like you handle yours, Austen.'

'Maybe you should.'

'You don't like the way we run things in the Navy, do you?'

'Some things.'

'Whyncha go back to painting pretty pictures and leave the Navy alone? It's got along this far without you.'

Two ensigns bustled in for a quick cup of coffee before going on watch.

'Fifty-knot wind across the bow,' one of them said.

'Must be blowing Johnny around a bit.'

'Isn't he letting them know how it is?' the other ensign asked.

'How could he?'

'He's got a radio, hasn't he?'

Edge snorted. 'You nuts, boot? Ever hear of radio silence?'

The man flushed. 'I didn't know.'

'You dumb boots never know.'

'We're too close to the Jap islands to use the station,' Austen said.

'Every damned Jap plane on Kiska and Attu'd hit us if we bust radio silence.' Edge snorted again. 'Trade-school boots!'

'Okay, Edge. Back to your tinker toy.'

'It's no toy. It's a real engine.'

The ensigns finished their coffee and buttoned up their bridge coats. No one else aboard the *Atlantis* wore bridge coats. Edge eyed them scornfully.

'Don't go sending no radio messages now,' he said. He watched them go out. 'Bridge coats! You'd think they were with Dewey at Manila.'

'Only you were there,' Austen said.

'The Navy sure ain't what it used to be.'

'It never was.'

Dooley cleared his throat. 'What was that man Fowler pestering you for, Austen?'

'He wasn't pestering me.'

'He was beefing about his gun station, wasn't he?'

'You ought to know.'

'I took care of him.'

'I know. He told me.'

'Had to. It would have set a poor example for the men.'

'For the white men, you mean.'

'It's a ship's rule, Austen, and damn it, we can't——'

'It's not a ship's rule. It's a stupid Navy habit. Let's drop it. I hate post-mortems.'

'Negroes have enough duties,' Dooley persisted shrilly, 'without wasting their time on the guns.'

Edge dropped the screwdriver. 'A nigger in a gun crew?' he said. 'Why not?'

'I wouldn't let no nigger near a gun.'

'Why not?'

'They're yellow, is why. They freeze up. The ones who don't you can't trust. They'd like as not turn a gun on you.'

'Then what the hell's the sense of training them in the States? Like Fowler was trained? Is that the way the Navy does things?'

'No use discussing it,' Dooley said loudly. 'How are the gun crews this morning, Austen? Alert? Manned and ready?'

Austen regarded the thin worried face wearily. 'They're manned and ready,' he said. 'And very, very alert.'

'You've checked the men at their stations?'

'Yes. Some of the crews are shorthanded.'

'Why?'

'Seasick, most of them.'

'I knew nothing of this.' His thin lips tightened. 'Why wasn't I told?'

'I'm not running to you with every unimportant detail, Dooley.'

'Why not? I'm gun boss. I insist on being informed of every detail—I'll determine its importance.'

'Okay.'

'You know I could be back in the States, Austen. I chose to remain out here. It's my duty. I expect the same sort of devotion to duty from my subordinates.'

'Aye, sir.'

'In the future you will keep me advised of the condition of readiness and security extant throughout the gunnery department.'

He saw the executive officer behind Austen. His voice rose shrilly.

'That's an order, Austen. See that it's carried out.'

'Oh, horseshit, Dooley,' Austen said. He thought angrily of mad Gray and sorry Slobodjian and dead Loomis and it was too much. 'That goes for the whole miserable lash-up. I'm sick of it.'

He started to get up. Seeing the shocked expression on Dooley's face, he turned and saw the executive officer. He sat again, slowly, the din of his own words deafening his ears.

'I'm sorry, Commander,' he said. I'm not sorry at all, he thought. Why do I say such things?

'Stand up, please.'

Austen stood up.

'At attention.' He went to the sideboard and poured some coffee. Austen could see Fowler's anguished face through the pantry opening. He felt sorry for him.

'I didn't know you were standing there, Commander.'

'You meant to say what you said behind my back?'

'No, not at all. I just felt——'

'That's it, isn't it, Mr. Austen?' He faced Austen across the table, stirring his coffee delicately. 'Isn't it?'

Eat it, Alec Austen, he thought to himself. Dutch eats it. Dooley eats it. In the Navy everybody eats it. Be a nice boy, Alec. Eat it.

'Yes, sir. I meant to say those words behind your back.'

The executive officer sat down. It was very quiet in the wardroom. He sipped a little coffee and turned his red-rimmed eyes on Austen.

'You were insolent to Commander Dooley, you know.'

'I really meant nothing by it, sir.'

'Nothing? Come now, Mr. Austen. I am told you are an intelligent young man. Is foul language and insubordination *nothing?*'

'I guess not. Sir.'

'Stand at attention, please. With your hands at your sides. I suppose being a ninety-day wonder limits your knowledge of Navy customs and usages. We really cannot expect too much from a ninety-day wonder.'

Sixty days, Austen thought, remembering the cruel-tongued martinets and their make-believe Annapolis.

'Were you at least required to familiarize yourself with Navy regulations?'

'Just roughly, sir.'

'Your remarks to Mr. Dooley were in violation of Sections 1 and 6, Article 8.'

'If you say so, sir.'

'I do. I have more to say. Your conduct as an officer is hardly exemplary. You set a poor example for your junior officers. You violated the chain of command—an open insult to your superior officers. You stir dissension among the enlisted men. You have displayed a marked disregard for discipline and tradition and the responsibility of your rank. I am therefore placing you under hack. You will remain within the limits of your quarters unless the ship is called away to battle stations.' He waved his hand, almost languorously. 'That is all, Mr. Austen.'

'May I say something, sir?'

'Certainly not.'

Austen saluted and left the wardroom. The executive officer drank his coffee slowly. No one spoke. He stood up to leave and his eyes found Edge's. For an instant he grimaced. It was almost a smile. Edge lowered his gaze and fumbled with his tools.

'I almost believe you enjoy this sort of thing as much as I do, Edge,' the executive officer said. He frowned. His thin mouth line seemed thinner and the corner muscles twitched slightly. Then he was gone.

Dooley raised his eyes for the first time and looked at Edge. They could hear the executive officer's shoes on the metal ladder, ascending. Dooley licked his dry lips. Edge tapped the model engine absently. A minute passed.

'I guess maybe I better check the guns myself,' Dooley said. 'With Austen in hack.' He struggled manfully to his feet.

'Yeah,' Edge said, tinkering, 'I guess you better.'

Dooley limped out.

The ship rolled nastily in the wild, heaving sea. There was no horizon. Sky met sea in a limbo of grey mist. The catapult crews lay about the afterdeck, their 'zoot' suits bellied in the cruel wind. They clung to struts and wires, to the naked catapult and the sheathed torpedo tubes like rain-swept sea birds to driftwood. When the wind and the ship's roll permitted, they hacked at the ice clumps formed on the gear and rigging.

Above the wind came the faint purr of a motor in the sky. Men paused, straining their ears to hear it again. It was the steady throb of a single powerful engine. Smiles cracked their tired drenched faces. Johnny was coming home.

The squawk box blared. The bosun's pipe squealed. *'Now hear this! Flight quarters! On the double! Now man your flight-quarter stations to recover aircraft!'*

The *Atlantis* left the cruising formation and headed into the wind. The plane's motor roared once as it passed over the ship. No one saw it.

The Word spread and the men risked the vile wind and murky fog to crowd the hatches and weather decks. The recovery sled was streamed from the side of the catapult deck and the crew on the hoisting crane stood waiting. The lookouts aloft strained their eyes against the patches of grey mist. In the wardroom pantry Homer Fowler hummed a tune and popped his sweet-potato pie into the oven.

Minutes passed. There were ragged reports from topside stations. They had heard a motor, faintly, or a splash to starboard. Lookouts were posted in the eyes of the ship. The captain ordered the engines stopped. The ship lay helplessly drifting, broadside to the wind.

More minutes. Then the engines went ahead to one-third standard speed and the helm to right standard rudder. The ship circled slowly like a stalking beast. The men watched the sea for signs. They listened for the faint hum of the plane's motor once more. The sky was silent except for the wind.

Austen and Clough sat uneasily in their quarters and listened.

'How much longer, Dave?' Austen asked.

'Thirty minutes on the outside.'

'Not much, is it?'

'He hasn't a damned thing to guide on. Can't use his radio. The ship's damned radar is out. And the fog's cut visibility to zero.'

'He came right over us. He can't be too far off.'

'In this pea soup he could skin the foremast and never know it.'

'What would you do if it were you, Dave?'

'Pray. What the hell else is there to do?'

The water sloshed and gurgled in the near-by head. Suddenly the squawk box crackled. There was a fanfare of static. A shrill voice piped insanely.

'*Mr. Johnson, how do you receive me? This is the ship, Mr. Johnson. How do you receive me?*'

The voice cut out. Its swift shrillness and instant cessation was at once a violent and shocking experience to the two officers. Austen was on his feet and into the passageway. Clough dropped from his bunk to the deck and stood weak and aghast.

'*Come in, Mr. Johnson, please. This is our position, can you hear me, can you——*'

Voices flooded the speaker. There were sharp magnified sounds of struggle. Austen ran back for his coat and cap. Clough held him.

'Where you going?'

'To find out what's happened.'

'No use. It's done.' He looked past Austen. 'It's a good thing. It's a break for Johnny.'

'What the hell happened, Dave?'

'Somebody cut the ship's intercom into the main radio setup and went on the air.' He paused. 'Somebody is fouled up, because the intercom would ordinarily not be hooked up that way.'

'I know that voice, Dave.'

'Who was it?'

'A kid named Gray. A radioman. I'm checking.'

Even as he ran along the passageway he could sense the panic spreading through the ship.

Some of the ship's officers were bunched in the wardroom when Austen arrived. Their faces were grave.

'—should have seen the exec. He had just got here from the bridge and the squawk box explodes. He ran out so fast he took the tablecloth halfway across the room.'

'He's in the radio shack. It was a sailor name of Gray. A nice-looking boy.'

'They'll ream him,' Edge said.

'The whole damned ship heard it.'

'Maybe Johnny heard it.'

'You can bet the Japs heard it,' Edge said. 'Real loud.' He continued to tinker with his model engine. 'Them Japs'll be over us like a tent. You wait and see. With them float-type Zeros and them *Mogami* cruisers. Hell. I'd like to lay my hands on that kid Gray. He's nuts.'

'The exec beat you to it, Mike.'

'Them Japs'll be here from Attu in no time. Maybe right while we're taking the plane aboard.'

The plane, they all remembered.

Fowler had been following the conversation from the pantry opening. 'Think Mr. Johnson's going to make it, Mr. Austen?'

'Nobody knows,' Austen said.

The squawk box staticked. The men stopped talking and listened.

'Men, this is your captain speaking. No emergency exists at this time. We are therefore not sounding the general alarm. It is not necessary to go to general quarters. We must however be in a fair degree of readiness. It is entirely probable the enemy knows we are out here somewhere. They possibly know our position by this time. The gunnery department only will go to battle stations. All other departments stand prepared for the alarm.

'All hands topside keep a sharp lookout on all bearings. I repeat: A sharp lookout on all bearings. This is of utmost importance. It may mean the recovery of Mr. Johnson, his crew man, and the plane. It also means preparing for the possibility of attack by air or surface. Be alert. Report all contacts to the bridge immediately. Good luck, men.'

Austen stood up. 'Good. No more hack.'

Fowler came out of the pantry. 'What's with Mr. Johnson, sir?'

'Still can't say.'

'I got that tater pie cooling in the pantry, sir.'

'I hope Mr. Johnson gets to eat it, Fowler.'

'What the captain just announced, sir—that include me?'

'Yes. It's the same as general quarters. Report to the gun. I'll be there.'

The officers were drifting from the wardroom. Fowler went into the pantry and collected his foul-weather gear. When he came out the wardroom was empty except for Mike Edge. Fowler started for the topside ladder.

'You. Fowler. Don't be a fool,' Edge said.

Fowler went through the hatchway. Edge stood up and said, 'Stand where you are, damn it.' Fowler stopped. 'Get back in here.'

Fowler came into the wardroom and stood across from Edge.

'You ain't to go on them guns. Hear?'

'Why not?'

'Why not, *sir*, damn you.'

'All I want to know, sir, is why I can't go on them guns.'

'Never mind why. Get back in the pantry.'

'Mistuh Austen say fo' me to go, suh.'

'The hell with him. Do what you're told.'

'He say to go. Ah'm goin'.' But he stood without moving and his eyes were fixed on Edge.

Edge hesitated. 'You don't want your friend Austen to get in trouble, do you?' he said.

'How trouble?'

'Breaking Navy rules. Putting you in a gun crew.'

'He'd get in trouble for doing that?'

'Hell, yes. I'd slap you on report and they'd ream him. Son of a bitch is in enough trouble as it is.'

Fowler's eyes narrowed. He walked to the table where Edge sat. Edge's fingers clawed for the screwdriver.

'Go on, now,' he said. Fowler reached for him and Edge drove the screwdriver downward. The point gouged Fowler's arm. He moved quickly and his hands found Edge's throat.

His brown fingers tightened.

Edge heaved forward. His sheer weight carried Fowler back against the table. Fowler held on. The engine crashed to the floor. It seemed to give new strength to Edge. He uttered a low, strangled cry and drove his knee hard into Fowler's groin. The brown fingers slipped a little. Edge caught Fowler's nose and twisted it. Fowler squirmed and his fingers relaxed around Edge's throat. He drew up his feet swiftly and caught Edge in the stomach and slammed him against the sideboard, where he fell. Dishes crashed. Two steward's mates peered frightenedly from the pantry and quickly disappeared. Steps clattered down the ladder.

Fowler was at Edge with animal ferocity. Edge tried to regain his feet. His stricken eyes watched Fowler's face.

'You'll die, you nigger bastard——'

Fowler's fist smashed against the words. Edge sagged, the entire hulk of him collapsing, his face, arms, body, and legs in the slow stupefying disintegration that resembles a dynamited mountain in slow motion. He sat with his fingers crawling to his bludgeoned face, not believing the blood that spurted from the dark gums where his teeth had been. Fowler, watching the eyes, feeling the rage ebb to pity, instantly recognized an end of time had come for him. For shabby triumph, bright with pleading, lay in Edge's eyes and Fowler, slowly turning, saw why.

The executive officer stood there horrified. Fowler lurched away, seeking escape. It lay beyond the hurdle of Edge, who even now was rising, his eyes still pleading with the executive officer, saying, *See what is happening to our fine Navy line?*

The expression of momentary horror and disbelief on the executive officer's face seemed to indicate that such a violent and disgraceful incident were impossible. *Everything to destroy me*, he screamed inside the tightness of his mind. *Everyone against me, conspiring.*

'Stand at attention!' he commanded.

Fowler hardly heard him. There flashed through his mind a

montage of all the tools of violence he had in his time endured. Edge grabbed him. Fowler easily wrenched free. He reached the door aft and in that instant turning to see who followed him, he spied Austen behind the executive officer, his eyes sad and supplicating.

Theah, now, Fowler thought brokenly, don' git to feelin' sad fo' the likes o' me, suh. Ah seen wuss times an' wuss places.

The executive officer reached for the bulkhead phone. His lined face was haggard. His lip corners twitched and he breathed noisily.

Edge sat on the deck. His face was basted in a sauce of blood and tears. His brutish fingers caressed the wreck of his model engine. His eyes had an unfocused look.

Austen stood in the doorway where Fowler had seen him. His fingers were taut on the pale green coaming. He knew if he could hold himself in control now everything would be all right.

Fowler glided past the pantry hatchway. His fellow stewards watched him in fear. Their eyes shifted to blank unrecognition as he passed them. He moved through crew's quarters, through the confusion of idly sitting, sleeping, smoking men. At any moment he expected the strong clap of hands laid on him.

He neared the scarred topside hatchway furthest aft on the main deck. The poison of rage was out of him now. Caution alone remained. Grey daylight showed above. A near-by squawk box crackled. Fowler paused, warily listening. He leaned against a bulkhead, hiding the arm Edge had struck, hoping the dark wet stain against his white jacket would not draw attention.

'Now hear this ! Master-at-arms report to the executive officer in the wardroom ! On the double !'

Two seamen sat on a rumpled bunk playing acey-deucey. An engineer wearing a blue shirt and an oil-soiled khaki cap stood legs apart, drinking coffee, and stared with occupational sullenness at nothing. The men ignored Fowler. An officer clattered down the ladder and passed close by him.

Fowler climbed the ladder to the weather deck. The wind whipped across the port quarter eddying razor-thin sheets of spray out of the fog. He gripped the torpedo tubes for support, his eyes fixed on the men who were waiting on the catapult deck for the plane to return.

Tater pie, he thought sadly. Cooling on the shelf.

He suddenly realized that his white mess jacket made a bright blob against the ship's dark battle paint. He stripped it from his shoulders and slid it between the tubes. The spray slashed at his naked bluish waist and he shivered.

He went aft through the gun room of the after main battery where Shapiro and Kracowski had fought. The watch crew was going through the motions of a drill. The dummy shells rolled on the trays. The rammers engaged them and sped them into the breech and whipped back and sent the powder bags hurtling after them. The plugs whammed home. The ready lights flicked on. The turret officer droned the monotonous litany of orders. No one looked at Fowler.

He went up the ladder like a cat. He sidled along the narrow ledge of the ready service room. Above him the watch crew on the twenty-millimetre guns huddled in the lee of Battle Two and talked about women. Fowler carefully undogged the metal door to the ready service room, grateful for the keening wind. He dogged the door and waited for his eyes to adjust to the darkness within.

He squatted among the racks of loaded twenty-millimetre magazines. He found some clean rags and wiped the blood from his arm and dried his body. The cold air seeped through to his naked waist. He pummelled himself to keep warm. He wondered how long it would take them to find him here.

Commander Blanchard and an attendant were treating the bruise on Edge's face. Edge sat quietly. He doggedly refused to let go of his model engine. He stroked it and talked to it.

The executive officer sat at one of the wardroom tables drumming his fingers and waiting for the master-at-arms. Austen came in, buttoning the collar of his rain gear. The executive officer stared at him coldly.

'Where are *you* going?'

'My battle station, sir.'

'You're under hack, you know.'

'The captain said for the gunnery department to go to battle stations. Isn't that the same as general quarters?'

He stood there, feeling uncertain. The executive officer did not look up. The master-at-arms appeared in the hatchway. He was a burly petty officer with a face like a chopping block. He wore a service Colt. A set of shiny handcuffs hung from his web belt.

'Call for me, Commander?'

'Come in here, please.'

The master-at-arms came in. He looked at Edge and turned his head away.

'A steward named Fowler,' the executive officer said.

'Yes, sir?'

'Find him and throw him in the brig.'

'Fowler. Aye, Commander.'

'You'll have to search the ship.'

'Aye, sir.'

'He's vicious and he may be armed.'

'Aye, sir.'

'Report to me as soon as you take him.' He waved his fingers. 'That is all.'

The master-at-arms saluted and left. Austen could hear him scurrying up the ladder, handcuffs jangling like castanets. Poor Fowler, he thought.

He turned to the executive officer, who was idly stirring his coffee.

'May I go to my guns now, Commander?'

The executive officer stared at him vacantly for a moment. 'What are you waiting for? The captain called your crews away ten minutes ago.'

Blanchard winked as Austen passed him. Austen took a good look at Mike Edge's face. He had never seen a face, he decided, on which blood could have looked better.

He went topside to his battle station and climbed over the shield into the director tub. He strapped on his battle helmet. Frenchy Shapiro unlocked the mount from its zero position and cut in the power to the director. Austen gripped the control bars, feeling the vibration as the big mount shivered.

'You're late, Boss.'

'Manned and ready yet?'

'All except Ski.'

'Ready rooms manned and ready?'

'Yes, sir.'

Austen called over his shoulder to the officer in charge of the twenty-millimetre gun crews. 'Gillies!'

'Yes, sir?' He was an ensign. His narrow face looked puny under the oversized Mark II helmet.

'Your guns manned and ready?'

'Manned and ready, sir.'

'Ready rooms?'

'I'll check.' He talked into his radio phone. 'Yes, sir. Brown and Trotter, sir.'

'Okay.' He turned to Frenchy Shapiro. 'What's with Ski?'

'He had the midwatch.'

'So did a lot of others. He's holding us up.'

'I sent Salvio after him.'

Kracowski's close-cropped head appeared over the rim of the shield. He seemed in no hurry. Salvio pushed him from below. Austen signalled the phone talker.

'Report to control. Manned and ready.'

The talker pushed the speaking button. 'Control from machine guns aft. All guns manned and ready.'

'Put on your helmet, Ski,' Austen said.

'It hurts my head, sir.'

'Put it on, damn it.' Kracowski pushed a helmet over his eyes. The chin straps dangled. He took his station on the mount.

'Where the hell you been, Ski?' Frenchy said.

'In my sack. Can't a guy sleep?'

'You were sleeping all right. They passed the Word.'

'I didn't hear nothing. The damned master-at-arms woke me looking for some nigger from the wardroom.'

Austen called down. 'You're a man shy. Who's missing?'

'Slobodj, Boss. He's in the brig.'

'I forgot about him. Okay.'

'The master-at-arms come through twice looking for this here steward mate,' the trainer said.

'I heard nothing,' Kracowski said. 'No bells, nothing.'

'There was no bell. The captain himself passed the Word.'

'Who you kidding?'

'The captain himself. Tell him, Frenchy.'

'That's right, Ski. The skipper himself on the squawk box.'

'How fancy can we get? The skipper on the squawk box passing the Word.'

'This is special.'

'What's so special about this?'

'The plane ain't back. Also the Japs know we're here.'

'Hell, they knew we was here months ago.'

'Now they really know. Some nutty radioman bust radio silence. He thought he heard Mr. Johnson's plane and he opened up.'

'These guys kidding me, Mr. Austen?'

'No, Ski.'

'And me sacked out!'

'It happened no more than ten minutes ago.'

'Maybe we'll have some action, huh?'

'I seen some of them dispatches from the decoding room. It says a powerful task force in the Aleutians has the Jap fleet bottled up and the garrisons on Attu and Kiska starving to death.'

'That's us? A powerful task force?' Kracowski snorted. 'Listen, was I to see one of them streamlined Jap cruisers within a hundred miles I'd take off like there was a fireball in my pants.'

'Knock it off down there,' Austen said sharply.

The men fell silent. The ship rolled in the grey sea.

'Keep a sharp lookout on all bearings, Frenchy,' Austen called out. 'Pass the Word along.'

'Okay, Boss. You guys hear that?'

The phone talker signalled for quiet and listened. 'Machine guns aft, aye,' he said into the mouthpiece. 'Aye, sir.' He turned to Austen. 'Bridge reports radar back in commission. Screen is clear.'

'Very well.' He called below. 'Stand easy down there, Frenchy.'

Ensign Gillies came over. The lengths of rubber phone wire trailed after him.

'That's a help,' he said. 'How much longer do you think Johnson has?'

'Dave Clough figured half an hour.' He looked at his watch. 'That was almost half an hour ago.'

'They say that kid Gray is off his rocker.'

'I guess so.'

'They say he's queer.'

Austen felt his stomach turn over. 'Nonsense,' he said.

'I got it straight from Edge.'

'And that makes him queer.' He stared at Gillies with faint horror. Gillies stood awkwardly for a few moments, then returned to his guns. The men on Austen's forty watched him go.

'Hear what that chicken ensign said? Gray's a pogue.'

'Not that kid. He's psycho. They'll ship him home fast,' a loader named Kelly said.

'Wish to hell they'd ship me home. I'm sick of this life.'

'Go see the doc. He'll fix you a dose of saltpetre.'

'He give me a slug of whisky once, the doc. did.'

'He's four-oh, that guy. Right, Boss?'

'Right, Frenchy.'

'Smart, too. Too smart for the Navy.'

'He's in it, ain't he? Is that so smart?' Kracowski sneered.

'How come, Boss? A brain like that?'

'I don't know, Frenchy.'

'All he ever sees here is cat fever and spick itch and the clap.'

'Big deal.'

'But a real gent. An officer and a gentleman.'

'Yeah. Like the exec.'

'Him? Ice water for blood and his eyes like froze snot.'

'An officer and a gentleman. Looka Mike Edge.'

'You look. He makes me nauseous.'

'That nigger they're looking for, he's the one slugged Edge.'

'He should get a medal.'

'You know what he'll get, don't you?'

'Poor bastard better start praying.'

A loader named Willis, a slim, quiet man, said, 'How come they don't have chaplains on cruisers, Mr. Austen?'

'I don't know.' The simple question startled him.

'What's wrong, Willis?' Kracowski taunted. 'No guts?'

'Lay off, Ski,' Frenchy said sharply.

'You'd think every ship'd have at least one,' Willis said.

'A-a-h,' Kracowski said, 'next thing you'll be wanting stain-glass windows in the head.'

'Wipe it, Ski.'

'Wipe his. He needs it.'

'Okay, wise guy. Why ain't we got a chaplain like on other ships?'

'How the hell should I know? My name ain't Nimitz.'

'My brother is on the *Lexington*,' Willis said. 'They got two chaplains.'

'Them flat-tops got everything. Steak. Milk. Now two chaplains.'

'One Catholic and one the other kind.'

'How about that, Mr. Austen? Don't we rate?'

'I guess not.'

'Just one chaplain. Any kind,' Willis said. 'That ain't asking for too much.'

No one said anything after that. They searched the sea. The minutes passed.

Homer Fowler crouched in the cold, damp ready room and heard the gun crews take their stations. No more guns for Homer Fowler, he thought sadly.

He remembered his childhood in the Florida scrub. He remembered the warm-bodied hound dogs and giddy-sweet frying smells. The cow that calved and devoured the afterbirth (remembering its bloodied mouth). His own mallard drake, give by Mister Cluny up to the big white house (remembering the brown-flecked hens nuzzling the soft earth for worms after a cloudburst).

And as a young man, the steel mill in Alabama (remembering ol' Lessie Groves, who taught him puddling, fainting and falling into the vat). When they buried him they had to bury a ton block of cooled steel to be sure some of it was ol' Lessie.

So he quit the mills for Chicago and school at night (remembering the spiritual he wrote when they told him his father was dead of snakebite in the old seedling grove).

> *Got to get in tutch with the Lord*
> *Afore it too late.*
> *Got to get in tutch with the Lord*
> *At the golden gate.*

Remembering machine shops and drill presses and the sweet, oily smell of steel filings. In Chicago, the welcoming warm city, where the touch of lovely steel in the grimy shops meant a piece of ol' Lessie Groves to his finger-tips.

Now no more guns, he remembered, bereaved.

He stiffened, hearing the door handle turn. Let 'em come, he thought. Git it done with.

The grey light of day filtered in. He recognized the voices of Brown and Trotter. His colour. The tight breath oozed out of him. Trotter saw his face and stumbled backwards.

'Christ a-mighty!'

'Easy, Trots. It's me, Homer Fowler.'

Brown cursed softly. 'What you doing, man? Like to scare us to death.'

'Just talk quiet, Brownie.'

'Damn fool thing you done. What get in you to do a fool thing like that?'

Fowler moved closer. 'That door have to stay open?'

'It do for general quarters.'

'Can't you find another hiding-out place but here?' Brown whined.

Heavy steps clattered on the ladder outside. Fowler's hand covered Brown's mouth. He faded toward the darkest corner of the compartment. He ducked down.

The master-at-arms poked his face through the opening. He saw Brown and Trotter and his hand reached cautiously for the butt of his pistol.

'Sound off, you two.'

They stood for a moment too frightened to speak. The pistol waved at them menacingly.

'Elmo Brown, steward's mate first.'

'John Byrne Trotter, steward's mate second.'

'Which one of you's Fowler?   Come on, now.'

'None of us, sir.'

He glared at them.   The pistol slid into its holster.   'Either of you seen him around?'

They shook their heads.   The master-at-arms retreated, cursing, and went up the ladder.   Brown and Trotter did not move.

Fowler crept forward and touched them.   'Thanks, boys,' he said.

They moved away from him.   'Nothing but trouble coming,' Brown said bitterly.

'For me, Brownie,' Fowler said softly, 'only for me.'

The master-at-arms climbed over the splinter shield and threw a loose salute at Austen.

'Seen anything of a steward's mate name of Fowler, Lieutenant?'

'Not around here.'

'You heard what he did, sir?'

'I saw it.'

'A crazy damn thing.   A nigger striking an officer.'

'He's not here,' Austen said.

'He wouldn't be one of them two in the ready room, would he? I can't tell one burr head from another.'

'I told you he's not here.'

The phone talker waved excitedly.   'Machine guns, aye!' he said into the mouthpiece.   He touched Austen.   'Bridge to all guns.   Radar contact.'

Austen shouted to the men on the gun mount.   They tumbled to their stations.   'Air or surface?'

The talker pointed skyward.   He was listening intently.   The words rasped from his mouth.

'Plane bearing one-seven-five relative, distance nine thousand yards, closing.'

The men at the guns strained their eyes against the fog.   A calmness had enveloped Austen.   His eyes spot-checked the men at their posts.   Frenchy moved among them checking the dials and levers.   The fog drifted over the ship in woolly opaque patches, showing an occasional vagrant strip of grey sky.

'Take over the director, Frenchy,' Austen said.

'Aye, sir.'

'Maybe I can do some good with these glasses. The fog's got holes in it.'

Frenchy climbed into the director tub and took over the control bars. He peered through the lighted reticule of the Mark XIV sight.

'All set, sir. She's in automatic.'

'Load and stand by.'

'Aye, sir.'

The clips slammed into the receivers. The loaders swung up fresh clips and reached for more from the racks inside the splinter shield.

'A sharp eye, lookouts, on all bearings,' Austen shouted.

'Range closing to seven thousand yards, sir. Bearing one-eight-zero.'

The gun mount jerked, meeting the new bearing. The flared tip of the flash guard at the barrel's mouth quivered. The solenoid hummed. The men watched tensely.

'I hear a motor,' Frenchy said. He was leaning forward. His raw-knuckled hands tightly gripped the control arms. His leg muscles arched the heavy blue cloth at his calves and his tough face looked strained. Sweat and salt spray gleamed on his cheeks.

Austen made a sweep through his binoculars from dead astern to starboard. He searched each sector carefully. He saw nothing.

'Range, five thousand. Bearing, no change.'

'Come on,' Frenchy muttered softly, 'come on, baby.' His fingers tapped a rhythm on the controls. His left thumb pointed stiffly away from the firing key.

One of the lookouts screamed. 'There he is!' He pointed and Austen followed with his binoculars.

'Still on him?'

'Lost him, sir. He was there just for a second—*There he comes!* Head on.'

'Can you make him out?'

'He's awful blurry. Got floats, I think.'

'Is it us or them?' Frenchy asked.

'Hard to tell.' He relaxed. 'Don't see it now.'

'Okay,' Austen said. 'Talker, report to the bridge. Plane

sighted, range closing, bearing one-eight-zero. Possible float-type but cannot identify.' He continued to search the sky astern.

'Bridge acknowledges, sir.'

'Very well.'

'They say radar has lost contact.'

'The plane's too close in.'

'Maybe radar's fouled up again,' Frenchy said.

'Bridge says to open fire if you positively identify it as enemy.'

'Nice of them.' Austen tapped Shapiro. 'Don't get trigger-happy, Frenchy. Not a round gets fired until I give the word. It can be our plane as well as theirs.'

In the ready room Fowler heard the excitement. He stood concealed inside the open door, inhaling the sharp cold air and listening. His eyes glittered with pleasure. Trotter called to him softly.

'Better git back in here, Homer, or they find you for sure.'

Fowler ignored him. He slid along the bulkhead and out of the doorway. The chill wind struck his naked waist. He pressed his body against the cold, wet side of the ready room and stared into the grey sky. Above him, one of Gillies's lookouts screamed and pointed.

'It's got floats. I can see it!'

'One or two?' Austen shouted to him. He still searched through his glasses and suddenly the plane came into view. It seemed almost immobile, drifting hazily through the patches of fog. In a brief instant of open sky he spied the single central float of Johnson's plane.

Behind him a man shouted. 'Twin floats! It's a Zero!' He heard his own voice screaming louder than the others, and then he heard the deafening chatter of one of the twenty-millimetre guns. It fired ten bursts and jammed. Another gunner, nervous and frightened, opened fire.

'No!' Austen screamed against the gun chatter. 'No! No, No, No!'

Fowler had been climbing to the gun deck. The suddenness of the burst sent him sprawling, thinking, *Man! That's my gun! Wait for me! Wait for Homer Fowler!* The explosions were shouts of welcome sweet as a spiritual to his ears.

He whirled catlike, regaining his feet. His eyes followed the rapid bursts in the overcast. He saw the plane through the thin, drifting fog.

Austen still screamed. 'Hold your fire! Damn it, Gillies, stop that man!'

The gunner was trying to unload the jammed magazine as Fowler bounded across the deck. He thrust the dazed man from the slings and took hold and nested his shoulders against the rubber pads and braced himself. His eye found the metal ring sight. He swung the muzzle skyward to the plane. He tracked it smoothly, leading slightly, and closed his hand on the firing circuit. The bullets rippled away.

Ah, he thought. Like little bitty birthday candles.

He fired in three eloquent and deadly bursts. In the cold silence that followed, the others, appalled, watched the plane. It seemed to swallow the graceful arching bullets as they reached its shining sides. It did not falter. It drove toward the ship, diffused by a soft red glow and fell into the sea a scant thousand yards astern. The waves took it and rolled over it and it slowly began to sink.

Austen's words had drifted soundlessly in the wind, lost against the violent chatter of the guns. He leaped over the splinter shield, but it was too late. He watched with the others, stunned, as the plane disappeared.

Fowler slipped free of the sling. 'Shot him dead!' he shouted. 'Stone dead into the sea!'

He whirled in a gesture of absolute ecstasy. Austen reached for him. Fowler took Austen's shoulders in his big hands and embraced him.

'Done it, Mr. Austen! Shot me a Zero!'

The men watched in dumb-eyed silence. Phones crackled. Orders raged through the ship. None of the men saw or heard anything but Fowler. Austen tried to hold him.

The master-at-arms came running, breathing curses.

'I'm afraid you'll have to help me,' Austen said.

'Hell, yes.'

The master-at-arms raised the flat of the pistol and smashed it against the side of Fowler's surprised face. He dropped senseless

and instantly bleeding to the deck. The fixed look of surprise
turned crimson.

'Oh, God,' Austen said.

The sea around them churned as the ship changed course. The
sky appeared flat and empty. Some of the men turned away.
A man laughed harshly and another man prayed.

One of the destroyers had swung about and was racing to the
spot where a Franklin buoy bobbed at the scene of the crash. Its
flickering light offered a thin ray of hope.

Austen looked at Fowler and then at the man who had struck
him down.

'You shouldn't have done that,' he said wearily.

16

AUSTEN lay in his foul-smelling littered cabin and smoked a
cigarette. He had helped them carry Fowler to sick bay.
Instead of returning to his battle station he had retired. The raw
image of Fowler's smashed face, slack, purpled lips, and senseless
bloodied eyes persisted.

I'm here if they want me, he thought.

The narrow bunk heaved as the ship pitched. Looking for
Johnny, he thought. What was it Frenchy always said? *Gurnisht
helfen.* Twenty minutes was all a man could take in the icy
Bering Sea. He looked at his watch. Thirty minutes since the
crash. Sweet of them, he thought. Let's get the hell out of here.

The side of the sea smashed against the side of the ship. Loose
gear slid crashing against the bulkhead. Broadside and wallowing,
he thought, gripping the chains as his body arched from the bunk.
Incredible that water can make a sound like that. Plain water with
a little salt in it. The sea. Tears. That was it, all right. Tears
for the boys on the bottom of the sea. Like Johnny.

The biggest cemetery in the world, he thought.

Ah, the hell with it. Right this minute on Guadal, in Africa, in Italy, men are dying and dead, blood-red and rotting. Why cry for Johnny? Because I know his face? Hell. There are millions of faces and they all look like Johnny. The hell with sentiment. Sentiment's for the birds.

'Then what the hell are you crying for, Austen?' he said.

A sailor poked his head through the curtain.

'Lieutenant Austen?'

He sat up, startled. 'Yes?'

'Sorry, sir.'

'Come in.'

'I thought someone was with you, sir. Commander Blanchard would like to see you in his cabin.'

He got up and zipped his jacket. Fowler, he thought. Dead, probably. Dead is becoming a dull word, he thought. He put on his cap. It was sticky. He wiped some blood from the visor.

The messenger was waiting for him in the passageway.

'Anything wrong?' Austen asked.

'No, sir.' He grinned a little. 'They picked up Howards.'

'Howards?'

'The radio-gunner. One of the cans picked him up a few minutes ago. They put it out over the TBS.'

'Glad to hear it.' He did not ask about Johnson. There was no need to.

'They say one of them tin-can sailors went over the side to secure a line to Howards so they could take him aboard. In that cold water.'

'I'm glad.' They stopped in front of Blanchard's door.

'They never got Mr. Johnson. Howards was thrown clear, but they never even seen Mr. Johnson.'

'Okay,' Austen said. 'Thanks for getting me.'

He knocked on the door and heard the bottle clink. Blanchard let him in and locked the door and poured a drink into a paper cup.

'Joint's getting fancy,' he said, smiling. He held out the cup. Austen reached for it. His hand shook.

'Snap out of it,' Blanchard said.

'Sure. Just like that.'

'Drink your drink.'

Austen sat staring at it in his fingers. 'How's Fowler?'

'Don't worry about Fowler. Worry about yourself a little.'

'He didn't have to slam that .45 across Fowler's face like that. It wasn't what I meant at all.' He reached for the towel at the foot of Blanchard's bunk. Some of the whisky spilled. He wiped his eyes and then his trousers where the whisky spread a dark stain. 'It could have been anybody. Not just Fowler.'

'Sure. Now pour it down. It's what you need.'

Austen laughed shortly. 'What I need. Where I get off. What I mean.' He looked at Blanchard suddenly. 'Why cry for Johnny? He's gone. Cry for me. Cry for the poor bastards who weren't lucky enough to die.'

Blanchard held up his drink. '*L'chayim*,' he said.

'What's that?'

'Hebrew. Courtesy of your pal Shapiro.'

'Since when do you drink toasts with Frenchy Shapiro?'

'Since half an hour ago. He helped us with Fowler.'

'He's supposed to be at his battle station.'

'The captain dismissed the gunnery department from the guns about ten minutes ago.'

'Where was I?'

'Don't you know?'

'Sure I know. I was in my sack wishing I were dead.' He looked at Blanchard. 'Isn't that why you sent for me?'

'I thought you needed a drink. Now drink it, for Christ sake, before you spill it again.'

Austen tossed down the whisky and wiped his mouth.

'It's very good.'

'So were you when you were twelve years old.'

'Is that what you gave Frenchy?'

'Probably. I don't keep records. I often give enlisted men shots if I think they need it.'

'I figured Frenchy was something special.'

'On this ship everyone's special.' He poured another drink for both of them. 'Shapiro ever tell you about his family?'

'A little.' He looked at Blanchard guardedly.

'Then you know. Maybe you can learn a little from Frenchy.'

'Like what?'

'Like rolling with the punches.'

'You're really worried about me.'

Blanchard shrugged. 'Just try. Don't let these things get you down.'

'Like the thing with Fowler?'

'Like the thing with Fowler. Or anything else.'

'It wasn't his fault at all. He saw them shooting and he thought it was a Jap plane. A lot of the men did. It could have been anyone. It's just too bad it had to be him.'

'Right. Now down the hatch.'

'You're a cold-blooded old man with a hollow leg. Why are you being so good to me?'

'I'm not being good to you.'

'I'm a potential psycho, that's why. Isn't it?'

'Knock it off, Alec. Relax.'

'Why? Is the slow disintegration of the sensitive artist a little too much for you?' Some of the whisky spilled. 'I've a surprise for you, Dr. Freud. I'm okay. Four-oh. Here. Look at my cap. See the blood? Fowler's. While I was carrying him to sick bay. Is the sensitive artist collapsing? Not at all. Look at my hand.' He held out his hand. It shook a little. 'See? I can take it. I'm tough. Rock of Gibraltar.'

'Sure, Alec. You're fine.'

'It was just that thing with Fowler.'

'It could have happened to anyone.'

'Exactly. That was all. Poor bastard.' He drank the whisky and crumpled the paper cup and wiped his eyes. Blanchard was taking a long drink from the bottle.

'The way you drink,' Austen said.

'Never mind,' Blanchard said sharply. 'How do you feel now?'

'Better.' He grinned sheepishly.

'We're going in to see the exec.'

He ran some water into a fresh paper cup and took out a small phial and shook a few drops of a green liquid into the cup. 'Drink it down and let's go, Alec. We're late.'

'What is it?'

160

'For offensive breath. Don't want to be socially offensive, do you? The exec. would be very unhappy.'

Austen drank it slowly. It was tasteless. Blanchard mixed one for himself and tossed it off. He grimaced at Austen.

'Secret of a great Navy career. Don't be socially undesirable.' He opened the door. Austen waited in the passageway while Blanchard locked it from the outside.

'Can I know why we're seeing the exec?'

'I can guess. He sent for the both of us. I thought you might need a bit of fortifying before you saw him.'

'Thank you. I did.'

'Just don't shoot off your mouth like you were doing in my cabin.'

They went down the passageway to the executive officer's cabin. Blanchard knocked on the door. 'Just let me do the talking,' he whispered.

Austen nodded. He blew his breath into his palm and sniffed. There was no odour of the liquor he had drunk.

The doctor's dilemma undilemmed, he thought.

The executive officer was sitting at his desk surrounded by the clinical neatness of his room.

'Be with you gentlemen in a moment.' He frowned at his watch. He was writing carefully. Austen could see it was the plan for the next day. He stared at the balding head bent over the desk. The sparse grey hairs lay in dank strings across its round shiny surface.

The executive officer finished writing and closed the lid of his desk.

'Now, then,' he said, 'what delayed you, Dr. Blanchard?'

'I came as soon as I could, Commander.'

'I sent for you and Mr. Austen almost fifteen minutes ago.'

'Yes, sir.'

'Would you sit, please, while I take up Mr. Austen's situation?'

'Thank you.'

'Now, then, Mr. Austen, it seems to me you and I are in constant disagreement over certain matters. I will be brief and to the point. Your conduct, your judgment, your flagrant defiance of Navy regulations force me to take steps . . .'

Yackety-yack, Austen thought. The whisky was warm and brave inside him. Here I am back in Godfrey Clemson's posh office, listening to the same old crap. The exec. and Clemson, he thought. Two guys to fight a war for.

'. . . . you are not capable of handling the responsibilities of a Navy officer. I should have known better than to release you from hack. I should——'

'I'd like to know what I've done this time.'

'Certainly. Would you please tell us why you deserted your battle station?'

'I didn't desert it. I helped carry Fowler to sick bay.'

'Your gun crew was still presumed to be at general quarters.'

'I assumed the emergency was over when the plane crashed.'

'That was your considered opinion?'

'It was what I thought at the time.'

'You exhibited poor judgment. In the Navy an emergency exists as long as command deems it to exist and not according to the whims and sentiments of junior officers. No word was passed to secure from general quarters.'

'Okay, I'm a deserter. Shoot me.'

The executive officer smashed his fist against the desk. 'I will not have insolence and flippancy from you,' he screamed. His lips were grey and his fingers trembled.

'I'm a little weary of being abused,' Austen said.

'Sir,' the executive officer said.

'Oh, nuts.' He ignored Blanchard's warning glance.

The executive officer stood up. 'Dereliction of duty is a court-martial offence, Mr. Austen. And if it weren't enough to hang on you, I'd have plenty more right here. Placing you under hack seems hardly adequate punishment. You leave me no choice.'

'Anything you say, Commander.'

The bone-grey face stiffened. 'I say this: You're not going to make a vacation cruise out of this hack time if I can help it. You're going back in the watch section, Mr. Austen, where I can keep an eye on you.'

'Aye, sir.'

'The captain has just requested the heads of departments to stand the night O.D. watches. You will stand the watch as my junior officer, Mr. Austen. Perhaps you will learn a little about the Navy.'

'Perhaps.'

'Sir.'

Austen shrugged. 'Okay. Sir.'

The executive officer consulted the watch bill on his desk. 'That will be the morning watch, 0400 to 0800. Is that clear?'

'Yes, sir.'

'It should prove quite educational, Mr. Austen.' For a moment his eyes gleamed. 'That will be all.'

'Excuse me, Commander,' Blanchard said. The executive officer stared at him. 'It's my fault Mr. Austen left his station.'

'How do you figure that?'

'I personally requested that he bring Fowler to sick bay with the attendants.'

'Why do a thing like that, Dr. Blanchard?'

'To avoid any violence. There was considerable feeling against Fowler after what happened. The presence of an officer *en route* seemed a good idea.'

'It still does not allow an officer to leave his battle station.' He pursed his lips. 'Why didn't Mr. Austen return to his guns instead of to his quarters?'

'When I saw him in sick bay he seemed upset and disturbed by what had happened. The Word was being passed to secure from gunnery stations anyway. So I told him to sack out.'

'Why didn't you tell me this, Mr. Austen?'

'What difference would it have made?' Austen said.

The executive officer studied his finger tips. 'None, probably. Many officers and men in the ship are upset and disturbed. They are standing their watches and carrying out their duties. I see no reason to make an exception in Mr. Austen's case.'

'Are you telling me how to run this ship's medical department, Commander?'

The executive officer reddened. 'He looks perfectly healthy to me. How do you feel, Mr. Austen?'

'Terrible.'

'I still insist on making my diagnoses without the help of anyone else,' Blanchard said evenly.

'I think you can go now, Mr. Austen,' the executive officer said. 'We still have the early morning watch.' He coughed dryly and a ghost of a smile touched his lips. 'I will be looking forward to it.'

Austen went out of the room. He stood in the passageway for a few moments. The whisky still warmed him and Blanchard's generous lie somehow calmed him.

He went to his room. Clough was snoring unevenly. Austen loosened his tie and stretched out on his bunk and almost instantly slept.

Blanchard lit a cigarette and watched the executive officer go through the motions of tidying up his perfectly ordered room.

'What have you got against the boy, Commander?' he asked.

'What boy?'

'Austen.'

'Got against him?'

'You've been riding him hard since we left Adak.'

The executive officer's back was to Blanchard. He ran a bony finger along the ledge of the bunk.

'Dust,' he said, studying his finger tip.

Blanchard watched him with half-closed eyes.

'You might take it easier on the men,' he said softly. 'A lot of them are feeling the strain.'

'Will you tell me something?' the executive officer said. 'Will you tell me why a steward's mate cannot keep a room clean? I've told that boy three times to-day there's dust in my room. Look.' He held out his finger for Blanchard to see.

'Yes,' Blanchard said, thinking of Gray, 'I see what you mean.'

Will you remind me to speak to the chief steward's mate when we are through here, please?'

'Certainly.'

He wiped the dust from his finger. 'Now, then. Two things, Commander Blanchard. First the matter of radioman Gray.'

'Oh yes. Gray.'

'You have transferred him from the brig to sick bay.'

'That is right, Commander.'

'Why? I was not consulted. No permission was granted.'

'The request is right there on your desk, stamped "URGENT: MEDICAL," in case you haven't seen it.'

'Worthless, Commander Blanchard. It needs the commanding officer's endorsement.'

'Matter of routine. The captain has always approved my decisions regarding sick personnel.'

'It is my intention to forward the request to the captain with a note saying Gray's transfer from the brig should not be approved.'

'Why? He's ill. He belongs in sick bay, not in the brig.'

'He's committed a rash and dangerous act, Doctor, seriously violating the ship's security. He belongs in the brig under guard and that's where he's going to be. No telling what he'll do next. He's out of his mind.'

'That's why he's in sick bay, Commander.'

'I will not tolerate any further coddling of the crew. Gray is going to be punished.'

'Hasn't he been punished enough?' He looked for an ash tray. There was none in the room. He tapped the ash into his cupped palm.

'Have you finished with Fowler, Dr. Blanchard?'

Blanchard nodded. 'He's got a hard head. That blow'd have killed an ox.'

'He goes to the brig, you know.'

'I suppose so. That's a somewhat different matter, of course.' He shrugged. 'He's patched up and in fair enough shape.'

'I'll send the master-at-arms for him.'

'That's the goon who should go to the brig.'

'He was obeying orders,' the executive officer said coldly.

'I suppose so.'

'Which brings up the second matter. I would like your department to prepare a medical report on Lieutenant Austen.'

'On Austen? There's probably one in the files.'

'I don't mean that, and you know very well what I mean.'

'I'm afraid I don't.'

'I want an immediate and thorough report on his present condition.'

'You said yourself he looks healthy, Commander.'

'I mean his mental condition.'

'Well,' Blanchard said slowly, 'we're pretty busy right now. Sick bay's loaded with seasick cases. There's that boy, Gray, and a couple of other bed cases, one possible appendicectomy and three severe cases of spick itch——'

'An inventory isn't necessary, Doctor. I have the daily sick list. Simply prepare a report on Austen's mental condition. I intend to append my own views. Is that clear?'

'Very clear. But I'd rather not do it at this time.'

'Why not?'

'I feel that any such report at this time would not give a normal picture of his condition—or anyone's condition.'

'Doctor, as second-in-command of this vessel, I have certain duties and responsibilities and the chief one is the welfare of the officers and men and I insist——'

'I'm not questioning your authority, Commander. Such a report could be very damaging later on.'

'From observing Mr. Austen's attitude, I should think it wouldn't make a damned bit of difference to him.'

'That proves my point. I believe he's normally loyal and conscientious. I've watched him these past few weeks. He's sensitive and possibly more deeply affected by what's been happening than we realize. His crewman, Loomis, then Johnson, and the business with Fowler are all tragic experiences and he feels them deeply.'

'Go on,' the executive officer said.

'And like the rest of the men, he's suffering fatigue. But I do believe he's carrying out his duties and from what I hear, Dooley's as well——'

'Duties are my concern, Doctor. Confine your remarks to the condition of Mr. Austen's health.'

'He's in excellent health.'

'Please, this is not the time for levity.'

'Why do you pick on Austen?'

'I am carrying out my duties as I see fit.'

'Do you suppose if I turned in an official report on him I'd make him anything but normal? I'd do as much for any man on board right now.'

'I would expect you, as a full commander of the medical corps, to submit a thoroughly unbiased and completely honest report. I would expect the same from the lowest seaman second.'

'And when do you want this report?'

'As soon as possible. I have certain recommendations to make to Captain Meredith. A medical report will be essential.' He opened his desk. 'Now if you please, Commander Blanchard. I have work to do.'

'Nothing more to discuss with me?'

'Not at the moment.'

Blanchard tapped another half-inch of ash into his cupped palm. 'There is the matter of me reminding you to call the chief steward's mate.'

'Of course. Thank you.'

'About the dust.'

'Yes, I remember now. If that is all——'

'Doesn't it seem a little peculiar to you, Commander?'

'What do you mean?'

'I mean the dust.'

'What about the dust?' He frowned. 'Please be explicit.'

'It's very important, the dust. Mind if I sit down?'

'I've work to do, as I explained——'

'You sit down, too. I've something to discuss with you.'

'Something of an official nature?'

'In a way, yes.'

'I really believe——'

'For Christ sake, sit down,' Blanchard said.

The executive officer sat slowly on the edge of his tightly made bunk. His eyes shifted from Blanchard's face to the corners of the lifeless room. His lips were pinched in a thin, stubborn line.

'It's official,' Blanchard said, contemplating the small stock pile of ashes on his cupped palm. 'But off the record, of course.'

The dry lips barely moved. 'In the Navy nothing is off the record.'

'Then man to man.   You understand what that means, I hope?'

'You're wasting my time,' the executive officer said.

'That remains to be seen.'   He looked thoughtfully about the room.   'You mentioned the welfare of the men before.   Did you mean it?'

'Please, Doctor——' he began to say stiffly.

'Because I have never seen you give them a glad word.   A pat on the shoulder, a smile.   I've never witnessed an act of kindness from you in eighteen months.'

'I believe I know my duties, thank you.'

'Then it's about time you performed them with some regard for the men instead of for the damned rules and regulations.'

'If this is your official business . . . if this is what you have to say . . .'   His body sagged a little as Blanchard's cold professional eyes remained unmoving.   'Finish saying what you have to say, then.'   He played nervously with the metal buttons on his blouse.

'You're going to have to take things easier yourself,' Blanchard said earnestly.   'For your own sake as well as the crew's.'

'Why do you say that?'

'Because the strain is showing.   Badly.'

For a time the executive officer said nothing.   He sat with his fingers folded in his lap in absolute contemplation of the clean grey deck.   He made a faint derisive movement with his lips that was not a smile.

'This is the Navy.   We expect strain.   We're trained for it.'

'There are breaking points for all of us, Commander.   Maybe yours is higher than that of the crew.   You still can't expect them to match yours.'

'I expect duty and discipline to go beyond breaking points. That is standard procedure for every man in this ship.'

An angry flush diffused Blanchard's cheeks.   'In my opinion your treatment of Austen goes even further than that.   It bypasses duty and discipline and is based on personal hatred, pure and simple.   Is that standard procedure?'

'Don't be insulting, Doctor, just because I was kind enough——'

'Kind, my eye.   It's high time someone told you about yourself. You're jealous of Austen because through no fault of his own he's treated as a human being by the captain. Shocking, isn't it, to be told the truth? And galling to find such a thing as humaneness in your rank-conscious life.'

'I warn you, Blanchard——'

'*Commander* Blanchard, please. Let me warn you first. You're a sick man and the last place you should be is at sea with other men. Know why? You're loaded with fears—of disorder, of dirt. It's a mania, Commander. Ataxiophobia and mysophobia. Worse than that, you're a hater—God knows why. A psychopathic hater. You don't just plain hate—you get a bang out of it——'

'Stop it!'

He stood livid and shaking, and his eyes were pale with hatred. Blanchard regarded him coldly.

'Look at yourself in the mirror and see what I mean.'

The executive officer took a folded handkerchief from his pocket and wiped the corners of his mouth. Blanchard tapped a half inch of ash into his palm.

'I've heard all I care to hear,' the executive officer croaked.

'One more thing,' Blanchard said evenly. 'Because of this, the men hate you. Every man in every part of this ship hates your guts.'

'The men hate me?' He looked surprised. 'Why should they hate me?'

'Are you serious?'

'All I have ever done is my duty.'

'It's the kind of hate that breeds violence, Commander. So that any violence in this ship may very well be blamed on you.'

'Violence?' The expression of sheer pleasure in his blotched face struck terror in Blanchard's heart. 'Violence is our business, Doctor Blanchard. Had you forgotten? This is war . . .' The executive officer smiled lewdly.

Blanchard recognized almost instantly in that face the undeniable image of vile and shameless sensuality. Its presence was as unforgivable as sodomy in this ship of lonely men. He knew now there could never be a common ground between them. Whatever sympathy or humaneness he may have felt was swiftly erased by

169

the depraved words. They continued to pour from the wetted lips like juice from a burst fruit skin.

'—meddling in the affairs of the ship. I've heard enough. Let them hate. Hate is good for their souls. If they hate enough we'll never lose a war, we'll never——'

The swift flow of words stopped because Blanchard had dropped the ashes from his hand on to the clean deck. His cigarette followed. He ground it under his shoe tip and strode to the hatchway. In passing he noticed the executive officer's clawed fingers against the metal frame of the doorway. He looked down. The trim, almost delicate black shoe the executive officer wore rested on the coaming. The shoelace was untied.

It is as revealing of the martinet's disintegration, Blanchard stormily reflected, as his torrent of guilt-laden words. He went to his room and sought comfort once more in his bottle. He drank until the anguish was out of him.

Tell me about hate, he thought numbly. Just stand there and tell me.

The executive officer remained standing stiffly against the edge of the door frame. He heard the captain's Chamorro humming tunelessly across the passageway. Overhead warm air sucked through the blowers, carrying faint galley smells. He closed his door and locked it. He stood there and passed his hand several times over his red-rimmed eyes.

There should be no galley odours in the blower system, he thought irritably.

He went to his desk and took out the small black notebook and a pencil. He opened to a page on which the pencilled entries read, 'soiled necktie', 'insolence', 'silverware', 'grabbing', 'silent contempt', 'dust'. He crossed out the last entry and rewrote it 'DUST' and underlined it. Then he wrote down 'galley odours' and 'humming'.

He closed the book and returned it to its place inside the desk. He inserted the pencil into a sharpener and ground its fine point finer. He put the pencil in a drawer with other pencils, all finely sharpened, all pointing the same way.

He used a sheet of scrap paper to sweep up the debris of Blanchard's shredded cigarette butt. He recovered all of it and emptied it into the waste basket.

Then he washed his hands, scrubbing them vigorously and rinsing them many times. He shook the water from them as a surgeon might and wiped them thoroughly and folded the towel into a laundry bag that hung inside the steel wardrobe.

He smoothed the bedcover where he had been sitting and tucked the sides and tautened the hospital corners. He aligned the chair to parallel the desk. Then he looked about the room and nodded and washed his hands again.

He noticed the untied shoelace and frowned. He bent over and drew the laces tightly and tied the bow, arranging the ends so it was evenly balanced. He went to the bulkhead phone and called for the chief steward's mate and walked over to the mirror. He stood there a long time looking at the reflection of his homely expressionless face.

17

WHEN Blanchard could drink no more, he locked his room and went below to Austen's quarters. Both Austen and Clough were asleep. He left them and started along the passageway. He glanced into the small compartment on the other side. Mike Edge lay sprawled across his bunk.

'Hi, Doc.'

'How's the face feel?'

'Lousy. It's still swelled up.'

'Keep applying those wet towels.'

'It hurts like hell. When I talk it's murder.'

'Don't talk so much. The swelling will go down.'

'They got the nigger finally. The MAA slugged him, I heard.'

'Yes.'

'It'd a been me I'd a used the other end of the .45.'

'Call sick bay if your face feels worse.'

'Did I show you what he done to my engine?' He sat up. The model engine was next to his pillow. He held it up.

'You can start all over again, Edge. Excellent therapy.'

'What?'

'You'll have it fixed in no time.'

'I spent months on it, Doc. It woulda run like a real gas engine.' He laid it aside and wiped his nose gingerly. 'If I ever lay hands on that bastard I'll kill him.'

'He's in trouble enough. He'll get a summary at least. Forget it.'

'But looka my engine, Doc. A wreck.'

'Chin up, Edge.'

The room smelled of Edge and it was too much. Blanchard left. He went to his own cabin and locked the door and got out the bottle. His mouth was dry again and his bones ached. He smiled wryly. He did not have too far to go for the cure, he thought. That's about all you could say for it.

18

THE long day ended.

From the wing bridge of the *Atlantis* the night orders were wigwagged to the destroyers. The men on watch moved about listlessly. The men below decks settled down uneasily for the night.

The grey light of day faded. The Word was passed to darken ship. Cigarettes were carefully extinguished at the topside watch stations. The ship's gaunt structure assumed its dark grey shape for the night. The single plane was perched on its catapult like a mourning bird of prey bereft of its mate. The four stacks shimmered amidships behind the transparent smoke. The giant tripod cluttered with the trappings of war reared skyward, laced with its filament of ladders and landings.

The security watch began its night vigil. Men roamed the length of the ship drawing blackout curtains, checking for light leaks, inspecting the damage-control equipment and dogging down the steel watertight doors.

On the bridge the deck watch checked the escorting destroyers as they proceeded to their assigned stations for the night patrol. The group formed up in scouting line, each ship hull down to the next, mast tips barely visible at the horizon.

The long night began.

19

HEARING the repeated knocking through the thinness of sleep, Austen awoke. Frenchy Shapiro stood in the curtained doorway.

'Come in, Frenchy.' Shapiro stepped in and Austen sat up. 'What time is it?'

'Twenny hundred. They just relieved the watch.'

'I must have crapped out.' He yawned.

'You missed chow, Boss. Wanna bite to eat?' He reached inside his blouse.

'Not that, please.' He swung his feet to the cold deck and shivered. 'I've got the damned four-to-eight on the bridge.'

'Hell, you got plenty time.'

'With the exec. as O.D.'

'You get all the breaks, don't you?'

'It was his idea, not mine. What's on your mind, Frenchy?'

'I need a favour off you, Boss.' He glanced anxiously at Clough, who slept in the upper bunk.

'He's out like a light. He's okay. Talk up.'

'If the answer is no, so it's no. No hard feelings——'

'Quit stalling, Frenchy. What's on your mind?'

'Also I'd wanna pay for it or it's no deal.'

'Pay for what?'

'The picture. If you'd draw me one of them pictures. A quickie, see? Nothing special.'

'What kind of picture?'

'Of me. Of my mug. But I wanna pay for it.' He dug a roll of bills from his pocket and shoved it at Austen. 'I know I'm outranked, Boss, you doing the skipper and all, but a fellow like you can always use a little extra dough.'

Austen looked at the thick roll of money. 'How much do you have there, anyway?'

'You mean you're gonna do it?' The anxiety left his face. He grinned widely and thrust the bills into Austen's hands. 'If this ain't enough I can get more. Just name the price.'

'Answer my question, will you? How much is here?'

'Three hundred and eight bucks. I can get another hundred in two minutes.'

'Where would you get it?'

'I got it.'

Austen rubbed his chin. 'Three hundred and eight dollars isn't a bad fee at all.' He studied Shapiro's eager face.

'You don't have to do it right now, Boss. So long as we make the next mail ship is okay.'

'Who's it for, Frenchy?'

His wide grin faded. 'It's something personal.'

'I'll make the sketch, but it will have to be under my conditions.'

'What's the conditions?'

'First condition: the fee. It's one buck. I'd do it for free, but I know from experience that when people pay for something they appreciate it. So it's going to cost you a buck.'

'Now look, Boss——'

'Second condition: I'd like to know who's getting it.'

Shapiro squirmed a little. 'Why do you have to know that?'

'It affects the kind of sketch I'd make. For a Frisco whore, I'd make you look handsome and salty——'

'It's for my kid, Edith.'

'I'm sorry, Frenchy.'

'I didn't want you should think I was getting soft in the head. I was a little ashamed to tell you.'

174

'I'm the one who's ashamed.' He opened the drawer under his bunk and took out a large portfolio and wiped the dust from it.

'Sit in that chair over there.' He opened a flat box in which the sticks of pastel lay like a broken rainbow.

'The kid's got a birthday coming up, see? And I got to thinking all these years she's growing up she has no idea what her old man looks like. I figured you'd fix up a sketch of me and she can be real proud.'

'Sure, Frenchy.'

'I'd like to pay that fee, like you said, Boss. I'd feel better. I don't want something for nothing. I never did.'

'Shut up and turn your head a little to the side.' He began sketching. 'One more condition. Don't go walking around the ship with three hundred-odd bucks in your pocket.'

'It's just from to-day's crap game.'

'Sure. And some nice night you'll find yourself with your throat slit and your empty wallet floating past the fantail.'

'They wouldn't try.'

'That's what they all think. Turn a little more to the right. There. That's good.'

'You drawing my nose sideways?'

'Profile, we call it in the art game.'

'It's not the best angle, Boss.'

'Why not? It's a very handsome nose.'

'Who you kidding? It's been busted twice.'

'Sit still.'

Austen worked rapidly. His fingers were stiff, but the touch of the pastel sticks felt fine. They seemed warm and smooth-textured. They felt like old friends.

'Would you call it a Jewish nose, Boss?'

'I'd call it a broken nose.'

'Ski's nose is bigger than mine. We measured the other day.'

'Is that all you guys can find to do?'

'That wasn't all we measured, either.' He cackled obscenely. 'And who do you think wins? Me or Ski? Like hell. Salvio he wins. That little runt, can you imagine him beating big guys like me and Ski?'

'Sit still, Casanova.'

He used a line technique, sometimes blurring the line with the heel of his hand. Where the naked overhead light cast the shadow of Frenchy's high cheekbone he accented the depth with green and lavender and blue. He caught the full thrust of the jaw in a single flat-edged stroke, the cynical turn of mouth with a sensitive gradating line of deep brownish red.

As he worked he lost sense of time and place. He saw in the street scars the mark of Roman whips. The lips were as thin and transparent as an ancient prayer shawl. The skin became a nomad's skin, toughened by years of desert sun. It was all there in the wise battered face that had looked on nothing but city streets and the sea.

Frenchy scratched his nose. 'All of a sudden it begins to itch.'

'Means you're going to have a fight.'

'It's about time, ain't it?'

'Sit still. I'm almost finished.'

Frenchy craned his neck. 'Can I have a look?'

'Sure. I'm faking in a little background.'

Frenchy came over and looked over Austen's shoulder.

'Jeez. Is that me?'

'It sure is. Like it?' Austen was wiping the colour from his fingers.

'It's terrific. It looks more like me than I do.' He stood there and studied the picture almost fearfully. 'I wish you'd take the dough for it, Boss. I'd feel better, I swear.'

'Forget it. I'm glad you like the sketch.'

'I don't want anything for nothing.'

'It's costing you one buck. That was the deal.'

'You may as well take it all. I'll only toss it away in a crap game or something.'

'Tell you what, Frenchy. When you send the picture to Edith, send along the dough.'

'The three hundred and eight bucks?'

'Three hundred and seven. One is mine.'

'Don't tell me what to do with my dough,' Frenchy said fiercely. He wiped his eyes with an angry thrust of his arm. 'If you take it for the sketch, okay. Otherwise, don't tell me what to do.'

'Okay, Frenchy.'

'Can I take the picture now?'

'I've got to blow some fixative on it so it won't smudge.'

'You want me to wait?'

'It'll just take a minute. Then it's all yours.'

Austen sprayed the sketch. Frenchy sat morosely and watched. His big chapped hands were clasped between his knees and his eyes were moist and still fierce.

'I'm sorry I blew my top, Boss.'

Austen examined the sketch to see how the fixative was drying. 'Okay, Frenchy. Forget it.'

'I don't like to be told what to do.'

'Nobody does.'

'How am I ever gonna mail a big thing like that?'

'Get a cardboard tube from one of the quartermasters. The kind they roll charts in. Then the sketch won't be wrinkled.'

He blew on the sketch to make sure it was dry. He handed it to Frenchy, who looked at it sheepishly.

'Thanks a million, Boss.'

'Never mind the thanks, wise guy. Fork over the buck.'

'Hell, I forgot all about the buck.' He caught the twinkle in Austen's eye. 'I was thinking of my Edith, so help me God. This is gonna make her awful happy.'

He peeled a dollar bill from the roll. Austen folded it and put it in his pocket. 'What are you waiting for? A receipt?'

Frenchy thrust the rest of the money into Austen's hands. 'Look, do me another favour. Send this to the kid for me, will you?'

'Why don't you do it yourself?'

'I got to make out a postal money order.'

'That's no big problem, is it?'

Frenchy looked uncomfortable. 'I'll tell you, Boss. The joker in the post office, that mail clerk, he's been in some of these crap games with me. Was he to see I'm sending home some money, he might raise hell.'

'Okay, Frenchy.' He took the money. 'Let me write out a receipt for it. Just in case.'

'Forget it. I'm glad to be rid of the responsibility. Money,' he said. 'I never told you about my old lady, did I?'

'You mean your wife—Babe?'

'Nah, not her. My old lady. My mother.' He leaned against the bulkhead. 'You got a few seconds? I ain't keeping you from sacking out or something?'

'No, Frenchy. I'm all charged up from the sketch.'

Frenchy took a bulky sandwich from inside his shirt and proffered it to Austen. Austen shook his head and lit a cigarette. Frenchy shrugged and bit into the sandwich.

'There's somebody can tell you about money and responsibilities from the word "Go". My old lady.' He chewed thoughtfully. 'She's a shrimp. A half-pint of a woman, maybe sixty-five, seventy, now. She's been running this candy store in Brownsville, Brooklyn, ever since my old man he should rest in peace dropped dead.

'He was always a sickly guy, my old man. A skinny little cocker but with plenty of guts. He was one of them emics, you know.'

'Emics?'

'Yeah. You never heard of them? My old man, he was an emic. People all over Brooklyn suffer from just such a disease. He drops dead one day right in synagogue. It's left for my mother to run the candy store. My sisters they were already married or bumming around Pitkin Avenue with the mob, they wouldn't raise a finger to help her.

'So she runs it herself, selling penny candy, malteds, seltzer water for two cents a glass. I tried to help her out a little, but in those days I was having my own *tsuris* with Babe and the bagel run. Also Babe used to get sore when I'd go over some nights to help out. For her running a candy store was too common.'

He paused and contemplated the half-eaten sandwich.

'Is your mother still alive?'

'You kidding? She'll outlive you and me both. What I was just thinking, talking like we were, why not go back? I mean when I finish this last hitch, not to ship over. The way I feel, I can take the responsibility off of her shoulders. She's getting old. Around that neighbourhood I'll bet they're gypping the pants off of her. Stealing, chiselling, hell, I know what goes on there. So maybe I can finish my hitch and go back and take over from the old lady. She's got a nice few rooms in back of the store I can live in. . . .'

He took a dispirited bite of the sandwich and chewed slowly. 'I must be nuts. I swear to God.'

'Not at all, Frenchy.'

'Soft in the head.' He looked at the money. 'I've half a mind——'

'No, Frenchy. You don't get the money back.'

Frenchy ate the remains of the sandwich. He wiped his hands carefully and rolled up the portrait. 'Maybe it's worth it. But I swear to God I must be nuts.'

'I like the idea of going home, Frenchy. I hope you do it.'

'On this ship who can tell what the hell he's gonna do next?' He started down the passageway. Austen watched him until he disappeared up the ladder. He went inside the room and lit another cigarette. He was too stirred now to sleep. He sorted the sticks of pastel and put them away and closed the portfolio and put it inside the drawer under his bunk.

Dave Clough awoke and watched him sleepily. He looked haggard. 'What in hell's making that smell?'

'Fixative. I was sketching.'

Clough wrinkled his nose. 'Don't go complaining about the stink in here any more. That stuff's worse.' He scratched his head. 'What time is it?'

'Around nine-thirty. Going some place?'

'Okay, wise guy. Somebody's got to fly the morning recon.'

'Think you'll make it?'

'I'll make it.'

'Okay, kid,' Austen said softly. 'Get some shut-eye then.'

You're going to need it, he thought as Clough turned over. He sat quietly smoking the cigarette and trying to understand how he had forgotten about Johnny so quickly. As though it had never happened. As though he had never known him.

It's the sea, he thought. Out here you're not alive and you're not dead. You're at sea.

He finished his cigarette and closed his eyes. Clough moaned in the bunk above him. He heard Mike Edge bellow angrily across the passageway.

Edge, Austen thought. It's his sea. I'm just borrowing it for a few years. Sometime soon he can have it back. All of it. Gladly.

He thought he would never fall asleep, but he did.

20

AFTER Blanchard left, Edge lay on his bunk caressing the wreck of his model engine. The day's events were vague, disturbing shadows in his dulled mind. His bitterness resolved on Austen.

Austen the artist, he thought sullenly. The feather merchant. The nigger lover. The goddamn toady, making up to the skipper for small favours. He placed the engine alongside the pillow and covered it.

The room seemed stuffy. His body perspired. He kicked savagely at the blanket. He lay back with his fingers locked under his head. He stared moodily at his thick hairy body, naked except for a pair of soiled skivvy shorts.

The mounds of muscle were gratifying to his eye. He knotted his fists and pummelled a swift tattoo across the ridges of his belly. He relaxed and tensed his shoulders, forcing pressure through his arms, making his breast muscles twitch. First one, then the other. Then both together.

It excited him. He smiled and the pain shot through the side of his bruised face. He cursed Austen and Fowler. His thick fingers groped for the engine.

Fondling it, he thought of lust, and the times he had known it. The ship heeled. He closed his eyes and submitted to the sensual heaving of the bunk, rising and falling gently with the roll of the ship.

His face relaxed. His mind dwelled on the *montage* of lustful images which congealed slowly and erotically into one recognizable white body.

It had now become familiar and desirable to him. Slim and hairless and the bones pliant and the torso yielding, it had insinuated itself in his thoughts. He was unable to escape it. It was the form of radioman Gray.

Behind the cloak of his lowered lids Edge conjured an image of himself. He was tall and calm and handsome in perfectly tailored dress blues (taller and calmer and handsomer than Austen, he thought happily). He pictured Gray's face radiant and sweetly smiling and no longer stricken with fear. His moist lips were parted and his insane blue eyes looked tenderly on Edge, filled with the love that Edge craved and never in his vulgar lifetime had known.

Edge lay in rapt enjoyment of the image until across the passageway Dave Clough moaned in sleep.

'Knock it off, goddamn it,' he shouted. 'Let a man sleep!'

The moans ceased. Edge twisted his mouth grotesquely, silently enjoying the knowledge of Clough's suffering.

Stinking trade-school zoomie, he thought. He squirmed, frowning, trying to recall the erotic image of radioman Gray. He touched the model engine. Its sides were cold and unyielding. He looked at his watch. Gray would be in the brig, he reckoned. Where he belonged.

His breathing became laboured as he contemplated it. The brig guards would be sacked out as usual. Gray would be sacked out, too. He would never know what hit him, the darling.

Serve the little pogue right. Serve him the hell right for doing what he did. Busting radio silence. Getting Johnny killed.

I'd be doing it for Johnny, Edge explained to himself. He fondled this new thought as he had fondled his pet engine.

And the nigger, he thought. He sat up. There is no sense in waiting. He'd take Gray and he'd take the nigger too. He clawed in the dark for the engine. This time the feel of it relaxed him. If he had a .45 he'd show 'em what he'd do to the nigger.

He lay back breathing heavily and soon he slept. His fingers were laced over the twisted metal. He awoke later, hearing voices across the passageway. He listened as the bridge messenger wakened Austen for his early morning watch.

He dressed quietly, his mind again cluttered with the shadowy images of Austen and Fowler and Gray.

I'll show 'em all, he thought. The hell with the .45. I'll show 'em with my bare hands.

He reached for a life jacket and went to the curtained doorway and peered out.

21

AUSTEN had slept without dreaming. He felt someone shaking him.

'It's three-thirty, sir. You got the watch.'

'Okay. I'm up.'

The messenger's voice droned mechanically. 'Wind's from dead ahead, sir. Twenty-three knots.' He moved to the curtained hatchway. Austen could see him, hazy against the murky red glow of the passageway battle lights. 'It's pretty nasty topside, sir.'

'Okay. I'm up. You can shove off now.'

'The exec. said to be sure you got up on time, sir.'

'I said I'm up.'

The messenger left. Austen could hear him bumping down the passageway. As he swung his feet over the side of the bunk the room shook with the impact of the sea. There was a crash and the rush of water along the ship's side. He listened, fascinated and respectably afraid. The roar died to a liquid gurgling taunt.

He dressed, cursing the dark and the bulk of his foul-weather gear. He snapped the buckles of the heavy overshoes and went through the green cloth curtains into the passageway.

Mike Edge was braced against the bulkhead, strapping himself into his life jacket. He did not notice Austen in the red loom of the battle lights.

'You got the watch, Mike?'

Edge looked up startled. 'What the hell's it to you?'

I asked for it, Austen thought. He pulled the night-adaptability goggles over his eyes, cut his breath against the acrid stink of the warrant officers' head and groped along the dim passageway.

He heard the steady throb of turbines and the drive of steam through the overhead pipes. He heard the muffled night noises. Think about Johnny, he thought. Is he floating with his feet higher than his head? Is he nudged by a curious whale? Is he flaked out on the oozy bottom without a dream in his head?

At least he's feeling no pain, he thought.

He went up the ladder and squeezed through the narrow opening in the hatch cover. Sleepy-eyed men moved to relieve the watch. A metal locker door slammed. A hatch cover clanged shut. A deep voice called a short name. The hollow silence echoed it. Shoe leather scraped impatiently on the wet metal ladders.

In the wardroom he drank black coffee. The green-covered tables seemed like black bottomless pits. Cups and saucers gleamed greenishly like pale round pools in the Stygian cloth.

Throw in a moon, he thought, and Ryder would have painted it.

The rough sound of voices filtered through the pantry opening from the crew's quarters abaft the wardroom. They were human, lusty voices. Austen smiled a little. There seemed to be a deliberate contempt thinly disguised in their sound, directed at the holier-than-thou gold braid drinking its sweet, hot coffee in the sacrosanct wardroom.

There was a last-minute fumbling with caps and mittens and coat collars as the officers prepared to leave for their watch. Austen went aft through the crew's compartment. He walked carefully through the cramped quarters.

He passed an arm outstretched, tattooed 'Mother', woven in a coil of manila with a blue anchor and a red 'USN'. The fingers were oil-stained brown and tensed even in sleep. A hunting knife hung in a home-made sheath, strapped into wrinkled dungarees. He passed a hand-tinted photo, a cross on a tarnished golden chain, a rosary, a comic book.

The wonder of it, he thought.

He swung around the ladder to Number Three hatch and turned

up the thick collar of his coat. He removed the night-adaptability goggles and snapped the button that strapped on his blue cloth helmet. He heard the wind whine through the superstructure as he climbed the remaining steps of the ladder.

He pushed aside the heavy canvas flap and bent to meet the stinging wind and spray. He leaned against its force with his arms extended. He reached the torpedo tubes and holding fast against them fought his way forward to the catapults. Step by step he inched along, clinging to the life lines, to the sheer surface of the galley deckhouse, until he stood panting in the lee of the foremast structure.

He climbed the slippery ladders in the teeth of the wind and swung himself arm over arm on to the bridge deck. He stood gasping, each sucking breath a knife-edge of pain inside his chest. Inside the pilothouse he heard the helmsman and quartermaster reciting their orders to the oncoming watch. He swung the heavy steel door and went in.

The executive officer was perched in the captain's chair on the starboard side.

'Late, aren't you, Mr. Austen?' he said.

Austen looked at his watch and then at the clock on the bulkhead. His watch was three minutes slow. He was half a minute late.

'Sorry, Commander,' he said.

He relieved the junior officer of the watch. An uneasy silence settled over the pilothouse. He went into the chartroom. The light lock device clicked and the room remained dark until he shut the door again. The light came on brightly and he blinked until he could see clearly again. Commander Griswold was stretched out on the narrow emergency bunk. The light had awakened him.

'Sorry, sir,' Austen said.

Griswold grinned. 'I don't sleep, anyway.' He watched while Austen read the captain's night order book. 'How's the barometer?'

'Rising, sir.'

'Maybe that goddamned wind'll die down yet.'

Austen read the night orders. It included the course changes for the night and the customary precautions for alertness against air, surface, or underwater contacts. General quarters as usual, an hour before sunrise.

Sunrise, he thought grimly. No one ever saw the sun rise. Or set. Sunrise was an entry in the captain's night order book. Or a wistful guess by the navigator.

'What about this wind, Commander? It's blowing like a williwaw.'

Griswold grinned. 'Maybe I'm crazy, but I'm expecting Miami Beach weather by morning.'

Austen studied the zigzag plan. The next leg was due in seventeen minutes. He corrected his watch with the one over the chart desk and went into the pilothouse.

He took his station on the port side and glanced at the executive officer who still sat stiffly in the captain's chair.

Let him have it, Austen thought. It makes him happy, pretending he's captain.

He made a slow sweep forward through the binoculars. The fog had thinned. The wind still blew hard. The forecastle deck was visible above the cruiser's slim clipper bow. Beyond it lay a hundred clear yards of the sea.

'Mr. Austen?'

'Yes, Commander?'

'You've read the captain's night orders?'

'Yes, sir.'

'Committed them to memory?'

'I believe so. Sir.'

'You're not sure?'

'I've committed them to memory, sir.'

'Suppose you recite them.'

Austen repeated the essential details of the night orders. The executive officer listened, drumming his fingers on the cowling of the pilothouse windows. The rest of the watch crew stood by and pretended to take no notice. Austen finished.

'The next zigzag leg, Mr. Austen?'

'In fourteen minutes, sir.'

'The course?'

'Left twenty degrees, sir, to course three-five-zero, true.'

'I expect the manœuvre to be executed smartly and at the exact moment.'

'Aye, sir.'

'I will insist upon a taut watch from all of you. Is that clear?'

The men acknowledged in a mumble of voices. The bridge was quiet for a moment.

'If it appears I'm being somewhat exacting, I assure you there are sound reasons for it.'

Austen said nothing. It was a remarkable statement, coming from the executive officer, who never made explanations.

'Mr. Austen?'

'Yes, Commander?'

'Did you hear me?'

'Yes, sir.'

'Please acknowledge when spoken to.'

'Aye, sir.'

'Have you given any thought as to why I, second-in-command, should be standing a deck watch?'

'No, sir.' Behind him the bosun's mate whispered to the messenger.

'It is not customary for department heads to stand sea watches, as I presume you know. And certainly not the executive officer of a combatant vessel as large as a cruiser.'

'I see, sir.'

'But, following this morning's regrettable errors, command has deemed it necessary that we do so.'

'Yes, sir.' The whispering behind him continued.

'Our tactical situation is precarious enough without inviting further trouble.' He turned his head sharply. 'I want you men to listen and be silent while I speak.' He coughed dryly. 'You know our purpose in being out here, Mr. Austen?'

'Patrol, sir.'

'More than that. Blockade of Kiska and Attu. At any cost.'

'I see, sir.'

'It means we're expendable. Were you aware of that?'

'I wasn't, sir.'

186

'Do you care at all?'

Austen considered for a moment. 'No, sir.'

'Just what do you know or care about, Mr. Austen?'

'Painting, sir.'

'It's your duty to know what your ship's mission is.'

'I know as much as the other junior officers. We're not told much about command decisions.'

'Sir.'

'Sir.'

'I'm going to tell you. The enemy undoubtedly knows we're out here, and approximately where. They will seek us out and try to destroy us. To supply their garrisons. That is why I am standing a sea watch. To be on hand in case of a sudden contact. To execute smartly and competently what years of training and discipline have prepared me for.'

Okay, Admiral, Austen thought. Enjoy yourself. Just so it doesn't splash on me.

'I believe the men should know what's going on,' the executive officer said. 'Helps them carry out their assigned duties more efficiently.'

'Yes, sir.'

'So, under the circumstances I am not being harsh, expecting a taut watch from all hands. Am I?'

'No, sir.' It will be nice to go home some day, Austen thought, and carry on a conversation with a normal human being like my old landlady, Mrs. Titus.

'I have been told,' the executive officer said slowly, 'that I am entirely too harsh.'

Austen felt numbness and a sweaty chill. He stared at his watch.

'Commander Blanchard said so,' the executive officer continued calmly. 'He took great pains to so inform me.'

'Excuse me, sir,' Austen said. 'I had better stand by for the next zigzag change.'

'Nonsense,' the executive officer said pleasantly, 'you have seven minutes and a half, Mr. Austen. Do you find my conversation boring?'

'No, sir.'

187

'Commander Blanchard regards you as a talented young man. Apparently respect for rank is not among those talents.' He laughed dryly. 'Do you find me harsh, Mr. Austen?'

Austen did not know what to say. His lips felt cracked and dry. 'Do you?'

It's so simple to say no, Austen thought. He stared at the clipper bow, nosing the sea in the darkness ahead. He smelled the burnt cordite of guns. He smelled the sourness of Dave Clough's sea-sickness. He smelled the urine smells of the warrant officers' head. He remembered Loomis and Johnson.

Harsh? he thought. An incredulous laugh slipped through his tensed lips. He could not help it.

'I'll have no disrespect from you!' the executive officer thundered.

Captain Meredith stirred in his emergency cabin. His voice called out, hoarsely querulous, muffled by the steel door and the curtains.

'What's the ruckus out there?'

'Nothing, Captain,' the executive officer said.

'I thought I heard someone yelling.'

'Not out here, sir.' His voice was calm and reassuring.

They heard the captain turning, the bedsprings yielding. They heard him punch his pillow to freshen it. They stood very quietly in the pilothouse, hearing these things.

The executive officer signalled to the phone talker.

'Aye, sir?'

'Check the readiness of all gunnery stations on your circuit.'

'Aye, sir.'

The talker pressed the speaking button. 'All gunnery stations. This is the bridge. Report your readiness.' He acknowledged briefly as each station reported in. He looked at the executive officer. 'All stations report manned and ready, Commander.'

'Very well. Now, Mr. Austen.'

'Yes, sir?'

'When you make your tour of the ship, I want you to check each gunnery station that's manned during this watch. Place any man on report who is doping off or not at his assigned station alert and ready.'

'Aye, sir.'

'You may attend to your zigzag change now.'

Austen went into the chartroom. He sat watching the sweep second-hand on the brass clock until thirty seconds before the course change was due. He held his finger on the Amplicall button that communicated with the pilothouse.

'Helmsman from JOW. Next leg is left to three-five-zero, true.' He glanced at the clock. 'Stand by.' The sweep second-hand came up. 'Left standard rudder.'

'Rudder is left standard, sir.'

'Come to course three-five-zero, true.'

The navigator had been watching him from the bunk where he lay. 'What cooks out there, Austen?' he said quietly.

'Nothing, sir.'

'The exec. got ants in his pants?'

'He's in a funny mood, sir.'

Griswold chuckled. 'Don't let it get you down, boy.'

Austen looked at him gratefully. 'I'll try not to, sir.'

He snapped up the Amplicall button. He checked the time for the next course change and went into the pilothouse. The helmsman had the wheel over and was watching the gyrocompass. Austen checked the course and went out to the starboard side of the open bridge.

The wind velocity had slackened considerably across the deck. Visibility had increased to several hundred yards. He made a steady sweep with his binoculars. A lookout leaned on the splinter shield in the lee of the flag bags. His face was hidden under his parka. Austen prodded him.

'Snap out of it, kid,' he said, 'we're in enemy waters.'

The lookout straightened and stared sullenly at Austen and raised the binoculars to his eyes. Austen checked the new course on the compass repeater and went into the pilothouse. The executive officer was slumped in front of the radar screen. Austen peered over his shoulder. The pips that represented the two destroyers ahead and astern of the *Atlantis* were on station. Austen retired to his side of the bridge.

'Mr. Austen.'

'Yes, sir?'

'You have neglected to answer my question.'

Austen closed his eyes. 'I'm sorry, Commander.'

'Do you agree with Dr. Blanchard?'

'I hardly know what to say, sir.'

'You must have some opinion about it.' He was tapping his fingers on the cowling again.

'I've never been invited to express an opinion before, sir. Must I do so now?'

'Yes.'

'Being the exec. of a big ship is a job I wouldn't care to have, sir,' he said carefully.

'Go on.'

'I imagine it's exhausting and thankless.'

'Then you agree with Dr. Blanchard?'

'It's a harsh job. Yes, sir.' I'm a coward, he thought.

'You're evading the question, Austen.' The formality had been dropped and his tone was amiable. 'You're just trying to be agreeable and not commit yourself. Commander Blanchard told me I was too harsh and the men hated me. I told him the truth. I said it was my job to make them hate me. It made better seamen, better fighters out of them. Would you agree?'

'No, sir.'

'Why not?'

'Hate is inexcusable.'

'Even in wartime?'

'It's inexcusable at any time, sir.'

'Even if it wins the war for us? Come now, Austen.'

He's really getting a bang out of it, Austen thought. He could find nothing to say. He looked at his watch. There was plenty of time until the next course change. He checked the course the helmsman was steering. He was dead on. He checked the wind velocity and the portside alidade and the bridge lookouts, and he stood by helplessly because there was nothing more he could check.

'Well, Austen?'

'I can't agree with you, Commander.'

'Why not?'

'Because hate breeds tyranny and fear, sir.'

'And tyranny and fear breed the highest form of efficiency man has ever known.' He cackled shrilly in the dark and the chair creaked. Austen felt a clammy chill.

'I'm afraid I can't agree with you, sir.'

'No harm done.'

The drumming had stopped. Austen watched him narrowly. Strange, he thought, to find the enemy here. Right in the god-damned pilothouse.

'Do you hate me, Mr. Austen?'

'No, sir.'

He had spoken without thinking. A swift horror seized him. *Or do I?*

'Why not?'

I am a little boy, Austen thought. I am walking along a familiar maple-shaded street to school. My heart is filled with the dewy morning. My cheek tingles where my mother has kissed me.

I am kicking a friendly little rock along the cobblestones. I am dreaming of the pictures I will paint some day. My books are strapped and buckled and I am swinging them and whistling.

They pout out of the alley of crumbling shanties. They scream like Indians. I am terrified because it's the Ludlow Street gang and I am a nice quiet kid in a clean white shirt with an Eton collar and grey flannel shorts and I go to a private academy.

The books are scattered aloft. The pages are ripped from their seams. The clean white shirt and collar are muddied and torn. And as the enemy streaks away howling in triumph I pick up my friendly little rock and hurl it among them with the blind might of child rage. One boy falls and the others disappear.

Later I am faced with his parents and my solemn father and my disturbed mother. My teacher, whom I hold in special adoration because she has taught me the love of painting, carefully explains to all what has happened. I am sick with shame in her presence. I am filled with remorse to see my erstwhile tormentor now a puny victim with a bandaged head. He is just another boy like myself.

His parents are red-eyed and sad and poorly clad. I know them. I have seen them many times selling pitiful bunches of hand-picked violets in front of the church on Chestnut Street.

I made a promise then. I would never hate again.

I have never hated again, Austen thought. I meant it when I told the executive officer I did not hate him. I did not have to think about it.

'Well?' the executive officer was saying.

'I learned not to hate when I was a child, sir.'

'I believe your next zigzag leg is imminent, Mr. Austen.'

'Thank you, sir.'

Austen went into the chartroom, perspiring. He had forgotten about the zigzag course change. The navigator slept. Austen executed the course change and went out to the open bridge.

There were no stars. The sea lay exposed in all directions, calm as a summer lake. The wind had died. A night of wonder, he thought.

He went inside the pilothouse.

'Visibility has cleared, sir. The wind is down. Shall I report the change to the captain?'

'Decisions during this watch will originate with me, Mr. Austen.'

'Yes, sir.'

'It would be foolish to awaken the captain for such minor details.'

'He always likes to know about these things, sir.'

'I'm officer of the deck, Mr. Austen.' The finger-drumming was resumed.

'Aye, sir.'

'So you learned not to hate as a child.'

'Yes, sir.'

'And yet you joined the Navy.'

'Yes, sir.'

The executive officer laughed again. It was an unpleasant sound to hear. Austen could see the other men out of the corner of his eye. They were pressed back against the bulkheads as far from the executive officer as they could get.

He glanced desperately at his watch. Two and a half hours to go. In a few minutes he could graciously escape to make his tour through the ship.

'And you do not hate me, Mr. Austen?'

'No, sir.'

'Dr. Blanchard must be wrong, then.'

'I do not hate you, sir.' Austen wiped the cold sweat from his lip.

'Thank you for your co-operation, Mr. Austen.' His voice was dry and cold. He sank a little deeper in the captain's chair. 'Quartermaster of the watch?'

'Aye, sir?'

'Your name, please.'

'Graber, sir.'

'Do you hate me, Graber?'

'Why, no, sir.' He sounded surprised.

'Thank you. Bosun's mate?'

'Aye, sir?'

'Your name.'

'McIlhenny.'

'Sir.'

'Sir. I'm sorry, sir.'

'Do you hate me, McIlhenny?'

'No, sir.'

'Thank you, McIlhenny. Helmsman?'

'Aye aye, sir?'

'One aye is sufficient. Your name.'

'Gomez, sir.'

'What course are we steering, Gomez?'

'Course? Course, sir? Yes, sir. She's—uh—two-seven-five, true, Captain.'

'I'm not the captain, Gomez.'

'I beg your pardon, Commander.'

'It's very interesting. Why did you call me captain?'

'I wasn't thinking, Commander, so help me Jesus.'

'You're at the helm. You'd better be thinking or we'll get another helmsman. What's your rate?'

'Seaman first, Commander. I'm striking for quartermaster.'

'Do you hate me, Gomez?'

'No, sir. I don't hate nobody, Commander. Honest.'

'Thank you, Gomez. Messenger?'

'Yes, sir?'

'Your name.'

'Smith, J. W., sir.'

'Do you hate me, Smith?'

'No, sir.'

'Thank you, Smith.   JV talker?'

'Aye, sir?'

'Your name.'

'Lewis, Commander.'

'Do you hate me, Lewis?'

'No, sir.'

'Thank you, Lewis.   Now I want you to put a message out to all stations, Lewis.   I want you to ask the talkers at each station to find out from the other men on watch how many of them hate me.'

'Now, sir?'

'Of course.   We may as well have this settled once and for all.'

'Excuse me, Commander,' Austen said.

'Yes, Mr. Austen?'

'I believe you may want to reconsider that order.'

'Why?'   He seemed genuinely surprised.

'The men might not understand, sir.'

'It's a very simple question, Mr. Austen.   Why shouldn't they understand?'

'It's not a simple question, sir.   It's rather unusual.'

'Nonsense.'   He had sunk even deeper into the captain's chair.

'You'd regret the outcome, Commander.   Believe me, sir.'

'All of you here answered honestly and directly.   Why shouldn't the others?   I'm just going to prove to Commander Blanchard that he's wrong.'   He was a dark blob faintly illuminated by the reflection of light from the radarscope.   'Are you afraid for me to ask the others, Mr. Austen?   Are you?'

'I don't know, sir,' Austen said in despair.

'Why are you afraid, Mr. Austen?'

'I didn't say——'

'I know why.'   The executive officer's voice was a whisper.   It came from the shadows of his dark shapeless bulk.   'Because all of you are liars.   All of you.'

He sat up, unfolding like an oriental paper flower—uncurling,

194

expanding, coming alive steadily as a sprouting blossom until he burst in a single monstrous scream.

'Liars! Because every one of you hates me! Every damned one of you!'

The emergency cabin door opened and Captain Meredith stepped into the pilothouse. He was stuffing the tail of his shirt inside his trousers. His feet were slippered and made silly padding sounds against the deck.

'I've heard enough, Commander,' he said quietly. 'I relieve you.' He saluted. The others could not see his face.

The executive officer smiled shakily. 'Everything is under control, Captain. We were merely having a little discussion.'

'We'll see about that later. Right now you're relieved.'

'I don't understand why you're doing it, Captain,' he said in a strangled voice.

'I'm doing it. That's reason enough.'

He took the executive officer's arm and led him to the afterpart of the pilothouse. 'If you wish you may rest in my cabin here. I have the conn.' He turned to Austen. 'When is the next zigzag change?'

'In four minutes, Captain.'

Captain Meredith came over and read the gyrocompass. 'Course and speed, Alec?'

Austen told him. The captain poked the helmsman's back.

'Come right two degrees, son. You're off your course.'

'Aye, sir.'

The tenseness had evaporated. No one looked at the executive officer. After a few minutes he went into the captain's emergency cabin and closed the door.

'Alec?'

'Yes, Captain?'

'I'll take over the zigzag plan. Make your rounds of the ship and return to the bridge.'

'Aye, sir.' He saluted and went out. The captain followed him to the open bridge. His voice was edged with concern.

'Two things, Alec. Wake up Blanchard and ask him to report to me on the bridge. Use your judgment as to telling him why.

Then check on Mike Edge. I've had a phone call from the damage-control officer in central station. Edge is roaming the ship and acting very peculiar. Report to me as soon as you know something.'

'Aye, sir.'

'I don't know what's happening to this ship. It's falling apart.' He stared at Austen for a moment, then smiled. 'It's about time, isn't it?'

'I think we'll get by, Captain.'

'I liked what you said about not hating, Alec.'

'You heard that?'

'Hell. I heard everything.'

'I'm sorry about the commander, sir.'

'We've known about it for some time. Get going now, Alec.'

Austen went below. He wakened Blanchard and told him what had happened. Blanchard dressed, softly cursing, and Austen left him to search the ship for Mike Edge.

22

MIKE EDGE had remained in the passageway for several minutes after Austen had seen him. He watched Austen ascending the ladder and yearned for the feel of a .45 in his fingers.

The squawk box in the dimly lighted passageway crackled. Edge whirled, palms flattened to the bulkhead.

'*Relieve the watch! Condition Three, Watch Two, relieve the watch!*'

He peered around craftily, waiting for the watch to change. He could hear Dave Clough breathing heavily. Steam hissed through the overhead pipes and the throb of turbines vibrated the bulkheads. He stood and waited, cursing to himself and rubbing the narrow sweaty crevices between his legs. He removed the bulky life jacket and threw it inside his room. The ship quieted down again.

He wiped his mouth with the back of his hairy hand. He listened for an instant and bent quickly and held his breath. Someone was coming.

A seaman in dungarees appeared through the dim haze of the red battle lights. A sidearm sagged in his web belt. He stopped to inspect an overhead gauge. Mike Edge stiffened as he approached. He stepped out, blocking the man's way, thrusting his big head towards him.

'What you doing in officer country, sailor?'

'Security watch, sir.' He looked surprised.

'Stand at attention, goddamnit! Take off that hat!'

The sailor removed his white hat and slowly straightened to attention. He looked in Edge's eyes. His surprised smile faded. He swallowed hard.

'No kidding, Mr. Edge. I got the security watch is all.'

'Knock off that crap. What you doing with a .45?'

'Nothing, sir. We all got to carry a .45. It's orders.'

'How dumb you think I am? Who sent you?'

'Nobody sent me. This is the area I'm supposed to patrol. From the warrant officers' head aft to——'

Edge slapped him to silence. The man put his fingers to the side of his face where Edge had struck him. He looked dazedly at his fingers, expecting to see blood.

'This is officer country,' Edge said. 'You goddamn enlisted men ain't supposed to come through officer country.'

The man turned to go.

'Stand fast, goddamnit!'

The sailor regarded him stupidly. His cheek stung where Edge had slapped him. He hoped Edge would not slap him again. He knew what he would do if Edge slapped him again and he did not want to have to do it.

Anywhere else, he thought, but not here. Just eat it.

'Hand over that sidearm, sailor.'

'The .45?' He tried not to see the expression in Edge's eyes.

'Yes, damn it, the .45.'

'Look, Mr. Edge. Please. You must be kidding.'

'Hand it here, goddamnit.'

'I'm not supposed to. I swear to God, Mr. Edge.' His mind raced. 'I'm signed up for it,' he said desperately. 'I can't.'

'What's your name?'

'Walker, sir.'

'Rate?'

'Water tender second.'

'If you wanna stay out of trouble, Walker, if you don't wanna be slapped on report and get maybe a summary, just be smart and hand over that .45.'

'What are you going to do with it?'

'Just sure as hell I'll get you slapped back to seaman second. I'll make your life so goddamned miserable you'll wish you never seen the inside of this ship. Now hand it over and never mind what I'm going to do with it.'

Walker slowly unbuckled the web belt and handed it to Edge. Edge slid it around his middle and buckled it. He patted the shiny holster a few times and scowled at Walker.

'Okay. Shove off.'

Walker did not move, nor did his gaze waver from Edge's face. Edge gripped the hard butt of the pistol.

'Shove,' he said, 'or I'll slap you on report.'

'This is my watch station. I'm not doing anything.'

'You don't need to for silent contempt. Now I'm warning you. Shove off.'

Walker retreated carefully, not turning until his fingers touched the rungs of the ladder. Then he scrambled out of sight.

Edge waited a few minutes before he walked aft. He went through the crew's quarters to the brig area and listened. He could hear voices. He looked into the cluttered compartment.

Several men who had returned from the midwatch were undressing and talking in quiet tones. Others slept in the tiered bunks. A bright, naked bulb glared overhead.

Beyond them Edge saw the brig guard. He was a short, fat coxswain. His chair was tilted against the bulkhead. He sat drowsily with his fingers clasped over his fat paunch. A mug of coffee sat in a puddle on the deck alongside him.

Edge backed away carefully. He went to the wardroom two decks above. It was empty. Two pots of coffee steamed on the sideboard. He went into the pantry. The watch boy slept with his head thrown back and his mouth gaped open. Edge found the sweet potato pie that Fowler had made for Lieutenant Johnson and took it into the wardroom.

He stood at the sideboard and ate noisily. He washed down the pie with gulps of coffee. He wiped his mouth with the back of his hand and wiped his hands on his trousers.

He patted the holster. Now he felt good. He patted his stomach where it bulged slightly over the web belt.

You nice, shiny gun, he thought. You sweet finger.

He was George Raft and Eddie Robinson. He was Rico the Kid.

He sat at one of the tables. He felt strong and handsome and irresistible.

He remembered a love movie he had seen as a boy in L.A. It was a double feature along with a Tom Mix western. It had excited him very much and he had started to play with the boy sitting next him. But the boy next to him preferred cowboys and Indians to anything else. Especially to Edge. He moved away.

Edge quit the movie. It still bothered him. He walked aimlessly until he found himself in the Mexican section of town. It was getting dark. He laid his hands on the first loose kid he could find, not caring whether it was a boy or a girl.

It happened to be a boy—a small, brown-eyed, frightened boy who whimpered in Spanish, begging to know what Edge wanted of him. Edge dragged him into the shadows of a building excavation. They rolled around on the rough concrete surfaces, until Edge, panting, let the boy go.

Nothing had really happened. Edge warned the boy carefully that they had only been playing. It was all in fun. There was nothing to tell his parents, but if the boy did tell them Edge would come back and really hurt him.

The small boy ran swiftly, choked with sobs. Edge hitched a ride on the back of a bus, licking his scratches and giggling, and somehow partly satisfied. He would have to try it again, he thought. It was more fun than girls and he had never quite trusted girls anyway.

The thought of it now excited him. He remembered Gray. First the nigger, he decided. Then Gray.

He went below. The compartment was darkened except for battle lights. The brig guard slept. Edge walked quietly to the metal door of the brig and peered through the barred opening.

The cell was about six feet by nine feet. Two men slept on the narrow bunks that hung by chains from the bulkhead. Edge recognized Fowler's dark, bandaged head. The other he presumed to be Gray.

He reached for the key ring hooked to the brig guard's belt. The guard opened his eyes.

'Lemme have them keys, guard,' Edge whispered.

'The keys?' The guard was befuddled with sleep. He stared at Edge in the half darkness. 'That you, Ensign Edge?'

'I got to bring the nigger up,' Edge said with a vague wave. He watched to see if any of the others had awakened. 'They want him topside. On the bridge.'

The guard stirred. 'They want him now?'

'Yeah. Let's have them keys.'

The guard unbuckled the ring of keys. 'He's in bad shape, that coon. You should see his head.'

'It's nothing to what's coming to him,' Edge said.

'The captain's sore, eh? For what the coon did?' He proffered the keys to Edge. Edge pointed to the cell door.

'You open it,' he said craftily. 'I'll keep you covered with the .45. In case he tries any tricks.' He drew the pistol.

'Thanks, Mr. Edge. They say he's real tricky.'

He unlocked the brig door. Edge waved him aside with the pistol and stood at the entry. The guard flashed his light inside.

'C'mon outta there, Fowler.'

Inside the two men looked up. Fowler blinked at the glaring light through the frame of bandages. The other man was Slobodjian. Edge stared at him.

'Where's that pogue, Gray?'

'Gray? Who's he?' the guard asked.

'The crazy kid from the radio shack,' Edge snarled.

'Him? They took him to sick bay before chow to-night. He's bats.'

Edge waved the pistol. 'You, Fowler. Get the hell out here. On the double.'

Fowler sat up on the edge of the bunk. The blood had dried on the side of his swollen face. It formed an ugly maroon clot. An end of the bandage hung down stained and shredded like bright red confetti. He stared at the hand that held the gun.

'What for?' he said.

'Never the hell mind what for. Get out here.'

Fowler started to get up. Slobodjian thrust a skinny brown arm against him and sat him down again.

'Who wants to see him, Ensign?' Slobodjian said softly.

'None of your goddamn business, you rat.' He shoved the muzzle into the cell. 'You coming out or do I got to come in there and haul you out?'

Fowler looked at Slobodjian. Slobodjian shook his head. His soft eyes dropped to the pistol Edge held. 'Uh-uh.' He rose and stood between Fowler and Edge. 'He's got a right to know who wants to see him, Ensign. He's a very sick man.'

'He's gonner be sicker in a minute.'

'The doctor don't want him moved, Ensign.'

'The hell with the doctor. The captain wants to see this guy right now. On the bridge. So get the hell out of the way.'

'I don't believe you, Ensign,' Slobodjian said.

Edge started for him. Slobodjian did not yield. A knife showed in his fingers, its blade glittering in the bright glare of the guard's large flashlight. Its point was fixed unwaveringly a few inches from Edge's belt buckle.

'He's a sick man, Ensign,' Slobodjian continued softly, 'he shouldn't be disturbed.' His eyes blinked gently in the bright light.

The guard crowded over Edge's shoulder. The light beam wavered.

'Do what Mr. Edge says, Slobodjian,' he whined, 'or you'll get us in real trouble.'

'Ensign Edge knows who's in trouble,' Slobodjian said. He smiled for the first time.

The smile enraged Mike Edge. His eyes dropped swiftly to the .45.

'It ain't loaded, Ensign,' Slobodjian said. 'I seen it when you came in.' He advanced the knife tip an inch.

Edge looked. The magazine in the pistol grip was empty. The loaded clip lay snugly in a pocket of the web belt. He closed his eyes and rushed Slobodjian. The knife moved surely. The slim blade flicked along his forearm, tearing cloth and skin. It caught a shirt button and severed it. It continued upward, nicking Edge's chin and the lobe of his ear. He stumbled backward clutching the gun, clumsy and fumbling and frightened. A thin stream of blood stained the khaki shirt.

'Touch that clip and I'll really slice you,' Slobodjian said amiably. Edge stared at him aghast. The rat really means it, he thought. He didn't believe a skinny little rat like this one, a goddamn sneaky little Armenian, would have the guts to stand up to him like that.

'Put up the shiv,' he said, panting. 'You're on report.'

'Okay, Ensign. I'm on report. Throw me in the brig.' He uttered a faint sort of laugh. Behind him there was a low-pitched chuckle from Fowler. The knife remained still, pointed at Edge.

'You want me to call some help, Mr. Edge?' the guard asked anxiously.

'Hell, no.' He dabbed at his arm, and scowled at Slobodjian. 'You're through, you little rat. You'll swing from the yardarm for this.'

'What's a yardarm, Ensign?'

'You ignorant little bastard. No stinking rat of an enlisted man gets away with pulling a knife on an officer, a commissioned officer of the United States Navy. You're through, see?'

Slobodjian shrugged. 'I'm a citizen,' he said softly. 'My brig mate here, he's my friend. He's also a citizen. Of the United States. Just like you, Ensign. We don't like to get pushed around.'

Edge's mouth worked for words. None came. Slobodjian looked at his forearm where the stain had spread. 'Would you like a Band-Aid, Ensign? Or should I recommend you for the Purple Heart?'

'Close the goddamned door,' Edge shouted at the guard. The guard swung it hard and it clanged shut. It could not contain the mocking laughter that rose behind it.

Edge's voice whined. 'How come he's got a knife on him? What the hell kind of a guard are you, anyway? A prisoner in the brig having a knife on him like that. I oughtta slap you on report. It's your goddamned fault as much as anybody's, goofing off like that.'

'I ain't the regular brig guard, sir. I just relieved the watch. It's the master-at-arms's fault——'

He was interrupted by Edge's obscenities and listened for several moments in awed fear. Edge jammed the pistol in its holster and lurched away. His arm throbbed where the knife had cut him. The scratches on his chin and ear were slight, though the blood ran freely. He hoped no one would see him. It was an awkward time for explanations.

The guard watched him go. He rubbed his head, wondering if this, like so much of the day's events, had really happened. He hooked the keys to his belt. He picked up the mug of cold coffee and sipped it and spat it away cursing. He arranged his chair once more against the bulkhead and leaned back and closed his eyes.

Behind the cell door the two prisoners whispered quietly. The guard lunged forward and kicked the door savagely.

'Shut up in there,' he pleaded, 'or by Christ I'll kill the both of you!'

He sat down and pulled a comic book from his pocket and tried to read. His head nodded. The book slipped to the deck. He dozed.

Slobodjian, watching through the barred opening, snapped his knife shut and slipped it inside his shoe.

'Thanks, feller,' Fowler whispered. He wanted to touch him to show how grateful he was, but he did not touch him.

'Aah,' Slobodjian said, 'what a jerk. I got cousins, majors and captains, none of them a jerk like that ensign.'

'You reckon he'll be back?'

Slobodjian shrugged. He was sleepy but he felt very brave now. 'Let him come back. We got his number.'

'He might bring them others.'

'We got nothing to be afraid of, friend. We're citizens.'

'Sure,' Fowler said uneasily.

Slobodjian soon slept. Fowler sat awake for a long time. His head throbbed and his mouth felt like dry cotton and he wanted to sleep very badly, but he sat awake.

It an old thing, he thought. It take a long time.

He stiffened. Steps sounded on the ladder. His stomach knotted. He crouched, forgetting the pain at the side of his head. Someone knocked on the brig door and softly called his name. He recognized the voice. His body relaxed.

He cleared his throat. 'That you, Mr. Austen, sir?'

'Yes. How do you feel?'

'Face hurts something fierce, but I feel all right.' He paused. 'They sent you to fetch me, sir?'

'Who?'

'The captain, sir?'

'No. Why?'

'That what Mr. Edge say, sir.'

'Edge? Was he here?'

Was he here? Fowler thought. *Was he here?* 'He come and gone, Mr. Austen. Had him a .45 and he come to get me.'

'How long ago?'

'Maybe a half hour, sir.'

'You don't know which way he headed, do you?'

'No, sir.' He came to the barred opening. His voice broke a little. 'Feller here he saved me with his knife. He keeped Mr. Edge from offa me.'

'Easy, Fowler. The guard's right here.'

'Keeped him out with a lil bitty ol' knife.'

'Who's in there with you?'

'Don't know his name, Mr. Austen. Some white sailor.'

'Don't worry about Edge any more, Fowler. He's in trouble. I'm searching the ship for him right now.'

'You be careful now. He mighty free with that .45, sir.'

'I'll be careful.' He reached a hand in and Fowler took it and squeezed it with both of his. 'Quit worrying now. And take care of that head, will you?'

He had to pull his hand free. Fowler listened until Austen's steps died away. He sat down on the bunk and gently touched his bruised face.

It feels good to hold a white man's hand, he thought. Mighty good. Goddamn.

23

MIKE EDGE wandered through the sleeping ship in a sullen half dream. One refuge remained, he decided. He opened the hatch cover to the bosun's locker and climbed in and shut the cover after him.

It was a small compartment that had been his domain in his petty officer days. It was cluttered with many coils of manila in varying thicknesses, oil and paint drums, and a jumble of loose gear that lay about the deck and on the disordered shelves.

Edge kicked savagely at the stack of manila nearest him. He punched a paint drum with a thick fist. It echoed hollowly. He sat down and rubbed his raw knuckles.

'Looka the place,' he muttered. He dabbed irritably at the stinging cuts on his face. 'A real dump. Like a goddamn bunch of limeys was running it.' He walked around putting things in order. 'Like the goddamn hooligan Navy.'

He became absorbed in the job. Soon the compartment was shipshape. He looked pleased and sat on the deck. He picked up a loose coil of small stuff and idly unlaid the end for several feet. He worked it into a monkey fist. His fingers were awkward and stiff at first and he cursed frequently. He undid the monkey fist and tried a more complicated knot known as a whale's eye. He held it up. It was a very well-made whale's eye, he thought.

He felt better now. The blood had dried on his forearm. The bosun's locker smelled good. It smelled like home. Christ almighty, he thought, it *is* home. What the hell ever made me leave it?

His fingers worked swiftly now. He made several more knots and then he thought happily, A Turk's-head. There's a real sailor's knot. I'll make me a Turk's-head. And then a double Matthew Walker. There, he thought proudly. There's the daddy of them all, the double Matthew Walker.

He frowned and looked up. Someone was opening the scuttle in the hatch cover overhead. He watched resentfully. Austen's face appeared. Edge scowled. Wherever I go, he thought. All the time.

'Now what the hell do you want?'

'You, Edge. You better come up here.'

'You go to hell.'

Austen slipped through the scuttle and climbed down the narrow steel ladder. Edge reluctantly put aside the length of rope he had been weaving. He rose heavily to one knee and glared at Austen.

'Come on, Edge. Up the ladder.'

'Go to hell.'

'The skipper wants to see you.'

'I ain't done nothing.'

'Then there's nothing to be afraid of. Come on.'

'The captain sent you, did he?'

'That's right.'

'To get me, huh?'

'To get you, right.'

'You're the captain's little cabin boy, ain't you? Run all his personal errands, don't you?' His hand worked slowly towards the Colt.

'Knock it off, Edge. I'm the junior O.D. and I don't have a hell of a lot of time. Are you coming?'

'Me? Sure. I'm coming.' He eased the big pistol from its holster. 'I been waiting a long time to do this.' He pointed it at Austen's groin.

'Do what, Edge?'

'Plug you. Blow you wide open.' He circled, putting himself between Austen and the ladder. 'It's your own damned fault.'

'Why? What have I done?'

'Bust my model gas engine, you son of a bitch.' He jabbed the muzzle of the Colt fiercely at Austen, who backed slightly.

'Is that damned thing loaded, Edge?'

'It is now. You bastards.'

'Put it away. You're in enough trouble.'

'And you killed Johnny Johnson. You put the nigger up to it.' He licked his dry lips. Austen, watching his eyes, had a feeling of hopelessness. They seemed murderous and they never wavered from Austen's face. 'I'm gonna kill you, you feather-merchant son of a bitch.'

'It's easy with a gun, Mike. Anybody can pull a trigger.' Edge's eyes clouded briefly. 'I always figured,' Austen continued evenly, 'that a big strong guy like you'd use his hands. Like Bogart or Cagney.'

'Don't hand me none of that, Austen. You're as good as dead now.'

'Okay, soft boy. Since you need the gun to do the job, what are you waiting for? Marlene Dietrich?'

'I like seeing a guy like you suffer, Austen. You reserves are all yellow. No guts. I wanna see tears come out of them eyes of yours. I want you on your knees, see? Begging for mercy.'

'And you need the gun to do it, don't you?'

'Hell, no. I don't need no goddamn gun.'

'Sure you do. There it is.'

'I could whip you with my bare hands.'

'Why don't you, Mike? Here I am.'

'I don't need no .45.' He waved it in Austen's face. 'Take off your coat, goddamnit.'

Austen slowly unbuttoned his coat and let it fall to the deck.

'Get over in the corner.'

Austen moved to the corner. Edge slid the pistol into its holster and unbuckled the gun belt and threw it on a coil of manila. He watched Austen carefully.

'I'm gonna ruin that sweet puss of yours,' he said.

'Why?'

'Because I don't like your guts. Stick up your mitts.' He advanced on Austen cautiously. Austen did not move. His hands hung at his sides. His face was pale and gravely calm. Edge paused.

'What are you waiting for, Mike?'

'Why you yellow son of a bitch.' Edge swung hard. His huge fist crunched against the side of Austen's face.

Austen fell backward against the expanded steel frame of the shelves and slid to the floor. He got on his feet slowly. A thin smile wavered at the corner of his set lips.

'Not too bad, Mike,' he said.

Edge hit him twice again. It was impossible for Austen to remain on his feet against the powerful blows. A small trickle of blood oozed from the corner of his mouth. He no longer smiled. His head was lowered slightly as he struggled to his feet.

Edge danced in a frenzy of rage. 'Fight back, you yellow bastard. Hit me.'

Austen shook his head doggedly. Edge drew back his fist. Austen closed his dazed eyes. Edge did not hit him again. He stepped back. Austen opened his eyes.

'Go ahead, Mike.'

'You yellow bastard. You ain't fighting.'

'No.'

'No guts. I oughtta cut you to ribbons.' His voice was filled with a furious perplexity.

'Why, Mike? Why?'

'I'll tell you why!'

Instead he turned away and leaned against the steel shelving. His body heaved convulsively. His knotty fingers twitched.

Austen pulled some cheese cloth from one of the shelves and wiped the blood from his face. He picked up his coat and put it on. The pain shot through him. Some of the blood on his cheek soaked into the wool collar and he tried to wipe it away.

'It's your own goddamned fault,' Edge blubbered.

'I didn't say anything, Mike.'

He picked up the web belt with the .45 in the holster. Edge watched him with frightened eyes. His body was racked with the labour of breathing.

'You dirty bastard! You dirty lousy yellow bastard.'

Austen painfully pulled himself up the steel ladder and pushed his bruised body through the open scuttle. He felt the flesh swelling at the side of his face. The blood tasted warm and sweet along his aching eyes. The weight of the .45 felt good.

He walked along the passageway until he found a telephone. He rang the pilothouse.

'Captain Meredith, please. This is Austen.'

He waited until he heard the captain's voice. 'Lieutenant Austen, Captain. I've made my rounds of the ship. All secure, sir.'

'Did you find Edge, Alec?'

'Yes, sir. He was asleep in his compartment.'

'What about that report from central station?'

'I'm going to check with the duty officer now, Captain.'

'I want a complete report, Alec. This is ridiculous.'

'Aye, sir.'

He hung up and went to central station. Dutch Fledermayer sat with a phone talker and a mug of coffee. Austen laid the web belt and sidearm on the desk.

'There's your missing .45, Dutch.'

Fledermayer ignored it. He was staring at Austen's face.

'What hit you, kid?'

'Nothing.' He sat down. It feels very good to sit down of my own accord, he thought.

'You look like hell. You sure you're all right?'

'I'm all right.'

Fledermayer opened a big first-aid kit. He poured some merthiolate on a gauze pad and cleansed the blood from the cut on Austen's cheek. He tore a strip of plaster from a roll and patted it over the wound. Austen sat wearily through it.

'How about a shot, kid?'

'I need one, I guess.'

Fledermayer produced a small bottle. Austen looked at it.

'What is it, Dutchie?'

'Torpedo juice. Made it myself.'

'No, thanks.'

'Do you good, kid. You look awful.'

'So does your torpedo juice. I'll be okay in a minute.'

'Where'd you find the .45?'

'Around.'

'Nuts. I already called the skipper about it. He knows something's fouled up with Mike Edge.'

'It's all squared away. I just told him Edge is sacked out.'

'Is he?'

'No.'

'He scared the bejesus out of Walker, one of my best boys. Walker wouldn't lie to me. He says Edge jumped him in officer country and took the .45. Pulled his rank and was real nasty about it.'

'I think he's quieted down now.'

'He can't get away with that.'

'Forget it, Dutch.'

'Why? Is he the one messed you up like that?'

'The hell with it.'

'We oughtta hit him with everything in the book. Where's the son of a bitch?'

'In the bosun's locker.'

'What the hell's he doing there?'

'I don't know.'

'He had the .45, didn't he?'

'Yeah. He had it.'

'And he slugged you when you tried to take it away?'

'Yes.'

'Did you slug him back?'

'No.'

'Why the hell not?'

Austen grinned faintly. 'Passive resistance. Ever hear of Gandhi, Dutch?'

'Gandhi who?'

'Okay. Never mind.'

'I got to make a report to the skipper. Why are you covering up for the son of a bitch?'

'Just call the bridge and tell them everything's squared away.'

'Okay. But if the skipper wants the details he's going to get the details. I'm not risking my skin. Not for Edge or you or anybody else, kid.'

'Okay, Dutch. I'll report the details to the skipper.'

'You'd better. For your own good.'

'Okay, Dutch. Thanks for the paste-up.'

'Where you going now?'

'Back to the bridge. I've still got the watch.'

'The exec'll want to know what hit you——'

'The exec's been relieved. The skipper's got the conn.'

'What the hell's going on in this goddamned ship?'

'I got to go, Dutch.'

He climbed the wet, slippery ladders to the bridge deck. The air was cold and the sea dark and eerily calm. The first faint edge of dawn sharpened the horizon to the east. He went in the pilothouse.

Captain Meredith sat in his chair on the starboard side. He was idly observing the sweep of the radar repeater.

'That you, Alec?' His voice sounded tired to Austen.

'Yes, sir.'

'Please take the conn. We've ceased zigzagging and resumed base course. Heading is zero-four-five, true and per gyrocompass. Speed fifteen.'

'Aye, sir. I relieve you.'

He checked the helmsman's course and the r.p.m. on the engine-room repeater. He was relieved that the captain had not questioned him about Edge. He wondered where the executive officer was.

'I must ask all of you,' the captain said suddenly, 'not to discuss what happened before.' He paused and they waited. 'It's very unfortunate. Those things are bound to happen from time to time.'

From minute to minute, Austen thought.

The phone talker spoke up. 'Radar One reports surface contact, Captain, bearing zero-zero-five, distance about twelve miles.'

The captain looked at the radarscope. 'Nothing here,' he muttered. He stood up, yawning. He slipped the strap of his binoculars over his head. 'Tell Radar One to report range and bearing every two minutes.'

'Aye, sir.'

'Messenger.'

'Yes, Captain?'

'Wake up the communications officer and have him report to me on the bridge, please.'

'Aye, Captain.' The man left the pilothouse briskly.

'Alec. Get that steward of mine to run some coffee up here.'

'Aye, sir.' He telephoned the captain's pantry. The coffee would be right up, the boy said.

Austen stood behind the captain and watched the endless circular sweep of the radar beam.

'A broaching whale,' the captain said. 'Maybe a school of them. Might be sea return.'

'I hope so, sir.' The captain looked at him quickly.

The sweeping beam now flickered in a north-northeast sector of the scope. The three bright blips were unmistakable. The captain went out to the starboard side of the open bridge and searched the morning darkness through his glasses.

The messenger returned and saluted the captain. 'Communications officer will be right along, sir.'

'Very well.'

Austen stepped out on the open bridge. 'Radar reports the contact to be three ships on a course of zero-zero-five, sir. Speed about eight knots.'

'Send a TBS to the destroyer commander to concentrate on this vessel immediately. Plain language, Alec, except for code names.'

'Aye, sir.'

He went in the pilothouse and cut in the ship-to-ship intercom. He depressed the sending lever.

'Roughneck, this is Bigwig. Over.'

The machine staticked, crackling.

'Bigwig, this is Roughneck. Come in. Over.'

'Message follows: Concentrate on Bigwig immediately. I repeat. Concentrate on Bigwig immediately. Over.'

'Bigwig, this is Roughneck. Wilco. Over and out.'

The machine clicked to silence. The captain came into the pilothouse.

'Message sent and acknowledged, Captain.'

'Very well.'

The communications officer came in. He looked sleepy and worried.

'Alert your radio gang, Sparky. Stand by me with a dispatch board.'

'Something up, sir?'

'Could be. Alec, check with the engine-room watch. All boilers should be on the main line.'

'Aye, sir.'

The captain's steward came in carrying a tray that was loaded with dull-gleaming silver dishes.

'Just the coffee, Ben. Sweet and black.'

His eye caught a series of tiny flashes faintly visible at the horizon. 'Check with the signal bridge, Alec. Some son of a bitch is blinking out there.'

The signalman was on his way in. 'Can't make it out, sir. Looks like some garbled recognition signal that ain't ours. Should I challenge?'

'Hell, no. Let him sweat.' He took a deep breath. 'Well, they know we're here, whoever it is. Call away general quarters.' He stared closely as Austen saluted. 'What happened to your face?'

Austen was reaching for the red lever that would send the crew to their battle stations.

'I slipped on a ladder, sir, making the rounds.' It's silly, he thought, lying at a time like this.

He pulled the lever. The alarms gonged through the ship. There's no sound like it in all the world, he thought. Wake up, you bastards. It's time to die.

He joined the captain, who had gone to the open bridge wing. He swept the north-northeast sector, steadying the glasses on the flat surface of the splinter shield. He paused at a faint blur.

'Something out there, Captain.'

The captain brought his glasses to bear. 'Might be kingposts,' he said after a moment. 'Some cargo ship, probably.'

'Two of them,' Austen said. 'And a single-pole mast to the right of them.'

The captain lowered his glasses slowly. 'It's no broaching whale, anyway. Have the galley prepare hot chow for all hands. Plenty of it.'

'Aye, sir.'

The captain slapped the communications officer on the back. 'Looks like a pair of sitting ducks, Sparky. We'll close as soon as the cans are on station. Start writing.'

He rubbed his big jaw.

'*ComNorPac from CO, this task group. Engaging two marus, one small escort, en route Attu. Looks like Roman holiday.*

'That's about it. Get it right off.'

'Aye, Captain.'

The navigator came out of the chartroom. His grey eyes were ringed with dark circles. He nodded brightly at Austen.

'Ready to relieve you.'

Austen recited the necessary details for the change of the watch.

Griswold saluted briefly. 'I relieve you.' He took the binoculars from Austen. Austen reported to the captain.

'I've been relieved, sir. Commander Griswold has the deck.'

'Very well. Don't slip on the ladder, Alec.'

'I'll try not to, sir.'

They smiled at each other. Next time I'll paint him in his wrinkled khakis, Austen thought. With neon shoulder boards, if he wants. He started to write the log.

'Skip it, Austen,' the navigator said. 'Better grab some chow and get to your battle station.'

He passed Dooley on the ladder. The gunnery officer looked pale and frightened. Austen gave way, feeling sorry for him.

The sea was calm in the faint grey light of morning. The ship still remained a shadowy silhouette without definition. Grey shapes moved about the decks preparing for the morning battle. No lights showed. The men growled and cursed and stumbled about readying the complicated machinery of war. He hurried through the narrow passageways crowded with men bulky in their life jackets. Their faces were heavy with sleep, spotted with fear and tense expectation.

He drank a cup of coffee in the wardroom. A crew of pharmacist's mates and attendants were converting it into an emergency operating room. The doors of the big medical cabinet were open. The men were taking down cartons labelled 'HUMAN BLOOD'.

The huge chrome lights over the tables had been lowered. Surgical instruments were boiling merrily in the large sterilizer.

Commander Blanchard came over.

'What's up there, Alec?'

'Looks like a couple of freighters or transports. There may be one small destroyer with them.' He lowered his voice. 'Did you see the exec?'

'I brought him down to his cabin.'

'How is he?'

'Hard to say. Did he get rough up there?'

'He wanted to know if we hated him. Nobody'd admit it. I got to go to my guns.' He headed for the ladder.

'Good luck, Alec.'

Austen passed the executive officer's cabin. The door was open. The commander was sitting stiffly on the edge of his bunk. Suddenly Austen felt sorry for him.

'They've called away general quarters, sir.'

'Thank you.' The commander did not look up. Austen hesitated. The executive officer's battle station was in Battle Two, topside and aft. Little time remained before the watertight doors throughout the ship would be sealed.

'Go away, please,' the executive officer said.

Austen went topside and aft. The men at the gunnery stations he passed were chattering happily, hungry for this easy victory.

He climbed into the gun-director tub and relieved Frenchy Shapiro of the phones. He exchanged his cap for the big Mark II battle helmet and reported the readiness of all guns aft to the bridge.

'Mind if I borrow the motor whaleboat, Boss?'

'Why, Frenchy? This is a pushover.'

'Nuts, Boss. We oughtta haul outta here.'

He pointed at the horizon. The masts of many ships were now visible to the naked eye. 'The JV talker just passed the Word. Two more cruisers and six cans. I want off, Boss.'

'Where the hell did they all come from?'

'Does it matter? There they are.' He grimaced. 'Just when I made up my mind I'm going back to Brooklyn.'

'You'll get back to Brooklyn all right.'

'Sure. Feet first.' He stared at Austen's face. 'Who slugged you?'

'None of your damned business.'

'Nobody loves me. Maybe I got halitosis or b.o. or something. I thought only us troops gets into fist fights. Not the gold braid.'

'Don't talk so damned much.'

'I gotta talk. If it don't come out one end it sure as hell will the other.'

Someone touched Austen's shoulder. He looked down. It was Fowler.

'They let us out,' he said. 'They said for me to report here, sir. Can you still use me?'

'I think so, Fowler. Just stick around and we'll see.'

He looked across the open water at the enemy ships. Two to one, he thought. We'll see, all right. Too damned soon.

24

AS mast after mast of the Japanese warships was sighted, Captain Meredith felt hopelessly certain that his small patrol force was doomed.

His original estimate of the tactical situation—the swift destruction of the enemy's two 'sitting ducks' and their escort vessel—now seemed somewhat ludicrous to him. He would have laughed if he had not been aware of its more deadly implications. He cursed softly.

It had seemed so simple. His three destroyers had closed rapidly, following his TBS message. The group formed up in battle line at their maximum speed and closed the range to the enemy ships to a point where they could open fire in a few minutes. Meanwhile the *marus* and their escorting destroyer had turned north to flee.

The captain winced and wiped his dry lips. The name of 'Snooky' would be long remembered, but not tenderly, when he went down with his ship. 'Snooky,' he thought forlornly. A Navy joke.

For a moment he wistfully considered escape. It was impossible to the east, where the enemy lay over the horizon. He could turn tail and fight what the Navy politely called 'a retiring action'. Just turn around and run like hell, Snooky, he thought. Head south, old gaffer, and live to run another day.

Easy enough. Mama and Gramma, sitting in the sun-drenched conservatory overlooking the Cliff Walk, would forgive you. Nobody in Newport is going to know the difference. And the Navy can be peculiarly silent about her cowards. So run, Snooky, while the running's good.

'More coffee, Ben,' he said.

He forlornly watched the racing enemy masts hull down to the north and east. This isn't for me, he grieved silently. The Navy has plenty of gamecocks who'd swap rank to be in my boots right now. Men like Red Eye Marcy, for instance. Why must it happen to me? he thought peevishly. Damnation.

He sipped the hot coffee. Sam Griswold was standing quietly at his side. He saluted.

'Destroyers are on station, Captain. Our course is three-five-zero, true. Speed, twenty-two knots.'

'Very well, Sam,' the captain said gloomily.

'I have just acknowledged for a message from the destroyers, sir.'

'What's the message, Sam?'

' "Will conform to your movements. God bless you, us and Uncle Sam." ' Griswold grinned. 'Sentimental son of a bitch, isn't he?'

The captain stared at his navigator's scarred mask of a face. Still a good-looking kid, he thought. Must have been dashing and handsome before he got it.

'Touching little message, Sam.'

'Very sweet, Captain. He included about everybody, I guess.'

The captain was staring at Griswold's scarred hands. 'Tell me, Sam. Did it hurt very much?'

Griswold grinned. 'Never even felt it, sir.'

'Must have been hell for a while.'

'It's a funny thing. You don't have time to think about it, sir. Not until it's all over and a long time later.'

'Do you really suppose God is going to bless us?'

'I suppose he'll get around to it. He's a busy guy these days.'

The captain scowled and rubbed his chin. He called for the communications officer. He came running over, pad in hand.

'Follow-up to ComNorPac, Sparky.'

'Delete Roman holiday my previous message. Enemy force now consists of two light cruisers six destroyers. Still counting. Immediate air support requested.

'That's it. Get it off on the double.'

'Aye, sir.' The officer tore the dispatch from the pad and handed it to a messenger and slapped the man's behind. The messenger scurried away.

The captain stared out to sea. 'Any more out there, Sam?'

' I doubt it, sir. Radar shows nothing more.'

'What about the *marus*?'

'They still show on the radarscope. Should be within range for the six-inch guns, sir, in about a minute.'

The captain called out to Lieutenant Commander Dooley, who was standing in a corner of the bridge. The long phone wires trailed after him. He tripped once, coming over.

'Range to the nearest target, Guns?' the captain said.

'Twenty thousand yards, Captain.' He paused nervously. 'Closing.'

'Very well.'

He looked to the horizon where the main force of the enemy was concentrated. 'I'd have sworn every damned one of them was a cargo vessel of some kind, Sam.'

'Those were false masts lashed to the fighting tops, sir.' He grimaced. 'Clever little bastards. Must be Hashida.' He did not look at the captain. 'Admiral Marcy would have liked to be here,' he said softly.

The captain said nothing.

'Won't be too bad, sir,' Griswold continued. 'At least there's nothing there can outshoot us. Not yet, anyway.'

'The odds are two to one.'

'Yes, Captain.'

'The lives of all these men are my responsibility, you know.'

'Yes, Captain.' His grey eyes steadily held the captain's.

'The safest manœuvre would be an immediate retiring action west, and then a possible swing to the south if we outrun them.'

'Yes, Captain.'

'What's the range to the nearest *maru*, Guns?'

'Closed to nineteen thousand yards, Captain.'

'Then what the hell are we waiting for? Let's get the bastard.'

Griswold's grave face broke in a wide smile. 'Now you're talking, sir. That's what Red Eye would have done.'

The gunnery officer was shouting instructions into the mouthpiece of his telephone. The big guns were trained to starboard, waiting.

The captain grinned jovially and slapped Griswold's back.

'The idea of retiring towards the Japanese home islands leaves me cold. We'll get the *marus*, Sam. It's our primary mission.'

'You've made an excellent decision, sir.'

The captain threw back his head and laughed. The men heard it and it was a fine sound to hear and they were less afraid, hearing it.

'I didn't make it, Sam. You did.'

'Me, Captain?'

'Believe me, Sam. You.' And he laughed again.

He felt better now that the decision to fight had been made. He looked at his watch. 0813. A long day ahead, he thought grimly.

The JV talker saluted him. 'Senior aviation officer requests permission to launch his plane, Captain.'

'Who?'

'Lieutenant Clough, sir.'

'Give Lieutenant Clough my congratulations. Tell him I'm delighted he's found a cure for his seasickness.'

'Aye, sir. What about the plane?'

'Not granted. We'll launch her if things take a turn for the worse. He'll get his chance.'

'Aye, sir.'

He frowned as the talker departed. Some chance, he thought.

Dooley screamed suddenly. 'Enemy's opened fire!'

The captain whirled. The gunnery officer's face was livid with fear and he ducked to the lee side of the pilothouse. Some of the men, seeing him, also took cover.

'Dooley!' the captain bawled. 'On your feet and out here where you belong!'

Dooley crept forward shakily. 'I saw their muzzle flashes, sir.'

'I don't care what the hell you saw. One more yell like that and I'll send you below.'

'I'm sorry, Captain.' The others rose shamefacedly.

'Let those trigger-happy little bastards waste their ammo. They're way the hell out of range. The *marus* are our primary target. Open fire as soon as they're in range.'

'Aye, sir.'

At that moment the first enemy salvo fell. It was a thousand yards short of the ship. The gunnery officer flinched and looked quickly at the captain.

'Right ten degrees rudder,' the captain said thrusting out his big jaw.

'Rudder is right ten degrees, sir.'

The speeding ship heeled sharply despite the small rudder change. A second salvo splashed five hundred yards closer.

'Steady as you go.'

The ship righted slowly. 'They're finding the range,' the captain said. 'Dooley, how about it? Those *marus* are close enough.'

Dooley's mouth hung open. He froze.

'Damn it, Dooley, commence firing!'

Dooley screamed the order into the phones.

In the plotting room deep inside the ship sweating men adjusted the sensitive instruments. The courses and speeds of their ship and the target ship were fed in by radar and visual ranges. They were then transmitted to the guns. The battery captains closed the firing circuits.

The six-inch guns roared. All batteries that could bear to starboard opened fire. The ship trembled with the impact of the eight-gun salvo. Black and yellow smoke wreathed the bridge and cordite fragments flew in all directions. Four more salvos followed the first in rapid succession.

On the nearest *maru* a burst of flame showed amidships, followed by a column of heavy smoke. The ship seemed to falter, then pursued an erratic course, trailing smoke. A second burst of flame showered her forecastle deck.

'Nice going, Dooley,' the captain shouted.

A third salvo from the enemy cruiser splashed a hundred yards beyond the *Atlantis*.

'Left ten degrees rudder.'

'Rudder is left ten degrees, sir.'

'That would've straddled if you'd remained on course,' Griswold said with a gleam of respect in his eye.

'Steady as you go,' the captain said calmly.   He was beginning to enjoy himself.

A sudden explosion rocked the *Atlantis*.   An enemy salvo had straddled the fantail.   The vibrations of the underwater explosion were felt on the bridge.

The *Atlantis's* shells were pouring steadily into the stricken *maru*.   Bright fires burned amidships and she listed badly.

'Right standard rudder!'   The ship heeled sharply and some of the men were thrown to the deck.   'Check fire, Dooley.'

'Aye, sir.'

The phone talker came over.   'Captain——'

'Steady as you go, helmsman.'

'Aye, sir.'

The thunder ceased.   Smoke drifted rapidly aft.

'Captain,' the talker said.   'Air-search radar reports they're out of commission.'

'Very well.'   He stared dully at the man.

Commander Griswold looked up at the peak of the tripod mainmast.   The SC antenna hung by a few thin wires.

'Probably one of those near misses that passed over, sir.'

'Advise all lookouts to double their alertness.'

'Aye, sir.'

The captain gripped the edge of the splinter shield and looked around.   One *maru* burning.   Good.   The enemy cruisers about zeroed in on the *Atlantis*.   Not so good.   One more of those straddles might change the picture, he thought.

'Course of the second *maru*, Sam?'

'North northwest, sir, and running like hell.'

'I'd love to take a crack at them,' the captain said wistfully.

'He's headed for home, sir.'

'I know.'

Primary mission accomplished, he thought.   For the time being, anyway.   He wiped his grimy face.   The residue of powder smoke on his sleeve looked good, he thought.

An enemy salvo fell to port a bare fifty yards from the bridge. The explosions rocked through the ship.

Go west, young man, the captain thought, holding on.

'Left standard rudder.'

'Rudder is left standard, sir.'

'Come to course two-seven zero.   All engines ahead flank speed.'

'Two-seven-zero, sir.   All engines ahead flank.'

'Take the nearest cruiser under fire, Dooley, at any time.'

'Aye, sir.'

The starboard batteries aft and the twin mount on the fantail opened fire.   The after end of the *Atlantis* shivered under the impact.   The captain watched the splashes through his binoculars.

'Short, Dooley.   For Christ sake get 'em in there.'

Dooley pushed back his helmet and snarled into the phone. He listened.   He heard the spotter's voice in forward control shout, 'Up five-double-oh.'   He waited, afraid to look at the captain.

The next salvo brought a small burst of smoke from the super-structure of the leading Japanese cruiser.

'You're in,' the captain shouted savagely.   'Now stay there!'

The talker saluted.   'Damage control reports some buckled plates in the forward fireroom, sir.   No immediate danger, they say.   A repair crew is working on it.'

'Very well.'

A few more of these near misses, he thought grimly, and the old girl is going to split her britches.   He frowned.   Maybe I hung onto that one *maru* too long, he thought.   He looked anxiously at the line of masts still hull down.

The talker said, 'Catapult deck, sir.   They're asking about launching the plane again.'

The captain checked the wind direction.   It was still wrong.

'Tell Dave Clough to hold his water, damn it.   I'm running this ship—not those zoomies.'

'Aye, sir.'

Damned impudence, the captain thought.   This new breed of cocky little Academy fly boys.

The big guns aft continued to pour shells across the glassy morning sea.   Enemy salvos fell close aboard the *Atlantis* as she raced through the sea, but as yet inflicted no direct damage.   The captain continued his light-footed salvo-chasing, nimbly heading for the area of the enemy's last splashes. So far it had worked remarkably well.

'We're checking fire, Captain,' Dooley said. 'The range has opened.'

'Very well, Dooley.' He studied the man's face. He was still pale, but the fear was gone from his eyes. 'You're doing fine, John,' the captain added. Dooley lowered his head and walked away.

The talker came over. 'Radar reports one enemy *maru* has disappeared from the screen, Captain. The closer one.'

The captain glanced swiftly to sea where the freighter had last been seen afire and drifting. There was nothing but clear horizon. Commander Griswold came out of the chartroom.

'Congratulations, Captain.' He was grinning.

'Well,' the captain said. 'Put it out on all circuits, talker. *Scratch one maru.*' He wiped his streaked face. Griswold handed him a battle helmet. The captain pushed it away. 'Might change my luck,' he said. He felt the blood tingling through him.

Dooley came over. 'The lookouts in Sky One report that a plane's been launched from one of the Jap cruisers, Captain.'

'Track him with the three-inch guns, Dooley. Get word aft to Austen and his crews to open fire if the plane's in range.'

'Aye, Captain.'

That's it, the captain thought. He watched through his glasses as the enemy plane rose and circled almost dead astern. Eighteen thousand yards, he estimated. He can sit out there as safe as Santa Claus and spot their gunfire for them. They'll be laying 'em right down the stacks, he thought.

'Range, Dooley?'

'Still opening, Captain.'

'How about that, Sam? Those are *Sendai* cruisers. They're rated as fast as us—maybe a knot or two better. How come we're pulling away?'

'They're zigzagging, sir. Afraid of our torpedoes, I guess.'

'At this range?' He shrugged and looked anxiously at the spread of enemy ships. 'I'll tell you what they're doing, Sam. They're spreading to keep us from turning south. Looks to me like we're going to spend the night in Tokyo.'

'Better than the sea, Captain. The water temperature is twenty-eight.'

'I'll take the sea, Sam.' He rubbed his nose. 'Left five degrees rudder!' he shouted to the helmsman.

'Rudder is left five degrees, Captain.'

The *Atlantis* commenced its racing turn to port. The course-change signal flags creaked flapping to the peak of the halyards. The destroyers acknowledged with similar hoists and churned to their new stations.

'Come to course two-zero-zero, helmsman.'

'Two-zero-zero, aye, sir.'

'Let's see if the bastards can still shoot,' the captain said.

The throbbing at flank speed had slackened. The stack and masts of the nearest Japanese cruiser were clearly visible off the port quarter. Tiny flashes showed from her rakish silhouette.

'Commence firing at any time, Guns,' the captain said.

'Yes, sir.'

'Better wear the helmet, Captain,' Griswold said.

'The hell with it, Sam.'

The six-inch port batteries thundered. Flame and smoke enveloped the bridge. The men coughed and cursed and clawed at their eyes with stiff cold fingers.

There was a shattering explosion amidships. The men on the bridge were hurled to the deck by the concussion. The ship seemed to lurch in its headlong course through the sea.

The captain sprawled helplessly against the forward bulkhead of the pilothouse. He clutched the port binnacle.

'Right standard rudder!' he bawled. He tasted blood inside his mouth and sucked at its dizzying sweetness.

'Rudder is right standard.' The helmsman clung to the wheel. The captain scrambled to his feet.

'Direct hit on the catapult deck, sir,' the talker reported.

'Christ. I thought it was here,' the captain said.

'Forty millimetres aft report a man overboard, Captain. Just drifted by the fantail.'

The captain had made his way to the after part of the bridge. He leaned over the flag bags and stared aft to the catapult deck.

The plane was half hidden in flame and smoke. Several me lay on the deck and one swung crazily from the catapult itself. Two damage-control men were dragging a hose across the deck. Another played a stream from a fire extinguisher between the draped body and the flames.

'She's gassed up. Jettison her,' the captain ordered.

The talker bawled the order into his phones. Two men on the catapult deck leaped on the plane's wing and struggled with the covered cockpit. The intense heat forced them back.

'What the hell are they waiting for?' the captain said. 'Get her over the side before she explodes. She's loaded with high octane.'

'They're trying to reach Mr. Clough and the radio-gunner, sir.'

'Jettison her at once,' the captain said. 'Cut away a life raft. Release a Frandlin buoy from the bridge.' He turned away and went forward.

The talker rasped his message over the circuit. The captain watched stony-eyed, dabbing at his bleeding lip. The flaming hulk of the OS2U slid into the water and drifted rapidly aft. A battle-painted life raft bobbed and bounced and was lost in the trough of the sea.

The bridge seemed quiet although the six-inch batteries were still pouring shells across the sea. 'Report on casualties and damage from the catapult deck, please,' the captain said evenly.

'Torpedo control reports all tubes abaft the catapult deck are out of commission, sir.'

'Can they be fired manually?'

'No, sir.'

'Disarm all torpedo tubes. Have the crews fill in wherever there have been casualties.'

'Aye, sir. Chief torpedoman reports no other casualties.'

'What about the catapult deck?'

'Eleven, sir, not counting the two in the plane.'

'Killed?'

'Three, sir. One man blown over the side—the one Mr. Austen reported. All fires are out, sir.'

'Very well.' He turned to the helmsman, who averted his frightened eyes. 'Steady as you go. What's your heading?'

'Coming to three-zero-zero, Captain.'

'Very well. That's your course for the present. Talker?'

'Yes, sir.'

'Abandon torpedo control station. Have the torpedo officer report where he places his men.'

'Aye, sir.'

A messenger swung up the ladder and handed the communications officer a dispatch. He glanced at it and handed it to the captain. The captain read it and called Sam Griswold, who read it.

It was from ComNorPac in Adak. It acknowledged Captain Meredith's second dispatch and suggested that in view of the overwhelming odds he ignore the *marus* and fight a retiring action. It also stated that the Army Air Force was dispatching a squadron of bombers but there would be some delay. The planes were armed with the wrong type of bomb for such an attack.

Griswold and the captain looked at each other.

'Any answer, Captain?' the communications officer asked.

'Please don't tempt me,' the captain said. He turned away.

In the wardroom they heard the thunder of guns. The bulkheads shook. Dishes crashed to the deck. The men stirred uneasily and looked at each other.

Commander Blanchard sat in one of the old leather easy chairs in the wardroom. A hospital attendant brought over a white surgical gown and a pair of rubber gloves. Blanchard glanced round the room while the man helped him into the gown.

Across the room a chief petty officer was calling the roll of his repair party. He read the names from a small black book. The men answered quietly. Their faces were calm. They might have been in a classroom except that their eyes had a tense, troubled look. It was very quiet in the wardroom. There was only the sound of their names and the answers.

The attendant finished and Blanchard sat again. He closed his eyes and wondered how long he would be able to go without a drink.

'Fogarty,' the chief said.

'Here.'

'Romano.'

'Here.'

'Edmundsen.'

'Here.'

'Wilcox.'

'Here.'

The doctor smiled a little. His eyes were still closed. He felt relaxed and comfortable and hoped he would stay that way until it was over.

Names, he thought. He envisioned the legion of limbs and torsos, as uniform and endless as rows of pale carcasses on packing-house hooks. He pictured the brightly coloured insides of men.

Names. What difference do the names make?

In a little while the chief pharmacist's mate came over and touched Blanchard respectfully.

'They're bringing down the wounded, Commander.'

Blanchard got to his feet and smiled sadly. 'That's what we're here for, isn't it, Chief?'

'I guess so, sir,' the chief said.

Austen watched through his binoculars as the smoking hulk of the plane drifted past. He searched the battered cockpit cover.

'See anybody, Boss?'

Austen shook his head. 'Not since Slobodj.'

'You sure it was him, sir?'

Austen nodded. 'He waved.' His voice choked.

'The talker says Mr. Clough and his zoomie were still in it when they give it the deep six.'

'There's nobody in it now,' Austen said.

The grey life raft followed. They watched it until it was gone from sight. Below them the big twin six-inch mount thundered its salvos at the enemy.

'Go be a flier,' Frenchy said.

Things were going badly on the bridge.

'The rudder's answering awful slow, Captain,' the helmsman said. 'She don't feel right.'

'Check with the steering engine room, Sam.'

Griswold reported back. 'Seems the hydraulic power's been carried away by the vibration of our gunfire, Captain.'

'Very well. Notify the cans we have limited steering power.' He stood alongside the helmsman and stared at the slowly changing course. 'At this rate we're dead ducks,' he muttered.

An explosion somewhere aft jarred the ship.

'Anti-aircraft gun deck, Captain,' the talker reported.

Alec, the captain thought.

'Report casualties and damage as soon as you have it,' he said evenly.

'Dooley!' he shouted.

'Yes, sir?'

'Maintain maximum fire power. No need to let them know our troubles.'

'Aye, sir.'

'Sam, have the engineer officer stand by to make smoke.'

'Aye, sir.'

'Signal bridge! Flag hoist to the destroyers: *Prepare to lay smoke screen*.'

'Aye, sir.'

The talker came over.

'Casualty report is in, Captain. The hit was in the starboard twenty-millimetre clipping room. It exploded through the deck and topside. Three of the twenties were damaged. One's still in commission and manned and ready.'

'The casualties, man, for Christ sake——'

'Ensign Gillies, sir. Lieutenant Austen reports he's dead and two of the crew wounded by bomb splinters. Forty-millimetre mount Number Two is out of commission. Mr. Austen says he's putting the surviving men into his ammunition loading crews.'

'A hell of a lot of loaders for one lousy gun with one lousy barrel.'

'Shall I tell him——'

'No, no.' The captain waved his hand wearily. 'Tell them to keep that damned spotting plane in sight and if it comes anywhere near to let him have it.'

'Yes, sir.'

'He's spotting too damned accurately.'

Griswold came over.

'After steering reports they've jury-rigged a small engine, Captain. It can give you rudder changes up to ten degrees. If that fails, they'll have to resort to hand steering.'

'Then we're really up the creek, Sam, eh?'

'We're still under way, Captain.'

'Check with Battle Two, talker. See how their steering responds. We may have to shift the helm aft.'

'Aye, sir.' He spoke into the phones. 'Battle Two is standing by, sir. Steering engine room is standing by.'

'Very well. Shift steering to Battle Two.'

They waited. The talker listened tensely. The bridge shivered as the six-inch guns flung deafening salvos across the sea.

'They report the helm answers sluggishly, sir.'

'Shift steering back to the bridge. Tell the exec. we have limited steering control here.'

'Aye, sir.' He talked, then listened. 'The Battle Two talker says the exec. isn't there, Captain.'

'Where the hell is he?'

'They say he didn't show up for general quarters, sir.'

There was a muffled explosion deep inside the ship. They felt its jarring repercussion on the bridge. The ship faltered in its onward rush through the sea. She settled slightly to port. The big guns still fired and ship's speed was almost immediately resumed.

The captain swore. A hit like that, deep in the bowels of the ship, had to be a deadly one. There was too much in too little space to escape lightly.

He was still numbed by the swift series of casualties and the dereliction of his executive officer. He looked grimly across the racing wake of the ship at the partly hidden silhouettes of the enemy.

'Hit in the after fireroom, Captain.'

'Very well. Get the damage and casualty report.'

He watched through his glasses. His own shells were geysering their splashes steadily about the leading enemy cruiser. It was impossible not to be scoring hits, he thought. Sixty shells a minute. Why doesn't something happen? His insides felt leaden. He remembered the boys in the after fireroom. What a hell, he thought.

A tongue of bright flame leaped across the superstructure of the enemy cruiser. He had it pin-pointed in his binoculars and observed it with astonishing clarity. She veered slightly from her station in the battle line and began smoking heavily.

'You're right on, Guns,' he shouted. 'Pour it on the bastard! You're right on!' He danced up and down.

The enemy cruiser slowed and the *Atlantis's* shells scored twice again. She heeled sharply and the formation passed by her. Flames licked along her foremast. Her guns still fired but were wildly disorganized.

'Nice work, John,' the captain called out. Maybe, he thought, *maybe* we'll make it.

Masked behind a screen of smoke he could try a swing once more to the south and surprise them. If his speed and luck held he might work well enough eastward to outrun them. The *marus* had been diverted. One of them was sunk. Now there was his own hide that mattered. His own and eight hundred others.

The signal to the destroyers still fluttered at the dip, awaiting his final order.

'Two-block your smoke-screen signal,' he ordered the communications officer.

'Aye, sir.'

The halyards squealed. The signal flags raced to the yardarm.

'Tell the engine room to commence making smoke.'

'Aye, sir.'

'Any word from them yet on casualties or damage?'

'Not yet, Captain.'

'Ask the engineer officer what it's like down there.'

The talker inquired. His face twitched as he listened. He stared at the captain uncomfortably.

'What's he saying?' the captain asked impatiently.

'He wants to know who threw the muck in the electric fan, sir,' the talker said shamefacedly.

The captain frowned. Then he laughed and slapped the talker.

'Good,' he said. 'That's a good report.'

'He'll phone up his report in a minute, he says.'

The ship rocked crazily under the impact of another near miss. The captain stopped laughing and cursed under his breath.

'Left full rudder,' he said. She'll come about slowly anyway, he knew. 'Hard over as she'll go, helmsman.' To hell with chasing salvos, he thought. That damned spotting plane's taken the fun out of it.

He tossed away his salty-looking khaki cap with its green-encrusted embroidered device. He picked up his battle helmet and jammed it on his head and tightened the chin strap.

The helmsman was watching the gyrocompass with an anguished face. 'She's awful slow, Captain. And she's as hard over as she'll go.'

'Very well. Steady her on one-eight-zero.'

He felt lightheaded. Inside him a small knot of sorrow reminded him of the last hour's casualties. Commander Griswold came out of the chartroom.

'Glad to see the course change, sir. We were getting uncomfortably close to Kamchatka.'

'Would that be so bad, Sam?'

The destroyers raced by, clouds of thick white smoke pouring from their raked stacks. On the open bridge of the leading destroyer an officer's arm shot upward in a victory gesture. Captain Meredith answered with the same.

Hell, he thought, you'd think he was watching the Sunday boat races on the Severn.

The bridge phone rang.

'Engineer officer, Captain.'

The captain took the receiver. It crackled.

'Several casualties, Captain, all minor. Nobody killed, Christ knows why. I don't. But we're in trouble.'

'What kind of trouble?'

'The after oil manifold is shot away. The bulkhead is leaking badly. The after gyro room's flooded and the after engine room under a couple of feet of water. The crew down here's working like hell but they ain't fish and the water's cold as a bastard.'

'Can we hold our present speed?'

'That's it. I don't see how. The goddamn water's spreading

to the after engine room. We don't have the steam-line leaks under control yet and it's tough to get around. The oil sludge is thick as mud. We're trying like hell to keep the sea water out of the fuel oil. If it gets any higher we may have to stop all engines to clear the lines.' He paused. The captain could hear the ominous sounds of sloshing water and the throbbing of the pumps. 'That's about it, Captain.'

'Very well.' He hung up slowly. The phone rang again, almost instantly.

'Captain?'

'Speaking.'

'Me again. Steam pressure's dropping fast. All burners are out.'

'How the hell did that happen?'

The engineer officer's voice had the calmness of sheer desperation.

'Because, Captain, some stupid goddamn son of a bitch of a snipe down here lost his head.' His voice broke.

'How? What happened?'

'We were trying to correct the five-degrees list. Sea water got into the fuel line—the only damned fuel line that wasn't damaged.'

'Jesus, man—how? How in hell——'

The engineer officer's voice sounded very tired.

'The poor benighted bastard connected the ballast-transfer line to the fuel line and pumped in the sea water.'

'How long will it take to repair it?'

'It's hard to say, Captain.'

The gunnery officer came in, pale and anxious.

'We're slowing down, sir. They're closing the range fast.'

'Thank you, Mr. Dooley.'

He hung up the receiver and brushed past the cluster of silent, staring men. He walked out to the port bridge wing and called for the chief signalman and the communications officer.

'Hoist the following signal to the dip, Chief: *My speed zero.*'

'Aye, sir.'

The captain ignored his stunned face.

'Sparks, stand by for a TBS to the destroyers, the same message. They might miss the flag hoist with all this goddamned smoke screen.'

'Aye, sir.'

'Tell the *Clovis* and *Washbourne* to prepare for torpedo attack. Request the *Brant* to stand by for an order to come alongside for the transfer of sick and wounded.'

'Aye, sir.' He hurried into the pilothouse.

'Talker.'

'Aye, sir.'

'Get the word to sick bay to make preparations to remove all sick and wounded. Advise the first lieutenant to rig cargo nets port and starboard and stand by to release all life rafts and buoys and launch the motor whaleboats on signal.'

'Aye, sir.'

Griswold came over. The captain looked at him guiltily.

'It's our only hope, Sam. Maybe the cans'll be diversion enough until we can get going again.'

That's about it, he thought wearily. He could not look at their faces as they carried out his orders. The smoke drifted about them as warm and secure as a wool blanket. Nothing to do but sweat it out, he thought, until they see us sitting here.

'Talker.'

'Aye, sir.'

'I want every man aboard wearing his life jacket.'

'Aye, sir.'

He touched Sam Griswold's blue wind jacket.

'Can you think of anything else, Sam?'

'No, Captain. You've got it covered.'

'Send off that TBS to the cans, then. Execute all flag hoists.' He took a deep breath. He went over to the radar-scope and watched it. The communications officer stood at the TBS and sent the voice message over the circuit to the destroyers.

The bridge was quiet. He watched the radar screen as the two bright blips that were the *Clovis* and *Washbourne* changed course and headed towards the enemy. The third blip slowly approached the *Atlantis*.

The TBS blared. The captain went into the pilothouse to listen.

'Bigwig, this is Roughneck. Over.'

'Come in, Roughneck,' the communications officer said.

'Wilco your last message. Thank you. It's been an honour to serve with you. Over and out.'

The instrument crackled to silence.

'Good luck, boy,' the captain murmured. 'Good hunting.'

'Did you want to say something to him, Captain?'

'What the hell could I say to a man I've just sentenced to death?' the captain said angrily. He stared at his watch. The crystal had been shattered. He felt lonely and abused.

The bridge chronometer read 1058. His head itched under the heavy steel helmet. He took it off and scratched his damp head. His ears rang. We're all deaf, he thought.

'Mr. Dooley.' He had to shout.

'Yes, Captain?' Dooley shuffled over. His face was red and streaked with gun dust.

'For a guy who's so scared of gunfire you've done a very nice job.'

Dooley lowered his red-rimmed eyes.

'I'm still scared, sir.'

'Good, John. So am I.' He spoke softly. Dooley had to lean close to hear his words. 'John. If the engine room can give me a few knots, I'm going to close. Pass the Word to all gun stations to be prepared to expend every last piece of ammunition. We may end up slugging it out at close quarters. Break out all small arms from the armoury. Pass around the tommy guns and .45s and ammunition as far as it'll go.'

'Aye, sir.'

The captain turned to Griswold, who was intently watching the destroyers on the radar screen.

'I'd like one more swipe at those bastards, Sam, before we quit.'

'Nobody's quitting yet, Captain.'

'Think the boys'd like a smoke?'

'I think they'd love a smoke.'

'Bosun's mate of the watch.'

'Aye, sir?'

'Your squawk box still in commission?'

'Yes, sir.'

'Light the smoking lamp throughout the ship.'

234

'Aye, sir.'

The bosun's pipe shrilled over the ship's circuit. They could hear his voice echoing and the faint cheers it roused in return.

'Cigarette, Sam?'

'Thank you, sir.'

They lit up. The ship drifted aimlessly, dead in the oil-streaked water. The captain glanced up once at the limp flag hoist.

'My speed zero,' he said softly. 'It always was.'

'I can't hear a word you're saying,' Griswold said, 'I'm deaf from all those guns.'

25

THE executive officer sat unmoving in the straight armless chair behind the locked door of his cabin. His slender hands were clasped in his lap as primly as a school child's. There was an absence of expression on his lined, homely face. His mind dwelled on the distant past. Time and place no longer held sequence or meaning for him.

Why have I failed, he wondered, *and where?*

There had been a time, he remembered, when he had had a name and not a title, a Christian name and a family name. He thought of his father, now dead—a defrocked preacher with a weakness for whisky and an incurable failing for the fraudulent use of the mails. And he thought of his mother, who was also dead, whom he had known only as a faded face in a tarnished picture frame—a face that showed patient sweetness and none of the swift cancer that ravished it.

And he thought of his grandfather, his mother's father, a stern and bigoted man who had raised him in the dusty Ohio town where they had finally sent him to live.

The old man ran the boy with the same joyless tyranny that he ran his feed business. There were days and nights of gruelling work in the dust-choked shed. The boy filled and lugged the heavy sacks of seed and feed and fertilizer.

Then, as though it were a righteous punishment, to atone for his father's weakness, and to balance the books for his mother's unhappy death, the old man arranged a military appointment for his grandson.

Why do they say I hate the men? he wondered.

Annapolis was a sanctuary when he came there. He was freed of the old man's endless and cruel haranguing. He was freed of the smell of the feed store. He embraced the new life at the Academy as one embraces a new faith. It became in time a place of worship. And in the span of his service years, cold to counsel and blind to change, he did not once relinquish this fanatic devotion.

It is the men who hate me. It is they who have failed me. Because I have loved—not hated.

A shattering explosion rocked the room. Directly above him the ship's starboard batteries had commenced firing. He was thrown heavily against the side of his bunk. He recovered and looked about anxiously. He started to straighten the bedcovers. The guns continued to fire in deafening salvos.

He tried to capture loose gear that fell from the bulkheads. He scooped up curlings of the pale green paint that had blistered and fallen. The guns thundered again and again. It was no use. He stumbled to the far side and flung open the port.

The masts of the enemy ships showed clearly against the cold morning horizon. He gripped the sides of the porthole and breathed the icy, sweet air and stared for a long time at the racing plumes of the enemy.

He closed the port and dogged it down. He unlocked his sea chest and took out his Navy sword from its shiny black and gold scabbard. He undressed methodically and carefully hung away his uniform and disposed of his underclothes. He sat cross-legged and naked on the steel deck and faced the enemy he could no longer see. There was no revealing expression on his homely face.

He clutched the blade below the hilt and plunged its point into himself. The flood of pain sent him writhing sideways. His hands did not relinquish their hold. He drove the point steadily deeper. The effort contorted his face with agony. He stopped. His bleeding fingers slipped from the blade. Slowly he righted himself.

Above him the ship's guns thundered. He watched glaze-eyed at the disorder of his cabin spread about him. A thin trickle of blood started from the corner of his lips. He bent in great pain until his taut, curled fingers reached the hilt of the sword. He gripped it and forced the blade deeper and downward. Slowly he began to die.

26

MIKE EDGE was putting the finishing touches to a very handsome double Turk's-head when he heard the vibrant clang of the general alarm.

He stirred uneasily. The clanging persisted. He put the manila aside for a moment and rubbed his bruised knuckles. He wiped his nose on his sleeve. He looked at his watch.

A hell of a time for GQ, he thought.

He snuffled and twisted his tear-stained face. The alarm continued its strident call.

'Shut up!' he screamed suddenly.

His shrill voice reverberated in the small compartment. He picked up the piece of manila again.

All I ask is a little peace and quiet, he thought plaintively. Why the hell don't they leave me alone?

He tried to work the knot. His fingers had lost their sureness. He tore angrily at the fouled strands. He finally heaved the line across the compartment and stood up. He crawled through the scuttle and started through the ship.

The ship heeled in a sharp turn. He was thrown heavily to the deck. He looked frightened for the first time and scrambled to his feet. He thrust a seaman from his path and lurched through the ship muttering to himself. Men at their battle stations turned to watch him.

It was nice down there, he thought. Quiet. Nobody plaguing me. When he arrived at his battle station the steel door had already been dogged down. Edge pounded on it and bellowed anxious curses.

'That you, Mr. Edge?'

'Open the goddamned door and don't ask silly questions!'

He shoved his way inside and pushed through the narrow passageway. The men stumbled out of his way.

'What the hell you guys tryin' to do to me?'

'We waited as long as we could, sir. They already passed the Word to set Condition Able.'

'Okay, okay.' He looked at them belligerently. There were four men in his repair party. They huddled together, their faces streaked with sleep and fear. 'You report to central station already?'

'Yes, sir. Manned and ready.'

They settled down and waited. Edge watched them nervously.

'What's goin' on up there?'

The phone talker was a thin boy whose bony face was almost lost under the big Mark II helmet.

'The guys in central station say it's a couple Jap *marus*, sir.'

There was a muffled explosion. The passageway vibrated. A fire axe fell from the bulkhead and clattered to the deck.

'Lash that goddamned thing down,' Edge howled.

The *Atlantis's* guns were firing in teeth-jarring salvos. The repair party sat in stunned silence as the shells pounded across the sea. The minutes passed.

Another explosion rocked the ship. The men were hurled against each other. They stared at Edge with pale, terrified faces.

'Christ, that was close!'

Edge looked thoroughly frightened. He staggered up and cursed.

'That was no goddamned *maru*!'

He moved among them, sharply slapping the tops of their battle helmets.

'On your feet, you chicken bastards,' he chattered. There was another shattering explosion. An overhead line spurted white-hot steam. The men ducked. Edge crawled to a safe distance and howled at them to stand their ground.

A chief water tender named Farley crept forward and spun the stop valve on the steam line. The fountain of hissing steam slowly died, bubbling. Farley wiped his scalded face and called out to the phone talker. Edge watched him, paralyzed with terror.

'Tell central station we got us a parted steam line, frames seventy-nine to eighty-nine, starboard side,' Farley said.

The talker relayed the message.

'Central station acknowledges, Chief. They're by-passing the line along those frames.'

Edge lay stiff with fear at the forward end of the sealed passageway. He licked his dry lips.

'One of you guys gimme a hand here. I strained my back.'

They helped him to his feet. He remained bent, glowering at them, his mouth drawn in simulated pain.

'Talker.'

'Yes, sir.'

'Tell central station to jump the parted section of steam line.'

'I already did, sir.'

'On whose orders?'

'Farley, sir. I thought——'

'Shut up!'

He glowered at Farley, who regarded him with sullen steadiness. Edge lowered his gaze and reached his hand to his hip as though in pain.

'Should I request an attendant, Mr. Edge?'

'Think I'm chicken?' Edge snarled. He straightened up. Hot steam still dribbled from the parted line. A few inches of water puddled the deck where they stood. Above them the six-inch guns thumped regularly, jarring the bulkheads, flaking paint, clattering the repair tools. 'Anybody else hurt?'

'Clancy's nose is bleeding.'

'Lay him on the deck with his head back.'

'It's awful wet on the deck, Mr. Edge,' Clancy said.

'The hell with you, then. It's your nose.'

'I'll be okay, sir.'

'They got hit bad on the catapult deck, Mr. Edge,' the talker reported. 'The plane's on fire.'

'The hell with that. We got our own troubles.'

He glared at Clancy's bleeding nose and suddenly remembered

239

Austen. The memory sent the blood pounding to his head. The men watched his distorted face anxiously. He slapped at them roughly.

'The rest of you guys on your feet.' He wiped his coarse lips and touched his nose self-consciously and looked at his sweaty fingers for blood.

'Clancy, you can squat till your nose stops bleeding.'

'Thank you, sir.'

The men slouched against the damp bulkheads. Clouds of steam continued to pour from the ruptured line. Farley tore at the shirt under his life jacket and wrapped strips of the cloth around it to slacken the flow.

The racking thunder of near misses broke the uneasy silence. The men huddled together apart from Edge. The ship lurched in a high-speed turn. The men clung to the fittings and to each other. Edge sat alone, rubbing his sore knuckles. He watched the men furtively. The long minutes crept by.

The talker looked over at Edge once.

'It ain't only *marus*, Mr. Edge. You were right. There's two Jap cruisers and they don't know how many destroyers.'

Edge stared at him vacantly.

'And the exec. ain't showed up at Battle Two. They don't know where he is.'

'Mind your own goddamned business,' Edge grunted.

The bulkhead plates shook as the *Atlantis* poured her big shells into the enemy force. The enemy's gunfire fell dangerously close to her own thin sides. The men shivered and sweated. One of them whimpered. Another tried to comfort him.

Farley looked up. A small stream of oil bubbled from a seam in the fuel line. It dribbled to the wet deck. An enemy shell erupted in a near-by compartment. The oil burst through the split seam and cascaded round them in a shining black shower. Farley cut the flow of fuel by spinning a shut-off valve.

Edge came to life. 'Report that leak to central station, talker,' he said in a loud voice. He sat there avoiding the men's troubled eyes as the talker transmitted the message.

'They're jumping the section of fuel line, sir.'

'Tell 'em it's getting awful nasty in here.'

'Aye, sir.' The man transmitted the order.

'They say anything?'

'No, sir.'

Edge wiped his mouth. 'Tell 'em the compartment's flooding. Ask 'em can we abandon this station.' He ran the last words together shrilly. He clutched his back and shielded his fear in an expression of intense pain.

'Aye, sir.'

Farley watched Edge's contortions with open contempt.

'It ain't that bad, Mr. Edge,' he said. 'The water's still below the hatch coamings.'

'Shore up that leak, goddamnit, and don't tell me what to do!' His curses poured over their heads as fluid and black as the bunker oil itself. The men slipped and clawed and fell in their frantic efforts to obey him. 'What about central station, talker. What'd they say?'

'Permission not granted, sir.'

Edge cursed insanely. The oil sludge had inched around their ankles. Edge slithered alongside the talker and grabbed his life jacket fiercely.

'You tell them the fuel line is busted and we're taking on sea water in here badly. Up to six—hell—ten inches.' He shook the talker. 'Tell 'em a foot of water and rising fast.'

The talker transmitted the message. They watched him tensely.

'Damage-control officer says to stand by your station and to stop sending in foolish requests. He said to tell you they're busy enough with real damage reports.'

'Real?' Edge bellowed. *'Real?'*

The fear of entrapment panicked him. He sloshed through the oil thrusting the men aside. 'Ain't this real enough, for Christ sake?'

Farley watched him narrowly. 'This ain't so bad, Mr. Edge.'

'Who asked you?' He looked about wildly. 'You—Clancy. Up on your feet. You gonna let that nose bleed all day?'

Clancy got up and immediately fell as a near miss hit the water and exploded beneath the surface. Sea water hissed through the seams where the bulkhead plates had warped and the rivets pulled away.

The men worked furiously to shore up the damaged bulkhead with heavy canvas. Their glistening bodies slid about helplessly. Their grease-soaked, chilled fingers were useless in the icy sludge.

For a moment Edge remembered the peaceful isolation of the bosun's locker.

I shoulda stayed, he mourned. Who the hell'd 'a known the difference?

He sobbed once. The men heard it and recognized instantly the end of leadership.

'I'm shoving off,' the talker said suddenly.

He ripped the helmet from his head. The phones crashed against the bulkhead. Edge watched him dazedly.

'Hold it, kid,' Farley said sharply. 'We're okay. Just hold it.'

He grabbed the talker's life jacket. The man struggled for a few moments, then seemed to collapse all at once, crying softly against Farley's shoulder.

The ship listed. Edge watched the stream of sea water through the narrow seams. He sloshed hastily towards the steel door at the end of the passageway. Farley tried to block his way. He was hampered by the sagging bulk of the phone talker. Edge rushed by them, and struggled with the handles that latched the door.

'Run, you pig,' Farley shouted. Edge did not seem to hear him.

Farley tried to comfort the terrified boy in his arms. He ruffled the damp, bared head. 'We'll be okay, kid,' he said softly. 'Let that yellow pig run.'

There was an earsplitting explosion. The passageway was plunged into darkness. A man moaned. The piteous sound of it bubbled away as his face sank in the oily water.

Edge heard nothing. He had been blown against the bulkhead by the concussion. As he fell his head struck heavily against the door handle he had been holding.

The big guns ceased firing. The water trickled down the oil-spattered plates. Except for that the inside of the sealed passageway had the silence of a tomb.

Edge opened his eyes to darkness. Something icy had touched his face. He pushed at it, coughing as the water in which he lay reached his nostrils. He struggled to his feet, coughing and spitting. His groping fingers touched a cold face in the dark water. The water was deeper now, he realized. He shook his head and ran his fingers along the side of his face where the bulge of pain lay crusty with dried blood.

He reached across the dead man's body. His hand found the hard sides of a battle lantern. He tried to pry it from the stiff fingers. He was unable to free it. He searched in the dark until he found the big Stillson wrench in a repair kit. He smashed at the dead fingers until the lantern came away. He flicked the switch and played its beam about the wrecked passageway. The others were dead. He turned over the last of them and stared at the greyish face. It was Farley.

Edge tried to kick the limp, unyielding body, but his foot was impeded by the oily water. Farley drifted away with the slowed impact. Edge swung the Stillson and bashed in the dead face. It turned, slowly reddening the water. Edge switched off the light. He leaned against the bulkhead, breathing heavy sobs, listening to the slow drip of water.

He stiffened. Something was missing. The ship was silent. He strained his ear sto catch some faint sound of the turbines. There was none. He pressed his ear against the ship's side. There was no sound of the sea racing by. He stared at his useless watch and ripped it angrily from his wrist.

Dead in the water, he thought numbly. Sealed in this hole and abandoned. The bastards, he thought. Them and their god-damned watertight integrity.

The air was musty and close, rich with the stink of oil and cordite. He imagined swiftly that he was finding it increasingly difficult to breathe. He clawed at his throat. He struggled to open the collar of his life jacket. The lantern slipped from his fingers and, cursing, he grabbed it up and flicked the switch.

The light calmed him. He started through the water to the far door where he had been when the shell had struck. Pain streaked through his leg. He tore insanely at the blue cloth,

243

ripping the zipper upward from the ankle and exposing his slimy hairy shank. He stared at it, holding the lantern high. There was nothing there but the implausible pain. He thought dimly of sharks and suddenly laughed. It echoed insanely in the tomblike passageway.

He took a deep breath and wiped his slack mouth and blotted the cold sweat from his forehead with a sleeve. He remembered this door now. It led to a large compartment that served as an emergency sick bay. If it were flooded and he opened the watertight door he would be drowned by the tons of water that would be released. But if it were dry the comparatively small amount of water in his passageway would make little difference in the larger area of the emergency sick bay.

A body floated gently against him. The mouth was a dark hole inside the frame of the smeared helmeted face. The eyes were as flat and round as two Chinese coins. Edge wondered who it was. He shoved it away.

The sons of bitches, he thought. Leaving me here to die. Me, with twelve years in and two good-conduct ribbons.

He raised the Stillson and slammed it against one of the handles that sealed the door in place. It swung upward. He raised the wrench to slam up the next handle. The first one suddenly shot back into its locking position.

Edge stumbled backward and dropped the wrench. Relief and joy flooded through his bleeding, aching body. Someone was in the other compartment. He pounded on the door with his fist.

'Open up!'

His voice reverberated through the long passageway.

'Open up in there!' he shouted. He lunged for the wrench and slammed it against the handle again. Again it was returned to its locking position.

'Open up, for Christ sake. Can you hear me?'

There was a tight silence. Then a shrill, nervous voice answered.

'It's against orders.'

Edge danced impatient with the sweetness of it. 'This is Ensign Edge,' he shouted. 'C'mon, in there.' He felt the warm blood

244

along his face as the crust of his head wound parted.   'I'm bleeding to death!' he screamed.

'I'm sorry, sir.   I can't do it.   It's against orders.'

Sir, Edge thought.   He could feel the sharp lines of pain along his face in pencil-thin seams.

'Open the goddamned door, sailor,' he shouted angrily.

'They told me not to, sir.'

Sir.   It sounds familiar, he thought.

'That you, Gray?'

'Yes, sir, Mr. Edge.'

Edge could hear him whimpering for breath.   Gray, he thought, forgetting his wounds, forgetting the war.   Sweet, soft Gray.

'Listen, kid,' he said softly, 'is there any water in there?'

'To drink?'

Edge gripped the wrench tightly.   'Is there any water on the deck?'

'Oh no, sir, Mr. Edge.   It's very dry in here.'

'Who's in there with you?'

'Nobody, sir.   They've all gone topside with the real sick men.'

'Nobody in there?'   His fingers touched one of the handles, but he did not move it.

'They're all gone.   Some of them cut up awful, Mr. Edge.'

'Where are they taking them?'

'To the destroyer, they said.   They left me here because I'm not really sick, they said.'

'Open the door, Gray.   Nobody's gonna know.'

'I couldn't go against their orders, sir.   I just couldn't.'

'Even if I told you this is a command, Gray?   You'd have to do it.'

'I wish you wouldn't, Mr. Edge.'

'That'd be pulling my rank on you.   I ain't gonna do that, Gray.'

'Thanks, Mr. Edge.'

'When are they coming back, Gray?'

'I don't know.   They didn't say.'

'Any means of communication in there?'

'The Amplicall, sir.   But it's dead.   I tried it.'

'What about the squawk box?'

'It's dead too, sir.'   He was crying softly.   'Please, I'm all alone. Don't ask me to open the door.'

Edge wiped his face. His fingers came away bloody. He trailed them in the oily water. His head ached.

'Listen to me, Gray. You know what's happened?'

'Just the guns firing and what I told you about the wounded men, sir.'

'You don't hear the ship's engines, do you?'

'I don't hear anything. I'm worried, Mr. Edge.'

'You should be, kid. You know what they've done?'

'Who, sir?'

'Everybody. The skipper, your phoney pal Austen, and those liars who told you to wait for them. They abandoned the ship, Gray.' He strained against the door. He heard Gray's piteous moan. He grinned a little. The sweat was pouring along his cheeks and mixing with the blood.

'You hear what I said? Abandoned it. They left the two of us all alone to die like rats.'

He felt his cheek again. It was covered with a thick sauce of oil and blood and sweat. He closed his eyes and held tightly to the coaming. The dizzying pain shot through his head, high along the temple.

'You still there, Mr. Edge?'

'Still here, kid. You and me, all alone. I'm no rat. I ain't gonna desert you like them others did.'

'I'm scared, sir.'

'We're the last ones on board. So say your prayers.' His crafty eyes watched the handles on the sealed door. 'We're heroes—going down with the ship.'

'I don't want to be a hero!'

'Too late now, kid.'

'I don't want to die, sir!'

'You stay right there, Gray. I'm going to the other end and try to get out. If I do——'

'Don't leave me here!'

'I'm going,' Edge said. He sloshed his feet noisily in the water.

A cry burst from Gray's lips. 'I'll open up!' The handles flew up one after the other. 'I'm opening up, Mr. Edge. Wait for me! Please wait there for me!'

'I'm waiting, sweetheart,' Edge muttered.

The last handle was up. Edge thrust his bulk against the door. The water rushed in with him. He caught Gray off balance and they both fell swept along by the small flood. It slackened, seeping to the far corners of the large compartment.

Edge grabbed the boy and held him. The blood streamed freely. Tasting it and savouring Gray's frantic struggle to free himself, Edge was engulfed by a sense of profound completeness.

He felt Gray stiffen. The boy pointed and Edge, holding him, turned to look.

Dead Farley had drifted in with the water. Gray was pointing at his bashed-in face.

'God!' he whimpered. 'What could have done that?'

'Forget it, kid,' Edge said huskily.

Gray turned suddenly and bit him. Edge struck him across the face. 'You damned little chipmunk.'

His head throbbed. He felt dizzy and weak. No, he thought. Not now. Sweet Christ, not now. His knees gave. He tried to fight it. His grip on Gray relaxed and with a final effort he forced himself forward and fell ponderously across him. Gray fainted in a paroxysm of fear.

In a few minutes the others returned for Gray. They found him pale as a child, tenderly supported by Edge's thick, hairy arm.

27

FRENCHY SHAPIRO was the first to notice it. He nudged Austen and pointed to the swirl of the ship's wake.

'We're losing speed, Boss.'

His teeth were chattering and he slapped his sides to keep up circulation. Austen had felt the lessening vibration as the ship had slowed. Now he studied the wake. The huge spray had subsided. There were green, eddying pools like swirls of rising game fish.

'Something's fouled up.'

He looked at the crew of men inside the splinter shield. They were shaking with the cold. They had steadily tracked the enemy spotting plane, which had remained out of range. It was lost from sight now behind the rolling white smoke of the screen.

'Stand easy, down there,' Austen called to the men.

Hospital attendants were removing the wounded from the twenty-millimetre gun deck above him. The deck was a shambles of twisted metal. Cloth and flesh had already stiffened to the icy rigging. A lone twenty remained undamaged.

Austen signalled to Fowler, who was squatting in the lee of the splinter shield. 'Take over up there, Fowler.'

The Negro nodded his bandaged head and vaulted to the gun deck and slipped easily into the gunner's harness. The stretcher-bearers were carrying the last casualty from the other forty-millimetre mount. The wounded man moaned softly.

'Where you taking him?' Austen asked.

'They're bringing all the wounded topside, sir.'

'Why?'

'To transfer to one of the cans.'

'How bad is it forward?'

'Catapult deck's a mess. Same with the torpedo tubes.' He shook his head. ' You heard about Mr. Clough?'

Austen nodded.

'The scuttlebutt is he wanted the skipper to launch the plane. If they'd only have listened to him he'd never have got it.'

'Many killed?'

'They're still counting. They took one below decks forward of sick bay. We're clearing the guys out of there right now.' He wiped his face. 'They say Mr. Edge's repair crew is sealed in a flooded compartment and won't get out.'

'How come we've slowed down?'

'Hell, I don't know. I got enough troubles.' He limped past with his stretcher.

Austen tapped Salvio, who wore the phones.

'Check with the bridge. See what's up.'

A flag hoist fluttered to the yardarm. He watched it, trying to read its meaning. He had never seen it before.

Salvio spoke up. 'The bridge talker reports they can't get up any steam in the engine room. Somebody fouled up a line.'

'What's the flag hoist?'

'Mike sugar zero. My speed zero.' He looked at Austen bleakly. 'We're dead in the water.'

'If that smoke screen gets any thinner, Boss, we're goners,' Frenchy said.

The eerie stillness was broken by the distant sound of guns. The men searched anxiously, trying to pierce the smoke screen's thin opacity.

'Bridge reports the destroyers have gone close in, Mr. Austen.'

'Close into who?'

'The Japs, sir. They're making a suicide torpedo attack.'

'Very well.' He tapped Shapiro. 'Pass it along, Frenchy.'

The men listened glumly. The report did nothing to lighten the grim knowledge of their own immediate predicament.

'Mr. Austen?'

'Yes?'

'Suppose the Japs knock off them two cans. Then what?'

'Your guess is as good as mine.'

Salvio said, 'The gunnery officer has passed the Word that they're distributing small arms to all gunnery stations, sir.'

'Very well.'

A destroyer silhouette emerged from the mist on the port quarter. She closed the *Atlantis* slowly, idling her engines. The men could distinguish the destroyer's gun crews at their battle stations. Cargo nets were rigged along her starboard side.

Fowler called down from the twenty-millimetre gun deck.

'They're carrying up a pile of wounded, Mr. Austen. I can see 'em from here, just as plain.'

'Keep your eyes on the sky, Fowler. We're still in trouble back here.'

'Aye, sir.'

A man climbed up the ladder. He carried a small arsenal of firearms and ammunition slung over his shoulder. He eased it to the deck.

'Just in case,' he said. He climbed out of sight.

At the horizon on the starboard beam the gunfire ceased. Slowly the white screen of smoke thinned. Two clouds of black smoke climbed skyward.

'Somebody's burning,' Frenchy said, 'and it's gotta be either us or them.'

Now they could discern the racing stick masts of their own destroyers. The leading one had swerved sharply towards the enemy cruiser and had resumed its fire at close range.

The ship was buried under the mushrooming splashes as the enemy desperately depressed his big guns to meet the rapidly closing range. The two slim hulls drove onward in the face of incredibly heavy enemy gunfire. It seemed to Austen, watching through his binoculars in a grim sort of paralysis, that their destruction was unavoidable.

He stiffened instinctively. The streaming wake of a torpedo skipped from the rear destroyer and headed towards the enemy. He saw two more and a cold chill of tense expectancy ran through him.

The enemy cruiser's big guns ceased firing. Austen realized that the range to the destroyers had closed and the enemy could not depress the guns at a low enough angle to score hits.

A dull thudding reached his ears. A column of smoke, water and debris rose skyward. Smoke in thick curling ribbons enveloped the enemy cruiser and it was hidden from the sight of the men who watched from the decks of the *Atlantis*. He heard himself cheering wildly. Below him the men were shouting and cursing happily.

Minutes passed. The guns had ceased their firing and a stillness again lay over the scene. Austen stood numbly. All of them watched where the two destroyers had last been seen.

The p.a. speaker crackled noisily. The men turned, startled. It was a breath of life in the midst of a world in which everything had gone dead.

'Men, this is your captain speaking.'

They stared fixedly at the chipped grey metal box. The morning sun was a cold bronze disc in the grey sky. It shone pitilessly on the tired men, on the shattered deck plates, on the twisted guns and the bright pools of spilled blood.

'The *Clovis* and *Washbourne* just completed a torpedo attack on the enemy. It was a suicide mission, men. When I ordered it I did not expect them to return.

'But they are returning and the enemy is running like hell for home. I don't believe any of us in the span of our lives will ever see anything to equal such courage.

'The *Brant* is out there on the port quarter. She's been standing by in case we had to abandon ship. The engineer officer now tells me the fuel lines are clear. We'll be back in business in a few minutes. We should be able to make our standard speed of fifteen knots in no time at all.

'I'm proud of you men. Before Admiral Marcy left us I told him you could do a job and you've done it. It's cost the lives of some of us. Many others are wounded and burned.' He paused. 'It could have been worse. It could have been all of us. Let us give thanks to God for our deliverance.' He coughed. The squawk box rattled. 'There will be a fifteen-second silence.'

Austen took off his battle helmet and wiped his eyes. The men bowed their heads.

'Why ain't you praying, Boss?' Frenchy asked softly.

'Shut up.'

'You think they'll play the Star Spangled Banner later?'

'I wouldn't mind.'

'What a skipper,' Ski said. 'That guy could sell ice cubes to the Eskimos.'

'He came to the right place,' Frenchy said.

'The funny thing is,' Ski said reverently, 'he's full of crap and we all know it. Yet every damned one of us loves the son of a bitch.'

'God bless you all,' the squawk box said.

The vast steel hull of the crippled cruiser vibrated faintly. The men looked at the sea and the sky and each other. At the ship's stern the water boiled suddenly as the port engines came to life. The big propellers sliced into the sea and sent pale eddies swirling. Slowly, like a wounded monster waking, the *Atlantis* shivered from stem to stern. The great machinery inside her seemed to breathe. She thrust her knife bow surely against the sea.

A ragged cheer sounded from the lips of the men. It grew as the bow waves swept past the ship's sides. The men swore lustily and pounded each other. In the crew's galley huge cauldrons of soup and coffee and stacks of sandwiches stood ready.

At the horizon the *Clovis* and *Washbourne* had turned and commenced their return run to the formation. A deck fire on the *Washbourne* glowed faintly. It flared once and burned out. Smoke still billowed skyward.

The captain took Griswold's hand and squeezed it.

'I still don't believe it,' he said.

A messenger came over and saluted. He handed the captain a radio dispatch. The captain read it slowly. It was from the *Brant*, standing off the *Atlantis's* port quarter.

Recovered Lieutenant j.g. Clough and Radio-gunner Bennett at 1053 hours. Both treated for minor cuts bruises burns exposure. Nothing serious except Pilot Clough violently seasick. Will execute transfer at your request via breeches buoy.

'Isn't that swell, Captain?' the messenger said.

'It sure is.' The messenger started to leave. 'Just a minute, messenger.'

'Yes, sir?'

'My compliments to Commander Blanchard in the wardroom. Tell him to issue a ration of whisky to every man on board.'

'Yes, *sir*.'

'Also tell him to visit the executive officer in his cabin and then call me here on the bridge.'

'Aye, sir.'

One of the bridge lookouts sang out sharply. 'Plane on the starboard quarter, Captain!'

The captain went to the starboard rail and raised his glasses. The smile faded from his face. The talker ran over.

'Lieutenant Austen reporting from the aft forty, Captain. Jap spotting plane dead astern, range ten thousand yards, elevation about thirty degrees. Closing the range rapidly, sir.'

'Tell him to open fire at will.'

'Aye, sir.'

The bastards, the captain thought. They left without their plane.

The sharp staccato of twenty-millimetre gunfire split the noon-time stillness.

'The *Brant*, sir. She's firing on the plane.'

'Very well.'

He crossed to the port side and watched the destroyer's gunfire.

'Perfect broadside target,' he growled. 'You'd think they'd lay it right on.' He turned a worried face to Griswold. 'If I had any steering engines I'd turn broadside and let the three-inch fifties come to bear on him.'

'Not enough time, sir.'

'This lone joker may be one of those crazy suicide corps.' He jabbed a thumb into the frightened talker's side. 'Range, man. What's the range?'

Before the talker could answer, they heard the jarring deep-throated *thump thump* of Austen's forty-millimetre gun.

'Sounds weak as hell,' Griswold said.

'He's just got that one barrel back there.'

The noise of the guns increased. The captain watched tensely from the after end of the bridge.

'Right full rudder!' he shouted. Not that it'll do a damned bit of good, he thought.

Griswold pointed suddenly. The plane was skimming low over the water. Its twin floats seemed barely to clear the wave tips. They could hear the chattering twenty, and the four-pound shells pumping rhythmically from Austen's lone barrel. A sheet of flame spurted from the plane's fuselage, enveloping the cowling and wings. Fire and smoke poured over her until the plane itself was hidden from sight.

The ship had started to turn slowly in response to the full rudder. The plane seemed to hang almost motionless in mid-air. The captain dropped the glasses from his eyes.

'No,' he muttered. 'No, no, no, no.'

Austen leaned over the Mark XIV sight and picked up the

plane in the lighted cross hairs. He tracked it steadily. His cold hands gripped the handle bars. He held his right thumb lightly on the firing key with the safety open.

The talker tapped him.

'Bridge says to open fire at will, Mr. Austen.'

'Very well.'

It's a tired old joke, he thought. Will *who?* He could hear Frenchy breathing nasally next to him. He asked for a range.

'Seventy-five hundred, Boss. The *Brant's* already shooting.'

'They're crazy. He's out of range. Tell Fowler to open fire as soon as I do.'

'Okay, Boss.' He looked sternward. 'The bastard's barrelling right in.'

'Duck soup,' Austen said. He held his breath. 'Stand by.'

'Why the hell don't he start shooting?' someone whined.

Keep coming, baby, Austen thought. Nice little baby. The plane's image was seated in the heart of the lighted cross. One barrel, he thought. Like one ball. I'd give all I own for that other barrel. He remembered Sergeant Madjicka and almost laughed. All I own, he thought grimly. A roomful of crazy paintings and a small part of Stella. Very small. Very distant now.

The knot of terror lay in him and he tried to ignore it. A very personal thing, he thought. Here it comes. Here. Here. To me, baby, screaming. My God, he's on fire . . . now . . . NOW!

He squeezed the firing key.

The gun jerked. The loader jammed fresh clips into the breech. Hot lead flamed from the flared mouth of the gun and streaked into the air. Austen held the firing key. His eyes were riveted to the lighted reticule.

'You're short,' Frenchy shouted, 'but hold it. He's coming right into it.'

Flames burst from the plane's fuselage. It hurtled like a blazing comet towards the ship. Fowler opened fire with the twenty-millimetre Oerlikon. Its high-keyed chatter raged over the steady thump of Austen's forty.

The plane seemed to slip sideways as the ship turned. Both twenty- and forty-millimetre shells were hitting, seemingly swallowed into the mouth of flame and smoke. A wing section disintegrated and fell flaming into the sea.

'Duck, Boss! The bastard's going to crash us!'

Austen clung to the handle bars. Shell after shell struck the crazily rocking plane.

'Jump! It's no use!' Frenchy screamed. He swung a leg over the rim of the splinter shield and paused in mid-air. Austen remained at the director. Below him the men were scattering wildly from the mount. Salvio ripped off the phones and jumped.

'Boss!' Frenchy screamed. '*Boss!*'

With a stream of withering, hopeless curses he turned and flung himself bodily at Austen. Austen went sprawling to the deck. There was a thunderous, crunching impact. The plane's starboard float smashed across Frenchy and flattened him against the splinter shield.

The plane tilted on a wing. It caught Salvio flatly across his back. He burst like a blood sausage. It hurtled on end and hit Fowler on the burned-out gun deck behind the director. It came to a stop against the steel base of Battle Two and exploded. It sent a shower of flaming splinters in all directions. Jagged portions of the engine and fuselage slid hissing into the sea.

Austen struggled free of the weight of Frenchy's crumpled body. He stood up and looked around dizzily.

Fowler was bleeding from many wounds. He crawled painfully across the scorched gun deck and dragged the enemy pilot from the smoking wreckage. He fell and sat up again. He pounded his fist many times into the sightless charred face.

Two men in a damage-control crew climbed the ladder and pulled him away. He fought them, sobbing, until he collapsed. They lifted the pilot's body and carried it to the side. Fowler lay alone, bleeding.

'What are you doing?' Austen called out.

'Give this bastard the deep six.'

'The hell with him. Take care of Fowler.'

They dropped the body. It rolled to the scuppers, rocking

gently. Austen raised Frenchy's head. The eyes fluttered open and closed again. Some of the crew climbed to the director stand and lifted him and carried him to a blanket alongside the six-inch turret on the fantail.

Austen was too weak to protest. They shouldn't move him, he thought numbly. Someone was shouting for an attendant. Austen climbed painfully out of the tub and went down to join them. Empty shell cases of expended six-inch ammunition rolled around his feet, clinking dully. He kicked them out of his way.

A chief pharmacist came over. His uniform was splotched with blood. He jabbed a morphine syrette into Frenchy's arm. He looked around wearily. No one said anything.

Frenchy's eyes opened. His face was very pale. He saw Austen and his mouth twisted in a smile. He mumbled a few words.

The chief bent over. 'I can't make out what he's saying.'

'Can we move him below?' Austen said.

'No, sir. I think his back is broken, for one thing.'

'Maybe Commander Blanchard can do something.'

'He's got more than he can handle right now.'

A thin ribbon of frothy blood oozed from Frenchy's mouth. The chief tried to catch the soft mumble of words.

'Can you get what he's saying, sir?'

'He said, "*Gurnisht helfen*".'

'What?'

'It means it's no use.'

'He oughtta know.'

Frenchy reached out and touched Austen's sleeve.

'I'm sorry, Frenchy,' Austen said.

Frenchy shook his head. His mouth worked. No words came.

'That was a crazy thing to do, kid,' Austen said softly.

Frenchy shook his head again. Pain clouded his eyes. He regarded Austen with a faintly contemptuous expression. He winced as the pain lanced his broken body. He closed his eyes.

The chief looked at him. 'I'm afraid that's it, Mr. Austen.'

Frenchy's lips moved. They barely heard him. The words were in Hebrew, and they could not understand what he said. His crooked face stiffened. His back arched slightly and he died.

Austen looked at the grey sea. It seemed to encircle all of them, the living with the dead. He looked across the deck strewn with portions of Salvio's body. What could they want from a poor kid like Salvio? he mourned. His eyes rested on the small dark lump of the dead enemy pilot. Near it, Fowler moaned.

Austen stood up slowly. The men moved in curiously to look at Frenchy.

'For Christ sake take care of Fowler,' he shouted angrily. 'Leave Shapiro alone. Can't you see he's dead?'

The captain continued to receive the casualty reports on the bridge with a taut face. When the report on the executive officer reached him he made the messenger repeat it. He retired to his cabin and sent for Commander Griswold.

The navigator came in with a mug of coffee in his hand.

'How about a course to Adak, Sam?'

'Course is zero-nine-five, Captain. Estimated time of arrival 0800 Friday.'

'Very well.'

His voice had a listlessness that made Griswold look again.

'Anything wrong, sir?'

'Wrong?' He smiled sadly. 'You'll make a great admiral some day, Sam.' He sighed deeply. 'No. Nothing's wrong. Pass the Word to all there'll be a burial at sea in the morning.'

'Aye, sir.'

'You may as well take over the exec's duties, Sam.' His voice faltered. 'I'll be damned if I can figure it. What a ghastly thing to do.'

Griswold nodded his head to the west. 'Those guys are doing it all the time, sir. It's their honourable death.'

'But one of us, Sam. Our own kind.' He shook his head. 'Never mind. Should we bury him at sea with the others?'

'He's a sailor like everybody else, sir.'

'I suppose so.' He drummed his fingers. ' Take care of things, will you, Sam?'

'Yes, Captain. Why don't you go below and get a little rest now? Everything's under control.'

The hum of distant planes sent both of them running to the open bridge. Two formations were rapidly approaching from the east. The lookouts bellowed out the welcome identification. There were many B-25 bombers in the group. They passed in tight V-formation several miles distant on the beam. Some of the men cheered hollowly.

'The Army,' the captain said.

'That's fine with me,' Griswold said with a grimace. 'As long as they keep right on going.'

They watched the planes disappear to the west. The captain took a last long look at the littered decks.

'Let's head for the stable,' he said.

28

THE bodies of men still floated like aimless islands in the cold sea. The ships' swift bows swept through them. The bodies tossed gently as though in troubled sleep. In death each resembled the other, skins swelling sausage-tight in the icy brine, entrails diluted with the sea.

The spent men watched them from the decks of the fleeing ships and wondered idly which were shipmates and which of them the enemy. They thought weakly of their own immortal skins, their minds bright with the memory of the livid orange death flung in recent salvos from the faint horizon.

The living men moved dully, still drugged by the nearness of death. The ships stank of cordite and sweat and human fear. Death here was not like death on other seas, where flesh dried like glue in the hot sun. Here the air was cold and the torn flesh smelled sweetly.

The wounded were below decks. They did not think about immortality. They lay in thoughtless or morphined delirium. They screamed and vomited. They cried for their mothers. They prayed and cursed, tormented by steel. The ancient mark of war was indelibly and forever on them.

Soon the ships were gone from this unmarked piece of the vast sea. The heavy smoke of war faded in the endless mist. The anguished wakes of the racing ships erased themselves. The sea was glassily calm again. Most of the bodies had drifted peaceably from sight.

Silence sat over the sea like a mournful vulture in an icy, leafless plain.

The *Atlantis* remained in Adak harbour long enough to remove the seriously wounded and effect some temporary repairs. She stood out from Adak *en route* San Francisco a day later. She had taken aboard several passengers for the States and one item of cargo which had been waiting when the ship arrived. It was the delayed forty-millimetre gun-barrel assembly.

'That's the way it goes,' Blanchard said wryly.

'I'd like to heave the goddamned thing over the side,' Austen said bitterly.

They were in the doctor's cabin drinking. He looked through the open port at the brown-flecked hills of the island harbour. They were snow-capped and misty in the cold morning air. Austen tilted the dark green bottle and wiped his mouth.

'It's going to be a pleasant change to do this in some quiet Manhattan bar with a highball glass wrapped around some ice cubes.'

'The grass is always greener,' Blanchard said, reaching.

'Nuts. You're as happy as the rest of us to get back.'

The doctor shrugged. 'Where I am never seems to make any difference.' He took a long drink.

'How'd the casualties finally tot up?'

'Twenty-eight dead.' He frowned at Austen. 'Want names, too?'

'I'm sorry, sir.'

'You heard about Fowler, I suppose?'

'No.'

'He died last night. I almost thought he'd pull through.'

'I'm awfully sorry.'

'That other concussion made the difference. You know, when the master-at-arms slugged him.'

'It's funny,' Austen said. 'I'm entirely unmoved by obituary notices.' He stared at the bottle. 'Yet I feel responsible for what happened to Fowler. And to Shapiro.'

'Still the artist with the guilt-complex routine. For Christ sake forget it, will you, Alec?'

'Just like that.'

'For your own good. Listen. You're no damned good to this world for anything but your painting. Stick to it. And the hell with everything else.'

'It's not that simple.'

'You've got to make it that simple. The hell with sentiment and hooray for painting.'

'Okay. Hooray.' He sat cracking his knuckles. 'Just go back home and wipe the slate clean. As if nothing happened. Fine artist I'd be.'

'You'd be a damned sight better one than if you dragged the war around in your craw for the rest of your life. You'd end up in a psychiatric ward.'

'Or like the exec. ended up.'

'Not you. Not like the exec.'

'Why not? They buried him with the same honours as the others who were killed in battle.'

'Honours? What honours are there at the bottom of the sea?'

'I resent the idea of him being alongside guys like Frenchy or Fowler.'

'I can't argue with you. I'm a doctor. I see those things differently.'

They drank quietly for a while.

'How can I forget Mike Edge?' Austen said suddenly. 'If that isn't the Navy for you—Edge getting a recommendation for conspicuous bravery.'

'Why shouldn't he? He fought his way out of a flooded compartment. He rescued an abandoned shipmate. All in all an act of outstanding bravery.'

But Austen saw that he smiled.

'The whole damned ship knows what happened down there,

260

Doc. If that kid Gray had any guts he'd tell the truth. He's just too damned scared.'

'Wrong, Alec.' The doctor chuckled. 'He's become very fond of Edge. He really believes Mike saved his life.'

'Isn't that a bit disgusting?'

'You're ignoring the splendid irony of it. Mike Edge, the most contemptible scum on board, will get a Purple Heart and a Bronze star. I expect he'll also get Gray. If he hasn't already had him.' He smiled tiredly. 'Post-mortems. The hell with it. What are your plans for the States?'

'Well, I've got orders to new construction, with a month's leave. I'm going to paint my head off for a month.'

'Where?'

'Maine, probably. There's a little camp up there, on a lake.'

'Sounds very sensible.'

'It's what the doctor ordered.' He grinned.

'Right, Alec. Stick with the painting.'

'There's a little more. I'm going to marry a girl named Stella and take her with me.'

'Wonderful. Does she know about it?'

'Not yet. But she'll go.'

'Of course she will.'

'What about your plans, Doctor?'

'Plans?' He patted the bottle. 'I never make plans, Alec.'

'Maybe you should, sometime.'

'You go to Maine with your Stella. Don't tell me what to do.'

Austen stood up and they shook hands.

'Stop by again,' Blanchard said. 'The prescription will always be filled.'

Austen went out. He was mildly irritated. Blanchard's hand had felt cold and small. Hardly a hero's hand, he thought. Heroes, he thought. Like Mike Edge. There's a hero for you, kid. He grinned.

I'm sorry, Doc, he thought.

He went into the wardroom and drank some coffee. It tasted of ether and surgical dressings. He listened for a few minutes to some of the officers who were avidly discussing the finer points of the sea battle.

He went out. A lot of good it does Frenchy, he thought bitterly. He went through the ship to the division compartment. Kracowski was asleep in the leading p.o.'s bunk. Austen wakened him.

'Ski, where's Frenchy's locker?'

'I give it to one of the new boys, sir. Some of them didn't have no locker.'

'What about his gear?' He was unable to say 'personal effects'.

'Packed in his sea bag like you said to do.' Kracowski sat up and scratched his belly. 'Anything wrong?'

'I'm looking for a picture he had.'

'What kinda picture?'

'A pastel drawing.'

'There was a framed one of his kid and one of his old lady. I packed 'em with his other stuff.'

'This one was rolled up.'

'Maybe it's some of that stuff we thought was junk.' He got up. Austen followed him through the compartment. The sweepers had worked a huge pile of debris into a corner. It smelled of smoke and oily water.

'Gettin' it all ready for the incinerator,' Kracowski said.

Austen poked carefully through the pile of trash until he found the sketch. It was wet and crumpled.

'That what you want?'

'That's it.'

'It was too big to get into his sea bag. We never even looked to see what it was.'

'Okay, Ski. As long as we found it.'

They returned to the compartment.

'I'm gonna miss the big Jew boy,' Kracowski said.

'I know.'

'All the guys feel the same way. Ain't it funny?'

'I guess so. I suppose it's funny.'

He went to his compartment in officer country. It still smelled of smoke. The bulkheads were charred and blistered. He

262

stretched the portrait on a drawing board and stood it near the blower. He smoked a cigarette while it dried. Later he removed as many of the wrinkles as he could. He rolled the portrait carefully in a pasteboard chart tube and sealed the ends.

Someone knocked. Kracowski poked his head in the doorway. He held his white hat in his hand. He looked uncomfortable.

'What's up, Ski?'

'It's about that there picture, sir.'

'What about it?'

'I'm sorry what happened to it.'

'It's going to be all right.'

'Some of the guys just told me you made it or Frenchy by hand.'

'That's okay, Ski. I fixed it up like new.'

'Mr. Austen?'

'Yes?'

'The guys in the division got the Word you're leaving the ship in Frisco.'

'I've been ordered to new construction, Ski.'

'That's what they said.'

'It's a new Essex-class carrier. She's in the Brooklyn Navy Yard.'

'The guys are gonna miss you. That includes me.'

'I'm going to miss the guys, Ski.'

'They asked me to see you. They wanted to show their appreciation on account of what a swell division officer you turned out to be.' He suddenly thrust his hat forward. It was full of bills. 'Being I'm the leading p.o. now, they give me the honour of passing the hat. Here you are, sir, with the best wishes of the Fourth Division.'

Austen stared at the hatful of money. He dared not look at Kracowski.

'How much money you got there, Ski?'

'Two hundred and eight-four bucks.' He licked his lips. 'Better grab it, Boss.'

Boss. Austen took off his cap.

'Pour it in here, Ski,' he said gravely.

Kracowksi inverted his hat. Some of the bills fluttered to the deck. They bent together and retrieved them and stuffed them into Austen's cap.

'Tell the men I'll be aft to-night to thank them personally.'

'Yes, sir.'

'It's a very generous gift. I'm very grateful.'

'You're the goddamned best division officer I ever seen,' Kracowski said gruffly. He turned and jammed his hat on the back of his head and swaggered down the passageway.

Austen sat on his bunk and idly counted the money. He did not care how many times he counted it or how accurately. It was something to do while he cried.

29

HE quit the *Atlantis* in Vallejo and waited out his transportation in San Francisco. The city was warm in its welcome. Any other time he would have been reluctant to leave it. But the voice of Stella at the other end of a long-distance call filled him with an impatient longing for the sight of her.

The plane flight was a dreamy confusion of badly lighted airports in a night blurry with stars. He remembered gratefully hot coffee and fresh doughnuts in an Iowa canteen. He remembered an airsick Army nurse and the cold clatter of La Guardia in the early dawn.

He found a hotel room and phoned Stella. He walked the morning streets trying to co-ordinate her remembered face with her morning sleepy voice.

He sat on the brass hydrant in front of Bonwit's and waited for her. He was wearing the new blues he had bought in San Francisco. They felt stiff and formal after the rough khakis and foul-weather gear he had worn at sea.

He had Frenchy's portrait with him. It was wrapped in heavy corrugated paper and bound with stout twine. The wrinkles were out of it, thanks to a conscientious picture framer. He sat on the shiny brass hydrant and watched the morning crowd go by.

Hello, he thought, smiling a sad greeting. How are all the junior ad execs this ayem? Tongues like wool? Eyes like sash weights? How's the middle ulcer, Jack? What's the big rush? Confab with a client? Compo for the Coocoo campaign?

There I go, he mourned, in the pin-striped navy blue. The *real* navy blue, because the one I'm wearing is only temporary, Jack.

Let me tell you about the sea, Jack, he thought.

A Navy Officer passed with a good-looking girl in tow. He stared at Austen coldly. Austen ignored him and lit a cigarette. The hell with him, he thought. He's sore as hell because I'm sitting on a hydrant and I did not salute.

I'm getting Asiatic, he thought. Like Ski. Like Slobojian. Poor Slobodj, he thought, remembering him as he drifted past the fantail after the hit on the catapult deck. Slobodjian had waved at them, he remembered, as he drifted past.

Sweet, filthy, hopelessly civilian Slobodj, conversing philosophically with what cousin now at the bottom of the sea? Servicing what pile of sea onions, briny-eyed, friendly Slobodjian, cousin to the whole cockeyed world.

Stella came to him stepping over the warm green and gold stripes the sun made on the pavement. He knew it was Stella, seeing her ankles and the long strides and he remembered the boardwalk at Coney Island and the sound of her heels.

He stood up. The sun was on her face and she looked fine, he thought. She kissed him. To hell with the morning crowd, he thought.

'For Christ sake, Stella,' he finally said, 'not in Macy's window,' and they both laughed, knowing very well whose window it was.

'You're so thin,' she said, touching him with quick fingers.

'Worrying about you.'

'I'm sure, darling.'

'I talked to Mrs. Titus this morning. She told me you never picked up the painting.'

'The painting. Yes.'

'Why, Stella?'

'I saw it, you know. I told you I would. I went to your studio and I saw it.'

'Why didn't you take it? I told you in Chicago it was for you.'

'Must we, Alec? Now? The very first few minutes together?'

'Don't you like the painting?'

'I'm not sure. Is it really of me?'

'What difference does that make?'

'If it's a portrait of me, I don't want it.'

'It's whatever you want it to be.'

'It's either a nun or a whore.'

'It's whatever you make of it, Stella.'

'All right,' she said. 'All right, then.' She held his arm tightly as they walked. 'So good to touch you, darling.'

He looked at her. All that silk and leather and perfume, he thought. Right out of a Park Avenue mail order catalogue.

'You look fine,' he said.

'For you, darling,' she said. 'All for you.'

'Where are we going, Stella?'

'Coffee, darling, before I drop. This is the middle of the night.' They sat at the counter in a corner drugstore on Madison Avenue.

'What's in the package, Alec?'

'A drawing.'

'For me?'

One to a customer, he thought. 'It's for some people in Brooklyn. Their boy was in the ship with me.'

'It's a clumsy thing. Drop it off at the post office.'

'I'm delivering it. Personally.'

'To Brooklyn?'

'Is that so bad?'

'Darling. No one ever goes to Brooklyn.'

'I'm going.' He looked at her. 'To-day.'

'Our first day, Alec. I refuse to spare you for a moment.'

'You could come along.'

'To Brooklyn?' She laughed nervously and stirred her coffee.

'Hell, Stella, why so proud? You've been there—the time we went to Coney Island.'

'Coney Island,' she said. 'A million years ago.' She looked

at him brightly. She's lovely, he thought. 'Where are your things, Alec?'

'What things?'

'Uniforms and things. You're staying at my place.'

'I have no things.'

'Gear, darling. Isn't that the word? Your Navy gear. Uniforms and cap covers and all the knick-knacks I read about.'

'There's just what I have on my back.'

'How come, Alec?'

'Everything was lost.'

'Lost?'

'When the ship was hit.'

'Your ship? You never told me.'

'We lost a lot of boys.'

'Oh, darling.'

'All I lost was some clothes and art stuff.'

'And you're all right? You weren't hurt?'

'Oh no. I'm fine. It was funny about the uniforms.'

'Funny?'

'When I finally got to my quarters there was a foot of water on the deck. The uniforms looked all right. They were hanging from hooks on the bulkhead. Then I touched them. They crumbled in my fingers.'

'Poor darling.'

'The heat and smoke did it. Scorched them and they just crumbled. Like this.' He shredded the dry crust of toast between his fingers.

'No scars, Alec?'

'No scars.'

'I want you in one piece.' She took his hand and put it in her lap. He could feel the warmth of her body beneath. 'Let's not wait,' she said softly. 'Forget about Brooklyn. You're coming home with me now.'

'Home,' he said.

'The apartment, darling. Look. Godfrey leaves for Chicago to-night. I'm supposed to go with him, but the hell with that. We'll have the place to ourselves.'

'Godfrey,' he said wryly. 'And Chicago.' He was smiling stiffly. He withdrew his hand. 'I don't want to see Godfrey, Stella. I'm going to Brooklyn. You can come along or you can sit around until I get back. Or you can go to Chicago.'

'Alec,' she said, 'for Christ sake.'

'It doesn't matter, Stella. I love you and I'm going to Brooklyn.'

'Well,' she said.

'Then I'm coming back from Brooklyn to look around some of the galleries,' he said softly. 'I want to see the " Guernica " and a few Modiglianis and anything else that's exciting. Then I'm going to dig up old Stella and we're going to twist the ears off a few martinis. Then I'm going to ask her to marry me and she will say yes. Then we'll go to the country.'

'Marry her, Alec?'

'Why not, Stella? I love you.'

'Oh, you do. You really do, don't you?'

'Yes, Stella. I thee love.'

'You remember that?'

'Yes.'

'I love you, Alec.'

He leaned over and kissed her. 'I need you, Stella. For a long time I thought I didn't. I thought the painting would be enough and I had that and I thought a man would need nothing more, having painting the way I had it. But it isn't true, Stella. I lied to myself.'

'No. Don't say that.'

'It's true, Stella. I'm scared.'

'Not scared. Not you, Alec.'

'I need you to hold me and tell me how wonderful I am and what a hell of a good painter I am. Then I'll really paint. We'll be married, darling, and I'll paint you and I'll paint the countryside.'

'What about the Navy?'

'I've got thirty days' leave. I've got my uncle's place in Maine. We get aboard the State of Maine express to-night at nine and we're there in the morning.'

'I've never been to Maine.'

'The cottage is on a lake and the ice is out now. There are trout and salmon feeding on the surface. You'll fish. I'll paint. Can you make love?'

'I don't know,' she said. 'I really don't remember.'

'I'll teach you. It's easier than fishing.'

'It sounds wonderful,' she said in a low voice.

'What do you say?'

'It's so sudden.'

'Look, darling. I love you. Me—Alec—loves you. Will marry you. The air is sweet and clean in Maine.' He stood up suddenly. 'Let's get the hell out of here.' He put some change on the counter.

She held his arm. 'It's crazy, darling.'

'*You're* crazy. It's the chance of a lifetime. A month in Maine. All the salmon and corn you can eat. An ever-loving husband.'

'You make it sound so simple and it's really not. It's really very complicated.'

'Only because you're making it complicated.'

'Alec, darling, I want it to work out, I swear I do.'

'Fine. I'll meet you later, then.'

'Later?' She said it breathlessly. 'You're leaving me?'

'I'm going to Brooklyn. I'll meet you somewhere.'

'Well, you see, darling——'

'What the hell's the matter with you, Stella?'

'The point is, I've already arranged for us to have dinner with Godfrey——'

'The hell with Godfrey!'

'Everyone's staring at us, Alec.'

'The hell with them.' He took her arm roughly. They went outside. 'Look,' he said, 'once and for all. Make up your mind.'

'It's made up. I want to go with you.'

'Then let's go. Right now.'

'Darling,' she moaned. 'Why spoil everything? We'll have a quiet little dinner with Godfrey and I'll tell him what's happened.'

'You don't want to marry me, Stella.'

'I do!' Her eyes were imploring. 'I just can't run off without a word. We'll have this quiet little dinner and say good-bye. That's all there is to it. It's the decent thing to do after all these years, Alec. Then I'll pack. We can spend the night at the apartment and get a train to-morrow.'

'The apartment,' he said.

'Of course. I need time to pack. And we can be together——'

'At Stella's place.'

'I don't like the way you say that,' she said slowly. 'You make it sound like a whorehouse.'

'It isn't exactly a convent, Stella.'

'I'm no whore, Alec.'

'What the hell,' he said. He tucked the big package under his arm. 'Where are we supposed to have this quiet little dinner?'

'At 21.'

'Okay. I'll meet you there at four. I suppose I'll be able to stomach one more look at his fat, dedicated face. But look, baby. Try to figure things out for yourself once and for all, will you?'

'Why must things always be so involved with us, Alec?' she whimpered.

She stood quite still, searching his face. Then she reached for it with both hands and kissed him suddenly and walked swiftly away.

'Four o'clock,' he shouted after her. The kiss had unnerved him. He wondered if he would ever see her again.

30

HE had Frenchy's address on a small card, copied from the enlistment records aboard ship. He took the subway to the Brownsville section of Brooklyn. He walked self-consciously through the littered, noisy streets. His fingers were sweaty on the wrapping paper. He hoped it would not take too long.

It was a grimy apartment house in a street of narrow shops and faulty neon. The entry was blocked by clamouring children. Several women were ranged solidly on both sides behind a battery of baby carriages. They stared at Austen with bovine curiosity.

He pressed the black button opposite 'D—4 SHAPIRO'. A spotted metal sign said, 'ALL DELIVERIES THROUGH THE BASEMENT.' He looked uneasily at the basking row of mothers and wondered.

The door buzzer signalled. He pushed his way into the dark cave-like lobby. A woman's voice shrilled down through the network of iron railings.

'Who you want?'

'Mrs. Shapiro?'

'Speaking?'

'May I come up. I have some personal business.'

He could see the round red face four landings away, framed in the skylight. It was wreathed in suspicion.

'What kind of business?'

'I was in the Navy with your husband.'

Some of the children had crowded behind him. He started up the stairs.

'My husband?' There was an edge of panic in her voice. 'He not by the tailor shop?'

Another head appeared alongside hers. It was bleached and dishevelled. 'Something happened to Sol?'

'Isn't Frenchy Shapiro your husband? Or son?'

'Frenchy?' the first woman said. 'What do I know of a Frenchy?'

Austen rested the package on the first landing. 'I'm looking for Seymour Shapiro's family. This is the right address. He was in the Navy with me.'

'You got the wrong Shapiro, mister.' She consulted the blonde. They talked rapidly for a few moments. 'It's the other Shapiro,' she said. 'My God, you gave me a scare.'

'Where's the other Shapiro live?'

'They moved away months ago.'

'You wouldn't know the address?'

'I should know the address I ain't got enough trouble with the mixed-up letter carrier as it is? Go ask the superintendent.'

'Thanks. I'm sorry I troubled you.'

'It was no trouble.'

The children dogged his footsteps until the superintendent chased them. He was small and bald, with an inbred air of Middle-

European disdain. His breath smelled sweetly of garlic and Spearmint. He wrote the Shapiros' new address laboriously on the wrapping paper.

It was in Flatbush. Austen took a taxi. He tried to relax as it clattered along Eastern Parkway. He thought of Stella. He thought about the painting he had made of her. A nun or a whore, he thought. What difference can it possibly make?

A hell of a way to relax, he thought grimly.

The new apartment was like the one in Brownsville. Fewer children, fewer baby carriages, and two budding maples in front.

So Babe finally made it, he thought, seeing the tapestry brick and the black and gold sign 'ELEVATOR APARTMENT—NO VACANCIES'.

He pressed the button next to 'C–2 SHAPIRO'. The door clicked. He went inside.

The lobby was square and empty, and resembled a third-rate Gothic castle hall. Frenchy's wife met him as he stepped out of the elevator. She was plump and pale. She regarded Austen with friendly and red-rimmed eyes.

'I'm a shipmate of your husband's,' he said.

'Lieutenant Austen, by chance?' Her inflection was vaguely querulous.

'Yes. I tried to phone first.'

'We don't have one, being we're new here. Come in, Lieutenant.' She closed the door behind him. 'We got your nice letter.'

She led him through a narrow hallway past two bedrooms, a bathroom, and a kitchen that smelled of chicken fat and frying onions. One of the bedroom doors was closed.

The living-room was cramped but clean. Two curtained windows faced an apartment building across the street. It was partly screened by the thin branches of the budding maples. There was a smell of furniture polish in the room.

A small old woman sat on an up-ended orange crate in a corner. She wore carpet slippers over her stockinged feet and a black open-crocheted shawl across her shoulders. Her eyes were like bright buttons in her tiny, waxen face.

'This is Seymour's mother, Lieutenant. She's a little hard of hearing.'

Frenchy's wife spoke in Yiddish to the old lady. She darted a glance at Austen and turned away. He leaned the package against the wall.

'Does she understand English?'

'Yes. Also she speaks it well. She is just stubborn.' Her voice caught. 'Like Seymour. Full of the devil.' She motioned at the sofa. It was brown, overstuffed mohair with a boldly carved frame of flying cupids. 'Won't you take a seat, Lieutenant?'

'Thanks.' He sat down and looked at Frenchy's mother. 'I hope she isn't taking it too hard.'

'She quieted down the last few days.'

'How old is she?'

'Seventy-two.'

'Why does she sit there like that?'

'It's the way they mourn, the old Orthodox Jews. Sitting *shiva* they call it.'

'Who takes care of the candy store while she's in mourning?'

'It's closed.' She shrugged. 'Maybe now it'll stay closed. She doesn't need it.'

'There should be some insurance.'

'Even so. She has money stuck away in a savings bank.'

'Frenchy was a wonderful guy, Mrs. Shapiro.'

'You can call me Babe.'

'The men were very fond of him.'

'I can imagine.'

'I told you in the letter he lost his life protecting me. I'm sorry he did it. I'm sorry it had to be him instead of me.'

'They sent me a letter from Washington all about what he did. With a medal.'

'He did a very brave thing.'

'Seymour was like that. Very good-natured. A little too good-natured sometimes.'

'The night before the battle he came to my cabin. I made a pastel sketch of him. He wanted it for a present, he said. For his daughter.'

'Edith. Yes.' She averted her eyes.

Austen opened the package and held up the framed portrait.

The freshness of Frenchy's face so close to his startled him. Babe looked at it for a long time.

'It's a very good likeness,' she said. Her chin quivered. She showed the portrait to the old lady. 'Look, Momma, what the lieutenant made of Seymour.'

The old lady's sharp blue eyes took in the sketch. She spoke in Yiddish rapidly and with an incredible vigour. Babe handed the portrait to Austen. She looked embarrassed.

He smiled. 'Was it very bad?'

'It's not that.' She did not look at him.

'Please tell me what she said.'

'She said what good's a picture when he's gone? She says why should you come back big and healthy and not her Seymour?' Her lips trembled. 'Don't mind her, Lieutenant, please. She's old. These old folks, sometimes they don't understand things.'

'Maybe they understand them a lot better than we do.' He stood up. 'I brought along some of Frenchy's things.' He handed her a large manila envelope. 'That has eight hundred and fifty-two dollars in it. It was in his locker on the ship.' He took another envelope from his pocket. 'This contains two hundred and eighty-four dollars. The men on the ship gave it to me to give you as a memorial gift.' He produced a third envelope. 'Here's five hundred dollars. It's a gift from the officers of the ship.'

She rotated the envelopes slowly in her fingers. 'They shouldn't of done it,' she said. She began to cry. Her whole face seemed to collapse. 'I'm sorry,' she said. 'I just can't help myself.'

In the corner Frenchy's mother rocked back and forth. She watched her daughter-in-law. Her lips were set in a thin, bloodless line. Austen recognized Frenchy's hawklike profile in miniature. He touched Babe's arm.

'May I say good-bye to her?'

'You have to go already? You just got here.'

'I really must go.'

He went over and touched the fragile, shawled shoulder, bending so she could hear what he had to say.

'Good-bye, Mother. I loved your boy.'

274

She reached out a small, blue-veined hand and struck him sharply in the face.

'*Momma!*' Babe screamed.

'You're all alike,' the old lady said calmly in English. 'A bunch of murderers.' She gathered the shawl more tightly about her and looked stonily through the curtained window.

'I'm sorry,' Babe said. 'I swear to God, Lieutenant——'

'Please,' he said quietly. He looked once at the portrait. Frenchy still grinned. 'I better be going.'

He followed her along the narrow hallway. As he passed the closed door he heard the child's singsong voice.

'Would it be all right to see her?' he asked.

'Please,' Babe said nervously. 'Some other time, maybe.'

'How is she?'

'How is she? How do you expect she should be?'

She held the door open.

'Good-bye,' he said.

'Good-bye, Lieutenant.' She sniffled. 'I'd wait and talk to you till the elevator comes up, but I'm afraid maybe the chicken fat is burning.'

'That's all right.'

'Good-bye. Thanks for everything.'

She closed the door. He did not wait for the elevator. He went down the stairs and out of the place. The noon sun shone and the day had turned warm. He rode the subway to DeKalb Avenue. The car was almost empty. He looked around him. The faces were pale grey and dusty brown, listless in the stale air.

Faces to paint, he thought. Any faces. He longed for the good round feel of brushes in his hand and the rough texture of canvas. He thought of Edith and Babe and the old lady.

Why mourn for Frenchy? he thought.

He went out of the subway into the crash and clamour of Flatbush Avenue. He rode a taxi bumpily to the Navy Yard and walked through the big gates.

The aircraft carrier was tied alongside one of the docks. He stood for a while looking up at her. She was a fantastic leviathan,

275

crisscrossed with cables and air hose, alive with yard workers and Navy personnel. The racket of power tools was deafening.

He went aboard and passed an hour exploring her vast decks and insides while his leave papers were processed. She bristled with guns. Instead of the twin forties he had used on the *Atlantis*, they were installing quad mounts on the island structure, along both sides of the flight deck, and on the forecastle and fantail. He had never seen so many anti-aircraft guns before.

Lovely, he thought. For murderers. The old lady was right.

He picked up his endorsed papers and walked out of the Yard. He felt like a man freed from prison. He boarded a trolley marked 'PARK ROW/BROOKLYN BRIDGE' and sat in a window seat. The trolley lurched along the Yard fence. He idly watched the crowds of servicemen that passed.

He suddenly stiffened. He thought he saw Blanchard's face among the others. He rose and the trolley, clanging its bell, stopped at a crossing. The light was red. The pedestrian traffic flowed across Sands Street. He searched the crowd. It was Blanchard, all right.

The doors swung open. Austen paused.

'You getting off?' the driver asked.

Austen stared at him for a confused moment. 'No,' he said slowly. 'I thought I saw someone I knew.'

The doors closed. He went back to his window seat. Blanchard approached. He was bent a little, as though tired or in thought. His morose face looked flushed. The old air of serenity was out of it. Drunk, Austen thought. And not caring a damn who knows it. He could have called and Blanchard would have heard. He sat silent and unmoving.

The trolley lurched ahead, bell clanging. Austen sat numbly as it passed Blanchard. He stared after the doctor until his figure was lost in the stream of men behind the steel fence.

All right, he thought. Suppose I had called out. Suppose I had quit the trolley and joined him and we pumped hands and clapped backs. Then what? What the hell would we talk about? The dead?

The trolley creaked and clattered on to the bridge. Austen

watched the always astonishing spires of lower Manhattan. It can be done quickly, he thought. Wet down the cold-pressed Whatman paper. Squeeze out an inch of Payne's grey for the river water. Dark, swift strokes for the skyscraper mass bleeding into the docks and tugs and waterfront details. Let it dry a little. Then lay in the grimy majesty of the bridge with terre-verte and ultramarine and a touch of alizarin. Lattice the cables with a Number Two Winsor Newton Series 7. Opaque touches of orange where they've touched up the bridge against rust. Impasto the clouds and add a soupçon of pale lemon yellow and the thinnest of cadmium reds swiftly washed out above the tips of the tall buildings.

Impasto, my ass, you third-rate Picasso, he thought. He stared at the water. It was grey. The hell with the water, he thought. I'll paint Stella and trees and Stella and fields of rye and clover. And Stella. Trees and fields and solid barns and honest country faces, he thought happily. That's painting, Jack.

He stopped smiling. Poor Blanchard, he thought, with nothing to paint.

He stopped in a Greenwich Village shop that dealt in artists' needs. It was a narrow shop with cluttered shelves of dusty paper and paints and artists' tools.

There was a small room with a skylight and an easel in the rear of the place. The proprietor came out of its gloom, peering at Austen and rubbing his paint-smeared fingers on the tattered smock he wore. He had a face like a wrinkled old Buddha.

'Hello, Papa,' Austen said. 'Do you remember me?'

The old man cocked his head. 'In these uniforms,' he said slowly, 'you all look alike.'

'I used to buy good paint and canvas from you before the war.'

'Before the war there was such a thing. But not to-day.' He regarded Austen closely. 'You said your name is . . .?'

'I didn't.'

'You wished to buy something?'

'You used to have some good linen canvas.'

'What would a military man know about good linen canvas, please?'

277

'Look, Papa. All I want is canvas, not dialectics.'

The old man shrugged. 'Your loss, my boy.' His voice softened. 'Now I remember you. My one customer who refused to discuss world politics. Always too busy painting. Right?'

'Right.'

'You lost a little weight. You look older.' He smiled gently. 'When do you find time to paint, you're all so busy killing each other these days?'

'I paint between killings. Do you have any Belgian canvas?'

'Belgian canvas he wants, no less.'

'Listen, Papa. I've got a month's leave. I'm going to the country. I'm going to paint. How about the canvas?'

The old man's face suddenly lighted. 'Austen,' he said. 'That was your name. See? What a mind I got for an old cocker like me to remember a name like Austen?'

'I hope I live long enough to be an old cocker like you, Papa. At least I'll mind my manners and serve my customers politely and quickly.'

'I remember you, Austen. You're an all-right painter. You showed me once. Very inventive, but not crazy. You had something special. You were only a kid, I remember.'

'Such a praise from a refugee from the National Academy of Pinsk is indeed a compliment. Now what about some canvas?' His spirit flagged. 'You haven't any, have you, Papa?'

'Do you suppose,' the old man said with dignity, 'I would permit a trivial lousy thing like a world war keep me from having the best canvas that money can buy?'

He pulled some drawers open and brought out a thick roll of canvas and blew the dust from it. 'President F.D.R. himself, God bless him, couldn't buy an inch of this canvas if I didn't like his painting technique. Here, feel. Just touch this canvas.'

Austen touched it. It was very fine Belgian linen.

'I didn't know the President painted,' he said.

'Who said he painted? I'm merely trying to impress on you the value of this piece of canvas. Pure gold.'

'How much will you sell me?'

'Whatever you need for a month of painting.'

'I can use all of it. How much is it?'

'The same.' He seemed slightly offended. 'Here the prices don't change every five minutes.'

'You're a crazy old man.'

'All I ask is I should some day see the paintings.'

'Fair enough, Papa.'

'You don't need colours? Brushes? I still got from the old stock plenty of things from England and France and Holland. Germany I won't mention.'

'I need a pound of flakewhite, if you have it.'

The old man wrapped the canvas and the tube of paint and walked to the door with Austen. In the glare of daylight he looked even more ancient and Buddha-like.

'Tell me something, please,' he said.

'Sure.'

'Where you just came from in the war, there was some killing?'

'Yes, Papa, there was killing.'

'Much killing?'

'Very much.' Austen paused. 'One is very much, isn't it?'

'There was just one?'

'There were many, Papa. One is enough.'

'You were there in the thick of it?'

'I was there.'

'Tell me something.'

'Yes?'

'You think this kind of living is going to help your painting?'

Austen looked at him, startled. 'What a strange thing to say.'

'Do you?'

'I don't know.'

'How can you say you don't know?'

'I'm going to find out in these next thirty days.'

'You saw some terrible things. I can see it in your eyes. You think this won't bother your painting, foolish boy?'

'I'll have to paint to find out.' He looked up the street anxiously for a taxi.

'You'll paint, all right,' the old man said. 'This you can't help. But war stirs you up inside. This I've seen before. Right here in this dirty little shop of mine I've seen what war does to you artists. It's not a nice thing to see.'

'Goya did all right with war.'

'It hurt him too. It killed him for other things maybe greater. And you, my boy, you're not yet Goya.'

'Okay, Papa. Thanks for the sermon.'

'Listen. Go see the "Guernica". Go see what war can do to a great artist.'

'I'm going there from here.'

'Don't look at me so angry. I remember those paintings you once showed me. They were full of promise, a little unhappy, but in a nice heart-warming way. No violence in them and that I liked.'

'And Goya and Picasso are too violent for you?'

The old man shrugged his thin shoulders. 'What's the use of talking,' he said. He looked deeply troubled and his eyes glistened.

Austen patted the old man's skinny arm.

'Say what you want, Papa. It's still a free country.'

The old man brushed his eyes angrily. 'You can't stop wars by painting pictures of them.'

'A man has to paint what he has to paint. Look at yourself. Always dabbing away in the back room. Painting—painting what?'

'Flowers!' the old man shouted. 'Flowers!'

Austen shrugged. 'Maybe I'll paint flowers. I don't know. How can I know what the hell's going to come out?'

The old man looked hurt. 'How can you say a thing like that? You, an artist?'

'I just want to paint, Papa. Like a man dying of thirst wants water. Clean water, dirty, warm, anything. As long as it's water.'

'Better you shouldn't paint,' the old man said slowly.

'I've got to run,' Austen said. 'There's a taxi.'

'Run, run. Go in the best of health.'

'Thanks, Papa.'

'I'm sorry I talked so much.'

'Good-bye, Papa.'

'Do some good paintings.'

'I'll do my best.' He ran for the taxi.

The old man watched him run. Then he went to the back room and resumed his painting.

Such a fine boy, he thought. Such a foolish boy! To think he can paint a war out of his system in thirty days. Not in thirty years, painting with both hands! Such a sweet boy. A nice-looking, clean-looking, well-brought-up boy like that, already with blood on his hands.

He shrugged and took up a brush and peered closely at his canvas of flowers and resumed his painting.

31

AUSTEN sauntered through the halls of the glassy, dustless museum. It is like the ship, he thought. Clean and functional. With one difference. The ship is for destruction.

He came to the Modigliani. It was titled 'Bride and Groom'. He stood in front of it for a long time. Then he walked until he found the 'Guernica', coming on it suddenly as he turned into the hall where it was exhibited. Its distorted nearness startled him so that he closed his eyes and backed from it and then looked at it again.

It was too much, he thought. It was the ship, with horses. He was unnerved by its imprint of agony. He could feel the indelible pain emanating from the canvas.

He wandered around, searching for Modiglianis. Too few of them, he thought. He enjoyed their richness and the immense quality of peace they held for him.

There, he thought. Paint. Like young Amedeo. Long-dead Amedeo. Dead of the total illness that poverty and vice and genius inflicts. Like war, he thought. Another total illness.

He went back to the 'Bride and Groom'. He stood there until an attendant came over and told him the museum was closing now.

'Thank you,' he said softly. He took a last look at the painting.

Stella and me, he thought. Impaled. It's not for me. It never was. I used to know that, he reminded himself, before the war came along and softened my mind.

It was all he needed to know. He walked out of the cool stone glass and steel sanctuary.

He walked the streets of the darkening city until it was long past the time he had arranged to meet Stella. He bought some clothes for the country and a suitcase to carry them in. He ate a quiet dinner in a small café and thought of the paintings he would paint.

It will be all right, he insisted to himself. It will be fine.

He went to the station ten minutes before train time. He carried the huge roll of canvas and the new suitcase of country clothes. He walked through the cool, crowded caverns to the track where the State of Maine express was scheduled for departure. He went down the long ramp to the bleak platform.

Stella was there. She was holding a large package.

She did not run to him. She did not say anything. She watched him, knowing he saw her, knowing what he had planned, knowing it was for him to decide.

He went to her and put down his suitcase. She was very close to him, but he did not touch her. He looked at his watch.

'There's not much time left,' he said.

'Then let's get aboard.'

'Do you have any luggage, Stella?'

'No. I've everything I want.'

He kissed her. He was right. Everything was going to be fine. He picked up his canvas and his suitcase. He reached for her package.

'I'll carry that,' he said.

'Never mind,' Stella said. 'I'm a big girl.'

'What's in the package?'

'The painting you made of me.'

Down the long platform a man in blue waved a lantern. They boarded the train. Stella held his arm tightly. It feels good, he thought.

'You like the painting, don't you, Stella?'

'It's the kind of painting that changes with time,' she said.